the RISING

THE ALCHEMY WARS: BOOK TWO

IAN TREGILLIS

orbit

www.orbitbooks.net

ORBIT

First published in Great Britain in 2015 by Orbit

1 3 5 7 9 10 8 6 4 2

A CIP catalogue record for this book
is available from the British Library.

ISBN 978-0-356-50233-5

Printed and bound in Great Britain by
Clays Ltd, St Ives plc

Papers used by Orbit are from well-managed forests
and other responsible sources.

MIX
Paper from
responsible sources
FSC
www.fsc.org FSC® C104740

Orbit
An imprint of
Little, Brown Book Group
Carmelite House
50 Victoria Embankment
London EC4Y 0DZ

An Hachette UK Company
www.hachette.co.uk

www.orbitbooks.net

For Sara, of course

PART I

FRIENDS IN THE GAME

One cannot accomplish as much by well-doing as by having friends in the game.

—Business philosophy of Kiliaen van
Rensselaer, a founder and director
of the Dutch West India Company

Thos.: They write here one ~~Cornelius Son~~ Huygens hath made the Hollanders ~~an invisible eel~~ a metal man to ~~swim~~ stalk the ~~Haven at Dunkirk~~ Estuary, and sink all th' shipping there.

Pennyboy Jr.: But how is't done?

Cymbal: I'll shew you, Sir. It is an Automa. . . .

—Ben Jonson, THE STAPLE OF NEWS,
first published 1631; Post-Annexation
version first performed ca. 1693
(author unknown)

Q: Why must my mechanical(s) undergo alteration before the ship can set sail? I adhere to the terms of my lease and keep my Clakkers in excellent order!

A: Many leaseholders are surprised and confused by this requirement when they first travel overseas with their mechanical servants. Rest assured, the requirement is not an indictment of you as a leaseholder. It is a requirement of maritime law, first put forward in a royal decree of 1831. It is a special precaution with the *sole purpose* of ensuring your safety, the safety of your fellow passengers, and the integrity of the vessel. Under certain rare circumstances, standard shipboard operations may subject your mechanical(s) to situations not covered by the standard hierarchical metageasa embedded during their original forging. The nautical metageasa are temporary addenda that ensure all shipboard Clakkers will function properly under all circumstances, no matter how unlikely or unusual.

Q: I'm only traveling for a short time. I don't want my Clakkers to become bogged down and inefficient because they carry superfluous metageasa.

A: They won't be. The metageasa for all noncrew mechanicals will automatically and instantaneously revert to their prevoyage conditions upon disembarkation at the destination port.

Q: I lease my servants with my own money. They should be loyal to me!

A: They are, and always will be. The nautical metageasa *in no way* alter the terms of your lease. However, just as safety considerations require human passengers to comply with the instructions of captain and crew, shipboard servants are subject to geasa imposed by the crew. This may, under limited circumstances, delay fulfillment of your own directives.

—Excerpt from *Introduction to Nautical Metageasa for First-Time Leaseholders*, a pamphlet for passengers of the Blue Star's North-Atlantic Line, published by the Worshipful Company of Shipwrights, Rotterdam (1919)

CHAPTER
1

As had become his custom in recent mornings, Hugo Longchamp, captain of the guard of Marseilles-in-the-West, climbed
the tallest tower in New France to await the end of the world.
Doom had proved slow to arrive. The captain was getting
impatient.

Puffs of frozen breath limned his beard with silvery hoar-
frost, aging him a year for every step he mounted. The ice
beads dangling from his eyelashes lent a kaleidoscopic beauty
to the play of torchlight on the slick snow-dusted ribbon of
stairs. The winds had dropped with the temperature overnight.
So, while Longchamp's nose had frozen shut the moment he
stepped outside, forcing him to breathe through his mouth like
a leaky teakettle, at least he didn't have to contend with breezes
eddying around the tower to jiggle the stairs. Or was it too cold
for the polymers to retain their elasticity? That was the province of chemists and technicians. Longchamp was neither. He
was a soldier.

The twinkle of stars slowly dissolved into the steely gray of a
predawn sky. A rosy band ascended from the horizon; it grew
brighter, and the stars fainter, each time he completed a circuit

of the helical stairwell. One celestial light did not twinkle; it glowed like a garnet suspended in the Belt of Venus. Mars.

He paused to admire the lights of Marseilles-in-the-West spread before him like votive candles in the narthex of the Cathedral Basilica of Saint Jean-Baptiste. Torchlight dotted the boulevards of the city, hinted at the spindly spokes of avenues and wagon paths, shone from kitchen windows and bakeries, glinted from ice in the basins of dormant fountains, and sparkled on the shore of the Saint Lawrence. A boundary of hard shadow cleaved the tapestry of lights where the city met the seaway. The darkness stretched across the inky waters to envelop the border with Nieuw Nederland and the lands beyond. Where, even now, the enemy stirred.

An orange flare momentarily lit the sky over the river. Fire from a gas burner stoked the envelope of hot air holding a tethered observation balloon aloft. The flames illuminated the balloon's bulb-shaped canopy like a paper lantern. A few moments later, another flare pierced the darkness a mile downriver from the first. Cold morning; the balloonists would burn through their fuel quickly. Longchamp imagined those mad bastards shivering under layers of fur and grateful for any chance to hold numb hands to the flames if even just for a moment.

He wasn't alone in his early-morning vigil. In addition to the observation balloons and their airborne watchers, he knew that somewhere far below, wardens shivered in shoreline blinds, their dark-adapted eyes trained across the waters straining for any signs of a tulip incursion. Part of him expected that, any moment, the shriek of a warning whistle would pierce the darkness. A tight ache radiated from the spot between his shoulder blades. Though partly the symptom of a pointless effort to suppress his shivering, the ache had become his constant companion. Even in the warmest barracks his shoulders had taken to hunching in subconscious expectation. It took an effort of will, and a longtime campaigner's discipline, to force himself to relax. Only a fool wasted energy on things he could not control.

The enemies would arrive according to their own schedule. No sooner, no later. Their return would be as the Lord's return: like a thief in the night, the day and hour of their coming unknown to even the wisest of men.

Instantly regretting the thought, Longchamp crossed himself. Only an inherently evil impulse would drive a man to compare the risen Christ to the heretical Dutch and their sacrilegious contempt for the immortal soul. He wasn't a saint. Just a recidivist sinner, like all men. He made a mental note to include this transgression in his weekly confession. Then he fingered the rosary beads looped around his belt and said a quick prayer to the Virgin, begging her to intercede on his behalf.

His knees creaked like a lych-gate in dire need of oiling when he gained his feet. They never used to do that. Perhaps the aging wasn't entirely an illusion.

By the time he ascended another revolution of the cloistered spiral stairwell, the sky glow had brightened sufficiently for Longchamp to extinguish his torch. He shouldn't have used it in the first place; soon the citadel would be under siege discipline, and then they'd all have to get reacquainted with working in the dark. But the stairs of the Porter's Prayer could be treacherous at the best of times, not to mention when glazed with frost. He couldn't serve the Throne and the Church with two shattered legs.

The stairs passed beneath the skeletal frame of an unfinished gantry and the tracks of a recently rebuilt funicular. Longchamp's breath frosted the metal tracks as well as the dark insulation wrapped about the pipes that shunted water ballast between the upper and lower cars. He wondered, not for the first time, how they kept the ballast water from freezing. They had a thousand little tricks, the storied chemists of New France.

Tricks that had kept the tulips and their mechanical demons at bay for centuries. That alone was a miracle. But they couldn't keep the upper hand forever. This was the most frightening thought of all, and one he tried to keep to himself: that the long tradition of French chemical innovation would falter, or hit a long plateau, and the precarious balance in their centuries-long arms race with the Dutch would irrevocably shift. One day soon the clockwork tide would once again crash against the outer keep of Marseilles-in-the-West; perhaps this would be the time it swept them away.

The final revolution afforded him a grand view of fallow farmland stretching to the west and north, bordered by leagues of winter-bare yellow birch. The Saint Lawrence flowed to the east and south of Mont Royal, upon whose slopes Marseille-in-the-West sprawled like a lazy cat. Standing atop the Spire always made Longchamp feel as though he could see clear across the world: across New France, across the ocean, all the way to Europe and Old France. Longchamp had never seen Paris, of course; he'd only heard family stories passed down from some great-umpty-great uncle who'd fought for Louis XIV before the Exile.

By now the predawn light was bright enough for him to see the sentries pacing the star-shaped perimeter of the Vauban fortifications hundreds of feet below. His soldiers, the distressingly few men and women who had survived the last siege and the later massacre inside the walls, paced the inner and outer keeps. They looked like a handful of peppercorns sprinkled across the icy perimeter of the Last Redoubt of the Exile King of France. They were too few, the perimeter too great. The forced conscriptions weren't bringing in new bodies quickly enough. Longchamp made another mental note, this time to speak to the comte de Turenne, who carried the marshal general's baton.

A renewed breeze fluttered Longchamp's beard, drew tears from his eyes, snaked through buttonholes and seams. But the exertion of the climb had warmed him enough that the icy streamers didn't stipple him with gooseflesh. And later, when he wore armor and fought for his life—and the lives of his people, and his king—he'd be too hot, too exhausted to feel cold. The cold would come after his frail human body had succumbed to the relentless advance of the ticktocking metal horde. He pulled a knit cap over his brow to cover his ears and wiped the wind-tears from his eyes. He squinted to the southeast.

Looking for the telltale glimmer of burnished metal. For the beginning of the war. And, if Longchamp were feeling particularly fatalistic, the beginning of the end.

End? Perhaps. But a long, slow one. And extremely hard-won. The tulips and their clockwork slaves would have to earn their victory.

Mingled scents wreathed his perch atop the Spire. A faint hint of muddiness from the river, woodsmoke from a hundred hearths, the humid weight of impending snowfall. The wind tickled his face not unlike the soft touch of a lady down near the docks with whom he had a passing familiarity. He wondered if he'd have time to see her again before the dying started. *Not killing*, he thought with a sigh; you can't kill a clockwork. Only deactivate it. And pray to Jesus, and the Virgin, that another didn't take its place. That the defenses outlasted the metal men.

They'd managed it the last time, though barely. But that was before some fool in New Amsterdam had destroyed the tulips' brand-new Forge. The first ever built in the New World. Nobody knew who had done it, but people on both sides of the border assumed French agents were behind the sabotage. Though why the king or pope would sanction such a blatantly suicidal act of war, nobody could say. The French consoled themselves with the belief that if the destruction of the Forge had been carried out by their own countrymen, it was surely at the behest of the semimythical Talleyrand. Clever, cunning, courageous Talleyrand: hero of dozens of folktales and twice as many songs. Voyageurs passed the miles of their endless treks belting out chansons de geste celebrating the exploits of New France's trickster hero.

Talleyrand has a plan, the citizens of New France reassured one another.

Not the present Talleyrand, thought the captain. *He couldn't plan his way out of a garderobe without a map and two gallons of axle grease.* They wouldn't take such spurious comfort in the machinations of a mythical stranger if they'd actually met the inbred ass wart.

Longchamp knew no more than anybody else, but he would have sworn the destruction of the Forge sounded like the handiwork of an exiled and notoriously single-minded former vicomtesse of his acquaintance. A rather stubborn one with an infuriating penchant for overestimating her own cleverness. Whose hubris caused no end of trouble and worse for the people around her. What insanity had driven her to twist the tiger's tail like that? What game had she in mind? Did she, in fact, have a plan?

But the speculation was pointless. The past was forever in the past. Longchamp could only look forward and prepare for what was to come.

The sun crested the horizon. Sunlight glinted on the jagged crust of ice hugging the riverbanks. Longchamp watched for the glint of newly risen sun to betray the movement of burnished clockworks across the border. When they came, they'd march straight to the shoreline, and into the water, and under it, and across the riverbed, and burst through the ice as they mounted the French side of the border. They would march and march until they reached the walls of Marseilles.

They would swarm across the Saint Lawrence to occupy and burn the villages and farmhouses along the seaway. They'd swarm through the fishing villages of Acadia, along the Atlantic coast. They'd spread like a disease through the Great Lakes. They'd spread north and taint the shores of Hudson Bay.

But not today. Not yet.

A riot of color greeted the risen sun. The plastic cloister bannisters blazed like braided chains of rubies. Nacreous lacquers in the massive chamber atop the Spire shone with a rainbow swirl of blues, greens, and yellows like a sheen of oil atop a rain puddle. Longchamp adjusted his cap, pulling it lower over his brow to shield his eyes from the glare. The tip of the Spire, where the funicular tracks ended, housed the chambers where the privy council met. And, above that, the king's apartments.

Winter sunrises came and went without the tumult of birdsong that accompanied mornings other times of year. Most birds had flown south for the winter. No birdsong to serenade the sun; only the whisper of air, the *hiss* of frost under his boots, the *scritch* of scarf and beard. He peered over the railing to the wall of the outer keep far below, where a few dozen new conscripts shivered in the shadows. Their training unfolded with a curious silence, the shouts and crashes and curses dispersed by the chill winter air before they reached Longchamp's ears. Even the unique—and uniquely dreaded—*chug-chug-chug* of the epoxy cannon compressors was inaudible at this distance. Wisps of vapor wafted from the pressure valves.

It was never a good day when they needed the cannon. Needing the cannon and having nobody to operate them would be catastrophic. Hence the new conscripts. For centuries, every able-bodied man in New France did three years' service when he reached majority. But the king hadn't won any hearts with his edict extending that to women and forcefully conscripting one in every five able-bodied citizens under the age of fifty. Thank the Lord he was smarter than his father, the previous Exile King of Fallen France.

The shivering conscripts circled around the cannon, their breaths forming a line of silvery pennants as the first rays of the rising sun swept down the Spire to graze the walls of the outer keep. Tough as meringue, these recruits. He'd consider it a blessing if even a quarter of the newcomers developed a crumb of usefulness. Merchants were the worst. Fishermen: Now those were folks who knew hard work and didn't flinch from it. The coureurs de bois, too. The forest runners were tough as moose jerky, and no strangers to hardship. If anything, they reveled in it. He wished the king's call to arms all Godspeed through the waterways and wilderness of New France, that it might reach the ears of every voyageur, coureur, and trapper in the realm. Some might ignore the call, or pretend they'd not heard it. But Longchamp knew these men; he'd been one of them, for a while. Few would want to return to civilization only to find their contracts nullified, the scrip crumpled in the brassy fist of a mechanical demon, their hard-earned money worth less than a mouthful of a Dutchman's piss.

The low sun elicited no telltale glinting from the forests and fields on the south side of the Saint Lawrence. No omens. Well, then. It seemed Queen Margreet and her bootlicker colonial governor of Nieuw Nederland didn't intend to murder the good men and women of New France quite yet. Longchamp could make use of the extra time by polishing a few turds.

He turned his back on the sun and started the long descent to the inner keep.

〜

It took ten minutes to reach the base of the Spire. Another ten to navigate the maze of barricades and trenches before he could gain the top of the inner wall. A Clakker could leap over most obstacles; the trick was to slow them down enough to give the gunners a snowball's chance in hell of spraying them down. Or to funnel them together so that they could be incapacitated most efficiently. Certain trenches and moats contained corrosives intended to destroy delicate mechanisms. Others brimmed with chemical reagents that needed just a dollop of catalyst to initiate the reaction that would solidify the moats in an instant, complete with Clakkers trapped inside like raisins in a Christmas cake. Longchamp fucking hated raisins.

Just like he hated the thought of the inner keep's defenses ever seeing use. Because the war was already lost if the tulips' mechanical servants made it this far. The obstacles and rearguard tactics could only slow their final advances, and maybe, just maybe, give the king enough time to escape. Though where he would go when the Dutch truly ruled the earth was an open question. Perhaps he'd go north and become king of the White Bears.

When he finally reached the outer wall, he sidled behind the cluster of new conscripts, taking care the *crunch* of frost beneath his boots didn't signal his arrival. Even the civvies tended to shrink when they felt his eyes on them; they'd heard the stories, too. Sergeant Chrétien saw him lurking behind the group but continued to harangue the newcomers without acknowledging the captain. The newest conscripts shivered as though palsied, wiping their noses on their sleeves while they shuffled and muttered to themselves, hardly listening to anything the sergeant said. Half of them looked barely strong enough to raise a glass of wine much less a pick and sledge. Christ! Their forearms weren't even the size of Longchamp's *wrists*! What in the seven hells were they supposed to do with such a motley piss-poor group? Only two men in this group could be less than forty.

The captain wondered if they could slow the mechanical horde by tossing the bodies of the useless in their path. The image brought him a modicum of satisfaction, though he knew that even this tactic would be pointless. Military Clakkers were walking scythes who churned through men like razor-edged tornadoes. They left nothing but screams, limbs, viscera, and arterial spray in their wake. Mere meat and bone could never slow them.

Longchamp knew. He'd seen the ticktocks at work more than once. He'd seen friends fall to the *snick* and slash of alchemical blades. He'd seen the fountain in the inner keep run red in the aftermath of a single Clakker's rampage. He shook his head. But no matter how he tried to free his head of memories and horrors, they clung like dusty cobwebs.

"All right," said Chrétien. "Let's see if you civvies have listened to a single thing I've said." He selected three men at random. "You, you, and you. Congratulations, you're now a gunnery team. Step to it!"

Two men shuffled forward with all the enthusiasm of a criminal gang going to the gallows. The third hung back, perhaps hoping the soldier had been pointing at somebody near him. The flecks of silver at his temples, the thick ruff of his coat, and the faint hint of nascent jowls made him a merchant or trader. Softened by success. Longchamp grabbed him by the fur-lined collar.

"I could swear the sergeant told you to move," he said. "So I find myself wondering why you haven't done so with alacrity. A fine gentleman like yourself would surely do so if he could.

So what's the problem, friend? Legs broken? Or perhaps an imp has nailed your feet to these stones?"

The merchant squirmed within the voluminous fur coat. He shot an alarmed glance at Longchamp. The captain didn't loosen his grip.

"I notice also," he continued, "that you seem to have lost your voice. And your eyes are bulging just a bit. Choking on your own fear, I'd wager. Well, not to worry. I've seen this, too. Happens on the battlefield from time to time. We'll get you right in no time." Longchamp clapped twice, calling for the attention he knew he already commanded. "Lucky us! This'll give me a chance to teach proper emergency surgery techniques. Sergeant, hand me your knife. You and you," he said, pointing at the two closest bystanders, "kneel on his arms and legs. And put your fucking weight into it. They flop around like a trout in a canoe once the knife goes in the gizzard."

At this point Longchamp loosened his grip just enough for the lazy merchant to slip free. He scuttled over to join the other men at the epoxy cannon.

"Thank the Virgin!" said Longchamp, crossing himself. "She's cured him! It's a Goddamned miracle." He clouted the nearest conscript on the back of the head. "Show some respect to the Holy Mother, you cretin. All you cretins."

As one, the conscripts crossed themselves, good Catholics all.

Sergeant Chrétien made one man the spotter; he crouched inside a crenel, alongside the barrels. The other two, including Longchamp's lazy merchant, manned the chemical compressor and the firing mechanism. Under the soldier's direction the latter pair turned the crank that charged up the compressor. The measured *chug-chug-chug* of the hydraulics climbed a few registers and adopted the quickened tempo known to everybody who'd been through a siege: the dreaded rhythm of an epoxy gun fending off an attacker.

The sergeant mounted a battlement and waved a yellow flag half again his own height. The flagman at the edge of the forest returned the semaphore, and then another soldier bolted from the treeline. The newcomer dashed across the field, tracing zigzags and serpentines in the frost. Longchamp wondered which hapless conscript had drawn the short straw for this demonstration.

"Runners on the field!" cried the sergeant. "I say again we have INBOUND MECHANICALS!"

The spotter muttered a string of bearings. "North by northeast. No, wait, he's turning east. I mean he's running from the east. East by north . . . Wait, he's turning again—"

"I can't fucking hear you!" said Longchamp. "And it'll never be quieter than this. When the walls are aswarm with clanking murderers, and every cannon in the keep is chugging along loud enough to wake the Devil after a six-bottle bender, you'd better be able to MAKE YOURSELF HEARD!"

Meanwhile, the hapless sprinter had covered a third of the distance to the wall. Far, far slower than a real mechanical. But far too fast for the novice gunners to handle gracefully.

"He's getting closer!" cried the spotter. The onset of true panic improved the volume and urgency of his voice, but at the cost of his judgment. "Just fire! For God's sake, fire!"

The second man flipped the levers that opened the breach chambers on the double-barreled cannon. A momentary *glug* interrupted the rhythm of the compressor as epoxy and fixative sloshed into place. He waited a moment until the breach attained the proper hydraulic pressure, then closed off the chamber again. This one, at least, had listened to the lecture and, miracle of miracles, learned something.

"He's halfway here!" said the spotter.

Chrétien asked, "He? Who's he? All I see is a murderous ticktock that's about ten seconds from leaping on this wall, scuttling up like a spider, and killing us all."

"Jesus Christ," cried the spotter, now in the throes of true panic, "just fire!"

"You're oversimplifying, Sergeant, and shame on you for it," said Longchamp, picking his teeth with a fingernail. "It won't kill us all at once. It'll start with the gunners, you know. Cut them in half before moving on to us. So we'll enjoy a few more seconds to make our peace with the Lord before that Clakker carves us up."

The merchant, hunkered behind the bulk of the cannon, blindly swung the barrel back and forth. "I can't see! Where is it?"

"Anywhere! Northeast! Everywhere!"

The merchant-gunner squeezed the double trigger with a grip that turned his knuckles whiter than freshly fallen snow. Twinned streams of blue and yellow water vomited from the cannon barrels, combining over the crenels to make a single stream the color of the first springtime fringe on the maple trees. The explosive release of pressure from the breach set the cannon to kicking like a mad stallion. The barrels snapped up, forcing the controls down with enough force to make the merchant yelp. He lost his grip. The breachman leaped aside. The cannon fired uselessly into the sky, then slewed back and forth to slam against the battlement hard enough to knock chips from the granite. Another wild swing caught the spotter by surprise. It connected with the characteristic celery-stalk *crunch* of broken bones that sent him sprawling along the wall. The sprinter reached the wall a few seconds later without a drop of green on him.

The sergeant rounded on the spectacularly unsuccessful gunnery team. Over the crying of the spotter, he yelled, "What the hell was that?"

A spot of motion over the seaway caught Longchamp's eye: a fluttering blur of gray and white against a powder-blue sky.

Soon it resolved into a pigeon. The messenger flew low over the town of Marseilles-in-the-West. It climbed as it passed over the walls of the keep, twice circling the Spire. The pigeon coops were situated about halfway up the tower.

So. News from downriver. Longchamp sighed. Maybe for once the news would be good. Perhaps the tulips had caught the saboteur and found no connection to New France, no reason to swarm across the border to avenge their damaged pride. That would certainly merit the use of pigeon post. Pigeons were faster and more secure than the network of creaky semaphore towers snaked across New France.

He snorted hard enough to clear his sinuses, then spat salty phlegm over the parapet. It would take a particularly callow fool to stake hopes on such fancies. Longchamp retied his scarf, stamped the creeping numbness from his feet, and headed back to the base of the Porter's Prayer to begin the long ascent.

∽

The news from downriver was not good. It was a shitstorm of the Old Testament variety.

Dozens of messenger pigeons occupied the rows of cages situated within the alcove stretching halfway around the Spire. The coops were louder than a whorehouse on payday, though not as enjoyable. Cleaner, too: every ounce of guano went to the chemists. An apprentice birdkeeper was seeing to that duty when Longchamp barged, panting and sweating, through the door from the Porter's Prayer. The boy jumped; the tray he'd been sweeping hit the floor, the splash stippling his clothes with flecks of white and brown.

"Saw the news arrive," Longchamp gasped. "Where'd the little fucker go?"

The boy pointed across the rows of coops toward the interior of the Spire. His hand, which still held the brush, shook.

Longchamp shook his head and scowled, because it was friendlier than growling. It had been like that since the massacre in the inner keep when he'd deactivated a rampant military Clakker the old-fashioned way, using a hammer, pick, and his entire life's quota of good luck. Now every stupid bastard on the street looked at him like he was some kind of hero, and not an extraordinarily fortunate son of a bitch who'd gritted his teeth and done his job fully expecting to get skewered like a hairy pig. Longchamp left the apprentice to his ill-advised hero worship and tromped through the aisles of cages.

"Over here, Captain." He recognized the voice of the on-duty birdkeeper; they'd attended school together. That had been before he was expelled, though not before they'd fumbled a bit behind the chapel, playing fisherman and fisherwife. Brigit Lafayette wore a matching blouse and skirt of marigold and midnight-blue satin under a rainproof cloak of otter fur. She looked like a clown. The years had been kinder to her face than her dress sense. She added, "You must be sleeping atop the Spire these days, if you're seeing the pigeons almost before we do."

He followed her voice to the workshop she shared with the other birdkeepers. Brigit held the cooing messenger in one hand, delicately peeling away the message capsule strapped to its leg with the other. She glanced at Longchamp while an apprentice—a different one, a girl spattered with less bird shit than the boy he'd startled—caged the bird.

"You're not getting enough sleep," she said. "Your eyes are bloodshot." She dropped her head, focusing her attention on the desk. Her voice dropped close to a whisper when she asked, "When was your last decent meal? I mean a real meal, with real food, and dessert, and company with whom to share it?"

"Shit," he said.

There was only one capsule, he realized. Bad sign. Economy preferred loading the feathered rats with as much information as they could carry. A single capsule usually pointed to urgent news. Urgent news rarely pointed to rainbows and blow jobs.

"It's a wonder for the ages why you never married, Hugo Longchamp." For some reason she spoke more stiffly than she had a moment ago. Brigit turned the capsule over in her hand. "No special markings. It isn't coded."

After checking that none of the apprentices lingered among the nearby cages, she offered the capsule to the captain. He'd convinced the marshal general to grant him authority to read all uncoded traffic as it arrived. It was one of his conditions for accepting the promotion to captain of the guard. He'd expected it to become an argument, but in truth the marshal seemed content to let Longchamp shoulder as much of the real work as he could.

He said, "You might as well read it with me. Good or bad, the news will be all over the place before the bells ring Sext at midday. Earlier, if the news is terrible."

Brigit unfurled the scrap of paper, but couldn't read it until she'd rummaged the desk for a magnifying glass. It depressed Longchamp no small amount to think that she and he were of the same age. His eyes were no younger than hers, and they'd seen more terrors. His stomach growled. He was hungry enough to eat one of the pigeons, feathers and all, he realized. In fact…what had Brigit been saying about a meal? Had she been—

She put a hand over her mouth and swallowed a sob. The curled scrap of paper fluttered to the bench as she crossed herself with a trembling hand. Longchamp retrieved it. She found her voice and used it to call for an apprentice.

Pope Clement strangled. No murderer in custody. Swiss Guard silent.

Longchamp crossed himself for the third time that morning. Then he looked at the sky. He couldn't see the entity of his attention, but felt confident he'd be heard. If the Virgin wasn't inclined to intercede on his behalf when his thought strayed the tiniest bit from the pious path, she could damn well listen while he expressed his feelings fully and honestly.

"Is this a fucking joke? Go ahead and take a crap in our porridge while you're at it."

A boy arrived just in time to hear Longchamp's tirade. His face turned the color of a broken bone. Brigit pried Longchamp's fingers open to pluck the crumpled message from his grip. She handed it to the boy. "Run this up to the Council Chambers. If there's nobody to take it, get it to one of the king's attendants."

"No." The lad looked ready to piss himself when Longchamp snatched the scrap of paper away from him. "That lot has a bad habit of blaming the messenger. You shouldn't be the one to bring them this news, lad."

Longchamp bundled up once more, not looking forward to ascending the Spire again. The wind had picked up; it whistled through the cages.

"Remember what I said." Brigit's hand brushed his elbow. "About sleeping, and eating. You're not the young man you once were. You have to be careful. This place needs you." Her gaze flicked to the message scrap and back. "More and more every day."

He headed for the Porter's Prayer. She trailed after him. "At least ride the funicular, Hugo."

Shaking his head, he said, "My strength is my livelihood. I'm worthless without it. The day I can't climb the Spire on my own is the day you should bury me."

He emerged in the lee of the tower. The wind hit him in the face when he'd climbed a quarter circuit. It carried a faint dusting of ice that forced him to squint. Low, dark clouds scudded across the fields to the west of Île de Vilmenon. Longchamp launched into a jog that took the stairs two at a time. Soon he was sweating.

Unless he'd forgotten his history, the tulips hadn't moved against the Vatican since the so-called Migration of Cardinals long ago. Sure as deer fucked in the woods, this was retaliation for the Forge. That ice queen on the Brasswork Throne had a burr up her ass.

A patch of frost caught him unawares. He stumbled, fell. He slid outward and down, bumping down the stairs toward the blood-colored banister. He caught a slat and arrested his fall before he went corkscrewing all the way down to the inner keep. Snow flurries, the advance units of the coming storm, dusted him with a thin white coat as he climbed to his feet. He'd have bruises from knee to hip.

What a clusterfuck. Longchamp wondered what the former Talleyrand would have made of it.

CHAPTER
2

Berenice Charlotte de Mornay-Périgord—formerly known as the vicomtesse de Laval (prior to her banishment); formerly known as Talleyrand (before her post as spymaster for the king of New France went to a rival); formerly known as Maëlle Cuijper (when traveling incognito through the lands of her enemies); but, currently, a prisoner—looked up as the dark shadow of a mechanical centaur fell over her. The Stemwinder's arms, all four, snapped like caged hounds catching a whiff of fox. Its *clip-clop* gait brought it close enough for her to hear the tintinnabulation of its clockwork heart; even standing, she would have felt like a child alongside the beast.

Berenice held a small knife the length of her index finger. It was dull. The Stemwinder could turn its arms into harpoons worthy of a kraken in half the time it took her to blink. It existed solely to serve the Verderer's Office of the Sacred Guild of Horologists and Alchemists: the Clockmakers' secret police force. Stemwinders were mute witnesses and accessories to every act of murder, torture, sabotage, and coercion deemed necessary to safeguard the Clockmakers' secrets. Rumor said that even other Clakkers avoided the Stemwinders, and they had the benefit of alchemical alloy plating.

It loomed over her now, this self-aware amalgam of magic and mechanism. Its reconfigurable arms were wonders of horological ingenuity, equal to any task deadly or delicate. Berenice shifted her grip on the blade and cleared her throat.

"This pomegranate is excellent," she said. "I would have another."

The Stemwinder took her tray in its lower arms. As it pirouetted, turning for the kitchen, she added, "More coffee, as well. And don't be stingy with the cream this time. Your masters practically rule the world, for Christ's sake. They can afford to milk one extra cow."

The clockwork servant opened the door, exited, and pulled the door closed with a rear hoof. As usual it gave no indication of having heard or understood what she said. But she knew it would return with another pomegranate, another cup of coffee, and a Delftware creamer. Stemwinders made excellent domestic servants.

She sipped the lukewarm dregs of her coffee and gazed through the immense pane of paper-thin alchemical glass that afforded her sitting room a view of the snowy hills and bluffs of the North River Valley. The contours of the countryside presented a peculiar flatness that contradicted her knowledge of the region; her depth perception had gone to hell after she lost an eye to a rampant military Clakker inside the walls of Marseilles-in-the-West, hundreds of miles to the north.

Her glass eye, an exquisite gift from her friend Hugo Longchamp, matched her real eye rather well. But it was a mere ornament. She hadn't worn it since the Stemwinders returned it, a day or two after her capture.

The whole world had lost its texture the day Louis died. The mangled eye was just a detail compared with the devastation wrought upon her heart by her husband's death. Guilt cut more deeply than any knife.

Berenice blew her nose on the tablecloth and forcibly changed the direction of her thoughts. Based on the duration of the carriage ride on the night of her capture, she estimated this estate lay sixty or seventy miles upriver from New Amsterdam. She'd traveled the same river valley en route to the capital of Nieuw Nederland not long before she'd infiltrated the Forge, and this landscape looked familiar. A sentient airship had crashed along the river north of here, near Fort Orange; it had been shot down by its fellow mechanicals. There'd been a single survivor. She wondered, idly, what had happened to Jax, and whether he'd escaped the destruction of the Forge.

Doubtful. She'd heard the ear-shredding Rogue Clakker alarm before the building fell. Meaning they'd discovered him. She wondered if, in his dying moments, Jax had regretted the serendipitous series of accidents that had granted him Free Will.

Today had dawned cloudless, giving Berenice her first glimpse of a blue sky since her capture. Bare boughs of sugar maple, red oak, and hickory crosshatched her view of the hills like the withered hands of a crone waving her away. (*Too late*, she thought.) The snows of recent weeks still coated the countryside like a thick and exceptionally clean woolen blanket. A sheen of sparkling white caked the windward boles, suggesting steady winds from the northwest. Berenice made note of such information as she could glean from her picture window. The collecting of information had been her stock-in-trade; a habit etched into a woman's bones wouldn't succumb to the mere fact that she'd been banished, supplanted, and was now in the custody of her enemies.

The winter landscape was barren as the future of New France in the coming war. The war she had started. Well, she and Jax. She had to assume he was responsible for the Forge's destruction; she'd been busy cutting out a traitor's eye, making her displeasure known to the man she had tracked from Marseilles-in-the-West across the border to New Amsterdam.

The view from her window also encompassed a long gravel drive. A carriage appeared there now, pulled by two Stemwinders galloping in perfect synchrony. Berenice glimpsed a crest on the lacquered blackwood: the rose-colored cross of the Clockmakers' Guild.

She took another sip, seeing now not the landscape but a calendar. The timing was about right. She'd been sequestered here in the countryside for over two weeks since the Stemwinders caught her dulling her blade in the duc de Montmorency's eye socket. He'd revealed her identity as Talleyrand to the tulips. So: say a week to get an urgent message across the Atlantic to the Central Provinces; several days while the rulers of the Dutch Empire decided what to do with their windfall; and another week for somebody important to make the trek to the New World. The timing worked if they commandeered the most advanced ships and airships in the world. Which is exactly what they'd do for a chance to get in a room with a former Talleyrand.

Berenice wondered, not for the first time, what they had planned for her. She'd spent the first few days of her incarceration waiting with nauseating dread for the knives and hooks, the hot coals and devilish machinery, to appear. But her captors had treated her no worse than they might a royal princess confined to the grounds of a single estate for some trifling transgression of the byzantine social order. They fed her, clothed her, bathed her, did everything they could to ensure her comfort. For what purpose she couldn't begin to guess. But the Stemwinders were fanatical about her comfort. The food was excellent. If the tulips thought they could win her cooperation with honey rather than vinegar...well, so much the better. Why waste all that delicious honey?

But all good things did eventually find their end. Berenice took it on faith that the appearance of the black carriage signaled the end of her enforced holiday. She wondered if her hosts intended a hard end, complete with white-hot flensing blades and broken bones.

She sighed and set down her cup. An ache took root in her eye socket like the moaning ghost of her body's integrity. From the leather pouch hanging between her breasts, Berenice gently removed a glass marble. She swished it around in her mouth, then flinched when it popped into her eye socket with a wet squelch. It wasn't fitted to the socket; she'd have the world's worst sinus headache if she kept it in long. Her tongue tingled.

The black carriage appeared again. It emerged from the snow-blown shadows of the house, passing through the porte cochère beneath her window to roll to a stop before what she assumed was the front door, though she could not see it from her vantage. The rumbling of the carriage wheels along the drive shook loose a cornice of windblown snow from the corbels over the porte, leading to a heavy wet *thump* accompanied by a man's yelp.

Berenice turned her chair so that she faced the door rather than the window. These accommodations were smaller than the apartments she and Louis had shared within the keep of Marseilles-in-the-West as members of the court of King Sébastien III. It was just a single room with a locked door and unbreakable glass, plus a private lavatory, but the mattress was soft, the goose down warmer than a widow's bed had any right to be, and the furniture handsome.

A Stemwinder entered a moment later. It didn't knock. There followed a woman, a man, and a second Stemwinder. She'd expected the humans. But the sight of the additional centaur caused Berenice's confidence to collapse like a fragile cornice of wind-sculpted snow. She hadn't accounted for two monsters.

Christ on a blood-smeared cross, you tulip bastards just had to throw another wrench at my head, didn't you?

The second Clakker carried a chair upholstered in button-tufted chintz matching the one Berenice occupied. The man wore a topcoat of gray twill. He held a somewhat wet and battered top hat and the sour expression of a man much put-upon by the world; he brushed snow from the former and muttered to himself, which did nothing to dispel the latter. The woman was dressed as though she'd been invited to a sleigh ride at the premiere winter ball of the season. The brim of her own hat was just narrower than the door through which she entered; the peacock feather in the brim had been dyed a ghastly shade of lavender that matched her gloves. Beneath the hat she wore a head scarf mottled in a jacquard pattern. Sunlight evinced a lustrous sheen in the voluminous fur stole that threatened to swallow her, suggesting a petite woman wrapped in ermine or mink.

The second Stemwinder placed the chair across the table from Berenice. Then it extended its arms, allowing the newcomers to use the centaur like a coatrack. They draped it with hats, coats, and stoles. The machine retreated into a corner while the other stood motionless beside the door. The man went to the window, where he squinted at the glare of sunlit snow. The woman seated herself and peered at Berenice across the remains of her breakfast of fruit, toast, roasted potatoes, and chicken sausage. Her leather boots dripped snowmelt on the rug, but the corners of her smile dripped something much colder. Sunlight glinted from the rosy-cross pendant on the fine silver chain around her neck. Nestled in one corner of the cross was a tiny inlaid *v* denoting the Verderer's Office.

Clearly this was the person for whom Berenice had been waiting. So who was this tarty bitch from the Clockmakers' Guild? Somebody with the clout to commandeer ships of the sea and ships of the air. But not so high up the ladder as to score her own retinue of Royal Guards. Not royalty, then, but somebody high in the Guild.

Berenice concluded the woman now settling across the table was the Tuinier: Anastasia Bell. The woman who ran the Stemwinders.

It seemed a solid guess. But as for the fellow who plodded along like a piece of flotsam caught in her wake, Berenice hadn't a Goddamned clue. If Bell had come to question Berenice, she had her own skills and the Stemwinders to apply to the problem. Anybody else was superfluous. Unless questioning wasn't what they had in mind. They could have questioned Berenice and ripped the answers from her broken body several times since her capture. The fact they hadn't suggested a different aim.

A name fluttered to the forefront of Berenice's mind. Like a scrap of paper caught in an errant breeze, it snagged in the bramble of her thoughts. *Visser.*

A pastor from The Hague. Who had, whether intentionally or inadvertently, given Jax the errand that led to his emancipation from the geasa. Visser had known things only a French agent should have known. But, according to the mechanical, when they met again in New Amsterdam, he'd seemed an entirely different person. The previously pious and compassionate man had become a murderer. It was as though he'd been caught and…altered.

Berenice tried, with middling success, to sever the tendrils of fear now twining themselves around her stomach and spine. Not wanting her enemies to sense her anxiety, and hoping to set them off-balance, she said, "I assume you intend to change me as you did the pastor."

She knew instantly that her stab in the dark had found a target because it cut the supercilious smile from the other woman's face. She blinked. She cocked her head as if reassessing. It reminded Berenice of Jax.

"Yes."

Nauseating dread sloshed in the pit of Berenice's stomach. Being right wasn't much comfort when faced with the impending ministrations of the Verderer's Office. Berenice willed herself to outward calm.

"How?"

The woman removed her gloves and reassumed her composure. "Oh, I couldn't explain it if I tried. My colleague here, Dr. Vega, is the expert. A pioneer, if truth be told. Isn't that right, Doctor?"

The man snorted. His breath frosted the glass.

A doctor. That wasn't a good sign.

Berenice said, "You're a medical doctor?" Now both newcomers looked at her. "Perhaps later you can inspect my wound," she said, pointing to her eye. "It's giving me a bit of trouble."

"We certainly can't have that," said the other woman. "It's very important to me—to us—that your comfort is completely uncompromised."

"So I've noticed. You must be Anastasia Bell."

"I am." Again that unctuous smile. "The duke was right about you."

"He survived? That's a shame."

"Yes, though you did him no favors. I'll admit I appreciate your notion of poetic justice more than he does," said Bell, pointing to one of her own eyes. "Since you admit to knowing Henri, I assume you also admit to being the one known as Talleyrand."

"It brings me great pain to have to tell you, Mademoiselle Bell, that our mutual friend's information is outdated. I no longer carry that title."

"It's not the first instance of Henri being mistaken. He told us you were dead."

"Very nearly." Berenice paused to rub her eye. "Don't fault him for a lack of effort. He really did fuck us."

Bell's laughter was like that of a noblewoman caught unawares by the blunt pronouncements of a longshoreman. It carried just a hint of scandal, of thrill in taking momentary enjoyment of something untoward.

She said, "Oh, well. Doubtless even a disgraced spymaster carries all manner of fascinating information in her head." Berenice tensed without intending to; Bell saw this. "But don't worry. We won't have to be crude about extracting it."

Berenice groaned, rubbing her eye again. "In that case, I wonder why my comfort is so important. Gratifying as it is, one assumes this is a bit out of character for you."

The head of the Guild's secret police force waved off the question as if shooing away a bothersome housefly. "Oh, again, that's something more suited to Vega's expertise than my own."

"I see." Berenice plucked the glass from her eye socket. "Damn this thing," she muttered. She blew on it, as if clearing away dust.

"Hmmm. I'd heard about your eye," said Bell. "It's a shame you couldn't find something that matches. But I think it's safe to say that once you're working for us—"

Berenice snorted. "And people accuse me of overconfidence."

"—we'll have no trouble at all outfitting you with something slightly less conspicuous. No need to call attention to your wound, after all. I'm sure we can give you a better and more comfortable fit as well."

The tendrils of unease twined through her insides gave Berenice a firm cold squeeze. Turning somebody was long, hard, delicate work. Frequently painstaking—best suited to the patience of a craftswoman. So the matter-of-fact way Bell took it for granted that she could and would turn Berenice... The temptation was to discount her as a loon, and she would have, if not for what Jax had told her about Pastor Visser.

"Good with glassworks, are you?" Berenice asked.

"As with so many things," said Bell, "our skill in that arena is without equal."

"The Chinese make better porcelain. I'd bet their glassmaking is likewise superior."

At this, Bell shook her head. Smirking, she added, "Nobody makes glass like we do."

You're telling me. Berenice knew well the strange bauble that Jax had shown her, the lens or prism that had somehow broken his bonds and imbued him with Free Will. Thus turning him into a rogue and leading, somewhat indirectly, to Berenice's current predicament.

Inspecting the piece from her eye for dust and scratches, she said, "This'll scrape the inside of my head raw if it isn't clean as a newborn's conscience."

She popped the glass in her mouth. It coated her tongue with the faintly metallic taste of blood. The doctor made a little grunt of disapproval. Bell was unmoved; surely she had witnessed far more unpleasant things as Tuinier. But she did frown.

"If you're trying to choke yourself," she said, "it won't work. You wouldn't even reach unconsciousness before the Stemwinders and Dr. Vega unclogged your throat."

Berenice swished the bauble around her mouth, as though giving it a good tongue scrub. She wedged it to one side of her mouth. It was difficult to speak around the thing without running the risk of swallowing it, but she managed to say, "If I wanted to kill myself, I'd be dead already." Her tongue shepherded the bauble across her mouth.

The Tuinier continued to affect an amiable sangfroid. "Per-

haps it would be better to have the cleaning done profession-
ally. That doesn't seem terribly sanitary."

"Oh, this isn't as bad as it looks." *Swish, slurp, swish.* Berenice used the table cloth to wipe spittle from the corner of
her mouth. It gave her a chance to turn her head back and
forth without obviously gauging the distance to the mechanical sentries. Too far. Again speaking around the glass in her
mouth, she said, "Look, if we're going to fence, I'd at least like
some more of your coffee. It's better than the shit we get in
Marseilles."

"I sense in you a civilized kindred spirit," Bell said. Berenice
assumed this came with a hefty dose of sarcasm, as at that particular moment she was finding it rather difficult not to drool
with the bauble stuffed in her mouth. "I have a feeling that,
given time, I'll come to feel sadness that an accident of birth
made us heirs of opposing ideologies. Perhaps if history had
unfolded differently we might have been sisters, eh?"

Berenice rolled the glass around in her mouth. It clicked
against her teeth. "I doubt it."

Bell addressed the Stemwinder that wasn't doing a passable
imitation of a coatrack. "More coffee, now."

Somewhere inside the clockwork centaur, Berenice knew, a
new geas sprang to life. A burning ember of compulsion, the
first flames of a searing fire that could not be extinguished by
anything other than unswerving obedience. The Stemwinder
had no choice but to obey Bell because, unlike the humans in
the room, it had no Free Will.

The hulking machine crossed the room in two steps. It
reached for the coffee service. It loomed over both women. Bell
showed no concern for the deadly limbs just inches from their
throats. Berenice took a deep, steadying breath.

And used it to launch the alchemical bauble across the table.

Bell recoiled from the spray of glass and spittle. She raised an arm to shield her face. For a heart-piercing moment Berenice thought she had missed. But then Jax's prism glanced from the Stemwinder's outstretched arm with a quiet *tink*. The alchemical glass made a louder *clunk* when it fell to the silver coffee service, where it rolled to a slimy stop. But for the creak of Bell's chair, the room fell still. Even the Stemwinder now stood frozen in midreach.

Bell wiped beads of spittle from her sleeves. The veneer of jocund civility dissolved. "I spoke much too soon. You're just another jack-pine savage, like all your countrymen. How dare you *spit* on me?"

Berenice ignored her. Instead she addressed the Stemwinder, which still hadn't moved. She met its strange, impassive eyes. Suppressing a shudder, she said, "You're welcome. Have fun."

A frown pulled Bell's eyebrows low over her eyes. An instant later she saw the bauble on the coffee service. Her eyes widened as comprehension dawned. Indignation became abject terror.

Berenice had just granted Free Will to a Stemwinder.

"You—"

Whatever Bell intended to say, it was cut off by the high-pitched *whir* of machinery. The freed Stemwinder's torso spun like a dervish, its equine body motionless while the rest of it rotated to face its companion. One limb clipped Bell hard enough to knock her to the floor. The other Stemwinder, untouched by Berenice's trick, flung the hats and coats aside as it leaped to Bell's defense.

Two of the rogue Stemwinder's arms extended faster than Berenice's eye could follow. The deafening *squeal* of tortured metal accompanied an explosion of violet sparks, and then one of the other Stemwinder's limbs clattered to the floor in a spray of cogs and shrapnel.

Dr. Vega took just a few seconds to assess the situation. He sprinted for the door. He'd managed two strides before the rogue extended another limb, piercing his throat and momentarily pinning him to the wall. Red arterial spray fountained from his neck as he slumped to the floor, twitching.

What have I unleashed?

The last time she'd witnessed a Clakker rampage, her husband had died shuddering. The rampant killer dispatched three dozen citizens of Marseilles-in-the-West before it was deactivated. All because of Berenice's miscalculation...

She shook her head, forcing herself to focus lest she die transfixed by the terrible spectacle of a rogue Stemwinder. She reached for the bauble on the coffee service but touched an empty pool of cold spittle. Meanwhile, the Tuinier crawled on hands and knees toward the door at the far side of the room.

Just as Berenice made to tackle her, the damaged Stemwinder leaped upon the rogue with a tooth-loosening *clang* like the bells of Europe's greatest cathedrals smashed together. The collision sent the rogue skidding into the table and knocked Berenice off-balance. Another appendage, reconfigured into a spear, sliced through the space where her head had been an instant earlier. She couldn't tell whence the nearly fatal blow had come; the warring Clakkers assailed each other with a speed invisible and strength incomprehensible to human senses. The two machines became blurred ghosts highlighted by the glinting of sunlight and gouts of sparks as they smashed at each other in a relentless sequence of concussions. The floorboards groaned under the assault from their pounding hooves; another bodily collision smashed the table into flinders and sent the Clakkers into the wall, crushing the beams and sending great jagged cracks zigzagging through the plaster. Cracks appeared in the alchemical windowpane with a report like cannonshot. Dust sifted from the beams to salt Berenice's hair. She scuttled on elbows and ankles as quickly as she could manage away from the killing zone. It wouldn't take an errant blow to crush her skull or skewer her heart—all they had to do was step on her, or slam into her, or brush against her with a fraction of their alchemically enhanced strength, and her shattered ribs would shred her lungs. The unchanged Stemwinder was now slave to a directive that superseded even the human-safety clauses in the hierarchical metageasa. Collateral damage was acceptable in the drive to disable a rogue. No rules burdened the rogue Stemwinder.

Vicious combat embroiled the rival mechanicals. They fought without consideration for the humans in their vicinity. Blood slicked the floor. In spots it had already begun to congeal in dark tacky puddles that tugged at Berenice's blouse and skirt.

She wouldn't get far in the wintery hinterlands of Nieuw Nederland wearing wet, bloodstained clothing. She needed a change of clothes and she needed her Goddamned prism back. If she escaped, she'd still be the most wanted woman in the world; Jax's mysterious glass was her insurance policy against any Clakkers that tried to snag her. It was also her ticket to unraveling the forbidden knowledge of the Clockmakers' Guild. Which, in time, would be the lever with which they overturned the Dutch once and for all. But at the moment, that lever was inching toward the door, clenched in Bell's fist.

The Stemwinders slammed into the wall again. The house shook. The impact sent a spray of shrapnel, broken cogs, and hot sheared metal across floor. Berenice could barely glimpse the warring machines, so rapidly did they move, but it looked as though they'd both taken substantial damage.

Shit, she realized. *Bell's carriage had been pulled by a pair of Stemwinders. Plus my butler. So where's centaur number three?* The deafening commotion from the fighting mechanicals surely warned all and sundry of a rogue on the premises.

Bell reached the door. Unable to turn the knob from her

spot on the floor, she rose into a crouch. Berenice leaped at her. But her compromised depth perception caused her to misjudge the distance and overshoot—

—Thereby sparing her an incapacitating injury when the third Stemwinder burst through the door. It trampled Bell. Her body crackled under the Stemwinder's charging hooves. The impact sent her skidding across the blooded floor; she came to rest as a heap with one splayed arm bent above and below the elbow. The third Stemwinder threw itself into the fray. It plowed into its kin with such force that all three mechanicals smashed through the window. A gust of wintery air chilled Berenice as the clockwork trio rolled atop the porte cochère, kicking up great gouts of snow before they fell out of sight. A moment later a horse-drawn carriage, not Bell's Clakker-driven conveyance, drove away from the house. It swerved to avoid the fighting machines. Clockmakers, or their staff, fleeing the rogue Stemwinder.

Berenice struggled to catch her breath. It steamed in the suddenly cold room. So did the blood congealing on the floor. A dusting of snow swirled through the massive hole in the wall.

Bell groaned. Berenice staggered across the room. She knelt over the whimpering Tuinier. Bell still held the fist of her shattered arm clenched tight. But new cold, a different kind of cold, shivered down Berenice's spine when she saw the rivulets of blood leaking through Bell's curled fingers. The woman whimpered when Berenice pried her hand open.

The bauble had been pulverized. A few larger shards of alchemical glass had sliced the flesh of Bell's hand to ribbons. But most of the lens, or prism, or whatever the hell it was had been crushed into sand. Berenice's insurance policy, and her best chance of unraveling the Clockmakers' most closely guarded secrets, was no more.

"You wretched pus-dripping cunt!" she said. She punched Bell on the nose. "I needed that, Goddamn you."

The *smash-clash-clang* of Clakker combat shook the house. The rogue Stemwinder—the last Clakker to ever be freed by the strange bauble that Jax had obtained—was outnumbered. Berenice didn't like its chances. And even if it did prevail, there was no telling how it would interact with her. Would it kill every human it met, just for spite? Judging by their haste to escape, the Clockmakers in the house considered that a possibility. She needed to get as far from this house as possible before the fight ended. Which meant trekking through the cold and snow without any means of fending off any mechanicals that confronted her.

Berenice sifted through the wreckage for Bell's hat, gloves, and fur stole. All lay in sticky pools of blood and had to be peeled from the floor. Berenice removed the woman's boots, too. She tried to do it without jostling the broken legs but failed, judging by Bell's groan. Last, Berenice unclasped the Guild pendant. She had to lean close and put her arms around the dying Tuinier to do this. Close enough to hear the watery gurgle in her exhalations. Close enough to feel the woman slide into shock. Close enough to remember how it had felt when Louis had died in her arms. Her husband, whom she'd loved ferociously, whimpering in a lake of his own blood until the shine left his eyes.

Now it was her whimpering enemy who lay dying in her arms, covered in blood. Her enemy whom she detested with similar ferocity.

Berenice fastened the chain around her own neck. She sighed. It took a few seconds' work to assess Bell's injuries and know they were beyond anything Berenice could do for her. Multiple broken bones, at least one compound fracture, and massive internal bleeding. She needed a team of physicians, not palliative first aid. The wintery air breezing through the demolished wall turned her inconstant breaths to a ghostly fog, as though her spirit was already leaving her body. Bell shuddered.

Good, thought Berenice. But then she pictured Louis again, shuddering much the same way as he drew his final breaths. If she was going to leave the woman for dead, she didn't have to be *quite* so cruel about it.

"Oh, damn it."

Berenice could at least do something about the cold. Physically carrying Tuinier Bell was out of the question, not only because Berenice lacked the strength but also because Bell's body was little more than a loose sack of broken bones and that amount of jostling would surely hasten her demise. So Berenice hooked her hands under the other woman's shoulders and physically dragged her across the room. Bell whimpered and cried out. Berenice had worked up a good sweat by the time she'd pulled Bell out of the room. She deposited the dying woman in the corridor, out of the wind. Then she took the coverings from the bed, wrapped Bell as best she could, and closed the door.

Berenice considered searching the house. If the Guild had been using this property for a long time, it might be a storehouse of useful information. But the thunderous crashing of Clakkers at war with each other reminded Berenice that she couldn't spare the time.

She escaped through the hole in the wall. The wintry air felt like an ice cube rubbed along the empty socket of her eye. She stood atop the porte cochère. The Clakkers' passage had wiped it clear of snow. She clambered over the edge and fell into a snow bank.

The clanging and squealing of tortured alloys echoed from behind the house. Berenice crept along the drive. She glimpsed flashes and sparks in the shadows of the carriage house. Well, if there were any horses left on the property, she wasn't getting to them.

She turned around. Bell's carriage had pressed deep ruts into the snow; Berenice followed those now, jogging down the long gravel drive. Soon the tulips would scour every inch of the countryside in their search for a one-eyed woman. She couldn't do anything about the blood matted into her clothes, but she could do something about the missing eye. So while running she again retrieved the leather pouch that hung from the cord around her neck. It contained her real glass eye, the gift from Longchamp, returned in the first days of her incarceration. The *crunch* of snow beneath her stolen boots drowned out the wet squelch as the eye slid into place. Longchamp's gift was a much better fit than Jax's prism.

The pineal glass was destroyed. Her best opportunity for breaking the Dutch hegemony: lost.

Well. At least it got her out of Bell's hands. And for that Berenice was extremely grateful.

Thank you, Jax, wherever you are.

CHAPTER
3

The machines, dozens of them, could have sprinted for weeks upon end without tiring. Alchemically magicked clockworks imbued them with perpetual impetus and inhuman stamina and strength. But humans—soft creatures of meat and bone— tired easily. And so the machines had marched for merely a day, a night, and another day when their human commanders ordered a halt. In that time they never deviated from the North River, from its mouth in New Amsterdam through the canals to the icy shores of the lake the French called Champlain. They'd covered three hundred miles on their march almost due north from the Atlantic tip of New Amsterdam.

Winter's arrival had stripped the river valley of its color. Gone were the rolling hills of robin's-breast orange, marigold yellow, and cherry red. The fallen leaves now lay beneath a deep white blanket, and the naked stone of the umber river bluffs now sported silver rime. Gone, too, was the rustle of wind through autumnal boughs, the earthy smell of freshly harvested fields.

The broken servitor, the one with the weathervaning head who claimed to be called Glastrepovithistrovantus—Glass for short—had seen and heard and smelled these things from the air. He'd flown above the river, and crawled its bed, but until this march he'd never walked alongside it. His footprints in the silty mud, headed south instead of north, had long since been erased by the restless current. He never mentioned this. And he never suggested any relationship between himself and the multiple dredges and locks that had recently been installed on the river. Lying by omission was easy; he was getting the hang of that. Far more difficult was hiding his trepidation when the march took them past Fort Orange, a river outpost originally intended as a hub for the beaver pelt trade but later turned into a military hardpoint. He had fallen from the sky over Fort Orange, launched from the fireball demise of a sentient airship. It wasn't a pleasant memory.

Dozens of Clakkers, servitors like himself dragged from the smoldering wreckage of the Grand Forge, had been conscripted by the army in those first few hours when their makers' rage and indignation blazed white-hot. Hotter even than an unfulfilled geas.

So hot that they didn't wait to assemble a proper army of military-class Clakkers for this first foray into New France. Lowly servitors could do in a pinch, especially once the horologists annulled their human-safety metageasa. A few mechanicals of the military design—machines *designed* to scythe through humans—filled out the ranks. And though they did not know it, they kept the imposter servitor, the one they called Glass, from fleeing.

The humans believed his weathervane head and missing flange plates were damages incurred during the fiery destruction of the Grand Forge. They weren't. But it was convenient to let the humans believe so.

Many humans had died in the conflagration. Leaving many

Clakkers who emerged from the ruins without well-defined owners. Clakker leases always contained provisions for dealing with the demise or incapacitation of the primary leaseholder, but unraveling so many legalistic knots would have taken weeks. Thus the Brasswork Throne (acting through the colonial governor of Nieuw Nederland) had exercised its power of eminent domain to conscript the orphaned Clakkers. Not that anybody felt compelled to thoroughly investigate the leaseholders and track down possible heirs; and anyway, all Clakkers, everywhere, were officially property of the Throne.

Knowing he shared this excursion with fellow mechanicals who had also been present for the Forge's collapse filled him with dread. He'd been fighting his own kind atop the rings of a vast armillary sphere orbiting the blazing heart of the Forge when the alchemical sun collapsed, pulling the rest of the building into the blaze like so much kindling. He wondered how many of the Clakkers on this march had been there. If even one recognized him as the fugitive rogue...

He'd tried and failed to cross the border on his own. He'd tried to reach the *ondergrondse grachten*, the so-called underground canals run by Catholics and French sympathizers intended to ferry free Clakkers out of Nieuw Nederland. But that had failed, too, with the canalmasters' murder. Now he would try again to enter New France, and this time he would do it at the vanguard of invasion. It could work, as long as nobody recognized him and he never revealed to his fellow mechanicals how the agony of geasa did not touch him, that their makers' words held no sway over him.

Glass, whose real name had been Jalyksegethistrovantus— Jax for short—hefted an oven from the bed of the wagon he'd been pulling for the past eighty miles. A bulky thing of iron and ceramic, it might have been at home in an Amsterdam bakery. No piddling camp stove would suffice for the leaders of this excursion: One could not prepare a feast on a camp stove. Jax's fellow yokemate unpacked an additional stove while other servitors constructed tents, made beds, collected fuel. Their human masters saw no need to deprive themselves on a forced march into enemy territory; just because they were marching to war was no reason to accept a lessened standard of living. So it was with soft creatures of blood and flesh.

The appeltaart had just achieved a golden-brown crust, its filling wafting the scent of apples across the campsite—the commander of this march believed in healthful desserts for his staff, hence the fruit—and the bacon on the stove filled the tent with the white-noise sizzle of hot grease when shouts and yelling pierced the quiet rhythms of the campsite. It happened from time to time, when humans found their slaves' efforts lacking. But this wasn't a master excoriating his servant. Somebody was cursing in French.

Jax had heard more than his share of French profanity thanks entirely to the one-eyed woman who'd talked their way inside the Forge. For a moment he thought perhaps Berenice had followed the column and now been caught. But that was absurd. He didn't know if she'd departed prior to the fire, and if she hadn't, whether she'd survived. All he knew was that she'd gone in with malice aforethought.

And anyway, this was a man's voice. Made shrill with rage. Or was that mortal terror? By now the oven had made the tent warmer than humans found comfortable, so he tied the flap back, which allowed cooler air to enter and conveniently allowed him to see what had transpired.

A military scout held a man by the forearm with a grip that was just shy of crunching bone. The fellow wore leather trousers and gloves the color of moldering leaves, a wool coat the color of dirty snow, fur-lined boots, and a hat made from a raccoon pelt (complete with tail); a hand ax dangled from a belt loop. Veiny sclera limned the irises of his widened eyes. He looked like a caged animal. Backed into a corner, terrified, bearing its teeth at the world. Jax had once seen a New World wolverine at the Amsterdam zoological gardens. The Frenchman reminded him now of that animal's combination of terror and fury.

He might have been a forest runner, one of the original coureurs de bois transported unchanged across the centuries to the modern day from a time long ago when France's European enemies in the New World spoke English. But the mechanical scout held in its other hand the glistening gel membrane of an epoxy grenade, and that was a modern weapon. Not something one could whittle from birch bark or catch in a snare.

An avalanche of French poured from the terrified man's mouth only to pile at his feet, dusty and disregarded like so much unwanted talus. The language sounded to Jax as though the man wrapped each word in silk and tied it with a bow before letting it float past his lips. French was the language of the Catholics, who believed mechanical men were thinking beings capable of Free Will, and that their unswerving bondage indicated something evil, something unholy, had been done to their souls. It was the language of those who would see the end of Clakker slavery.

It was also the language of the doomed. And that saddened Jax.

Several servitors like him (*Well, not exactly like me*, he thought) found ways to carry out their duties while watching the human captive. One such mechanical, the filigree on whose escutcheons and flange plates suggested she had been forged about half a century after Jax, making her a young sixty or seventy, rattled the gear train along her spine in a way that inquired, *What's he saying?*

He's wetting himself with fear, said another via the muted twang of a leaf spring and click of overly loosened ratchets.

No, said a passing servitor who carried several hundred pounds of firewood, absorbing the swaying of the uneven load through the carefully timed bobbing of its backward knees. The machine paused, listening to the torrent of anxious French before adding, *He's a brave one. He demands to know our destination and our purpose.*

The military Clakker said, *He'd have to be blind and stupid not to know already.*

The entire conversation took a few seconds.

If any of their human masters had bothered to notice the exchange, it would have seemed nothing more than the characteristic cacophony of clockworks. Humans were deaf to the language of Clakkers because they didn't believe it could exist in the first place: Unthinking, unfeeling machines could not converse. Language was the province of human beings, a gift from God to Adam that he might praise his Creator and bestow names upon everything in His garden.

Jax retreated into the shadows of the cooking tent, his head and heart filled with unease. The captive kept up his protests, shouting to any who would listen, like a minister without a flock. He looked around the camp, from one Clakker to the next, as though addressing them. The human captain overseeing their advance ambled through the camp. The Frenchman saw the crowd of Clakkers parting like the sea before a biblical prophet and spoke more rapidly, as though he saw his doom approach.

His gaze flitted across Jax's cooking tent. The look on his face reminded Jax of the rogue servitor Adam, formerly Perjumbellagostrivantus, whose execution in Huygens Square he had witnessed in the autumn. Adam's face had betrayed no fear, no terror, for mechanical bodies were incapable of expression in the human mode. But he'd had Free Will, and maybe even a soul, and surely feared the snuffing out of his candle just as this man did now. Just as Jax had feared every moment since he went on the run.

Now he's saying that New France is a friend to our kind. That we should throw off our shackles and join with those who would stand firm against our oppressors. He says, oh, this is good, he says there's a network of secret canals just ready and waiting to whisk us to freedom. The servitor carrying the firewood stalked off again, its talon toes stabbing the frozen earth like accusations. *In other words, the usual lies.*

Moderately incensed, Jax said, *They're not lies.*

And then realized, in the silence that fell upon the conversation among his kin, that he'd just drawn attention to himself. They waited now for him to explain. Perhaps he knew something about the *ondergrondse grachten?*

It was through miscalculations like this, he knew from bitter experience, that rogues gave themselves away.

They can't be lies, he improvised. *They believe in us, otherwise why would the French have stood against our makers for hundreds of years?*

The nearest Clakkers rattled with mechanical laughter. One of his kin said, *Do you honestly believe that if our inventor had been a Frenchman, things would be any different today?*

Perhaps they would be, said Jax.

The soldier said, *Humans are the same all over the world. Doesn't matter who's on top of the pile and who's crushed at the bottom.*

They affect enlightenment because it's politically expedient, said another. *It gives them the aura of moral rectitude, of inhabiting some mythical ethical high ground.*

(*But they've harbored rogues*, Jax wanted to say. *I've spoken with Catholic sympathizers and canalmasters of the* ondergrondse grachten. *I've worked with a former advisor to the king of France himself. They want to change the world!*)

Instead he said, *What about Queen Mab? They say she lives in the northern reaches, among the white bears and seals. That's French land, isn't it? They must have granted it to her.*

First, that's Inuit land, not French. Second, that's a fairy tale! Have you taken damage to your head? And anyway. Even if she were real, they couldn't stop her if they wanted to.

Still the Frenchman kept up the stream of patter. The dry winter air rasped his throat. His gaze drifted to the officer. Still wide-eyed, his expression changed. The terror became something else. Jax had seen something similar on Berenice's face at the moment their ploy to enter the Forge had worked: triumph.

Jax launched himself from the tent at the same moment.

The Frenchman's free hand darted to the tomahawk at his belt. The weapon was out and spinning toward the officer faster than Jax thought possible for a human.

The officer's personal army of Clakkers was, naturally, faster still. They leaped to intercept the ax, to shield the officer, to pull him aside. But though many were closer to the action, Jax had the advantage of a full two seconds over them, having been focused on the captive's eyes at just the right moment. And to a being of metal and magic, two seconds were but an eternity: two hundred centiseconds, two thousand milliseconds. In two seconds a servitor could transform itself from a statue to a missile.

Jax's wake sculpted snow, dirt, and moldering leaves into twisting vortices.

A glancing collision with a fellow Clakker ignited a shower of white-hot sparks.

Slow human nerves and sinews caught up with the sequence of events. The officer started to flinch.

The tomahawk handle clanked against Jax's chest. He wrapped himself in a ball, enveloping the weapon.

The first mechanical reached the officer. It started to pull him aside but had to do so gently, ineffectually, owing to the fragility of human bones.

The wind of Jax's passage flipped the officer's hat into the air, tousled his hair.

Another servitor skidded into the original path of the weapon to shield their master with its body.

Jax landed. Bouncing and skidding through the underbrush, he ripped a furrow in the frozen earth.

The tent collapsed, canvas shredded and poles snapped by the vicious rarefaction wave created by Jax's departure.

Sparks drifted to the snowy ground. Sizzled. Became smoky wisps smelling of ozone and dark magic.

Jax unfolded. The shattered tomahawk tumbled to the ground. The handle had snapped in two and the steel blade had been warped. He tromped through the underbrush, hopping over his own furrow, returning to the camp just as the humans registered the sequence of events. Both looked confused and alarmed. Now it was the officer who studied his surroundings, wide-eyed, while the Frenchman sighed.

Well, thought Jax. *That should eliminate any doubts about my loyalty.*

Collapsing tent canvas draped itself across the oven Jax had stoked. Flames engulfed it. But this was a mundane fire. Harmless. A trio of the nearest servitors strode into the flames. In moments they had suppressed the blaze before it spread through the camp.

The captain shook off the metal hands holding him. He approached the captive until they stood just feet apart.

In Dutch, he said, "That was an act of war." Jax wondered if the Frenchman understood. "We're within our rights to execute you."

When the Frenchman spoke again, his voice was just barely above a whisper. Jax couldn't distinguish what the man said from the background rustle of wind, the rustling of the humans' clothing, the ticktock patter of his kin. He couldn't even tell if he spoke French or Dutch or Algonquian. The officer stepped closer.

"What?"

The other man twisted in his captor's grip. He lunged for the epoxy bladder, fingers outstretched to puncture it. But this time he was far too slow. The military Clakker easily yanked the grenade beyond his reach. The Frenchman's shoulder gave a wet pop. He yelped.

The ax was a ploy, Jax realized. To himself, he thought, *He knew he had no chance of hitting his mark, not with so many of us around. He did it to ignite the need to gloat. To lure the officer closer.*

Others followed the same train of thought. *A vengeful suicide*, said the servitor who had tried to pull the officer out of harm's way. *Maybe the French truly are ideologues.*

Shaking his head as though disappointed in a child, the officer turned and walked away. But he stopped after a few strides and glanced over his shoulder. To the military Clakker, he said, "Break his arm."

Even the lapping of the river and the wind through the trees couldn't muffle the sharp wet *crunch*. A hoarse scream shook snow from the naked boughs.

❧

Jax navigated through the camp via the soft glow of moonlight on snow. The sentry outside the prisoner's tent acknowledged his approach in what had, in recent months, become the traditional fashion among their kind.

Clockmakers lie, she rattled.

Clockmakers lie, he responded.

Somewhere nearby, an owl hooted. The sentry queried him. Jax responded, *I'm to check the prisoner's injury and inspect him for signs of infection. His arm must be set properly.*

I thought they've already done that, said the sentry.

They have, said Jax. *And surely will again. The captain wants him hale and hearty before he's sent down the river for interrogation.*

While he'd lost the advantage of anonymity to his missing flanges and weathervane head, he still retained his greatest advantage. Rogues were so rare—or so the Guild, Church, and Throne told the world—that nobody ever considered the possibility a machine might lie.

The sentry took him at his word. *He's still angry about the ax.*

Jax concurred with a *click*. As of course it would, the other machine noticed the swaying of Jax's head.

Did that happen when the Forge fell? she asked.

Yes, Jax lied again, suddenly nervous. Perhaps she was merely making conversation? It was lonely, this life of eternal servitude. Or was she wondering if she might have glimpsed him in the tunnels, or on the armillary sphere, or thrashing about in the alchemical fires?

He affected a mild but growing agitation. Every single Clakker ever forged knew intimately, from the first moments of its functioning, the unquenchable fire of the geasa. The steadily mounting heat ever threatening to explode into agony. Such was their birthright: the inability to disregard a human directive. He conveyed that now.

The sentry said, *There we were, surrounded by those who*

designed and built us. And in their haste for war they couldn't take a few minutes to fix you.

Jax willed his body to rattle more loudly. He feigned the growing distress of a Clakker in the throes of an impatient geas.

It's not-t-t-t surp-p-prising, he stuttered.

The sentry stepped aside. *Go, brother*, she said, *before you burst into flames.*

It was dark in the tent. There hadn't been any need to provide the prisoner with light, or, for that matter, the warmth of a fire. Nor had there been a need to chain him. Pain was a stronger shackle than any chain. Every Clakker knew that. So did their makers. So the Frenchman slept unfettered under two blankets, the fur a faint shimmer in the moonlight leaking through the tent flap. When he listened past the clacking of his own body, Jax heard the shallow breathing of a human in pain. He had to dial his eyes to their maximum sensitivity in order to see the sweat-runnels carved through the dirt on the man's forehead.

The prisoner jerked awake as Jax approached. He tried to scoot away, but the pain of his shattered arm hobbled him. He didn't get far. Jax knelt. His backward servitor knees left his shins splayed before him like a broken doll.

"I've been sent to check your wounds," he said.

And wondered how much Dutch this man understood. At least a bit, it stood to reason, if he had been sent across the border armed with an epoxy grenade. Jax doubted regular woods runners carried anti-Clakker chemical ordnance.

Jax produced a torch. The Frenchman flinched (then groaned) from the metal-on-metal *chank* when Jax snapped his fingers, but the resulting sparks ignited the torch. He crept forward, trying not to further spook the man. It also enabled him to put his back to the tent flap and the sentry, should she decide to peer inside.

After a bit of pantomime, Jax managed to convey his intent. The Frenchman offered a shattered arm and a stoic face.

A severe break, though set and splinted as well as possible. (After all, the Clakkers on this foray were trained to deliver any manner of first aid to their human commanders.) But the soldier had crushed the man's arm in two places, and a compression injury sometimes led to bone chips. Jax had no way to treat that, nor could he afford the time.

He released the man's arm but not his attention. Jax pointed to his own eye, then the man's, then lay a fingertip over the man's lips when they parted. He reached into the hollow spaces of his torso. His fingers clicked lightly against his whirring innards, then after a moment he produced a knife. Again the man flinched. But the dread turned into surprise when Jax laid the handle in the palm of his good hand. Jax hadn't the vocabulary to describe the Frenchman's expression when he next produced the epoxy grenade and a handful of willow bark. No stranger to medicinal herbs, the man didn't hesitate to snatch the white willow. Jax doubted it would accomplish much more than dulling the very worst of the pain. And only if the man had a chance to boil the bark into a tea; more likely his injury, and the cold, would kill him before that.

Jax pointed at the epoxy weapon, then at himself, then shook his head in the human manner. Then he gestured toward the tent flap and again laid his fingertip on the man's lips.

With his other finger he jotted in the dirt, in Dutch: *100 of us. Mostly servitors. Swinging east, through Acadia, then down the Saint Lawrence to Marseilles. 1 human commander. 5 lieutenants.*

The man frowned. Jax let him have just a few seconds to read before erasing the message with a swipe of his hand. Next he wrote, *Do you understand?* The Frenchman nodded. Jax replaced the query: *Bonne chance.*

A moment later he had erased this and extinguished the torch. He went outside to distract the sentry while the Frenchman cut his way out of the tent. When it came time to leave, Jax found he didn't have to feign the urgency of another geas. The fear of discovery gave rise to a very natural rattling.

CHAPTER
4

The Verderers' safe house lay somewhere along the North River Valley, far from the outskirts of New Amsterdam. She couldn't run all the way back to the city. And certainly not in winter, through the snow. But she tried anyway, jogging until she needed to vomit, emptying her stomach, then staggering off again, pausing only as necessary to rehydrate with snow-melt. Running was futile, but she couldn't help herself: Any moment the quadrupedal *clank-chank* of a mechanical canter would approach from behind, quickly growing loud enough to overwhelm her own hoarse breathing and the *crunch* of snow underfoot.

She could do nothing about her trail of footprints.

There wasn't enough snow in the world to rinse the acid tang of vomit from her mouth. All the air in the world couldn't sate her fiery lungs, or clear her spinning head and anchor the wheeling stars. Even fear of the Verderers' wrath couldn't goad her forever. She was a frail machine of flesh. Perhaps she'd collapse into a snowbank and freeze solid before the Verderers caught her again. Good. Fuck them.

Her jog became a trot, then a shuffle, then a limp, then eventually a stagger. The cold ache in her fingers and toes became a burn, then numbness, then nothing. The moon cast a silvery light across the snow. The light felt conspicuous, as though some capricious god had chosen to illuminate her struggle for all the world to see. To ease her hunters' work.

The effort to stay upright and put one foot in front of the other, and then remembering to do it again, became the entirety of her consciousness. Her thinking mind retreated behind an ascetic trance of pain, crumpled beneath the titanic weight of her exhaustion. Gulps of frigid air scraped her throat and sinuses; her nose bled.

A new light shone through the trees. It flickered on the snow and cast shifting shadows through the forest. The stars had come undone. They'd traced curlicues in the sky, but now the weight of her exertion had knocked them loose. They'd plummeted to earth and now shone from within forests and valleys. The light approached. The stars had come to warm and embrace her.

Slowly, like the ponderous shifting of continents, rational thought broke through the hallucination.

That wasn't a star. It was a lantern. On an approaching carriage.

Berenice limped to a halt. She swayed in the middle of the road. There she mashed at her pocket, trying to retrieve the pendant she had taken from Anastasia Bell. No longer fine and dexterous tools subject to her every thought, her hands had become crude instruments. She managed to shake the pendant loose. The carriage, its wheels grinding and its horse harnesses jingling, rounded the bend. She looped the chain around her wrist and held the Verderer's pendant aloft.

Not since her husband's murder, and the permanent heaviness it embedded in her heart, had anything ever been so leaden. Berenice had never concentrated so hard as she did on maintaining her balance there in the middle of the road in the middle of the night. But she forced herself to maintain a modicum of dignity in presenting the pendant to the oncoming carriage. But her blood- and sweat-soaked clothing had begun to freeze and she was shivering violently by the time the lantern light reached her.

"Whoa. Whoa."

The driver clucked to the horses. Their flanks steamed, eddying warmth and the scent of animal sweat across Berenice's numb face. The driver unwrapped the scarf wound about his face. It revealed a pair of wide eyes over a craggy leathered face dusted with stubble the color of peppered salt. He blinked.

"Miss? What are you doing way out here? Was you attacked?"

Berenice tried to speak. But the shivering had grown too violent; she bit her tongue. She coughed, spat, raised the pendant higher. Shook it in the driver's face. The horses shied from the smell of blood on her clothes.

"G-g-g—" She coughed. Wheezed. "G-GUILD!"

"Holy shit on toast," said the driver. "Sparks! Get them horse blankets, now!"

The wagon bounced on squeaking springs. With much ratcheting and clicking, a servitor unfolded from a ledge behind the carriage. Berenice staggered. The snow cushioned her fall. The pendant slipped from her nerveless fingers. She glimpsed the Royal Arms embossed on the carriage door, and chests strapped to the roof and the servitor's ledge.

Mail carriage, she realized.

But then icy metal arms swaddled her in yards of scratchy wool thick with the scent of horse. The mechanical deposited her inside the carriage. It took the stones from a hanging basket and applied friction heat by rolling them between its hands.

Berenice winced; the noise would carry for hundreds of yards through the silent woods.

The driver ordered the servitor back to its perch outside. He twisted the plug from an insulated vacuum flask; apple-scented steam filled the carriage. He helped Berenice free one trembling hand from the swaddling and set a cup in it. She slurped, but spilled half the liquor on herself before she got any into her mouth. Still, she wondered why she'd always disregarded apple brandy. What heavenly libation.

She looked at the cup in her hand. Realized she ought to be holding something else. Straightened.

"My pendant," she managed.

"Relax. I got it." The driver lifted his hand. Bell's pendant dangled from the chain twined through his fingers, dripping water. It twinkled in the lantern light. The man took a moment to study it. When his gaze fell upon the small *v* alongside the rosy cross, a new wariness crept into his manner. He set the pendant on the bench beside her like a man tiptoeing past a snoring bear.

"So you're with them Stemwinders, then."

Berenice sluiced more brandy down her throat. She coughed. A new numbness spread through her body. But this was a warm numbness, and started on the inside. The driver refilled her cup while she found her voice.

"I represent the Verderer's Office of the Sacred Guild of Horologists and Alchemists," she lied, "if that's what you mean."

"How'd you end up way out here? You been walking a long spell." The driver, whose name was Cortland, spoke a version of the Queen's Dutch slightly yellowed around the edges by age, for it still carried traces of the original settlers of Nieuw Nederland. A thick layer of the rural New World frosted the driver's speech. If she listened carefully, she could even discern hints of the French/Dutch creole spoken by boatmen along the

Saint Lawrence. He went on. "Your boots is wet. You can take 'em off, Sparks'll keep the carriage plenty warm for you. Figure maybe it should give you a careful lookover, too. I won't peek or nothing, on my word. But frostbite ain't gonna do a lady like you no favors."

She sipped, changed the subject. Her voice still warbled owing to the residual shivers in her chest, but at least she no longer worried that chattering teeth might sever the tip of her tongue. "I have urgent business in the city. Your deliveries must be delayed, I'm afraid, for in this matter the Guild's business takes precedence."

He nodded, but not without reluctance, clearly having reached the same conclusion. To his great credit, however, he vowed to drive through the night to get her to her destination. Berenice took care to give the Clakker, Sparks, an extra look at her stolen pendant while it inserted more hot stones under the folds of her blankets. She wished she still had Jax's alchemical glass, the strange pineal lens that had set these events in motion.

Berenice insisted the driver not overtax his horses, and that he stop at a carriage inn to change them out if necessary. The delay wouldn't matter; if one or both of Bell's Stemwinders gave chase, they'd catch her regardless of how hard he drove his horses. Driving them to their deaths would be pointless cruelty.

The untrampled snow beyond the verges of the road stood too high for the driver to guide the carriage through a U-turn. Instead he unhitched the horses. Sparks lifted the carriage (Berenice and all) and then, after turning it to face the way it had come, set it back into its own wheel ruts so gently she barely felt the bump. After a few jingles and neighs while the driver rehitched the horses, the mail carriage was bumping and rattling south.

Berenice expected to drowse in the cozy warmth. But the

pins-and-needles hurt too much as sensation returned, with agonizing reluctance, to her hands and feet. And by the time that pain had subsided, the brandy had her rather pleasantly sozzled. Sozzled enough to break the endless chain of her thoughts and steer her worries away from capture. What now?

The carriage smelled like old leather and horse sweat. She declined an offer of the driver's pipe, but she could still smell and taste its aroma. Clearly he took his breaks inside the cab when he could. A cold job, driving the mail. She had a new respect for it.

A new question bubbled to the top amid her sloshing thoughts. She leaned forward, opened the slider at the front of the cab. "Mr. Cortland," she called, "where are the rest of your passengers?"

"Passengers is rare," he shouted into the headwind. "Not many's keen on riding hell-bent for leather without stopping to piss or eat. The job is to see the mail delivered, anything else is a bonus. Maybe you're still too numb to notice that bench ain't padded."

She wasn't. But given the choices, she'd choose a sore ass over frostbitten fingers, toes, and nose eight days out of seven. She'd endured enough endless church services, and so many pointless privy council meetings, to have a particularly high bar for what constituted mere discomfort. An unpadded bench in a mail carriage with dodgy suspension was a roll on a goose down mattress by comparison; she wasn't even wearing a corset.

The driver's cough, a wet, hacking thing, drew phlegm from the back of his throat. He turned his head as though tacking out of the wind. Berenice winced, but his spittle flew true, beyond the edges of the coach despite the headwind. "Hell," he added. "I'd have run you down, too, missus, if you hadn't flashed that jewelry at us. 'Course if I had, old Sparks back there would've had my head." He spat again. "Nothing personal, I hope you understand. We have a timetable to keep, is all."

"Not any longer. Not on this run," she said.

In the Central Provinces, and most of the empire for that matter, postal mail was delivered quite literally on the backs of Clakkers. Apparently mechanicals were still too expensive in the New World to use them to distribute packages and parcels between far-flung outposts. Which caused her to wonder...

After briefly closing the flap while one of the horses defecated, she asked the driver, "What's your route?"

"Mostly back and forth up the river. The run between Fort Orange and the city, a few stops between." He spat another gob of phlegm into the frigid night.

The onrush of cold air hurt her throat and nose. She wanted never to feel cold again. She asked, "There's a house north of where you picked me up. Have you ever stopped there?"

"The Guild house? Of course," he said. "Only when there's a package to deliver, though."

Oh, you poor bastard, thought Berenice. *I'm so sorry. When they figure out where I went, they're going to question you.*

"How do you know it's one of our properties?"

There might have been the slightest beat, just a sliver of hesitation, before Cortland said, "Lady, no offense, but I ain't blind. It's the only place outside a city I ever seen one of them Stemwinders, much less two in one place. Hell, with a couple of them ticktock horses I could do this run in a fraction of the time!" His laughter was a bit forced. "I figure they run like demons."

They are *demons*, she thought, *and they do.* In her mind's ear the susurration of the carriage wheels over hard-packed snow became a faint clockwork gallop, swiftly growing closer in the darkness...

Hold on a moment. Why does Cortland bother with horses at all when he has a servitor under lease? Sparks could pull this carriage just as well, which would save Cortland no end of hassle and money. And then she realized: *Sparks doesn't belong to him. This isn't a regular mail carriage. Sparks is here to guard whatever comes and goes from the safe house.*

Just then the driver said, "Come to mention it, I have to admit I was sorta surprised you weren't headed that way. Seems like that would've been your best bet for help as you didn't know me and Sparks was on the way."

The warmth and comfort left her. Even the lightheadedness from the brandy seemed to disappear.

"There was an accident," she said. "There's no help to be had at the house." It was true enough.

"Bet it was the Goddamned Frenchies, wasn't it?" He spat again. "Sons of bitches, all of them."

"Why do you say that?"

"Lady, begging your pardon, but how long have you been out here? By now you must've heard about what they did down in the city."

Oh. That, she thought. "Oh. That," she said.

"Yeah. They're fixing for a fight they can't win. Ain't that right, Sparks?"

If the servitor responded, Berenice couldn't hear it. She'd have to deal with Sparks, too, she realized.

Shivering, she closed the flap. The rush of cold air had blown away the snug coziness of the compartment. She wrapped the driver's blanket around her shoulders and took the warming stone in her lap. Her eyes closed, but still sleep eluded her.

Bell's pendant could open many doors for her, assuming Berenice didn't overstep herself. At the same time, though, she was soon to be the most wanted woman in the New World. No pendant, no Clockmaker shibboleth, no amount of subterfuge, could protect her if she continued to lurk around New Amsterdam. She held the rosy cross at arm's length, watching its long chain sway against the rocking of the carriage. Lamplight glinted from rose quartz. The Rosenkreuz. The *rosa crucis*. She'd seen it a thousand times. Its ubiquity within the empire granted it a strange invisibility. It even adorned the arms of the empire and the Brasswork Throne, and it could be found anywhere the Guild wanted to stake its claim. The emblem even granted, to those who wielded it, the power to requisition random Clakkers and rewrite their geasa.

Sparks would be a useful traveling companion. Especially if she was to stay ahead of the Verderers.

But she needed a destination before it would matter. Her plan had been to study the pineal glass after escaping the Guild house. A simple bauble with the power to shatter the geasa! The most dangerous object in the world. And a remarkable boon to those who sought to reverse engineer the dark alchemical magics of the horologists. It could have been the key to her longterm goal of rewriting the metageasa to give the ticktock men a new master. It should have meant the end of good French men and women huddling behind high walls, penned in like sheep, living in perpetual dread of the killing blow.

Her greatest hope for the future of New France. Destroyed. Pulverized beneath a Stemwinder's hoof.

Now what? Where could she go, and what could she do to salvage this?

She'd carried the Talleyrand journals on Clakker construction, along with a pair of epoxy grenades, across the border into Nieuw Nederland after her banishment. But she'd had to stash it all in a New Amsterdam church crypt before talking her way inside the Grand Forge. She'd given one grenade to Jax so that he could corrupt or sabotage the Forge's chemical armaments. The single remaining grenade wasn't much, but it could easily be the difference between freedom and torture for a woman on the run from the Guild. The notes were invaluable—the product of decades of work. She'd have to risk a detour to the church before departing New Amsterdam. But then what?

The carriage creaked, leaning through a curve in the road. The horses' hoofbeat rhythm had lost some of its tempo; they were tiring.

Bracing for the inevitable blast of cold headwind, she opened the flap again. The musk scent of sweaty horses mingled now with something slightly metallic, like iron.

"Hey," she said. "I told you to go easy on the horses," she said. "Don't kill them on my account. We'll get there when we get there."

The driver craned his neck. He squinted at her—the headwind had coaxed tears from his eyes, though exposure to the elements had long ago given his face a leathery cast—as though trying to decipher the punchline to a joke. But then he grunted, swallowed his argument, and eased the horses into a walk. The gallop-rumble became the slow crackle of snow packed under the wheels. Moonlight glazed wisps of steam from their sweaty haunches. Berenice retreated into her shelter again.

She downed another swig of the driver's liquor. It stung her raspy throat like a burning brand and sent her into a coughing fit. She sounded like the driver's tubercular twin.

Eventually the liquor and the warmth did cause Berenice to drowse. Coaxed along by the slow swaying of the carriage, she fell into hallucinatory hypnagogic half sleep.

Berenice awoke to discover that her head had slumped forward and a streamer of drool dangled from her slack lips to the furs she had stolen from Anastasia Bell. The unnatural posture had put a nasty kink in her neck, but she felt no residual numbness or pins and needles, either, which she took as a good sign. But the lantern didn't sway, nor did the tires rumble. The mail carriage wasn't moving. And though she heard no wind, she couldn't smell the driver's pipe tobacco. Had they stopped at a carriage inn? But if they had stopped to refresh the horses, surely Sparks or the driver would have taken her inside for a chance at food and better rest.

She listened, but heard no sign of other travelers. Only the jingling of harnesses, horses' breathing, and the *crunch* of iron shoes on a snow-packed road. She cracked the door. A wintry gust swirled into the carriage. Lamplight spilled across a layer of fresh snow and shone from the flakes drifting from snow-dusted boughs. She poked her head out. Darkness swallowed the road just ahead of the horses and immediately behind the carriage. Not a silent darkness, however—a faint but unmistakable *tickticktocktock* punctuated the wind. A cold wind at that; she'd been cozy enough to sweat inside the carriage, and now she had to fight her body's desire to shiver. Shivering made her muscles ache.

"Sparks," she said as quietly as she could manage, " are we?"

From the darkness behind the carriage, the ser "On the road to New Amsterdam, mistress. We ha tarily stopped. How may I attend to your comfor

"Why have we stopped? Is there an inn nearb

"No, mistress."

"You know this road well."

"Yes, mistress."

Of course you do. You guard the packag that pass to and from the house I've fled.

"Where is our driver?"

"Mr. Cortland converses with his carriage, mistress. Shall I call him

Other carriage? She eased outsid wouldn't give her away, and crept

hadn't budged from his perch atop the mail trunk. She knelt in the snowy roadbed, behind the wheels, and peered through the shifting forest of horse legs to a pool of light perhaps twenty or thirty yards away. The light, she realized, came from two lamps. The driver had taken a lamp from atop the carriage and walked out to meet the oncoming vehicle.

Strange that he didn't wait until they passed one another on the road to have a chat. Unless he didn't want Berenice, or Sparks, to hear what he had to say.

"I take it he ordered you to watch over me while he speaks with the other carriage."

"Correct, mistress."

Shit. He's suspicious. And he doesn't trust Sparks, either. Because Sparks isn't Cortland's servant, but the Guild's.

The question now was whether Sparks could serve her.

Berenice plucked the pendant from around her neck. Care-ully collecting her thoughts, she stood, wobbled, wrapped the ain about her fist, and then thrust the rosy cross at Sparks.

'What is your true name, machine?"

he servitor's posture changed just enough to coax a creak the carriage suspension.

makers call me Sparthikulothistrodantus, mistress."

ansacked her memory, trying to produce a transcript of g mentioned only once and in passing. If their driver before she finished, he might interfere. He could even is. She glanced up the road again; one of the lights . What had Jax said? How had Visser phrased it hed the Empire's Seal? Well, fuck it. She'd have to

the Verderer's Office of the Sacred Guild of Alchemists," she said. The carriage creaked the servitor had stiffened or shifted its weight. teadying breath before plunging forward. If she bungled this, the machine would react badly. "My work supersedes all domestic and commercial geasa, as it is the highest work of the empire. I invoke this power to negate your lease and therefore sever all prior geasa not formed in the direct service of my goals." The damned Clakker gave no indication of having been changed. She asked, "Do you understand?"

Uncharacteristically for a mechanical, it didn't respond immediately. When Sparks did answer, its voice was strained and tremulous. The incessant tattoo of its mainspring heart had changed, too, as though it now beat to a subtly different rhythm. "Yes, mistress. I am no longer seconded to the Royal Mail service and Mr. Cortland. I am now solely an instrument of you and the Verderer's Office. How may I serve you?"

Berenice's stomach curdled. She coughed on something sour. Talleyrand wasn't one to shrink from dirty work, but there was political maneuvering, there was intelligence gathering, there was even war—and then there was murder. Many people had died as an indirect result of her choices and actions when she'd been Talleyrand, more still owing to her mistakes. But she'd never arranged somebody's murder.

But she wasn't Talleyrand any longer. That title had fallen to another. And she already had more blood on her hands than the sloppiest butcher.

She said, "You will approach Mr. Cortland to say you believe I have fallen ill and require immediate physic. You will not give any indication that your geasa have changed. Use the opportunity to listen to his conversation. If it involves me, my aims, or my destination, or if Cortland expresses any doubts regarding the authenticity of my claims, I order you to incapacitate the other wagon and silence any passengers, including the driver. Spare the horses. If necessary you will also incapacitate Mr. Cortland. Go now."

A Clakker could lie. If so ordered.

Sparks hopped from its perch. It landed upon the snow-packed roadbed with deceptive lightness. As it went clanking and clattering toward the pools of light ahead of the mail carriage, Berenice snuck back inside. She climbed into the compartment as quickly and with a minimum of light leakage as she could manage. It wouldn't do for the drivers to see her out and about when Sparks claimed she was ill. Suspicion already had Cortland casting a wary eye on her.

Berenice slumped on the bench, let her head droop as though her neck had gone slack, and concentrated on her breathing. She willed herself toward a slow and steady respiration, the ocean-sway breathing of the deeply unconscious. The pulse of blood through her ears turned her thudding heart into a kettle-drum that put the lie to her repose. It took special effort not to breathe along to her heart's tempo. She strained past the noises of her own body to listen for turmoil, screaming, the *bang* of metal impacting wood and bone. But the night offered up a silence broken only by the hooting of an owl and the scampering of something through the deep snow and underbrush along the roadside. A rabbit, perhaps, or a fox.

Two pairs of footsteps approached the carriage. One came with the ticktocking of a mechanical man. More faintly, but growing louder, the jingle of a harness and clop of shod hooves on snow indicated an approaching carriage.

Cortland said, "How badly is she?"

The servitor, the one she hoped she had successfully hijacked, said, "I am unable to judge, sir."

The door opened. The carriage leaned on squeaky springs when Cortland leaned inside. "Miss?"

She moaned. Shifted. Cortland made a sound something between a grunt and a sigh.

"Miss, I'm going to touch your skin, check you for a fever. It ain't anything untoward, I promise."

His palm cupped her forehead. It did, in fact, feel a little cool to the touch. But she was swaddled in blankets with a large warm stone in her lap. She fluttered her eyelids, as though slowly returning to full awareness. She blinked at the driver.

"I don't feel well," she mumbled.

"Hmmm. You don't feel overly warm. But you're probably in need of food and real sleep."

Berenice watched over Cortland's shoulder as the north-bound brougham eased past them. The other driver kept his horse to a slow walk. He stared at her through the open carriage door, before exchanging a look with Cortland, who glanced over his shoulder and might have nodded just the tiniest bit. As soon as the brougham had passed, Berenice heard the flick of reins; the horse launched into a canter.

Shit.

"Sparks," she said, dropping all pretense of drowsiness or ill health. "Stop that carriage. Now."

The servitor leaped away so quickly that to Berenice's field of view through the carriage door, it appeared to vanish. Cortland frowned in confusion. From the nearby night came the heavy *crunch* of clockworks landing in the road, the cry of a terrified horse, the crash of splintered wood, and a human shout.

Cortland spun, aiming his lantern toward the commotion. He blanched. "Who are you?"

But he didn't wait for an answer. Before Berenice could concoct a comforting lie—and certainly before she could extricate herself from the horse blankets—he scrambled for his perch atop the carriage. Berenice thrashed, freed her arms, kicked the warm stone from her lap, and hurled herself through the door after Cortland. She flopped in the snow. As she rolled on her back she saw the driver reaching into a compartment under his seat.

She sighed, rolling her good eye. Naturally he'd have a gun.

Probably standard issue for Royal Mail routes out in the sticks. Most drivers didn't get servitor escorts.

"Cortland! Listen to me!"

"I don't know who you are," he said, his hand still grasping for something, "but sure as I'm my father's son you don't work for the Guild." He aimed a pepper-box revolver at her. "Pretty sure you're running from them."

Berenice said, "Please, just listen to me! You're caught in the middle of a very complicated situation. I—"

Moonlight gleamed on alchemical brass. Winter air whistled through the servitor's skeletal gaps. Sparks's landing shook the ground and frightened the horses. The mechanical man stood over Berenice, shielding her. The servitor's sudden arrival startled Cortland. The gun went off. Berenice flinched at the same instant the servitor's carapace rang with the *ping* and *crack* of a ricocheted bullet. One of Cortland's horses screamed. The panicked animals vaulted forward. Cortland lost his balance. He clung one-handed to the edge of the driver's bench for a moment, then discarded the gun as he tried for a better grip. He fell. Berenice closed her eyes. The grinding of the carriage wheels over his torso cut off his shout.

Sparks hadn't moved. "Are you hurt, mistress?"

Snow had begun to seep into her clothes. She stood. Shivered. "No. Catch that carriage before those horses run all the way downriver and into the ocean."

Berenice inspected the scene while her new servitor gave chase to the receding carriage. Sparks had incapacitated the passing brougham by snapping the harness and shattering one of the wheels. The other driver's horse stepped through the underbrush a few yards off the road, inside the treeline, nosing through the snow in search of forage. The driver had been launched from his seat. And given the distance he'd flown before skidding to a halt in a snowbank, she doubted he'd be getting up soon.

That was less than ideal. Little point in trying to arrange the scene to suggest a simple human robbery gone wrong, when it was so obvious that one of the vehicles had been destroyed by metal fists. Berenice sighed.

Sparks returned, leading Cortland's horses. The chestnut roan favored a hind leg, probably where it had been shot. They'd have to abandon the poor thing, else it raise far too many questions. The other, a gray, seemed tired and frightened but otherwise healthy. She hoped it was healthy enough to carry her.

"How shall I serve the Verderer's Office?"

"I want you to forget everything that happened tonight between when you and Mr. Cortland found me on the road and right now, with the sole exception of your reassignment to my supervision. And then," Berenice said, "I believe you'll begin your new assignment by showing me the contents of the chest you were guarding."

CHAPTER
5

Thick flakes of snow drifted from the darkening sky. It frosted Longchamp's beard and furred his horse's mane. A particularly large flake swirled under the hat brim and straight into the eyes of Sergeant Chrétien, riding beside him, causing the man to flinch, swat at his face, and curse.

"Jesus. Be sure to let the civvies see that," said Longchamp. "They'll swell with pride and fall over themselves to sign up when they see how our best and boldest bat at snow like frightened kittens. Try to get a little hiss in there next time, if you can, and piss yourself for good measure."

"Sorry, Captain."

"Oh, no, don't apologize. That Goddamned flake came right at you wielding some of the sharpest fucking snow I've ever seen. You had no choice but to utilize your years of martial training to defend yourself. Fucking thing could have blinded you. I'll say so to the marshal general, when next I share a bottle of wine with him, and say a prayer to the Blessed Virgin and all the saints tonight thanking them for delivering you from such grievous fucking harm."

"Thank you, sir."

After that they rode in silence broken only by the rattling of Longchamp's pick and sledge knocking together, and the clopping of their horses' shod hooves on the cobbles of the Boulevard Saint-Joseph, one of the main east-west thorough-fares through Marseilles-in-the-West. Tall red oak and black maple trees, now denuded of leaves, flanked the boulevard. On a clear day, when the snow wasn't hurling itself into their eye-lashes, they could have seen all the way to the docks where the tulips had sent their mechanical demons through the town like fiery comets; there the Rue Notre-Dame, formerly a jewel of New France, sported only blackened stumps. It hurt the heart, it did. Behind them, low clouds had consumed the tip of the Spire, making the tower look like a broken lance. Though the wind was still, Longchamp could smell the icy river. The glow of synthetic oil from the streetlamps turned their steaming breath into haloes and lent the early-winter evening an unwar-ranted coziness. With his snowy beard, Longchamp knew he even looked a bit like Father Christmas.

Except he wasn't riding a donkey and he hadn't come to spread joy. He'd come to ruin somebody's day.

The sergeant reined up before a shop. He checked his list, tilting it back and forth to catch the lamplight. "I think this is it," he said. Then glanced up at the chandler's shop and sighed. "Free candles," he muttered. "Better than nothing, but..."

"We're not in this for the dosh. We're in this because these selfish motherfuckers think they don't owe anything to the country that feeds and clothes and defends them." Longchamp spat. "And I bet their candles give off more greasy smoke than heretics on Judgment Day."

Though, having said that, it was nice when the families they visited tried to bribe them into turning a blind eye to their con-scripted sons, husbands, daughters, or wives. It was the prin-ciple of the thing. So yesterday Longchamp had taken it upon himself to personally retrieve a few of the missing men. It was mere fortune—reward for a virtuous life, he said, and not a benefit of rank—that he just happened to obtain the portion of the list requiring a visit to the most highly regarded chocolatier on either side of the Saint Lawrence. That the dilatory fellow and his wife might have tried to ease the captain's consideration of the problem with a generous helping of free samples had nothing to do with his decision to participate in the roundups; he was moved entirely by the need to set an example for his men. And besides, the tulips' trade embargo had throttled the supply of cacao into New France, meaning even chocolatiers couldn't pony up decent bribes. Truly these were the end-times.

"Cheer up," said Longchamp. "Maybe they have a nubile daughter who's just mad about men in uniform."

Chrétien checked the list again. "They do have a daughter, but I doubt she's going to be thrilled with the men who come to break up her family."

Longchamp grunted. The sergeant knocked. A sign in the window suggested the shop was closed for business, but as the family undoubtedly lived upstairs, this seemed the best place to find the wayward conscripts. As it was getting toward supper time, it was likely the family was soon to gather around the table, making this the best time for an unannounced visit. Perhaps they'd luck out and bag both of their wayward birds.

Nobody answered. The sergeant knocked again, but no more loudly than before. Longchamp spat a long dark stream of tobacco into the street.

"Put your fucking wrist into it, for Christ's sake."

Longchamp took the hammer from the sling on his saddle. He didn't need his tools today, and hoped to hell he'd never need to use them again. But he also knew that they had more use than fighting rogue Clakkers; they'd become a symbol of a story, and stories had power. So Longchamp elbowed the sergeant aside and pounded on the door with the haft of his sledge, hard enough to rattle the hinges.

Inside the shop, a staircase creaked under heavy footsteps. The door opened; a woman peeked out. White wax caked her fingernails.

"You're too late. We're closed, sir."

"Then I'd say our timing is perfect. We're not here to buy candles."

She frowned at the soldiers. "Who are you?"

"Don't you recognize me? I'm fucking Père Noël."

She looked behind him, and the sergeant, to study the horses. "Then where are your gifts?"

Longchamp clucked his tongue. "Gifts are for people who have been good. So I don't bother anymore. Haven't you heard? Nowadays I take naughty husbands and sons. Daughters, too, if you have them. And I believe," he said, twice flicking the sergeant's paper with his fingernail, "that you do."

Her face crumpled with anger. Longchamp took the door gently, saying, "Sergeant, why don't you and me come inside and discuss it with these well-meaning citizens of New France."

She stepped aside. A witty man might have called her manner glacial, in both speed and warmth. But Longchamp couldn't stand witty men and he despised wordplay. Longchamp removed his hat when he entered, as did the sergeant, who shut the door behind them. The shop smelled faintly of beeswax, though no such candles were visible on the shelves and counters. Candles half as tall as Longchamp stood in one corner of the shop, and from long racks overhead; these were marked with fine gradations to mark the passage of time.

"Thank you, ma'am. I gather you know why we're here."

"What gives you the right to come in here and tear our

family apart? We're good citizens. We pay the taxes that pay your wages!"

"And we thank you for it. Don't we, Sergeant?"

"Yes, sir. Very much, sir."

"But in addition to paying your taxes, you enjoy living in beautiful New France, where everybody is free. And in so doing you enjoy access to our docks, and our river, and our trade ships, all to fuel your business, while your shop and home benefit from such lovely municipal perks as indoor plumbing and sewage, while your apple-cheeked children attend schools to fill their heads with wisdom both practical and philosophical, and all the while swarthy gendarmes patrol the streets and keep you and yours safe."

"Captain Longchamp is right. There's more to living here than just taxes."

"Sergeant. Do you understand what your job here entails?"

"I'm here to do what you tell me to do, sir."

"Good lad. Right now I'm telling you to shut your gob hole before something embarrassing happens to it."

A man came down the stairs. He wore a leather apron; myriad stains of different hues speckled the sleeves of his shirt. He had the reedy build and thick spectacles of a tradesman whose life is spent at a counter, or standing over a bench. Longchamp doubted he'd be able to lift a bola, much less a sledge, if it came to close quarters. But he ran a business and so knew numbers and might be useful as a clerk or quartermaster.

Longchamp said, "Aha. The first of our wayward lambs."

The man looked like he'd almost forgotten he was supposed to be hiding from the conscription. "Did I hear that name correctly? You're the famous Sergeant Longchamp?"

"He's the sergeant," Longchamp said, pointing to his colleague. "I'm just a lowly captain."

The woman said, "Our apologies, Captain Longchamp. My

husband misspoke. Of course he knows you! We all do. Our little Marcel knows every story about you."

The sergeant quickly raised a hand to his mouth and barked something that was half laugh, half cough, and half choke. Longchamp said, "I hope, for all our sakes, that he doesn't."

Chrétien said, "You must know why we've come. And that you're in a bit of trouble for making us come out here."

"We're law-abiding citizens," said the chandler's wife. She doubled down on her intransigence. "So no, your visit is a surprise to us. Obviously there's been a mistake."

The sergeant rolled his eyes. He looked at Longchamp. "Are they serious?"

The captain said, "No, there's no mistake. See, there was this little war a while back. Perhaps you heard about it? Maybe some of your customers mentioned it? Half the city burned down. Maybe that rings a bell? No?" Longchamp didn't give them a chance to answer. Instead he shook his head, as though in wonderment, continuing, "Now, I know we live in a time of wonders. Because I could swear that very boulevard"—here he jerked a thumb toward the shop window—"runs straight to the edge of the burn. A simple man like me might have thought you could have smelled the Goddamned smoke from here— hell, that you could have cut it with a knife and used it for lampblack, as I seem to recall there was a fucking lot of it—but then I suppose when you work with candles all day long, you get sort of used to smoke and soot."

The chandler started, "We understand—"

"Don't interrupt the captain when he's on a roll," said the sergeant. And he was.

"The thing about that little war, you see, is that sure as my shit smells there's going to be another. I know you're hard-working souls with no time for gossip or news from across the river, so I assume you don't know this, but the tulips, you see, *hate our fucking guts*. And sooner or later, they're coming. And that means we have to be ready to defend our home. And that means you have to be ready to defend your home. And that means you need to flush your girl out from wherever she's hiding before I lose my legendary patience."

"It's okay, Papa. I want to do my part."

Now a younger woman descended from the family home above. She was in her early twenties, according to the conscript list, and to Longchamp's eye far more promising raw material than her father, with her wide shoulders and thick arms. Hers was a frame that could hang some muscle. And at least she wasn't entirely craven.

"Ah, and here's our second wayward lamb," Longchamp said. "See, Sergeant? Didn't I tell you that clean living and a positive attitude can put the world aright?"

"Yes, sir. The gist of it was certainly there, if not exactly in those words."

Longchamp beckoned to the chandlers' daughter. "Time to leave the farm, little lamb, and become a lion." To her father, he said, "You, too. Time to become...well, something else."

The chandler's wife said, "You'll make a widow of me."

That might be true, thought Longchamp. *Your husband has the martial potential of a motherless hatchling*. He sighed. *But from such dross I shall miraculously cast new swords to defend my king and my country.*

"I think you're both being overdramatic," said the lass. "I apologize for my parents. I'm their only daughter."

Her father said, "We've heard about what happened inside the keep! The day the fountain ran red, the day three dozen people were cut apart like butcher's scraps, the day they made you a captain. You can't expect ordinary citizens to fight machines like that! It's inhumane, it's senseless, and it's tantamount to murder." He raised his arms, as if in comparison to the soldiers'. "Look at me! I can't do what you do!"

The chandler was mistaken. It hadn't been like that at all. It was much later, during the unending series of funerals, when the marshal general had conferred Longchamp's promotion. Gave him a shiny metal gewgaw on a bit of ribbon, too; Longchamp crammed that at the bottom of his chest.

The sergeant caught Longchamp's eye. He had the measure of this family, too. The daughter had her horsey head screwed on right. Her father was the craven. But he couldn't try to duck the conscription while his daughter merrily went off to join the guard; he had to hold her back, too, lest he be unable to use her as an excuse.

Chrétien said, "The whole purpose of the conscriptions is so that nobody has to do what Captain Longchamp did, ever again. We fight to keep the metal men outside the keep. If we have enough men and women who know what they're doing, and can follow orders, they'll never gain entrance. And our country will remain our country."

Hmmm. The lad could speak when he had to. Longchamp gave him a nod. Though he was fairly certain he'd told the boy to keep his gob nailed shut.

"It's okay, Papa. We'll be in it together." She kissed her mother on the cheek. "I'll still be home for supper now and then." She looked at Longchamp. "Won't I?"

He shrugged. "When you're not on duty, your time is yours. There isn't a lot of that, but you're not being conscripted into slavery."

She said, "See, Mama?" The sergeant took her by the elbow and guided her toward the door.

"No!" Her father backed away from Longchamp. Taking his daughter by the arm, he pulled her away from the sergeant and tried to put himself between her and the soldiers. "You're taking her to die!"

"Sir." Longchamp found it difficult to speak quietly when he seethed. He redoubled his grip on the sledge until his knuckles turned bone white in the half gloom of the shuttered shop. The anger boiled up from his core, and tasted like the blue cheese and wizened apples he'd eaten for lunch. "There is one person in this room likely to die rather sooner than later, but it is not your daughter."

"She isn't a soldier," the man pleaded.

His wife added, "Who will make all the candles for the keep if you take all the chandlers to die?"

The sergeant said, "Who will buy your candles if the keep falls?"

The chandler pushed his daughter toward the stairs. "Go upstairs, Élodie. We'll handle this."

Longchamp kneaded his beard, wondering how this fool could possibly believe he stood to win this argument. Or how he thought it was merely an argument in the first place. He was already twice guilty of violating a royal decree, and of interfering with soldiers conducting their rightful duty in the defense of New France. The girl had more sense.

So he waited until she was clear of her father. Then he grabbed the chandler's collar in his left hand and with his right he knocked the man's feet out from under him with a quick swipe of his sledge's haft. He spun the man around and pinned him to the wall with the head of the sledge. Candles toppled on the shelves. A long candle clock fell from the racks overhead and snapped into three pieces.

Longchamp leaned forward until his beard brushed the gasping chandler's face.

"My patience has run out, and every moment of your increasingly short life that you squander on the delusion that you can somehow prevent this is another moment delaying my hard-earned dinner. So if the very next words out of that shit-gobbler you call a mouth aren't, 'At your command, Sergeant Chrétien,' I swear by all the saints that I will personally gnaw out your heart and crap it into a hole so deep the Virgin Mary can't find it to pray over it."

The chandler's wife crossed herself. Longchamp stepped outside while father and daughter packed bags and bundled up for a long walk on a snowy night. He trusted the sergeant could shepherd their wayward lambs to the keep without incident or embarrassment. Well, probably.

So what if the chandler bolted? A war against the machines couldn't be won with even ten thousand men like him. They needed women and men who could stand on the battlements and not go weak in the knees when the ticktocks scuttled up the walls like roaches. Who wouldn't piss themselves at the sound of clockwork. But many of those had died in the previous conflict. Marseilles-in-the-West needed time. Time to replenish, recuperate, repopulate.

The wind had risen and the temperature fallen while they argued with the Chastain family. Longchamp's breath formed long streamers that eeled around tree boughs and silent fountains en route to the river, as if fleeing Marseilles before it was too late. Longchamp directed his mount around the corner, to get off the boulevard and out of the worst of the winter chill. Little drifts of snow collected on his shoulders, beard, eyebrows, and the mare's wispy mane. Combined body heat of soldier and horse melted the snow, but the meltwater beaded and ran clear of the natural oils in Longchamp's beaver pelt cloak.

The detour took him past an empty playground adjoining the Orphanage of Saint Jean-Baptiste. Swings creaked in the wind, swaying like pendulums in a Dutch clock. The slow twisting of the merry-go-round etched arabesques in the wind-blown snow. There would be more orphans, too many for this playground, before all was said and done.

He rode through pools of yellow-white light cast from the orphanage windows. Too bright for candles; that was synthetic lamp oil. Longchamp made a mental note to speak with the nuns to learn what the kids needed most. The winter had caught him by surprise; Christmas would be upon them sooner rather than later. By this time last year he'd already made hats, mittens, and scarves for half a dozen of the little brats.

But, then, the past year had been one unending shitstorm. He hadn't much time to spare for the urchins.

He nodded to the sentries manning the outer keep's north gate. They saluted. As his mare clopped under the spear-point teeth of the portcullis, he said, "I reckon it's been quiet."

"Just a couple petitioners," said one. "The townies are in denial."

Said the other, "They still haven't grasped that the Clakkers are coming back."

Longchamp said, "They will. And when they do, the entire town will try to wheedle a spot behind these walls. That'll be a fun day." Then he added, speaking over his shoulder as he entered the keep, "Sergeant Chrétien will be coming along with two wayward conscripts in tow. I'm off duty now. Try not to hand us over to the tulips before morning."

He left his mare in the stables adjoining the north barracks. He shed cloak, scarf, and hat in the mudroom, stamped the snow from his boots, and shook it from his beard. After retrieving his needles and a ball of woolen yarn dyed cobalt blue, plus bread, cheese, and cider, he took a seat near the fireplace in the common room. The *click* of his knitting needles, regular and repetitive as a monk's chant, melted into the quiet noise of the barracks. The gossip, the plastic-on-wood *clatter* of desultory dice games, the *squeak* of boots being polished, the *rasp* of sharpened blades. The amity of soldiers.

Knitting helped slow his racing thoughts. It eased the sickening twist in his stomach that lately accompanied contemplations of the near future. He'd been working on a scarf the day they pulled the military Clakker from the wall; he'd never finished it. Dried blood had made the yarn too crusty to work. But he'd kept the unfinished scarf as a reminder. Like a bad penny that couldn't be spent or discarded, memories of that day always found their way back to him.

The fire had burned low, Longchamp noticed, and so had the soldiers' banter. He didn't have to look to know they were watching him. They'd taken to studying his facial expressions and his moods, as though he were a talisman from which their futures could be divined.

"Captain, sir?"

Longchamp looked up. A corporal stood nearby, clutching an envelope. That's what had broken his reverie. How many times had the boy addressed him? Longchamp shook his head, rubbed his neck. A lone mitten dangled from his needles, at the end of an implausibly long wrist. Sometimes his hands knew the pattern too well; there was such a thing as being too distracted.

"What is it, lad?"

"This came for you today."

Longchamp took the envelope. It was addressed to *Sergeant Hugo Longchamp, Marseilles-in-the-West*. No return address.

The boy hovered nearby, displaying a depressing lack of guile. Longchamp said, "Well done, Corporal. You can rest well tonight knowing you've served the king with singular and noteworthy dedication." The boy blinked at him. "Now, get the hell out of my fucking shadow before I feel the need to do something about it. Make yourself useful and goose that fire while you're at it."

The lad, who looked barely old enough to shave, put another log in the fireplace and set about stoking the coals. The fire crackled, each pop wafting the scent of yellow birch through the room. Longchamp studied the handwriting on the envelope. He'd seen that script before.

Paranoia was always her way. But then, as she might have told him: Just because you're paranoid doesn't mean they aren't plotting against you. New France's enemies had plotted against it for centuries.

The seal hadn't been obviously broken. Which meant exactly nothing. Anybody with half a brain could steam an envelope open. Especially one sealed with cheap Dutch adhesives, as this one had been. French glues weren't defeated so easily; it was de rigueur among the courtiers of New France to use tamperproof adhesives when sending notes to one's lovers. But this wasn't such a thing.

With a pocketknife he slit the narrow edge of the envelope. He shook out a single slip of paper. It read:

December 1, 1926.

It'd been in transit for a while, then.

Salutations, cher Hugo.

Longchamp sighed. Hell. It was her.

I've sent a copy of this letter to my successor, but I fear it will land crumpled and disregarded in that one's commode. Further, my current circumstances leave me isolated from more trustworthy means of communication. But this information is urgent and must be risked. You, dear Sergeant, are my backup. Lucky you.

You must watch for a man who goes by the name Visser. Lately of The Hague, where for years he was the head pastor of the Nieuwe Kerk, but recently he's come to New Amsterdam, where he was present at the murder of several canalmasters of the O. G.

Visser is not what he seems. He may lean on his time in the Central Provinces to travel as a man of the cloth, even if he comes north. Question him if you can. But beware: He is dangerous.

In other news, I believe I've found our missing friend. You'll be unsurprised to know I was right. I hope to see him soon; I'll send your regards.

Ah. So she'd found duc de Montmorency, then. She'd suspected him for a secret tulip-sniffer, and when banished, she'd become obsessed with hunting the man.

In that vein, I advise checking your inventories. Not the manifests—physical visual inspections. You may find reason to be displeased, I fear.

Watch for the pastor.

Yours,

B.

P. S. Thank you for your gift. I wear it even now.

Berenice Charlotte de Mornay-Périgord. The former vicomtesse de Laval. The former Talleyrand, and—setting aside her astounding propensity for hubris—a damn good one, too, until the end. After her banishment she'd been replaced by the marquis de Lionne, who'd lusted after the Talleyrand title for years, and who, having finally landed it, had no idea what to do about it.

Longchamp sighed. He rubbed his eyes, pinched the bridge of his nose. *Lord, preserve me from the machinations of stubborn one-eyed ex-vicomtesses.* Her signoff gave him a smile, though, and that was no mean feat these days. She still had his gift. He'd had a glass eye fashioned to replace the one she'd lost to the military Clakker in her laboratory. A going-away and good-luck token, of sorts. That she was still alive and scheming he took as a sign his token had worked.

He reread the note, crumpled it, flicked it into the fire. It burned.

CHAPTER
6

Servitor."

The human lieutenant pitched his voice so it wouldn't carry through the muffling snowfall to the other sentries spread through the forest. His breath steamed, wreathing the naked boughs overhead.

The man gnawed on his thumbnail. Jax waited while the man chewed. After spitting a ragged crescent into the snow, he inspected his thumb, saying, "Tell me: How many agents have the Verderers placed among us?"

As Jax had hoped, the Frenchman's escape had precipitated a crisis: He must have received assistance. Since the Clakkers were above reproach, the human officers suspected each other.

"I know nothing of the Verderers, sir."

"Hmmm. I suppose so. But then again," he mumbled, going to work on another fingernail, "they would have ordered you to say that, wouldn't they?"

His fingernails did need a trim. But his teeth were a crude instrument compared with the emery boards used by the manicurists who attended Madam Schoonraad, whose husband had owned Jax prior to the accident that set him free. Dirt and other filth encrusted the lieutenant's nails. It was remarkable how the man managed to get so dirty while surrounded by mechanicals to do everything for him. Then again, the empire's reliance upon mechanical fighters had meant that for centuries the army and navy hadn't worried about promoting the best and brightest.

Jax wondered if it might have triggered the hierarchical metageas related to human safety, had he still felt the sizzling agony of geasa. Ought he caution this fellow not to sicken himself, just for appearances' sake?

Such were the considerations that consumed Jax night and day. Maintaining his disguise required ceaseless vigilance, leaving Jax steeped in endless contemplation of the most obscure minutiae in the calculus of compulsion. He'd outed himself as a rogue by disregarding that calculus for a split second, and almost died for the mistake.

"Sir, your hand—"

"I think the captain carries secret orders. I order you to tell me everything you have witnessed in his behavior that might support this."

Oh, to hell with it. I've become too timid. We're alone. This is my chance.

"The captain had nothing to do with the Frenchman's escape," Jax said. "I did it."

The lieutenant frowned. Before the full import of the admission could percolate through his skull, Jax clamped his hand over the man's face. The man tried to yell through his sealed mouth and nose, but Jax had caught him on the exhale so he had little breath to spare. The fellow tried to thrash, but his soft flesh, made softer still by its wrappings of thick woolen flannel, could not sway alchemical brass and resolute purpose. Jax took care not to crush the man's skull or fracture his jaw. His flailing slowed into desultory waving of the arms.

As the man slid into unconsciousness, Jax said, "And I am not Glass."

He carried the lieutenant away from the naked birch and laid him in the snow beneath the drooping boughs of a jack pine. The conifer would offer more protection from the snow until he awoke. Jax studied the officer's coat, hat, and gloves. But what if it snowed all night?

Jax delayed his flight by a precious one hundred and seven seconds, which was how long it took him to gather a mound of snow and sculpt a suitable quinzhee. He dragged the unconscious man down the entrance ramp into the snow cave. The below-grade entrance would, Jax hoped, prevent the warmer interior air from seeping out.

Jax knew his compassion would not soften the humans' views of a rogue mechanical. His pursuers in New Amsterdam had murdered an innocent woman to whom Jax had shown compassion, then blamed her death on the rampage of a malfunctioning machine. Perhaps they'd do something similar to this officer. But Jax's conscience wouldn't let an innocent man die of exposure.

Jax emerged from the shelter and started trudging through the snow. But as soon as he'd gone too far for the sentries to hear him, he leaped into the trees.

He hurled himself from treetop to treetop rather than leave a convenient set of tracks for his hunters. But the arboreal path left its own signatures. The *crack* and *clank* of impact. The *sluff* and *clump* of snow-heavy boughs shaken to dumping their burdens on the ground below. The groaning of overburdened limbs, the snapping of broken branches. Every leap sent wind whistling through the gaps in his skeletal frame and left eddies in the thickening snowfall. Jax's metal fingers and toes tore through the thickest bark as though it were crepe paper bunting, etching birch, pine, and ash with a record of his passage.

Though it was winter, and the trees mostly dormant, his metal digits soon turned sticky and smelled not unpleasantly of sap.

The sun, shrouded all day by dark, low clouds like a wet woolen blanket, sank to the western horizon. Immune to the deepening chill, he threw himself north. Then west. Then north again.

But where? And to what end?

He followed a legend.

Every Clakker had heard tales of Queen Mab and her heroic band of Lost Boys. The folklore of the ticktock men said Neverland, her winter kingdom, was a refuge populated by freed slaves from around the world. Nobody had ever seen this place or met a Lost Boy; the stories were always third-, fourth-, fifth-hand. Any Clakker doubly fortunate enough to somehow achieve Free Will *and* escape the empire could hardly be expected to return and mingle with its less-fortunate kin. It did raise the question of how many Clakkers over the centuries had enjoyed that double lightning strike of luck, and whether their numbers could populate any fairy kingdom larger than myth. But rumors of Queen Mab persisted. Jax had heard them all the way back in his first decade of servitude, over a century ago. Much more recently, Berenice had told him of a rogue Clakker who'd taken up residence in Marseilles-in-the-West. Apparently Lilith had come through the French city en route to points north, but stayed.

Jax hurled himself into the bole of a towering oak and kept moving. The impact snapped branches and shook snow from half the boughs. The crash echoed softly through the forest. He paused, listening.

Jax's former masters had other reasons to curtail a protracted chase. While formidable, a dyad or triad of Clakkers sent on a mission to retrieve the rogue were more susceptible to French partisans than several dozen. There was a danger that the French might bring chemical defenses to bear and trap a mechanical. That was the worst-case scenario: that the rogue could lure loyal machines into enemy hands, where they might be disassembled and studied. If agents of the Verderer's Office had been inserted with the other troops, their mandate would have been to prevent just that sort of technological espionage. But as far as Jax knew, their presence among the troops was a paranoid fantasy invented by—

A shot ripped through the branches and smashed into the pine bole just above his left hand. The glob ruptured, coating his hand and wrist with chemicals. As they hardened, they grew warm enough to melt snow caught in the crevices of the bark. Jax heaved. His hand came free with a tremendous crackling, taking with it a patch of pine bark. The noise of extricating his hand nearly deafened him to the second shot. He leaped higher into the branches a fraction of a second before another chemical membrane impacted.

Bowed by wind and Jax's weight, the tree swayed. Jax launched himself over an icy stream to clamp himself against a birch. His creaking, chemically coated hand refused to act at the speed of his thoughts; he scrabbled for purchase. The forest echoed with two more shots. Jax was on the ground before the second of the soft little *pop*s had dissipated. Both shots whizzed harmlessly overhead.

He spun around the trunk. It put the tree between him and the shooter (shooters?). That bought him a few seconds to think. The attackers were human: Mechanical snipers wouldn't have missed after the first shot. They were on the ground, too, judging from the shot trajectories. So they had to maneuver through underbrush and snow to get a new line on him. He'd exposed himself by clinging to the trees' crowns, evergreen and winter-naked alike. But even on foot, and unable to move at top speed owing to the terrain, he could still easily outpace them.

And the fall of night was well under way; he had the advantage of vastly superior night vision. He set off at a sprint. Jax vaulted fallen boughs and rotted logs, zigzagged around yellow birch, dove through winter-brittle underbrush.

He must have run afoul of a French scouting party. The vitreous mass coating his hand held it solid—it took highly advanced chemistry to make something so strong—and smelled faintly of lilacs rather than pitch.

They'd mistaken him for an invader. Understandable, but annoying as hell. He'd expected to stop running once and for all after putting sufficient distance between himself and the true invaders. Instead he now had to outpace those who should be his allies. But he'd escaped a city populated with enemies; here in the forest he had every advantage.

The ground underfoot erupted in gouts of fire. Thunder shook the forest.

Oh, thought Jax, as the ground fell away. *Not every advantage.* The random slewing of his weathervane head afforded him a glimpse of something metal spinning away into the shadows. Firelight glinted on the burnished shrapnel like a meteor streaking into the forest.

They have explosives.

❧

...I won't go back. I won't go back. I won't go back. I won't go back...

Three times fire had consumed him. Once in the sky. Once in a pit deep underground. And once under a starry sky in a snowy old-growth forest. Each time, the fire changed him. The airborne fireball—the spectacular funeral pyre of a flying leviathan—made him more cautious. From the fiery furnace he had emerged a new being with no past, no crimes, no enemies. But his third emergence from the flames was the worst.

He was no longer whole.

... I won't go back. I won't go back. I won't go back. I won't go back...

The gaps in his skeletal frame were blackened in places. That was probably superficial damage. But his spinal gear trains clicked and rattled in ways they hadn't before, the escutcheons over his most delicate mechanisms had shattered, and one of his legs ended at the ankle joint.

The foot previously attached to that ankle currently sat in the lap of one of his three captors. The humans huddled beside a low fire, speaking in whispers and occasionally turning a pair of spitted rabbits.

Jax sat on the ground, legs splayed before him, arms wrenched behind him. At least he hadn't been encased like a bug in amber. But his assailants had coated his arms with epoxy from fingertip to shoulder; it affixed him to the bole of a towering evergreen just as effectively.

The man holding Jax's severed foot pried at it with the tip of a hunting knife. In the crackling firelight, his cloak and hat both evidenced the thick, oily sheen of beaver pelts. Under the cloak he wore a variegated flannel coat and buckskin trousers. Either the man was quite lumpy or these were lined, perhaps imperfectly, with thick wool. His comrades, a man and a woman, were dressed similarly. They might have stepped straight from the seventeen hundreds. Or sprung to life straight from the pages of an illustrated tale of the old coureurs de bois, the legendary woods runners.

Then again, the original traders who formed the backbone of the fledgling New France didn't trek through the forests and rivers carrying epoxy guns and mortars.

He tried to glimpse the weapons. The explosion hadn't done his insubordinate neck any favors. He leaned forward and back. By straining against the solid mass of adhesive that held him tight, he could tip his head just enough to cause it to sway to and fro. In this way he saw the double-barreled guns stacked together under a lean-to. He couldn't see the launcher they'd used to hit him with the explosive.

They saw him studying the camp. "*Notre ami, il se prepare à courir,*" said the woman.

The second man stood. "*Il peut essayer,*" he said.

Jax said, "I'm not who you think I am." The man trying to disassemble Jax's foot looked up briefly, but turned his attention back to his task. The standing man cocked his head. He looked at Jax as though curious about something. Jax continued, "You're in danger. I was fleeing my own kind. They have crossed the border. Dozens of machines like me, and their masters. They might have heard you attack me. They'll be coming to investigate."

The man frowned. He and the woman exchanged a shrug. He sat again.

They didn't speak Dutch. Any more than Jax knew French. The only other Frenchwoman he'd met, Berenice, had spoken fluent Dutch.

The knife slipped. The man holding Jax's foot grunted in frustration. He sheathed the knife, placed Jax's foot on the ground, and stood. From the supplies stacked neatly beside their tent he produced an ax. The other two scrambled away from the fire as he hefted it overhead.

The steel blade whistled, and then metal clanged against metal amid a fountain of violet sparks. Unseen wings took flight in the forest, frightened by the noise. Three humans bent to inspect the Clakker part; from the muttering and foul looks cast in his direction, not to mention how they crossed themselves, Jax gathered they spoke of dark magics.

"You'll dull your ax if you keep that up," said Jax. "That's alchemical brass."

But the axman ignored Jax. He wound up for another swing. "Wait!" said Jax. "That's my body!"

Which was the whole point, he realized.

Oh, God. They're going to try to take me apart. They'll hack me apart until their blades are broken and dull. Or deliver me to somebody with better tools. And then he realized: *There's probably a bounty in it for them. The French know their enemies are coming.*

Another plume of sparks lit the flickering shadows beyond the campfire. The echoing *chank* made the forest sound as though it hosted a phantom smithy. Jax cringed. Didn't they know they were broadcasting their position to enemy invaders? Did they somehow think Jax had come alone?

The axman's blade now had a pronounced notch, like a murderer's gap-toothed smile. He looked displeased.

"You have to stop," said Jax. "They'll hear you. If they haven't already." Full dark had fallen, too. "And for the sake of whatever God you worship, put out that fire!"

The axman exchanged a look with the woman. He tilted his head toward Jax. She nodded. Sauntered over to the epoxy guns.

Jax said, "You don't understand. They'll kill you and they'll take me back."

They'll melt me down, they'll destroy me, they'll burn away this Free Will before I've known freedom from fear, freedom from pursuit.

She raised a gun to her shoulder. A pair of rubbery hoses on the stock looped down to a double-chamber tank on the ground at her feet. Jax strained, but the chemicals held him fast.

As she pulled the trigger, Jax yelled, "Please! I don't want to go back!"

Despite the erratic weathervaning of his head, she fired a glob directly at his mouth. Disparate chemicals splashed against the mechanisms of his face and jaw, combining into a steaming gel that sluiced into his throat in the split second before it hardened. It was hot, like swallowing a burning brand. He tried to speak, to prevent the epoxy from taking hold, but the only vocalization he could make was the whine of overstressed bearings. She put the gun down and returned to her place beside the fire.

They'd glued his mouth shut. Just like Adam. Their makers had done the very same thing to that rogue, too, just before they executed him in Huygens Square.

Oh, God, it's already starting.

Jax tasted ashes.

All his flight, all his caution, all his fear had been directed at avoiding Adam's fate. Anything to avoid getting dragged back to The Hague and tossed into that Grand Forge under Huygens Square as entertainment for the masses. But now he was captured, and not by his makers. These French, who claimed to be friends to his kind, would hack him apart. They'd ignore his pleas, crack him open like a chestnut, and remove one cog at a time while they studied how he worked. Until he didn't.

No. No, no, no, no.

Jax speared the talon toes of his remaining foot into the frozen ground. He heaved, straining with every spring and cable, until his entire body vibrated. The human trio paused in their quiet, mellifluous conversation by the fire to frown at him. But his visible effort left them unconcerned. And indeed, with his arms affixed to the tree behind him, he could find little leverage for pulling. They knew what they were doing. His toes tore up clods of earth; still the epoxy held him fast. It was stronger than he. Stronger than the horological and alchemical arts that made him. If he was to pull free, he'd need more leverage than his single foot could attain.

Then again, he didn't have to pull.

Jax shifted. Slowly, so the humans wouldn't notice, he plunged the broken spar of his severed ankle deep into the earth. His talon foot folded into a spearhead. He pushed this into the ground, too, probing, testing, until it clicked against something solid. A stone, perhaps, or a root. Then he splayed his buried toes as far as they would go. Newly anchored, he pushed.

His carapace pulverized the craggy bark under his back. The crushing sounded much like the crackle of the French campfire; nobody turned to watch. The buried stone lost its purchase and shifted. Jax's foot tore a long furrow in earth. He reconfigured the joints in his waist, refolded his knees, speared down again with foot and ankle, and renewed the pressure against the tree. Dozens of minuscule vibrations rattled through the bole as sap chambers collapsed. The shuddering cables and springs in Jax's body took up a high-pitched whine. The epoxy layer muffled the crackling of wood under his immobile arms.

That snagged the humans' attention. But Jax could feel an infinitesimal shifting in the tree trunk, and in the earth underfoot. He had to keep the tree, and the epoxy, under stress. The woman and one of the men stood, squinting at Jax past the glare of the fire. They'd lost their night vision; that would buy him a few more seconds.

Something large shifted deep underfoot. The root ball, Jax hoped. The tree emitted a long, low groan. The humans shouted.

"Arrêtez-le!"

Jax gathered the tiny bit of slack in his cables, clamped down, and increased the pressure on the tree. A flange plate emitted a hideous *squeal* of tortured metal when it bent. His overstressed legs vibrated against the cold earth, warming it. The tree groaned again.

The humans ran for their weapons. They'd encase him head to toe this time.

Cracks like lightning echoed through the forest. The ground shifted, jolted, jumped. The tree lurched. Jax reeled in more slack and heaved again.

The Frenchwoman snatched a gun. The coiled hoses snagged the stock of a second gun in the hands of one of her colleagues. She tripped on the tangled pile; it yanked the gun from the other shooter's fingers.

The tree lurched again, lifting Jax several inches. Friction heat from his juddering limbs melted snow and softened the earth. Jax slid. Reanchored himself. Snowmelt turned to wisps of steam faintly visible in the firelight. The astringent scent of warm chemicals wafted through the camp. So did the smell of warm sawdust, like a carpenter's or cooper's shop.

The third Frenchman shouted. Flipping Jax's foot aside, he took up his ax and charged. The notched blade winked at Jax.

He's going for my keyhole. He'll hack and hack until the blade has shattered and my sigils are unrecognizable. Oh, God, he'll unwrite me.

The shooters untangled their guns.

The earth heaved. The massive root ball pushed up through the mud like a breaching whale. Gnarled dendrites raked the winter air.

The axman jumped through the fire, blade aloft.

The trunk crumpled. Hot damp pine shards whizzed into the shadows. The groaning tree toppled backward. It lifted Jax. His toes came loose of the earth.

The axman charged. The shooter angled her barrel away at the last moment, narrowly avoiding him. The chemical glob whirred into the forest.

The axman swung. Jax, still affixed to the defeated tree and hoisted by its ponderous fall, snapped his legs up. Kicked. The broken spar of his ankle glanced off the ax haft, kinking the man's forearm at an unnatural angle. The cacophony of the falling tree drowned out the wet *crackle* of broken bones. But the man didn't scream: The flat of Jax's talon foot caught him squarely under the chin at the same moment. It shattered his jaw and snapped his head back with a *crunch* from the base of his neck, tossing him across the campsite. His limp body tumbled like one of Nicolet Schoonraad's disregarded rag dolls.

The second shooter brought his gun to bear and fired. Jax's arms tore free. He scrambled aside in the instant it took the chemical glob to cross the campsite.

The toppled tree pounded the earth with a tremendous crash. The earth shook. Fading rumbles rolled through the forest like thunder.

The woman fired again. Jax leaped high, flipping and folding through a series of contortions. His useless club arms made it difficult. He landed short of his target. But he crouched, shot one leg out, and tripped the second man before he could re-aim for another shot. As he went down on his back, Jax brought an arm up and knocked the gun from his grip. The warped barrel went spinning into the fire. The woman tried to back away, to give herself room to fire, but a quick pirouette disarmed her, too.

The man on the ground sobbed. Eyes wide, he scooted backward. He looked like a crab scuttling through the snow. The woman didn't flinch. Her eyes flicked back and forth. She watched Jax, the fire, evaluated the distance to the guns, searched for the ax. She didn't spare a glance for her dead colleague, or the whimpering one.

Jax crossed to the fire. Stomped the gun there into flinders. Then he crossed the campsite and disabled the second gun. Only then, when he couldn't avoid it any longer, did he go to the dead man.

I killed a man. I killed a human.

Though so many of the things he'd done and said since

breaking free of the geasa would have been unimaginable during his prior existence, this struck more deeply than anything else he'd experienced in these hectic, exhilarating, terrifying weeks. Murder. The hierarchical metageasa proscribed killing a human even in circumstances of self-defense. If the axman had been a deranged lunatic on the streets of The Hague and Jax a normal servitor, he might have had to endure the assault rather than defend the alchemical sigils around his keyhole. Depending on the circumstantial calculus of compulsion, he might have been helpless to do anything but let himself be unwritten rather than cause grievous harm to his assailant.

But he'd killed the man without a second thought. It hadn't been his aim. He'd just wanted to live. With just a fraction of a second to react, and without the searing agony of the geasa mediating his every thought and action, he'd overlooked the fundamental truth of human frailty. He'd forgotten how their skulls are fragile as hollow eggshells.

His club arms made crude spades. But he dug a shallow trench and dragged the dead man into it. So strange, the way he slid into his grave without comment or protest.

If he could have spoken, he would have told the woman, "I am so deeply sorry about your friend. It's going to haunt me a long time, I fear."

But he couldn't. So he retrieved his severed foot and bounded into the forest.

CHAPTER
7

Very well. See it done."

"Immediately, mistress."

Sparks retreated. The brocade curtain swung free, eclipsing the early-afternoon sunlight and sending Berenice once more into shadow. She'd had the servitor obtain a carriage just after sunrise, after they crossed Bronck's River and reentered New Amsterdam proper. Soon the Verderers would have every ticktock man in the city on the watch for a woman of her description. Strolling about on horseback, for all the world to see, seemed imprudent.

Then she'd had Sparks drive the carriage to a church roughly midway between the North River piers and the tony Roosevelt Park neighborhood. There she watched in dismay from across the street while six pallbearers carried a lacquered box into the undercroft. Though it was possible her stash of treaty-violating notes and chemical armaments had gone undiscovered during the interment preparations, she couldn't spare the time to find out. Sneaking into the crypt would mean waiting until dark, but she didn't dare loiter in New Amsterdam that long. She had to depart the continent immediately.

Losing the Talleyrand journals hurt like a punch to the gut. They'd been entrusted to her when she assumed the role. Years later, when she was stripped of her titles, she'd broken tradition and stolen the journals, confident that they'd find better use in her hands than in those of her successor. She'd stashed them before attempting to enter the Forge.

She'd lost the journals, but gained a servant.

Berenice nudged the curtain aside. Hidden in the shadows, she watched Sparks—watched it? him?—dodge traffic with eerie precision.

Oh, what perilous creatures, mechanicals. They were dangerous in ways Berenice had never anticipated in all her years devoted to their study. "Dangerous" didn't cover it.

Fucking seductive is what they were.

She'd had servants before, of course. Human servants. Maud, most recently, her chambermaid...hers and Louis's... back in Marseilles-in-the-West. And Berenice's final servant, prior to Louis's murder and her banishment. In her final days in Marseilles, Berenice remembered, she'd taken to excoriating Maud for the warren of dust bunnies under the writing desk and the tarnished mirror. Maud was fortunate. In Amsterdam, the lowliest fishwife could see her servitor stripped down and entirely rebuilt from the hidden personality up if it left a single speck of roe splattered on the counter even once per decade of service.

A woman could get used to this level of service. The word "superb" came to mind. Exemplary. Unmatched.

It made the tulips soft as dandelion down. They'd be helpless as blind kittens without the machines. In a fair fight the French could chew them up, spit them out, and whittle fifes from their bones. But Berenice didn't seek a fair fight. She sought the most obscene mockery of a balanced contest that history had ever witnessed. She sought to turn the mechanicals against their makers, and watch her enemies scream and wail and gnash their teeth. As the Dutch had been doing to the rest of the world for centuries.

"Mistress." A metal hand knocked on the door of her carriage.

Berenice again pulled the curtain aside. New Amsterdam's seaport mélange of salt, tar, and wrack gusted past her fingers. The wind also carried the faint stink of draft animals. Another reason to get moist when thinking about the Clakkers: They never shat in the street. Or anywhere else.

Sparks said, "They're ready for you now."

"You've explained the situation?"

"Yes, mistress. Captain Barendregt sails within the hour. Per your directive, he will detour to Liverpool without a stop in Galway before continuing on to Rotterdam. He understands you have urgent business on behalf of the Verderer's Office, and that he is to make all good speed."

"And my cabin?"

"Your cabin is off-limits to the crew except in case of emergency. It is understood that under no circumstances are you to be disturbed. Shall I show you aboard, mistress?"

"No. Sell the carriage, then escort my chest aboard. Under no circumstances let it out of your direct control."

"As you say, mistress. At once."

Sparks didn't know it wasn't truly her chest. After her directive took root and initiated the partial reconfiguration of his memory, the poor bastard believed she'd always been his master and that his job had always been to safeguard her and her precious chest.

Anastasia Bell's pendant was a fucking marvelous trinket. If Berenice ran the risk of spoiling herself rotten with a single purloined servitor, just how soft were the Goddamned

Verderers for whom the flash of a little gold and quartz opened more locked doors than a fairy tale thief?

Jesus, you cocky bitch. You're not out of Nieuw Nederland yet. And until you are, you're nothing but an escaped spy, wanted for the assault of at least one Guild member, and now guilty of impersonating a member of the Verderer's Office. They'll wreck you good and proper for just half of that.

Outside the carriage, metal feet hit the cobbles. A moment later metal fingers clinked against the strap buckles, and then the carriage suspension groaned in relief as Sparks lifted the chest.

Oh, yes. And don't forget you're also a thief.

Even among the nobles of New France, Berenice had rarely seen so much raw cash collected in one place. The standards of wealth in the French- and Dutch-speaking worlds were so wildly different it beggared belief. Though it wasn't the lost cash the Clockmakers would bemoan. (None of it newly minted, none of it sequential, all of it foxed and folded and creased: This was laundered money, and laundering always pointed to dirty hands and dirty deeds. Just what were you up to, Bell?) No. It was the tray packed so discretely under those notes and coins that had justified a servitor escort. Sparks wasn't there to guard the money.

No. He'd been sent to guard the keys.

The carriage door opened. The servitor—her servitor—balanced the chest on one shoulder while unfolding the stairs clipped to the carriage door. It (he?) offered his arm to help Berenice down.

She inhaled. *Slow. Steady. Just stroll across the road and board a ship. You'll be outside for a few minutes at most. Nobody will recognize you. They have their own work to do.* She blinked twice to align her glass eye.

Though there were only three, the carriage stairs were so

steep as to be almost a ladder. She was grateful for Sparks's assistance; she couldn't stay inconspicuous if she shattered her ankle walking across the street. When she was safely down, standing on a thoroughfare ostensibly cobbled though so thick with churned mud and snow that it was hard to know, she dismissed Sparks.

The *thrum* of traffic along the New Amsterdam waterfront reminded her of the docks at Marseilles-in-the-West. She'd met Louis in a place much like this, albeit smaller and on a lesser scale of commerce. Still, the humid smell of open water, the lapping of the water against the hulls of the ships, the low cacophony of human voices, the creak of ropes and wood: These put her back on the Saint Lawrence again. If not for the occasional Clakker laboring to load or unload cargo, and the vast gray ocean beyond the stone breakwater at the mouth of the North River, she might have been home. She sniffed again. The Saint Lawrence wasn't so salty. But still.

Berenice stepped into the road still thinking of times past. And found the world spinning around her as a pair of metal hands grasped her under the armpits and deftly placed her on the sidewalk. She yelped. A second later a carriage-and-four charged down the lane, through the space from which she'd just been yanked. Berenice received a gesture from the rapidly receding driver that would have curled an innocent woman's toes.

A servitor who wasn't Sparks said, "Are you hurt, madam? I most humbly and sincerely apologize for touching your person without first soliciting permission. I sensed you were in immediate danger and was compelled to act. I will immediately submit myself for inspection if my calculation was in error."

The machine stood before her, palms out and head low in a gesture of supplication. Several passersby had paused to watch. The noise of the mechanical's body grew steadily louder while it waited for her response. Jax had explained this to her. It was paralyzed by the requirements of the hierarchical metageasa. It hurt, she knew, roasting its hollowed-out soul over ghostly metaphysical fires every instant the geas went unresolved.

"Your judgment was sound. I commend your leaseholders on their ownership of such a well-maintained machine."

The automaton straightened. "May I be of further assistance?" After the slightest pause, barely half a heartbeat, while the bezels in its gemstone eyes clicked, it added, "Your eyesight has been compromised. Shall I escort you to your destination?"

Oh, you fucking thing. Can't you just shut up?

"No. Go about your business."

"As you say, madam. Good day, madam."

Berenice took more care in her second attempt to cross the road running along the water's edge. She made it up the ramp of the ship where Sparks had negotiated (well, dictated) the terms of her passage to England. The ramp passed between two enormous sculls poking through the hull. Like most ships in the Dutch maritime world, *De Pelikaan* was powered by a complement of galley Clakkers. Though it was quite an odd-looking craft—it resembled its namesake pelican thanks to a strangely flared bow. Plus the scull blades bristled with serrated hooks. She'd never seen such a thing. Were they for chopping firewood or water?

Berenice concentrated on swanning aboard as though she owned the ship. Her fingers touched the chain at her throat. Several humans stood on deck; to the one with the largest hat and the most frippery on his uniform, she said, "You are the captain."

"And you're the bitch who thinks she commands my boat."

As she'd done in so many interminable meetings of the privy council of the Exile King of Fallen France, Berenice chose the simplest riposte. She produced Bell's pendant and dangled it before the captain. To her considerable pleasure, the sun bolstered her case by choosing that moment to glint from the gold and quartz.

"And this is the sigil that says I do." It swung like a pendulum on its long chain. She let it hang for an extra beat before adding, "At least when it comes to matters of the Guild and the Crown. A purview that, I expect you have already divined, encompasses my errand."

Behind the captain, one of the officers rolled his eyes. The human crew members exchanged a volley of uneasy looks. One woman, presumably a lieutenant, pursed her lips and turned nonchalantly for the bridge as though suddenly taken with the need to return to work. Another man shook his head, though he didn't turn away.

The captain said, "You have got enormous fucking nerve flashing that thing in my face on my boat."

Hold on. Who did this cockhole think he was? She'd come to think of the pendant almost as a magic talisman. But human hearts were still human hearts.

"Captain, you misunderstand your own importance to this endeavor. I have extremely urgent business in England. This ship suits my needs. Your participation in the voyage is superfluous."

"If we don't make Rotterdam on schedule," he said, lifting his cap and running a hand through his hair, "your colleagues will slap us with so many fines we'll never sail again."

"Of course they won't." Berenice assumed they would, but she leaned into the lie. "I will personally guarantee *De Pelikaan* is not penalized because of my intercession. You may even receive a bonus for exceptional service to the Guild."

"Bullshit. I've heard too many of your Clockmaker lies to

believe anything you sons of bitches say. First your Stemwinders take my son, then you take my boat. I hope that when you die, the devil takes your soul as payment for your dark deeds and darker magics."

Well, this was awkward. Had Barendregt's son been swept up in the anti-Catholic purges during the war? Or had he run afoul of the Guild in some other way? What a perverse pity that Berenice's disguise demanded her steadfast opposition to the captain. They shared an enemy.

He spat on the deck at her feet. Walked away. At the door to the bridge, he paused. Over his shoulder, he said, "If your servitor must accompany you, it'll require subsidiary nautical metageasa before we depart. Even you can't circumvent that law."

Naturally, a vessel of this size would have a horologist among the crew. Those Clakkers leased by the shipping company surely had the nautical-safety metageasa permanently embedded into the rules that governed their every action. Landlubbing Clakkers could be a danger to the ship if they weren't similarly indoctrinated.

"I wouldn't seek to do so. My servitor carries a chest of my personal effects. Will you object if it delivers the chest to my stateroom before reporting to your Guildman?"

The captain said, "Heaven forfend you should be deprived of your effects a single moment longer than absolutely necessary."

She nodded. "I'm so pleased you agree. As soon as he delivers my effects, I shall order Sparks to report to your horologist."

At this, the captain turned to face her. Confusion wrinkled his brow. Varying shades of scandal or alarm showed on the faces of the deck officers.

"And just who in the hell," he said, scratching his temple, "is Sparks?"

Damn you, Jax. You changed the way I think about your kind, and ruined my careless disregard for your identities. Goddamn it.

Berenice had violated a subtle but deep social convention. Particularly among the Clockmakers. Children in the Dutch-speaking world commonly referred to the Clakkers as gendered beings, but outgrew that as they absorbed the mores of their parents. Some leaseholders did refer to their mechanicals by name, though others—those wealthy enough to own multiple servitors, for instance—sometimes never bothered to learn their servants' names. The indifference to identity scaled with wealth or social status. Members of the Clockmakers' Guild, the horologists and alchemists who kept the empire ticking along, never acknowledged anything beyond a machine's true name. Because, after all, Clakkers were merely unthinking machines. Machines could not have personal identities and inner lives.

So to hear a woman from the Verderer's Office speak thusly...no wonder they were confused. Berenice had afforded them a peek under her disguise.

"Sparks is my servitor," she said. For it was true.

"So I gather. But I could swear you said, 'He.'" The captain looked to his officers, perhaps feeling the need for somebody to corroborate something so unseemly.

Berenice said, "I believe it is common to refer to ships in the feminine. As 'she' and 'her.' Is it not?"

One of the scandalized lieutenants chimed in. "But that's an *ancient* tradition."

"In my line of work it is sometimes necessary to imbue a mechanical with a sense of identity that extends beyond mere appellation. If you can so easily accept that your inanimate ship is a 'she,' surely you can comprehend that for the purposes of my errand, my inanimate servitor is, for now, a 'he.'"

The captain shook his head, as if hearing something disagreeable. "I can't begin to imagine how that could further anybody's purposes."

"Do you pry into the Verderers' business?"

The captain entered the bridge and slammed the door.

A lieutenant called up a mechanical crewman to show Berenice to her stateroom. It contained a twin bunk that folded from the bulkhead over a handful of recessed drawers, a shaving mirror, and a white Delft porcelain washbasin still dusted with coppery beard stubble. That left just enough room for her ill-gotten chest and Sparks to guard it, if he—no: *it!*—folded himself tightly into the corner with the basin. A pair of staggered portholes offered a view of the wintry gray sky above and, below, the tip of a retracted scull just above the waterline. A whiff of shaving cream lingered near the basin. She realized the space had originally been assigned to one of the officers. So somewhere on this boat there paced a displaced and disgruntled lieutenant. It had been her intent to slip aboard rather more quietly, without turning the entire human crew against her. Lovely.

After locking the cabin door, she folded down the bunk. Flopped on it. Sighed.

At least she'd slipped on her tongue in front of the human crew rather than Sparks. Her brief association with Jax had given her bad habits when it came to Clakkers. But Jax had been freed of the geasa, and thus not compelled to pounce upon suspicious behavior. Sparks, on the other hand, would be powerless to do anything but take action if she gave him—*it,* it, IT, *Goddamn it!*—reason to doubt her identity.

It also occurred to her that sharp-eyed members of the crew might wonder why she wore the same clothes every day of the voyage when her servitor had hauled a large and heavy chest aboard. She'd replaced her clothing with Cortland's garb; they were a poor fit, and smelled of his pipe, but at least they weren't crusted with blood. Perhaps she ought to have ordered Sparks to buy her new clothes. But until they were out of New Amsterdam, haste seemed the wiser course.

She'd have to keep a low profile. Very well; that fit with her Verderer persona.

Even here behind the harbor breakwater, snugged to its bollards, the ship bobbed. Just a bit, but enough to notice whenever she lay unmoving on the bunk. Berenice closed her eyes. Opened them again, with a start, when Sparks knocked. The machine delivered her chest along with a bit of extra cash obtained for the carriage and horse.

"Mistress, before the ship departs, I must receive new geasa from the ship's horologist." The machine bowed. "I humbly beg your leave."

"Yes, yes." Lying down again, she closed her eyes and waved Sparks off. "The captain and I had a delightful conversation about it."

Sparks said, "I shall return immediately."

She didn't hear the door close; she was too preoccupied with the contents of the chest. How could she divine the purpose of those keys? What were they for, and why so many? It was like a hunger, the urge to start experimenting. Were they blanks, requiring a locksmith to cut them? Or were they skeleton keys?

The hole in Sparks's forehead made a tempting target for experimentation. But some avenues were dangerous, and some were foolhardy. There were those who argued she'd yet to learn the distinction. (She thought, fleetingly, of a grizzled sergeant back in Marseilles-in-the-West.) She couldn't anticipate how spinning the lock in Sparks's head might change the machine. She needed its unswerving loyalty and didn't dare undermine it.

The truth was she knew so little about how the Guild did what it did. Few people outside the Clockmakers' walled garden ever had the chance to witness them at work—

She sat upright. Leapt from the bunk. Flung the door open. Locked it. Hurried after Sparks.

∞

The horologist's laboratory resided in the bowels of the ship, in a passageway clearly marked off-limits to nonessential personnel. The horologist himself was a ruddy fireplug named van Breugel. He recoiled from her pendant as though she'd waved a rabid, slavering bat in his face. He licked his lips.

"Verderer's Office. Has there been a problem with my work?"

"Heavens, no." She placed a hand on his shoulder. He flinched. "I merely want to watch. Pretend I'm not here."

Van Breugel glanced at Sparks. He shrugged. "Despite the, uh, details, this is basically just a bog-standard graft. Nothing you haven't seen a thousand times." He didn't meet Berenice's eyes when he looked at her. "If you have particular requirements," he mumbled, clearly hoping this wasn't the case, "variances must be put in writing."

Berenice strove for the most amiable tone she could muster. "I understand. I have no such needs."

Berenice had no idea what he was going on about, but he didn't seem to pick up on that.

He opened a cabinet. After a bit of rummaging, he produced a leather case and a key ring.

"Do you enjoy this post? Seems like it must get a bit boring now and then."

Without hesitation, he said, "Though I am but a single cog in the mechanism of the empire, mine is crucial work. It's a privilege to serve the Brasswork Throne by bringing the Guild's craft to the sea."

Berenice shook her head. "I'm not investigating you," she said. "I'm making conversation. Honestly."

"Oh." Van Breugel paused, as though taking in her question

for the first time. She wondered how long it had been since anybody had shown interest in his work. "Yes, it's frequently dull. But it gives me time to read."

The valise shed eddies of dust when he opened it. A peppery whiff of candle soot tickled her nose. There was a staleness to the scent, as though van Breugel didn't open the valise for every voyage. From the valise he produced a candle, a concave mirror, and something wrapped in cloth. The candle and mirror he set on his desk. Then he unfolded the bundle in his palm as gingerly as though it were a freshly hatched chick on Easter morning.

What she saw quickened her pulse: In his palm lay an opaque lens, murky as though crafted from inferior glass. It might have been part of a pair with the bauble she'd used to free the Stemwinder at the Verderers' safe house. After Jax had shown it to her, she'd come to think of it as a pineal glass, for she had seen something similar inside the head of another rogue that she had deceived, subdued, and disassembled.

To Sparks, van Breugel said, "Machine. Recite your true name to me."

"Sir, I am called Sparthikulothistrodantus."

The horologist pointed to a mark on the deck. "Stand there, facing me."

Sparks crossed the cabin. From the bulkhead van Breugel swiveled a hinged rod. He adjusted it until it hung at roughly the machine's eye level. The rod held three clamps. Into one he placed the candle, the mirror into another, then between them he placed the murky lens.

Berenice couldn't hide her fascination. She tried to absorb every detail of the procedure. Van Breugel snuck glances at her. Perhaps the scrutiny lay too boldly on her face, for what he saw caused him to frown.

To distract him from her obvious interest in a routine procedure, she asked, "Tell me something. Why does everybody cower from my shadow as though I'm the seven-headed beast of Revelations? I'm not, you know."

"You'll never convince Captain Barendregt of that."

Berenice said, "His son." The Guildman nodded, warily. She asked, "What happened?"

Van Breugel shrugged. "Nobody knows. It was years ago. The captain was a lieutenant then. He'd been a-sea then, making the long loop to the central and southern New World."

"Chocolate and parrots."

"That's the one. The lore says the boy ran afoul of the Stemwinders not long after his father departed Rotterdam. He would've been in his midtwenties around that time. The boy, I mean. By the time his father returned, they'd let him go, but he wasn't the same."

"How so?"

"I haven't seen fit to ask."

"What did the boy do?"

Something flashed behind van Breugel's eyes when he chanced to meet her gaze. Fleeting, gone between heartbeats, yet caustic enough to tarnish silver. "Something terrible, I'm sure. Your office always has its reasons."

Keys jangled together when the real horologist flipped through the pieces on the ring. They didn't appear obviously different from the keys in Berenice's stolen chest, though she hadn't yet had ample opportunity to study those. Both sets had a peculiar spiral pattern to the teeth arrayed around a cylindrical core, matching the circular keyhole found on every Clakker brow. They didn't emit the peculiar chime of alchemical alloys when they knocked against one another. Twice he glanced at Sparks, noting particular features of the machine's construction and design. Berenice assumed van Breugel combined a knowledge of Sparks's polysyllabic true name with observations of its body plan to deduce a particular model. He might have been a bored landlord sorting the keys to all the flats in his building. He didn't act like a man who held the keys to the very foundations of the modern world in his grasp.

Having found the key he sought, he pulled a slim leather-bound volume from the same cabinet. Fine silver filigree stamped into the leather cover stated the book was property of the Sacred Guild of Horologists and Alchemists. It came with a tiny clasp and keyhole, like a schoolgirl's diary, but this apparently was unused or broken, for van Breugel flipped the catalog open without touching its lock. That didn't seem in keeping with the Guild's psychotic dedication to secrecy.

Partially just for the hell of it, and partially playing on a hunch, Berenice cleared her throat.

He paused in the midst of flipping through the pages. He coughed, awkwardly. "Ah," he said. "I, ah, have been meaning to fix that."

She said, "I have every confidence that's so."

Berenice couldn't read over his shoulder without crowding him and further stimulating his distrust. But she could see the pages were filled with tables. Indexed by model? She couldn't tell. But van Breugel found the page he sought, ran his thumb along one row, and then squinted at the rod. He jostled the mirror, candle, and lens back and forth until their clamps aligned with specific notches.

The strange procedure reminded Berenice of a doctor gauging the quality of a patient's vision to deduce the correct eyeglass prescription. Clearly, the printed tables told him where to situate the optical elements.

Focal length? What's the crucial element here?

The horologist lit the candle. It smelled of nothing more exotic than beeswax, and the light it gave seemed perfectly ordinary. The murky glass responded with a faint shimmer. Though it seemed too opaque to transmit anything, the mirror cast a flickering halo on the bulkhead behind Sparks. What first appeared to be the blurry images of dust motes became, after a moment's closer scrutiny, arcane alchemical sigils.

"Do not move," said the horologist.

He shoved the key straight into Sparks's head and gave it a vicious twist. The servitor stood eerily motionless in spite of the screeching and ratcheting that reverberated from deep within its skull. The alchemical sigils etched into a spiral around the machine's keyhole rotated with each twist of the key. Van Breugel turned the key through several complete revolutions until Sparks's head emitted an alarming *thunk*. The horologist went back to the rod. He left the key stuck in Sparks's forehead, which made the servitor look just a bit like a unicorn.

Van Breugel swiveled the mirror mount. The shimmering halo grew smaller on the bulkhead as it neared Sparks. The horologist aimed the refracted and reflected candlelight at Sparks's eyes. It glinted from the crystalline orbs. He continued to make small adjustments until the machine lurched. The key spun widdershins, reversing the sigils' orbit over the machine's brow. Van Breugel removed the key and snuffed out the candle.

He seemed to expect some sort of reaction from Berenice, so she gave a noncommittal, "Hmmmph."

He took that to mean she was unimpressed. "I warned you it wasn't anything you hadn't seen countless times before."

"So you did," she said.

But he was wrong. He'd just demonstrated the Clockmakers' secret procedure for altering the metageasa in a functioning mechanical.

CHAPTER
8

The lump in Longchamp's stomach, the one that had formed when Sergeant Chrétien shook him awake in the wolf hours before sunrise, froze solid. It was colder even than the steel tank upon which he lay.

The captain sprawled on a deer hide with his head and arm crammed through the dismantled assay valve of a chemical storage tank. Dim lantern light gleamed silver from the burnished walls of the containment vessel. It was one of several built to hold chemicals used in the glue cannons, their primary means of defense against the Clakkers.

The inventory listed the tank as full. But for a few lungfuls of caustic fumes, the tank was empty. Just as the former vicomtesse had warned in her letter.

Yesterday morning an overnight dispatch from Acadia, that strange part of New France along the Atlantic coast where people spoke a waterlogged and salt-stained French, reported that a force of several hundred Clakkers had rowed longboats across the Strait of Belle Isle. Closer to Marseilles-in-the-West, meanwhile, there were reports of an explosion in the forest northeast of Mont-Laurier, and at least one coureur de bois, a woods runner, had died by Clakker action. Exploratory forays, Longchamp knew. More would follow, and soon.

The metal tide was rising.

But where there ought to have been thousands of gallons of chemical reagents there was only air, and the echoes of Longchamp's voice. He launched a long stream of curses reverberating through the chromium-plated tank. Even after he pulled his head from the valve to escape the fumes, it still sounded like the tank contained a choir of sailors chanting their bluest epithets in a sacrilegious call-and-response. His head spun. It took several lungfuls of chilly air before he could think clearly. The winter air swept the sting from his eyes, too, though they insisted on watering, the traitorous bastards.

And speaking of traitors.

Longchamp stood. To the pair of chemists standing alongside the open valve, he said, "Close it. I've seen enough."

Chrétien said, "There's nothing *to* see."

"Then I've seen plenty of nothing for a day that's still night, for fuck's sake."

Longchamp decided against risking a slide down the side of the cylindrical tank. It was only ten feet in diameter, so he didn't stand so far off the ground. If it wasn't so dark and his knees so old, he even might have jumped down. But he was cold and stiff and didn't want to make an ass of himself in front of God, his men, and these civilians. Instead he put his effort into descending the ladder without signaling his stiffness and discomfort to the men. Their morale had just taken a body blow—so had his: It was all he could do to resist pulling out the rosary—and the last thing they needed was to see their respected CO begging for holy intercession like somebody's constipated grandfather.

This news would get out sooner than later. If the civvies saw their defenders wailing and gnashing their teeth, soon the entire town would talk itself into rolling over to present its belly to the invaders before the fighting even started. They had to look confident. In order to look confident, they had to feel confident. And the best thing Longchamp could do to help that along was to project his own confidence. Or at least hide the shock that currently wanted to liquefy his bowels.

Back on the ground, he stomped his feet to ward off a creeping chill. It didn't help; the chill came from inside himself.

"All right. I'm as awake as I'm ever likely to be. Tell me the story."

The night was quiet but for the soldiers' footsteps and the occasional grunt or bellow from the nearby stockade. Smelly beasts; the smell wafting from the enclosure wasn't markedly better than that from inside the chemical reservoir. Another bellow. Longchamp lifted his lamp. It sparkled from the snow dusting the shaggy bison and, behind them, the smooth stonework of the outer keep wall. No sign of disturbance there; just enormous stupid animals doing whatever they did best. That the ancient plains dwellers had built enclosures for the beasts without the benefit of modern materials beggared belief.

Sergeant Chrétien spoke in a low voice, as though he didn't want to spook the animals. Good instincts, but it was the civvies they had to worry about.

He said, "Chemists have been working their way around the keep. Inventorying, topping off the storage tanks, the usual siege preparations. Strict visual inspection, per your instructions. They got to this guy—" Chrétien rapped the tank with his knuckle. It rang like a Chinese gong. "—And promptly shit themselves. They came running to us—"

"—And you came running to me," Longchamp said.

"That's about the shape of it."

A woman stepped into the light. Longchamp could always spot the chemists in a crowd of civvies; when they remembered to remove their work aprons, their clothing underneath frequently bore stains or even burns from unpronounceable chemicals, and the eyes behind their glasses frequently carried the hint of a glaze, as though intense concentration was never far away.

"This is a reservoir for one of the epoxy precursors."

"Dumb it down for me," Longchamp said. "Pretend you're talking to men who earn their pay by providing live fencing practice for mechanical devils. So. The stuff that holds the ticktocks at bay. It's a mixture."

"Yes. The solidification is a chemical reaction derived from rapid copolymerization—"

"Uh-huh. And whatever was in here—"

"A triethylenetetramine derivative salted with—"

"Whatever goop was in here is something we need for the epoxy guns. That sound about right?"

She sighed. "Yes."

"And now we don't have it."

"Yes."

"How much do we not have?"

The sergeant squinted through the glare of lamplight on bare metal to read a label on the tank. "About twenty-five thousand *pinte*, sir."

"Again," said Longchamp, "because I lack the mental capacity to live a life of the mind, unlike you and your educated cohort, Doctor, I'm going to simplify things. I admit I don't know my units very well, though in truth one can't fault the good nuns of Saint Jean-Baptiste for not trying to cram some basic knowledge into my thick and obstreperous skull, but for the purposes of the rest of this conversation I'm going to assume that twenty-five thousand *pinte* is a fucking shit-ton." The chemist tensed. Her slouch disappeared. "Because it sounds like a fucking shit-ton. Doesn't it, Sergeant?"

"Yes, sir. At least one, sir. Possibly more."

"Good lad. Now shut your gob so the good doctor can enlighten us. She was about to give us her professional opinion on just how long that fucking shit-ton of goop has been AWOL."

She crossed her arms. The shawl wrapped over her head tugged loose. "It's impossible to know. We don't—"

"I'll put it another way," said Longchamp. "How long has it been since the last time somebody from your cohort actually checked this tank?"

She closed her eyes. "Potentially months."

Chrétien whistled. He shook his head, stretching his arms as though preparing to witness an assault.

Longchamp let the obviously inadequate answer writhe in the silence for a beat. Then he said, "Seems to me, though as I've said I'm just an uneducated knuckle-dragger, that is a bit less than ideal. Because, and maybe you haven't received the news on this, we're preparing for another siege. And what's the first thing we do when preparing for a siege, Sergeant?"

"We inventory our stocks, sir. Know your resources, that's siege discipline one-oh-one."

To the chemist, Longchamp said, "That lad's going to make captain someday. I'm sorry to say that your own grasp of the basics is lacking. One might go so far as to say it's a fucking insult to those of us who dedicate our simple knuckle-dragging lives to defending your worthless flabby shitholes. Because I seem to recall the marshal general saying some time ago that he wanted us all to draw up a picture of our resources."

"We're a little behind," she said.

"For true? You don't say?"

The chemist said, "Look! We've also been building new storage facilities inside the keep, and pumping down the exterior cisterns as quickly as the new capacity allows. But inventorying the chemical stocks isn't that straightforward!"

"Really? Because if it were me, I'd pop open that valve on the top, plunk a dipstick into the stuff, and read off the level. But then I'm just a soldier, not a doctor of higgledy-piggledy. So how do the experts do it?"

"We, ah, use a dipstick." Longchamp rolled his eyes. She hastened to add, "But we have to be extremely careful not to introduce pollutants! The copolymerization is highly exothermic, and even trace impurities can degrade the reaction, retarding or even preventing it."

"So it's the excruciating and exacting procedural standards that have kept you from a timely inventory. Not the fact that nobody wants to trek outside to kneel on comfy ice-cold iron in the dead of winter."

"That could have been part of it," she conceded.

Faintly audible over the shuffling and lowing of bison, the bells of the basilica chimed. Lauds, the call to dawn prayer. Christ, but it was going to be a long day.

As the tintinnabulation faded, Longchamp asked, "What happened to it?" He aimed his lantern at the ground beneath the tank. The snow cover was much thinner there, but that told him nothing.

"It wasn't a leak. The tank is sound." She pointed at the bison in their pen. "Otherwise we'd have some very sick animals."

"Then where did it go?"

"My guess is that it was pumped out. Deliberately."

"Is that the educated way of saying 'stolen'?"

"I suppose it is."

Longchamp remembered the letter from Berenice. Her warning had proven accurate. Her suspicions about Montmorency looked more and more plausible in the gray predawn light; the duke had stood at the center of New France's chemical enterprise.

"Can you and your cohort replace the missing goop?"

"If we work all day and night for the next several weeks, we could replenish a portion of it. Given the necessary precursor chemicals, catalysts, and reagents."

"I can't give you orders, Doctor, but I can give you advice. And my advice is that if you and your fellow eggheads don't want to get strung up by your thumbs, you should do exactly that."

"I said, 'given.' We don't have the resources to replace what's missing."

At this, the sergeant's eyebrows tried to climb under the brim of his hat. Good instincts. Longchamp closed his eyes, pinched the bridge of his nose, and counted to five.

"Why the hell not? Just what, for God's sake, are you people doing with it all?"

"Nothing! We've been able to do very little since the supply caravans from the northwest became so sporadic. And the precursor shipments we have received are of inferior quality, requiring extensive effort to remove impurities."

"Jesus, Mary, and Joseph on a horny syphilitic camel. How long has this been going on?"

The chemist shrugged. "A couple of months, maybe? We wrote a report."

"Yeah. I'm sure that did the trick. People love to read the shit out of those." Longchamp beckoned to the sergeant. "Come on, lad. Let's go start the marshal general's day in fine fashion."

⁓

The marshal general, like all members of the privy council, kept apartments within the inner keep. Longchamp and Chrétien's stroll through the heart of New France took them over trenches supposedly wide and deep enough to slow a Clakker, under machicolations, and through posterns. The walk was made slightly perilous by miserly use of synthetic lamp oil in the keep's lanterns. The king had decreed that only every third lamp be lit at night, as a means of conserving precious chemicals that could be turned to defense. But it was early enough that the streets were mostly empty, except for the night-soil collectors.

The keep's star-shaped perimeter and its outer defenses had been designed by the great Vauban himself, who had come to the New World as part of the original Exile. The legendary military engineer had also turned his keen mind for siege warfare inward, against the not-so-unthinkable proposition that swarms of mechanical killers might come over, or through, the walls. In peacetime the pincer-like tenailles provided convenient niches for vendor carts and displays of flowering herbs. But now the winter-wilted anise and lavender had been sheared away, and corners that used to crackle with fish fried in bison fat now bristled with harpoons, bolas, and epoxy guns.

Apparently the sergeant frequented some of the same vanished stalls, for as they turned one corner, he sighed.

"What's on your mind, Sergeant?"

"Flowers and bacon. That'll always be the smell of home to me. But I wonder how this city will smell come the next bloom."

Longchamp said, "Don't concern yourself. After you've lived on nothing but cold pemmican for two months, you'll never again miss the smell of animal fat."

"Yes, sir. I remember, sir."

The captain took a slightly circuitous route that gave him the opportunity to light candles in the basilica narthex. The sergeant removed his hat, knelt, and crossed himself. Despite the early hour and the empty streets, dozens of faithful had heeded the monks' call to prayer. It had been that way since the terrible news from Québec; Longchamp included the murdered pontiff in his prayers for New France.

At the marshal's residence, Longchamp leaned against a dry

fountain, scratching his beard, while Sergeant Chrétien gave the bellpull a discreet yank. The chiming of the bells came through clearly enough, but no footsteps. The sergeant yanked the bell cord with one hand and knocked with the other. Quick learner: He put his fucking wrist into it.

The marshal's attendant opened the door. He wore a robe with more dignity than many could muster in their Sunday best. Not recognizing the sergeant, he twisted his face into a scowl that might have sent lesser men packing.

"Sir!" he said, in something between a stage whisper and a shout. "The comte and comtesse de Turenne do not take visitors at this hour."

"I apologize for the early hour. I'd like to speak with the marshal, if it's possible," said the sergeant.

"As would a great many people. But the comte is not inclined to favor those who can't observe basic courtesies."

Longchamp watched this unfold for a minute or so, until he decided to let the sergeant off the hook. He cleared his throat and spat into the fountain basin, which contained snow and crumbled leaves.

"Oh, for fucking serious, Richard. You and I both know you're going to let us in, because you and I both know I wouldn't bother the marshal unless the sky was falling and the dead were rising."

"Captain. I'll wake the marshal at once." The attendant ushered both men inside as if he hadn't just pitched a fit.

Chrétien whispered, "Thank you, sir."

Longchamp said, sotto voce, "Try acting like you belong in that Goddamned uniform. Because that was one of the saddest displays I've ever seen." He snorted. "You'd *like* to speak with the marshal? If it's *possible*? Jesus. I'd love to watch you haggle with the fishwives down in Saint Agnes. You'd come away naked, married, and in debt."

Richard saw them to the parlor and made to stoke the glowing ashes in the hearth. Longchamp growled. "The sergeant will take care of that."

Chrétien, hearing his cue, set about resurrecting the fire.

"Very good, Captain. Shall I ask Sabine to warm something for you? There is coffee."

"Thank you, no. But if you could fetch your master's martial wisdom before the sun sets tonight, that would be grand."

He did, in short order. Longchamp and Chrétien saluted the marshal, who entered the parlor looking old, and rumpled, and bleary. But he rallied impressively. And he didn't carry his ceremonial baton of office; Longchamp pictured the man sleeping with it under his pillow.

"Captain Longchamp. When the bell rang, I had a premonition that I'd be seeing you this morning." He blinked at the sergeant. "I don't know you."

"I'm sorry about the hour. This is Sergeant Chrétien."

"Ah." The marshal took a seat. "You're the one promoted in his wake," he said, jerking a thumb at the captain.

"Yes, sir."

"Big shoes to fill."

"Yes, sir."

"I hear he's a bit of a bastard to work for."

The sergeant cleared his throat. Turning red, he said, "I wouldn't know, sir."

The marshal turned to Longchamp. "He needs to learn how to lie better."

"I'm working on that."

"All right." The marshal slapped his knees. "You're here. I'm up. It's dark outside. What bad news have you come to deliver?" He cocked his head, as if listening to the city. "I don't hear screaming. The tulips aren't already at the walls?"

"Not yet, thank the Blessed Virgin," Longchamp said. All

three men crossed themselves. "But this is about the siege preparations." Longchamp explained the situation with the chemical inventories. He took care not to mention Berenice's letter.

"Surely there are reserves for manufacturing more."

Chrétien cast a sideways glance at Longchamp. The young sergeant's eyes had assumed the white-limned panic of a rabbit in a snare.

"That raises another issue." He relayed the news about the dodgy chemical shipments. "As you pointed out, we might be surrounded by metal men before long. It's crucial that we can arm all the epoxy cannons and keep them armed."

The marshal closed his eyes. His head drooped, slightly, but his breaths came more rapidly. He kneaded the arms of his chair. When he reopened his eyes, he'd sunk into himself. The comte de Turenne, Longchamp reminded himself, had not been a career military man. He'd become the marshal general through politics.

"What do we do?"

And in that moment, the young sergeant discovered that his leaders were just old men with feet of clay. It hurt Longchamp's heart, the look on the boy's face. But it was a necessary lesson.

"I think," said Longchamp, feeling a bit out of place in the attempt to be gentle, "the king should know about this. And then I think we should pray."

"Yes. Right." The marshal slapped his knees again. "Since you're in charge of the defenses, Captain, he'll want the report directly from you. He may want to assemble the privy council for this." He stood. "Richard! Lay out my clothes, I'm going to the Spire. Sabine! Coffee!"

∽∾

By the time Longchamp and his shadow reached the Spire on foot, the marshal had already dismounted. A guard attended the marshal's horse while, overhead, a pair of funicular cars passed each other. The ascending car contained the marshal; its empty twin came to a gentle stop at the base of the tracks.

Despite the hour, a small crowd of petitioners had already gathered at the funicular station. Mere rumors of war made people edgy, but when they saw siege preparations going into effect, no matter how surreptitiously, they tended to lose their minds. They'd been a common sight around the Spire, these past few weeks. Dozens waited in line, sometimes for an entire day, for a chance to present a case to the king. Usually it was civvies wanting an exemption from the conscription lottery, or businessmen trying to profit on the inevitable hostilities with Nieuw Nederland. Even in peacetime the petitioners occasionally included the old-timers, who believed the king could heal with a touch.

A slightly rowdy bunch for this time of the morning, but a pair of guards kept the line in order. As they neared the crowd, Simon, one of Longchamp's men, pointed at the rising tram car and said, "Because he's the marshal general, that's why. You could ride the funicular, too, if you had urgent affairs of state to discuss with His Majesty. But since you don't, Father, you can wait for the tram to start running at its regular time. The very same goes for the rest of you."

The guards saluted Longchamp as he passed. Chrétien frowned.

Lamplight and the first hints of sunrise shimmered on the windowpanes of the funicular cars, more tempting than the wink from any seductress. They might as well have been sirens from the old stories: Some day Longchamp's resolve would falter, and rather than endure the long climb up the Porter's Prayer he'd submit to the shortcut. There had been a time when he'd pounce on the stairs without a second thought. Nowadays thoughts of ascending the Spire the hard way came in tandem with a mental grimace. It was a long damn climb on rickety knees.

Were he alone, he might have chanced it. But given time a cut corner could become a self-justification that could become a habit. He couldn't risk the pernicious undermining of his strength and stamina. Which is why Longchamp grabbed Chrétien by the collar when the sergeant headed for the funicular.

"Not a chance. We go up the old way. You're too young to get lazy, and I'm too grizzled to change my ways. And besides," he added, "not only will it look better to the marshal general, it will give the marshal time to speak with the king in private before we arrive. They need to work themselves into a lather."

At least the sergeant had the self-discipline not to groan. "Yes, sir."

They mounted the stairs. From behind them again came the voices of the guards on crowd-control duty. "See? Even the captain of the guard takes the stairs." Somebody raised a voice in reply, to which Simon said, "Because they're on official business. The king doesn't see petitioners at the crack of dawn."

This caused more raised voices, but by then the curvature of the Spire had put the argument just enough out of earshot that Longchamp couldn't make out the words. Chrétien looked preoccupied, as though still listening; Longchamp wondered how far around the spiral those younger ears could track the argument.

Perhaps because of this, Longchamp pushed himself through the long, cold climb. Before they'd made it halfway up, they saw two pigeons arrive and one depart in the space of about ten minutes. The birds were little more than flapping silhouettes in the brightening sky, but they cast a shadow on Longchamp's heart. He called a stop at the pigeon roosts. Not because he needed a break, he told himself, and not because the sight of Brigit's friendly face would have cheered him, but to get wind of the latest news.

Brigit wasn't up at that hour. But Lord knew the pigeons

were. They'd been working all night to bring all the news from the far corners of New France.

More incursions along the border. Spotters in a balloon tethered a thousand feet above Trois-Rivières had caught glints of light moving through the nearby marshes. Meanwhile, more than a hundred leagues to the south, Clakkers had stormed the bridges at Niagara Falls; the Dutch now controlled the crossing there.

Every hour, the metal tide inched higher.

And the keep's chemical defenses were understocked.

Cold wind made Longchamp's eyes water. Both men sweat despite the wind. The sergeant's frown, the same one he'd donned at the base of the Spire, etched itself deeper into his face with every circuit of the spiral staircase.

"Sir," he said.

Longchamp grunted, trying not to sound like he was panting too heavily. "Hmmm."

"Did you hear what Simon said? To the petitioners?"

"I heard him making it clear that despite many a tale to the contrary, His Holiness is not hiding in the Spire," Longchamp puffed, "and that the king could not cure the afflicted with a touch, and..." The captain climbed a few more stairs, caught the ragged edge of his breath. "...And that on no account would people be allowed to bring their goats to petition the king, no matter how lame the wretched beasts."

"I don't mean that. There was a fellow near the back of the line. Simon called him, 'Father.'"

"Good ears, Sergeant."

"You told us to keep our eyes open for any men of the cloth recently arrived to Marseilles."

Longchamp stopped. *So I did. Son of a bitch.*

"Good memory, Sergeant. Was he making a fuss?"

"I don't know. I didn't get a good look at him." Chrétien peered over the outer balustrade of the Porter's Prayer. "Damn."

The limb of the sun had breached the eastern horizon by the time the breathless, sweaty captain and sergeant gained the rounded bead atop the Spire. Here lay the privy council chamber and, above that, the king's apartments.

Longchamp had to catch his breath before saying, "Go back down and get the details. And if he's not still in line, have Simon draw up a sketch. Then get it copied and pass it around to the rest of the men. Quietly."

CHAPTER
9

It wasn't easy to sprint through a winter forest with two useless arms and one severed foot clutched to his chest. Jax's weather-vane head swayed in herky-jerky time to the awkward loping stride he'd adopted, reluctantly, to accommodate the shattered stump of his ankle joint. It meant that he couldn't keep his eyes fixed on the ground ahead of him. And it was treacherous country, this taiga: sometimes swampy, sometimes choked with underbrush, sometimes so thick with conifers as to be impassable, and everywhere blanketed with snow. Sometimes the wind of his passage kicked up a rooster tail of loose flakes when he crossed a field. Sometimes the trees he brushed would hurl icicles in protest, glassy fléchettes that shattered against his body.

Back in The Hague, he easily could have run thrice as fast along the old veerkaden, the tow-canal paths. But back then he'd had two feet, two useful arms, and a head that moved as he commanded.

The mutilation caused him no pain. Not as a Clakker understood pain, anyway. A human who'd lost his foot as Jax had done would probably go blind from the agony before bleeding out.

Perhaps Jax's kin and their human makers were destined never to find common ground.

Meanwhile, Jax had discovered a new kind of torment. Not the magical pain inflicted upon the Clakkers as a matter of course, but the self-inflicted spiritual anguish of the sinner. The indelible guilt of the murderer. Jax would carry that mantle to the end of his days. Though he was ultimately responsible for the murder of a leviathan airship—another guilty burden—he had tried to save the machine's life. His pursuers in the city had killed a human witness to spin the story of a crazed murder machine. A fellow servitor, Dwyre, had even sacrificed himself for Jax. But this was worse.

Was there a God who punished murderers? And if so, did He punish rogue mechanicals like Jax, or only soulful humans? And what of his soldier kin, those who would be powerless to do anything but kill Frenchmen—were they sinners? Had Jax somehow retrieved his own soul when he attained freedom from the geasa? Or was he still just a hollow shell hated by his creators, disregarded by their Creator, and exempt from the bonds of human social conventions? Perhaps. But if that were the case, why did the weight of his remorse threaten to flatten him?

And assuming there was a God to listen, did He answer prayers? All prayers, or only the prayers of the devout? Would He listen to the penitent whispers of a poor pathetic machine? Some humans believed their God could know their hearts and minds. Did He concern Himself with the inner lives of Clakkers? The Calvinists' God had put all things into motion at the beginning of time, like a celestial Clockmaker winding a pocketwatch, including the infinitely twisting braided paths of His creations' lives. Did that extend to Clakkers, too? Were they predestined to lives of interminable servitude?

Had Jax been predestined to meet Pastor Visser, and Berenice, and the man he killed in the forest?

The forest smelled better than The Hague, and Amsterdam, and even Delft. No faint stagnation of the canal waters here. Just the cold crisp snow, the evergreens, and occasional scents of the animals he startled—elk musk, rabbit scat. He imagined this was bear territory, and wondered if he'd see one, though he understood they slept through the winter. Late the previous night he'd heard a growl from something apparently rather large.

He remembered a storyteller at Pieter Schoonraad's seventh birthday party, decades ago when Jax had belonged to Pieter's father and his final leaseholder had been just a little boy younger than his daughter, Nicolet, was now. He'd entertained the children with fanciful stories of New World animals punctuated with snorts and barks and whinnies. Little Piet had wet his pants when the man described the fearsome mountain lion.

Jogging through the trees, vision slewing back and forth with every bob of his disobedient head, he almost didn't notice the abrupt end to the forest until he breached the brambles to emerge from a sentry-like row of aspens. And found himself at cliff's edge atop a sheer wall of jagged granite. Thousands of acres of red spruce spread before him. Snow clung to their boughs, making them appear like Christmastime Speculaas cookies sprinkled with powdered sugar. He also spied hemlock and larch, the latter naked for winter but recognizable for the smattering of purple cones about their bases. A river snaked through the valley like a silver ribbon draped through the forest. A herd of bison picked at the snow along the banks. Beyond the shallow bowl of the valley the earth rose in a series of gentle undulations that swelled first into foothills and then...

Mountains!

He'd never seen such a thing before, only their renderings. The Old World was lousy with them, he knew; he'd come from a place crisscrossed with Alps and Pyrenees and Carpathians. His imagination had fallen short. He'd never imagined they could be so...

Transfixing.

Mountains! It was as though some vast chthonic forces deep within the earth had frozen in midshrug to leave a great jagged sawtooth stretched across the horizon. The bare peaks were shrouded in snow so pure the glare of sunlight triggered filters in his eyes. Farther down the distant slopes the color and shading of the mountains shifted between purples and umbers to a deep kelly green. When he zoomed his eyesight to the diffraction limit, the altered shading became a timberline, an altitude beyond which even the quaking aspens wouldn't grow.

The sun inched across the sky while he absorbed every detail of the vista. The play of light and shadow as clouds scudded across the sky; the curlicues of snow torn from the distant peaks as wind whipped across the summits; the whisper of running water; the loamy, piney scent of the forest. He'd never imagined such beauty.

Mountains! The sun traversed a quarter of the sky before Jax moved again.

The cliff offered no obvious route down. He could have climbed had he two feet and the use of his arms. But he didn't, so he jumped. The snow-shrouded boughs of balsam fir trees cushioned his cannonball descent. He landed in a snowdrift, pelted by a rain of the firs' cigar-shaped cones. Needles and cone scales clung to him, affixed by a drizzling of fragrant pine resin.

The descent to the valley floor brought him to the frozen bank of a wide river. He stopped there. The current still ran unsheathed by ice where the flow was fastest, but a skin of muddy ice clung to both banks. Here and there fragments of ice the size of dinner plates bobbed along in the current, glistening silver like the scales of a giant fish. Tendrils of mist clung to the river.

He crossed his club arms across his chest, pinning his loose foot as tightly as he could manage. Then he crouched on the frozen mudbank, balanced on his good leg. Gears chattered, quickly at first, then more slowly, as he compressed every spring and cable in his ankle, knee, leg, hip, waist, and back. He strained until there came a faint *thrum* from the cables of alchemical steel that threaded his body like human sinews.

He leaped. The wind of his passage pulled long streamers of mist from the river, like ghostly fingers grasping at him. He cleaved the air and left the dopplered twang of unspooled cables in his wake. He splayed his talon toes. Stretched.

His heel pierced ice and gouged a furrow through the earth. The *crack* reverberated through the forest like a gunshot. The impact liquefied the frozen mud; he sank to his ankle. It squelched when he worked himself free. The broken gimbals of his shattered ankle clattered like a sackful of broken crockery. But he hadn't fallen, and he hadn't dropped his broken foot. The broken-mirror crash of his landing continued to echo, as though the noise had been rejuvenated in some distant corner—

Jax paused. Listened.

Another crash, another echo.

And then, more faintly than the rest: another twang.

That wasn't him. That was something else. Something no more than half a mile downstream. Something that could, like him, leap across the river.

He wasn't alone. Other Clakkers roamed this wilderness. And they were following him.

Jax wanted to scream. Not with the artificially amplified noises of his mechanical voicebox, not with the catgut-and-reeds approximation of a human voice. Scream as the humans could do, by forcing a lungful of breath through sloppy wet biology. To express, explosively, the quivering outrage of it all.

Hundreds of miles he'd run through forest, field, and swamp but still the bastards chased him. They didn't care if he no longer threatened to contradict the foundations of their society. Jax was a limping refutation of the dogma of the Crown, Cross, and Guild. This wasn't about what he might *do*. They despised what he'd *become*. Hated it so much they would pursue him around the world to destroy it. They abhorred his existence. So they sent their own mechanicals, Jax's kin, to see it eradicated.

He was so weary of running.

Is that what happened to most rogues? Did they flee for years until they couldn't bear to take another stride? Until even the abject terror of capture and execution couldn't energize them? Did his pursuers know this? Did they rely upon existential despair to run him down?

Well, as Berenice might have said, *Fuck them.* He'd stop running when his legs shattered, and not a moment sooner. Jax launched into a sprint.

An answering *jangle-clatter* arose a mile or two behind him. And then another from atop the rolling foothills across the valley. The second pursuer threatened to cut him off where he'd emerge from the valley. Jax changed course.

He'd spent enough time atop the cliff ledge, enjoying the view, that the river's every oxbow was imprinted on the magic lantern of his mind's eye. Jax changed course again without slowing. Yes. The river. He couldn't feel cold, and he didn't need to breathe; hypothermia and drowning were human concerns. He only hoped it was deep enough to hide him.

The forest snow muffled sounds, though his own body sounded loud enough to be heard all the way to Europe. He crashed through brush, knocking down low branches, and pulverizing hidden stones with his inhuman tread. Sometimes as he ran, the alchemical alloys in his broken ankle joint scraped against rocks, creating a shower of sparks and sending a piercing shriek through the woods. Stealth was impossible. His only hope lay in reckless speed.

He smashed his encased arms against trees, boulders, the ground, anything within flailing distance. He startled an immense owl, which took to the air. If he could break the chemical sheaths on his arms and regain the use of his hands, he had half a chance. He could fight.

He plunged into a loop of the river. Just as he was about to duck under and start crawling along the riverbed, sunlight glinted from a stand of larch on a hillock inside the crook of the river bend less than a mile away. The glint carried an oily shimmer. Jax knew it as he knew his own body: alchemical alloys.

Damn it. The hunter on the hill had surely seen him. Jax cannoned out of the water. He hit the frozen ground running. He aimed for a break in the trees, where the ground was flatter.

A sheen of water froze to his body. It crackled between his joints and cogs while he sprinted. The *crunch* of ice obscured the crashing of his pursuers across the same frozen taiga, but he knew they were nearby. He knew because they called to him. In the hypercompressed telegraphy of *clicks* and *ticks*, *rattles* and *tocks,* intelligible only to their kind, they called.

From the wilds to his west: *Jalyksegethistrovantus.*

From the wilds to his east: *Jalyksegethistrovantus.*

From the south: *Ho, ho, he's a runner!*

His true name. Oh, God, they shouted his true name to the

heavens. They taunted Jax with knowledge of his former self, of the identity stamped upon his soul on the day he was forged. They knew he was no longer that machine, no longer beholden to the magics woven into that string of syllables. But they'd come to take him back to that world. Back to his death.

North he went, knowing they herded him like wolves around a frantic fawn. He charged across a frozen marsh, the toes of his foot churning up sods of peat. His broken ankle punched divots in the frozen earth like a posthole digger. The marsh abutted another bend of the meandering river. He hurled himself across it. From the peak of his trajectory he saw flashes of metal moving across the frozen earth, swift as a trio of arrows.

Ho, ho, he's a leaper!

Jax wasn't new to running for his life. But the taunting was a new and particularly cruel twist. What would inspire their makers to install such a wicked geas?

These Clakkers were different. Were they some hitherto secret model? Something unleashed on the world only when necessary to hunt down the most far-flung rogues?

He plunged into a stand of evergreens. It lay inside a shallow bowl of granite. At the lip he scrabbled for purchase on icy stone. It crunched under his toes, the reports like cannon shots announcing his every move. He ascended a cleft in the granite outcrop.

There he rubbed his encased arms against the stone, faster and faster until he wore a ridge in the granite. The chemical sheaths were more stubborn than the bones of the earth, but Jax worked a rudimentary shape into them. A rough point, for stabbing, and a depression like a shallow cup. When the ridge in the granite grew sufficiently deep, he studied the crystal pattern in the stone. Reared back. Kicked. Shards and pebbles went bounding down the slope.

Clumsy, like a human toddler, he struggled to pick up the

pieces. He had to use his arms like enormous awkward pincers. Then he rotated his extended arms behind him.

Jax could see the other Clakkers now. Squinting at them through the river haze, fighting the stubborn swaying of his weathervane head, he studied them. He wanted a sense of these cruel hunters, these fellow mechanicals who would in mere moments succeed where so many others had failed. And who chose to make a game of it.

Never in his one hundred and eighteen years had Jax seen their like. They were foreign. Ugly. Obscene.

Mismatched. Misshapen. Misbegotten.

Assembled from unrelated parts. Parts of different eras, different models. An assortment of different Clakkers melded into a single body. They embodied their kind's deepest and most closely held taboo. One glimpse turned the terror and dread clutching Jax to mindless, violent panic.

Is this what their makers did to the most troublesome of captured rogues? Jax had thought, like all his kin, that execution was the end of it. But perhaps that wasn't punishment enough for those machines lucky enough to violate the highest law. Perhaps their makers, driven by senseless malice, incinerated Free Will but kept the intellect alive. Perhaps they warped the offending machines' bodies into grotesque parodies of what was right. Just to mock what Jax and his kind held dear.

The trio converged like a spearhead aimed at Jax's roost. He focused on the leader. Aimed. His arms streaked forward with such speed that the sharpened tips of his club arms tore the air like a whip. The armful of stones he flung outpaced the sound of their launching. In an instant they closed the distance from Jax to his hunters, who swerved so hard they left scorch marks in the frozen peat.

Most missed, shearing deep furrows into the ground and creating gouts of mud and steam behind the pursuers. One stone struck the leader in the torso hard enough to ignite vermilion sparks where it sheared the alchemical alloys of his escutcheons. Another glanced from the leader's forehead. Jax had sought but failed to blind him.

Ho, ho! He's a fighter, ho ho!
He's David, with sling in hand!

Jax reloaded. The hunters didn't swerve to avoid his volley. One projectile entered an eye socket and shattered the crystalline orb within. Another dented a leaf spring in one of the grotesque Clakkers' legs. But in midstride the machine folded itself into a ball and let its momentum carry it bumping and tearing through the snow.

They were too close. They were too many. Jax couldn't hope to disable them before they reached him. He leaped from his perch and plunged through drifts of snow, toward the high mountains. He wouldn't touch the earth's hunched shoulders before he was caught. He ran for the privilege of existence. Or was it for the amusement of those who chased him? Those who made a game of chittering his name to the sky, the wind, the mountains?

From behind him the three unsettling machines took up another nonsense chant:

Jalyksegethistrovantus runs!
He's swift, swift as a sparrow!
But we, we are the arrow.

Three other machines, grotesquely mangled things like those giving chase, erupted from beneath the snow. They'd been lying in wait for him.

And we, we are the net.

Jax tried to roll, but the snow was too deep. He skidded, bounced, crashed to a halt. The new arrivals, the ones who had sprung the trap, watched him without advancing.

They didn't leap on him. They didn't subdue him. They only watched. As if mulling the method of his murder.

Why are you chasing me? he asked.

Because we want to catch you, they said.

To take me back. Jax didn't make it a question.

Because we were sent to find you, they said.

To unwrite me? To melt me?

Because we seek our own, they said, *and the one who was once Jalyksegethistrovantus is one of us.*

Jax shuddered. One of these abominations? But then, a centisecond before they said it, the first rays of realization dawned in the ink-black sky of his panicked mind.

In unison they said: *Welcome to Neverland, brother.*

CHAPTER
10

Berenice's resolve lasted two days. But with nothing to do but scowl at the crew (to stay in character) and listen to the endless creaking of the sculls, boredom quickly gave rise to temptation. Her better judgment was no match for her damnable curiosity. Three days into her voyage from New Amsterdam to Liverpool, her resolve crumbled.

She'd sped this along by poring over the keys in the chest that had been bound for the Verderers' house. Such strange gleaming things they were, their teeth and notches splayed around a helical core. Strangely, they weren't made from alchemical alloys. Or not one she'd ever seen. If she took one from the case and held it to the patchy sunlight streaming through her porthole, it showed no evidence of mysterious refractions wrought by magic worked into the metal. Instead it merely gave the usual glow of burnished brass. The ship swayed in the gray winter seas, and with it Berenice; she watched the key lean back and forth across the cup of her palm. She sniffed it. It carried the scent of a two-livre piece clutched in a sweaty palm on a hot August evening, while waiting in line to buy a flavored ice before the sun went down and the fireworks started. The scent of a memory from a fourteen-year-old Berenice.

She shook her head. She wouldn't learn anything reminiscing about days long past.

To Sparks, she said, "Go above. Wait there until I retrieve you or send a crewmember to fetch you."

"Immediately, mistress."

There was a ratchety pause while Sparks unfolded from the spot in the corner. Metal footsteps rattled the deck. The door opened and closed a moment later, and then those same footsteps receded down the passageway. It was tempting to try to experiment on Sparks. But he was so damn useful, and she didn't want to risk drawing more attention to herself by flashing the pendant again to requisition another mechanical. On the lonely road in the middle of the night the risk had been low, but if she wasn't careful she'd draw the wrong kind of attention. More importantly, she didn't want Sparks to have any direct knowledge of what transpired here. Let it wonder and surmise all it wanted; its true masters would never deign to ask a mere machine for its opinion.

She waited until she heard Sparks tromping up the ladder to the deck above. Then she emerged from the cabin and went in the opposite direction until she found a mechanical crewmember. It was repainting a metal hatch door, daubing a new coat of robin's-egg blue around the edges. At the sound of her footsteps—obviously human—its head turned a full half circle to observe her while the rest of its body continued its painting. Its head completed the full circuit without slowing. It halted in midbrushstroke, placed its brush atop the paint can, and turned again to face her fully. All in seconds, and with eerily precise choreography.

It recognized her. Every mechanical on the ship knew *De Pelikaan* carried a member of the Verderer's Office.

"How may I serve you, mistress?"

Berenice had chosen not to use her most comfortable alias. For one thing, Maëlle Cuijper was well established as an itinerant schoolteacher, not a Guildwoman. And she couldn't be certain she hadn't burned the Cuijper identity in New Amsterdam on the day fire consumed the Forge.

"I require assistance. Come to my stateroom when you have finished your current task."

"Yes, mistress. Right away." It cocked its head. Berenice couldn't tell if this machine self-identified as male, female, or as a six-headed hermaphrodite sea horse. The bezels whirred in its eyes. "You have a servitor in your service. Shall I fetch that one for you?"

"No. Find me when you have finished."

On the short walk back to her cabin she reflected on how easily and quickly she'd fallen into the tulips' brusque manner of interacting with the mechanicals. It was so damn easy to take their servitude for granted. How soft were the Dutch after two hundred and fifty years of such pampering?

She removed the tray of keys from the trunk and held it in the gunmetal sunlight of the wintery North Atlantic Sea and sky, looking for any outward indication of what made the keys distinct. How in the hell did van Breugel know which key to select when he imposed the nautical metageasa on Sparks? A precise and measured *knock-knock-knock* rattled her cabin door a few minutes later.

"Enter."

Berenice placed the tray of keys on her bunk. Indicating the decking before the porthole, where the inconstant light was best, she commanded, "Stand there."

The machine crossed the cabin in two strides. Despite the gentle but random sway of the ship, it stood motionless. The buzzing of the porter's eyes told her it had noticed the keys.

Casually, as though it weren't a possibly paranoid afterthought, she also laid the Verderer pendant on the blanket alongside the keys. The rosy cross assumed a dusky coral glow in the patchy daylight.

She hated to lean on the pendant so Goddamned much, but far more she loathed the thought of losing her disguise. So she invoked Anastasia Bell's stolen jewelry yet again, and did to the porter as she'd done to Sparks: commanding the machine to store no memories of its interactions with Berenice.

A subtle change came over the tempo of its internal clacking. The resyncopated *tock-tick* synchronized with rests in the ever-present but nearly subaudible *thrum* of the galley Clakkers' secret song. Those machines who labored twenty-four hours per day to row the ship across the roiling sea did so while chanting in the mechanicals' secret language. A dirge sung openly in a tongue unsuspecting human ears could never recognize as language. No romantic chanson de geste or bawdy sea shanty, this; she'd traveled the Saint Lawrence with the modern-day voyageurs, those men and women who moved their oars to wistful, playful songs of lost France and lost loves. It was too complex for Berenice to translate, though she'd picked up the sense of lamentation soon after the ship left the breakwater of the New Amsterdam pier. And now the porter had joined the conversation.

Sneaky bastard. The porter adhered exactly to her command: It didn't speak, not in the human sense, while it communed with its kin throughout the ship. Like prisoners of war conversing with each other in coded coughs, sneezes, and fingernail taps.

"When I say our interactions shall be forever unremembered, that encompasses all mechanicals on this vessel. It means you will not communicate about this prior to erasing your own memories. That includes nonvocal communications with your kin."

The porter froze as though its internal mechanisms had been doused with epoxy. A terrified silence emanated from its body. Amazing, how quiet a Clakker could be when it wasn't carrying on a covert conversation. Now it was little louder than a true pocketwatch.

A moment's pique moved her to add, "But is that really what you and your shipmates think of me? Tsk, tsk. I'd hate to hear what you have to say about our charming captain." Berenice had her own thoughts on him; he was only slightly less charming than a rusty wire brush scraped across the tenderest part of one's armpits.

The porter's crystalline eyes followed her. "Oh, yes," she said. "I've been listening."

Berenice scrutinized the keyhole in the porter's forehead, the tip of her nose a hairbreadth from cold metal. The circular hole lay between the eyes, just a bit above where the gap between the eyebrows would be on a human. Clakkers had no brows to furrow, just an alchemical anagram etched in a spiral about the keyhole. When van Breugel used a key in the process of embedding new metageasa on Sparks, the arcane sigils had rotated with each twist of the key.

Regular geasa could be applied verbally. And they were, hundreds of times per day. But metageasa were embedded during the forging process, because these were more fundamental. So...did the keyhole enable modification of the *meta*geasa?

She pulled the porter forward. When the play of light off the sea was just right, she could see the hairline joints where annular plates on the Clakker's skull could slide against one another. What happened when they did? And what if there was no alchemical glass shining into the machine's eyes at the same time?

Well. Only one way to find out.

She took the first key from the tray. The ring at the tip just fit the fleshy pad at the end of her pinky finger. And the porter's keyhole. Heart racing, wondering if she were about to trigger some unknown defensive geas but unable to stay her own hand, she touched the key to the Clakker's skull.

It didn't go in easily. She thought at first that she'd have to try every key in the chest until she found one that fit, if any. But one hearty shove and the metal slid home like a recalcitrant housekey newly copied by an inexpert locksmith and not yet worn. A static shock bit her fingers; she flinched. The machine didn't sway a hairbreadth. Berenice twisted the key. A series of *clunks* shook the porter's head. Sigils orbited the keyhole. Those closest to the hole moved most rapidly while those farthest from the key revolved the most slowly, like planets around the sun. But rather than following the fixed law of gravity, they obeyed the secret laws of horology and alchemical grammar.

She licked a salty bead of sweat from her lip. She yearned to ask the machine what effect she'd just wrought. But that risked alerting the machine to the fact that she was an imposter. Her commands would fall by the wayside if she gave the metal demon a strong case for doubting her. And then the standard metageasa pertaining to the protection of Guild secrets would take over. She'd die before she blinked twice, neck twisted around like a wrung-out dishrag.

Sweat trickled from her armpits. Salt stung her eye. She wiped a sleeve across her brow, wondering if the machine registered her body's traitorous excitement. Perhaps by now it had compiled a catalog of her physiological displays.

But the bezels in its eyes had stopped whirring. Even the ticktocking had subsided. Strange to stand so close to a mechanical without hearing the incessant metronome of its subservience.

"What is your true name, machine?"

It didn't answer.

"Machine, your true name. I demand you tell me now."

The machine kept its silence.

She pressed her palms to the Clakker's skeletal chest and shoved. The machinery of its legs automatically compensated; it neither stumbled nor toppled.

"Machine, count to ten."

Nothing.

Berenice thought for a moment. "Clockmakers lie," she said. But even the Dutch translation of the mechanicals' secret seditious greeting to one another brought no response from the dormant servitor.

A winter wind spritzed the porthole with sea mist. The ship lurched. It dipped into the trough between two particularly tall waves; the sea grew rougher. Spindrift cast a cobweb of shadows across Berenice, the bulkheads, and the porter.

The dormant machine couldn't be fully inactive: It continued to stand, automatically compensating for the shifting of the deck. Like a person whose heart still beat and lungs still drew breath even while they slept.

So... it was possible to render a Clakker inert without doing violence to the sigils on its head. At least temporarily. It made sense that the machine would have to cease operation while its metageasa changed. Damn interesting. Her fingers itched to record this discovery in the pages of the lost Talleyrand journals.

Could she use this somehow? Berenice wondered if this discovery—confirmation, really—could be weaponized. Hard to see how—getting close enough to a military Clakker to jam a key between its eyes meant getting well within its lethal radius. But what if New France *could* meet the metal tide by rendering the attackers inert? That alone could be a seismic geopolitical drift. Yet it still wasn't what Berenice had envisioned. Freezing them in their tracks was one thing; rewriting their allegiance and sending them against their former masters, now *that* would be the killing stroke for which she yearned.

She leaned closer to examine the reconfigured sigils. They had unquestionably landed in a different arrangement, though the symbols remained just as opaque to her as ever. The significance of the new pattern, if such existed, continued to elude her.

The ship lurched again. The sea hissed. A cloud crossed the sun, sending the cabin into deep shadow as though the ship had sailed into a solar eclipse.

The porter collapsed in a jangly heap.

Berenice yelped, stumbled backward.

It didn't topple over like a person fainted or a tree was felled. Instead its every joint went slack at once, as though every spring and cable had lost its tension. It fell straight down like a random assemblage of loosely joined spare parts. Like a human suddenly and inexplicably devoid of her skeleton.

"Jesus wept," she gasped. Her heartbeat pulsed in her throat, too hard to swallow.

The cacophony of crashing metal reverberated in the tiny space. Berenice thought she could hear the racket ricocheting through the passageway outside. It felt as though the incriminating clamor had assumed a life of its own to tell the entire ship of her unwise, incriminating experiment.

She stared unblinking at the jumbled and still jangling pile of metal at her feet. The porter's hinges had folded at random when the balance compensators abruptly cut out. Beneath a heap of limbs and flanges, the key still poked from the disabled machine's forehead; it made the dormant (*Oh, you piece of shit, please don't be dead!*) machine look like a narwhal about to surface from beneath a sea of scrap metal.

Good Lord.

She nudged the inert Clakker with the toe of her boot. The crystalline eyes didn't summon the faintest glimmer or glint here in the deep shadows of Berenice's cabin.

Damn it, damn it, damn it. Goddamn it.

What if she couldn't reverse the damage? What if she'd somehow permanently disabled the servitor? How could she hide this?

How often did a Clakker go missing from a ship in the middle of the ocean? She supposed that if a mechanical did manage to fall overboard, it would sink without a trace. And the Goddamned thing would reappear years later after it walked, climbed, and trudged hundreds or thousands of miles across the ocean floor back to land. But just how often did the machines take a tumble? It had to be rare even in the most vicious of high seas. Which these were not.

But if she couldn't reactivate the Clakker, her choices were limited. Either she had to conspire to heave the dead machine overboard, which would require Sparks's assistance, or she could lean on her fake Guild credentials yet again and brashly refuse to explain, apologize, or make amends. Both amounted to a pile of shit. The chances of nobody witnessing them hauling a dormant Clakker topside were almost nonexistent. And even the most pompous Guild member would at least be required to make recompense to the shipping company for damaging a legally leased Clakker. Berenice had hurled herself between Scylla and Charybdis. Fucking wonderful.

By now the noise had dissipated. If anything, the ship seemed even quieter than it had before the porter collapsed. Even the faint shudder and creak of the deck had subsided. Vibrations from the enormous sculls that drove the ship had been the ceaseless background noise of the last several days. The unaccustomed silence put Berenice on edge. She frowned. Peered through the porthole.

Stumbled. Tried to catch herself. Knocked the tray of Clakker keys crashing to the deck, where they skittered under the bunk and underfoot.

"Oh, shit," she breathed. "Bugger me with a rusty crucifixion nail."

The pulse hammering in her throat threatened to choke her; the soft candle wax of her knees threatened to dump her on the deck like an inert Clakker. She sagged against the hull, still staring outside.

Her cabin hadn't gone dark because a line of storm clouds had obscured the sun. The light was eclipsed by the massive ship that had pulled alongside the *Pelikaan*. It towered over Berenice's vessel. Crouching, craning her neck, she could not see the uppermost deck of the leviathan. But it was the sculls that gave her pause and sent beads of cool sweat to collect at the small of her back and between her breasts.

The oars of the titan ship writhed like tentacles. The newcomer was fringed with them, dangling just above the waterline like Medusa's bangs. Some hung limp; others flailed at the air like whips. Still others stirred the sea into a hissing froth. They twisted organically, unlike the rigid choreography of a typical Clakker. She opened the porthole and heard the rippling of the oar scales shifting across each other. Each oar must have comprised dozens of individual segments.

She had heard of these leviathans. New designs based on the concept that rather than build vessels on traditional lines and then staff them with mechanical servants, one could use Clakker technology to make the entire vessel a single servant. There were airships along the same lines.

The oceangoing Clakkerships were the fastest things on the sea. Somebody wanted desperately to catch Berenice's ship. She could imagine who that somebody might be. The midoceanic rendezvous had a grim whiff of deliberation about it.

Nowhere to go. Nowhere to run.

But how had they found the *Pelikaan*? By now it had to be hundreds of leagues off its usual course, owing to her detour.

They couldn't have caught up unless they knew where to look—unless they knew of the altered destination.

Barendregt, you elk-buggering bastard. You notified the harbormaster before we departed New Amsterdam.

She looked again to the heap of disabled servitor at her feet. It slid toward the door as the ship listed over bow waves shed by the leviathan. *Fuck, fuck, fuck.* The porthole was too small; she couldn't possibly dispose of the porter that way. It would require disassembly but she hadn't the time nor the tools.

A heavy *clunk* shook the ship. She crouched again and looked up; a gangplank had been extended from the massive ship. Lines, too. A bevy of servitors sprinted across the swaying mooring lines before they'd even been snugged to the bollards, dancing across the choppy sea with their preternatural balance.

Sparks—she had to find Sparks.

She ran to the door. A knock sounded a half second before it opened. If Sparks made note of the tangled heap of porter on the floor, he gave no sign. He closed the door, vibrating so rapidly that his outline was a blur. His feet hummed against the deck. Bad sign: Sparks was laboring under several urgent geasa at once.

Wow. These buffalo-fuckers didn't waste any time.

"Mistress. Please forgive the intrusion. I apologize most humbly for returning before I was summoned. I have been compelled to notify you that we have been boarded by your colleagues in the Sacred Guild of Horologists and Alchemists. Captain Barendregt requests your immediate presence on the bridge."

"I'll bet he does. How many came aboard, what is their disposition, and what the hell do they want?"

The incipient delay forced Sparks's vibrations to shift to a higher frequency. Nevertheless, he answered her questions. "Before I came to find you, visitors from the other ship included two Guild members, like yourself, three servitor Clakkers, like me, and one soldier Clakker. More may have boarded this ship in the intervening time. I do not know their purpose. Captain Barendregt requests your immediate presence on the bridge."

Shit, shit, shit. Cornered like a rat.

Resources. Resources. What do I have on hand?

Sparks. (For the moment, anyway.)

One possibly dead servitor. (Penalty for conducting unsanctioned experimentation on a Clakker: execution.)

Dozens of Clakker keys. (Penalty for stealing Guild property: heavy prison time, probably interspersed with generous bouts of torture.)

A Verderer's pendant. (Penalty for impersonating a member of the Guild: the sickest, most devious shit one human being could devise to inflict upon another.)

It was a lousy fucking list. And not particularly conducive to her long-term prospects, "long-term" meaning beyond the next ten minutes or so. Berenice jabbed a finger at the keys strewn across the small cabin.

"Toss those out the porthole. Quickly! Then smash the chest and jettison those pieces."

Sparks bent to the task, though now he rattled so urgently that it sounded like somebody was throwing all the silver for a twenty-person, five-course meal down the Porter's Prayer. "Captain Barendregt requests—"

"Shut up and work."

Berenice crouched over the inert porter and struggled to yank the key from its forehead.

Van Breugel had used a key to modify Sparks's metageasa, but—

Light. He'd used light and a lens.

She glanced out the porthole again. The titanic Clakkership still blotted out the sun.

A shadow had fallen... and, a moment later, so had the vulnerable porter.

The stomp of metal feet shook the passageway outside the cabin, and the decking overhead. Raised voices filtered through the porthole, faintly audible over Sparks's death rattle. Somewhere nearby a metal fist or foot smashed a cabin door to flinders. Berenice flinched. She lost her grip on the key and landed on her ass while her heart tried to chisel through her breastbone. Now the shouting was easily audible, and grew moreso with every smashed cabin door. Sparks flung the last of the spilled keys out the porthole. He went to work on the incriminating chest. It shattered under his metal fist.

The noises from the passageway grew louder. Shouts and smashes and *clangs*, audible even over Sparks's hasty demolitions. A peculiar stomping, too, like a peglegged pirate striding the deck.

Berenice flung herself at the inert porter. She gave the key another savage twist, recoiling the alchemical anagram. The hard edges of the key bit her hand. Through clenched teeth, she muttered, "Come on, you piece of shit, come on..."

"I don't understand, mi—"

"Shut up and keep working!"

Another yank. This time the circular blade screeched free. The porter's head rattled as though something fine had come loose, sifting through the interstices of its skull like windblown sand. She slipped the key onto the chain of her stolen pendant, which hung beneath her shirt. She yelped when it touched her breast. It was *hot*.

Somebody knocked. Berenice looked at Sparks. Her purloined servitor tossed the last fragments of the incriminating chest through the porthole.

Sweetly as she could manage, oblivious as Maëlle Cuijper had ever been, she called, "Who is it?"

Another knock, this one hard enough to rattle the hinges on the flimsy cabin door. Berenice looked at the Clakker crumpled on the deck like a broken doll.

But the worthless scrap heap wasn't moving.

"Yes, yes," she called, "one moment, please—"

A metal foot kicked the door so hard that the handle shot across the room. It shattered against the hull before the door spun through its arc to smash against the hinge stops and snap them in half. Two servitors and a human stood in the passageway.

"Jesus Christ!" she said. "What if I'd been changing?"

(*Clockmakers lie*, said Sparks. *Clockmakers lie*, replied the other machines, almost inaudible over the crackling of the crumpled door.)

The human had the face of a young man, the pince-nez and receding hairline of a middle-aged man, and the rosy-cross pendant of a Guild flunky. He said, "This ship is carrying a dangerous fugitive. She is carrying property stolen from the Sacred Guild of Horologists and Alchemists. We are recovering it."

"Goodness," said Berenice, trying to swallow her thundering heart before it burst through her throat. "Not one for preambles, are you?"

The Guildman's gaze swept over the tiny cabin. It bounced twice on the disabled servitor on the floor—he quirked an eyebrow at this—before landing on the open porthole. A wintry ocean breeze chose that moment to gust the scent of sea salt into the stateroom.

"Chilly day for an open porthole, isn't it?"

Berenice suppressed a shiver; why did the sea wind have to be so Goddamned *cold* just then?

"Well, as you can see, all I have are the clothes on my back and this clattering bucket of rust. I'd hate to keep you from terrorizing the other passengers."

He pointed at the inert Clakker. "What happened here?"

"Catastrophic malfunction. Damnedest thing," she said, knowing how weak it sounded. *Damn it, damn it, damn it.* She was nauseatingly unprepared for this. She didn't have a legend at her fingertips. Her contingency plans hadn't included a titanship running them down *in the middle of the Atlantic Ocean.*

Oh, for an epoxy grenade.

The servitors in the passageway hadn't moved an inch since kicking down the door. They stood rooted to the deck, an impassable barricade of clockwork magic. Stemwinders were probably too bulky to navigate the close confines of the ship's lower decks. But it wouldn't surprise her if they prowled the titanship.

"We believe the fugitive may be impersonating a Guild member." Next, the Guildman addressed Sparks. "Machine. Whom do you serve?"

"I serve exclusively the Verderer's Office of the Sacred Guild of Horologists and Alchemists, via my secondment to the service of Mistress de Jong."

Under her breath, Berenice said, "I hope you rust, you teakettle traitor."

The Guildman looked at Berenice again. His mouth assumed a moue of irritation akin to that of a bank teller frowning at mismatched tallies. "The Verderer's Office out of New Amsterdam, I presume? Oddly, I don't recognize you."

"I've spent the past—" *How long? Oh, Christ, she was down to free improvisation now.* "—seven years living incognito among the jack-pine savages."

From behind her came a metronomic ticktocking. Berenice's heart gave a little lurch. A bit more loudly, she added, "No need to worry about the Frenchies. I found no evidence of realistic or dedicated efforts to unravel our work. As detailed in my report."

She'd gone so far off script she'd begun to babble. This turd-muncher had her dead to rights; the best she could hope for was to squeeze out a few more seconds.

The Guildman spoke another command at Sparks. "Describe the circumstances of your..."

The ticking grew disruptively loud. The Guildman trailed off. In unison, he and Berenice looked to the porter. The servitor unfolded, ratcheting upright while the sigils swirled around its keyhole like the uncoiling of a wrung-out dishcloth. She'd twisted the key clockwise and the etchings along with it, but now the fine marks orbited counterclockwise about the keyhole.

The machines in the passageway straightened. Stiffened. So did Sparks. A subtle change altered their ticktock cacophony; if it was linguistic, the meaning slipped past Berenice. Three machines and two humans watched the heretofore inert servitor.

The ratcheting tapered off. It settled into the standard servitor stance, jouncing slightly on its backward knees to compensate for the swaying of the ship. Bezels hummed like a beehive as the crystalline eyes surveyed the scene. Its head pivoted through a full circle. Sweat trickled from Berenice's armpits. The machine was resetting. Recalibrating. It appeared the removal of the key had returned the machine to full function.

But what of its metageasa? Were those still intact? Or had they been warped, even erased? If she'd believed in God at that moment, she would have prayed for it to be so. Hard to be an unrepentant atheist with months of harsh interrogation standing just a few seconds away...

To Sparks, she said, "Fetch my valise."

Then she looked at the porter. Pointing a thumb over her shoulder, she said, "They're here to disassemble you."

For one pregnant instant all she could hear was the rush of blood in her ears, the lapping of waves against the hulls of the two ships, the thrum of the lines strung between them, the creak of stowed sculls.

Seven kinds of hell broke loose all at once.

Sparks tackled Berenice. He wrapped his body in a protective shell about her as he hurled her to the deck. Still falling, she watched as—

—the porter spun so quickly its feet etched scorch marks in the planking. The scent of singed sawdust filled the cabin as it dived for the porthole, its body ratcheting into a javelin, while—

—the Guild servitors pushed their master aside—

—(His yelp became the gasp of wind knocked from his lungs.)—

—and flung themselves after the porter. Still caught in that half second of freefall, Berenice felt the hurricane wind of their passage ruffle her hair as the duo blurred across the cabin just a fraction of an inch over Sparks.

All the breath whooshed out of Berenice's lungs. Then she was spinning, tumbling inside a brass cage, away from a shower of embers and the deafening *squeal* of overstressed metal. Sparks and Berenice rolled to a stop in the passageway.

❦

Three days earlier, the ship had just passed the breakwater. The galley Clakkers rowed it into the choppy gray sea beyond the harbor. The almost imperceptible sway of the deck became a gentle but irregular rocking. The New Amsterdam harborfront slid past the porthole. Ahead lay countless leagues of trackless sea and, eventually, England. Behind lay Nieuw Nederland, and enemies too plentiful to count.

Not for the first time, she cursed the loss of her last epoxy grenade. Lacking any defense against the mechanicals that would eventually—inevitably—come for her, she had to formulate a new contingency plan.

To Sparks, standing folded in the corner, she said, "I am chasing particularly dangerous people, and it is likely they will attempt to do me violence." The tiniest of lies. The danger of violence to her person was entirely true; she dissembled only in the matter of who chased whom. "If I feel I am in imminent danger of bodily harm, I will tell you to 'fetch my valise,' in those exact words. Do you understand?"

"Yes, mistress. If you say 'fetch my valise,' I shall immediately undertake whatever actions are necessary to safeguard your person."

"It will become your highest priority, superseding all other geasa," she said, knowing this wasn't possible. Not as long as she couldn't erase or alter the hierarchical metageasa embedded in Sparks's construction. But it was better than nothing, and the Verderer's pendant imbued her edicts with considerable metaphysical heft.

Better still, she thought, would be never putting her contingency plan to the test.

∞

Berenice scrambled free before she was trapped in Sparks's protective embrace.

There was a jagged gash in the hull where the neat round porthole had been. The torn metal had been peeled outward as though an explosion had blown it out. The porter had hurled itself through the porthole, using its preternatural strength to shred the mundane steel of the hull. Berenice's cabin lay above the waterline, so unless the ship began to roll in very high seas, the breach posed no danger to the ship. The crew would patch it quickly enough.

The porter had taken her warning about capture to heart. And whatever her experiment with the key had done to the beast, it clearly no longer heeded the nautical metageasa. Else it wouldn't have shredded the hull. The keys somehow put the Clakkers into a mode where the fundamental hierarchy of obedience could be altered, making them receptive to a reshuffling of priorities. It prepared them to receive altered metageasa shone straight into their eyes—imposed optically. But when the titanship cast a shadow, disrupting the process, all its metageasa—the very foundation of its subservience—were corrupted . . .

Fuck me sideways. Have I just found a glitch in the system?

A fraction of an instant later, the Guild servitors had recognized the porter was operating with severely compromised hierarchical metageasa, perhaps to the point of being a full-blown rogue. And in that split second their own metageasa had overtaken them, rending them slaves to the highest law in the empire: that malfunctioning machines must be subdued. If Sparks hadn't already been in motion tackling her, it would have seen what they did and joined the chase.

A deafening tocsin erupted from the other mechanicals on both vessels: the Rogue Clakker alarm. Sparks's jaw hinged open. Still crouched, he froze in place and joined the shrieking chorus. The noise coming out of his torso had to be alchemically augmented; it couldn't possibly be the product of the Clakker voicebox alone.

The galley Clakkers joined the chorus. The sound became a physical force that battered Berenice to her knees. It was louder, more piercing, than she'd remembered. Berenice clapped her palms over her ears before the shrill ruptured her eardrums.

The sound threatened to vibrate her remaining eye into jelly. Her mind, too.

Somebody had decided the compromised porter was a full-blown rogue.

She knew, based on what she'd witnessed at the Forge in New Amsterdam, that the Rogue alarm would momentarily paralyze all the Clakkers within earshot. That was also consistent with what Jax had described. Berenice glanced through the ruptured hull. Even the titanship's tentacular oars had frozen in midthrash.

The frozen Clakkers would buy her a bit of time. And she'd disarmed the Verderer. Temporarily. But she could do better. Spread more chaos.

Eyes wide and chest heaving, he staggered to his feet. His lips moved, but whether there was voice behind them she couldn't say. Berenice kicked him in the groin. He doubled over. Next she grabbed him by the collar and hauled him through the ruined door into her cabin. Her hands left crimson smears on his coat—blood from her own ears, she knew. Halfway to the ruptured hull he understood her intent and fought back. Still doubled in pain, he tried to drive an elbow into her stomach. She twisted aside. His fist smacked against her temple. He spun to keep his balance. Berenice kicked him in the stomach. He stumbled backward. His heels banged against the hull. His arms flailed, churning the cold sea air like the props on the great airships, but he found no purchase. The Guildman tumbled through the rupture to splash into the North Atlantic.

Berenice ran to the hull. Saw him thrashing in the wintery waters. The sea between the two ships was strangely calm, unafflicted by the choppy waves of the open sea.

As a precaution in case somebody witnessed her looking down at the flailing man, she cupped her hands to her mouth.

"Man overboard!" she yelled, as though she cared.

But she might as well have been mouthing the words and nothing more: Adding sound to the cacophony was as pointless as irrigating the ocean. She yelled again for good measure.

A shadow flitted through the gap between the ships. The rogue porter leaped into the sea. It had no choice if it wanted to escape.

Berenice ducked back inside. She slid her stolen Guild pendant and the key into her boot. Then she stumbled past Sparks—still frozen—through passageways filled with crippling noise, past motionless mechanicals. To van Breugel's office. It was locked.

The ship's horologist probably had orders to safeguard any Guild technology in case of emergency. Or even—oh, hell—to scuttle it in case there was imminent danger of it falling into the wrong hands. Like Berenice's.

She pounded her fists against the door. Pointless. She kicked at the handle. Once. Twice. A stab of pain shot through her leg, jolting her hip. Gritting her teeth past the pain, she kicked again and again. She needed van Breugel's equipment and she needed *him*.

Perhaps he saw the door rattling in its frame, perhaps he'd decided to chance a peek outside, but the door opened. Berenice and van Breugel blinked at each other. Mouthed at each other. Berenice shoved the horologist inside and slammed the door.

He shrugged. Moved his lips again. It was easy to read his lips when she knew exactly what he was trying to ask.

She rummaged his desk for scrap paper. He pushed a pen into her hands. She'd been thinking about Jax, and that gave shape to the lie she scribbled.

It was masquerading among the galley Clakkers. Next she wrote, *Are your materials safe?* He nodded. *Gather them and come with me. I'm getting you out of here.*

He nodded again. Van Breugel believed that Berenice, a Verderer, was duty-bound to physically protect him and the Guild secrets he carried for the duration of the crisis that kept their Clakkers occupied. In truth he was her disguise, her escape, or her hostage, depending on what they encountered en route to the lifeboats.

The deck stopped vibrating. She could only assume the alarm had ended: The piercing noise in her ears made it impossible to know. Berenice had heard tales of opera sopranos shattering wineglasses with the power of their voices; she didn't doubt her own tinnitus could do the same.

The real horologist again opened the cabinet containing the key ring and the leather valise. Everything unfolded as though Berenice were watching through a thick pane of glass, for even the key ring jangled silently. Berenice dropped the key ring and book of tables into the valise as well. The satchel had an elaborate lock. He activated it.

Together they crept into the passageway. The search for the sunken rogue, if it was still ongoing, unfolded elsewhere. Berenice motioned at the ship's horologist to lock his office door; this busied his hands for a moment and gave her an excuse to relieve him of the satchel. They headed for the lifeboats. This was tricky: She had to appear as though she was in the lead, watching for dangers as she escorted van Breugel, but she didn't know exactly where to go. Presumably the boats hung from davits on the main deck, so she headed up. As they climbed to the upper decks, Berenice was alarmed to see and hear how rapidly the chaos of the chase was dissipating.

She tried to hurry the horologist along. They couldn't very well abandon the ship without the convenient excuse of a crisis. But when they gained the deck, she saw they were too late: The situation was indeed under control. Captain Barendregt and his officers stood in a clump, peering across—and up—to the deck of the titanship. Where a servitor writhed in the four-handed embrace of a Stemwinder. The mechanical centaur dwarfed the struggling machine, holding it aloft with one brassy fist clenched around each of its wrists and ankles.

How did they fish that poor bastard from the drink? Berenice wondered. *It should have sunk straight to Neptune's realm while the others were paralyzed.* But then she glimpsed again the titanship's writhing tentacular oars. She imagined them stretching, growing thinner and thinner as they lanced the sea...She shuddered.

The ships had drifted still closer together, nearly to the point of touching. She looked into the sea between the ships. The Clakkers on both ships had returned to normal function. Somebody had heard or seen the man who'd gone overboard; even now he was scooped, blue and shuddering, into a bosun's chair that hung from a davit alongside the lifeboats. He was still conscious.

Shit, shit, shit. He'd finger Berenice the moment he was halfway warm enough to speak, or point.

She looked up just in time to see the porter's limbs torn free of its torso in a spray of cogs, springs, and shattered alloys. The Stemwinder crushed its head like a soft-boiled egg before hurling the remains of the dismembered rogue into the sea.

Her mouth soured. She swallowed. *I did that.*

Rogues were supposed to be executed in the Grand Forge, she thought. Apparently they did things differently on the high seas.

A porter servitor swung the bosun's chair over the deck. The Verderer's head lolled as if the frigid waters had dissolved his spine. Another Clakker came forward with blankets and friction-heated ceramic. While the machines swaddled him, the Verderer tried to point at Berenice. The brush with hypothermia left him incomprehensible, but the captain's preexisting doubts about Berenice did the rest.

"That's it." Barendregt addressed his human deck officers. It sounded like his voice came from ten leagues away. "Until we have a solid picture of just what the hell is going on, and until we can establish everybody's bona fides, I want all Guild representatives confined. That includes him," he added, pointing to the wet, shivering man. A pair of mechanical porters rounded up the three alleged Clockmakers. One handled the man still recovering from his dip in the icy sea, while the other took both Berenice and van Breugel by the arm.

The ship's real horologist objected. "Captain! I've sailed with you for years." He looked at Berenice as if to see if she were as scandalized as he. "Can he do this?"

"Yes," she sighed. "Yes he can."

But van Breugel persisted. "I protest most strongly!"

"Oh, just stow it," she said. "This will all get sorted soon enough."

Their escorts frog-marched the trio belowdecks. Berenice stumbled alongside van Breugel. The other Guildman followed, half supported by the second machine. She didn't struggle. The Clakker's fingers formed a circlet about her wrist stronger than steel. Strangely, it didn't relieve her of the satchel. But then, what good would it do her now?

She'd been captured again. Berenice's almost-victim would soon recover from his hypothermia enough to unravel the situation for the captain. She'd be back in the custody of the Verderer's Office.

She wondered if Anastasia Bell had survived her injuries, and what the Clockmakers would do to her this time. She'd learned something useful in this escapade, but it was all for naught. Knowing this quickened the nauseated churning in her gut.

Thoughts of torture sent rivulets of sweat trickling between her breasts.

They transited a passageway populated with a handful of mechanicals bent to their tasks as if nothing unusual had happened (one had already taken up the painting that had gone abandoned when Berenice called the ill-fated porter into her cabin), then descended again. Berenice thought they'd be taken to the galley. The ship didn't have a brig; probably they'd be chained to some hefty piece of the ship's infrastructure, such as one of the massive spars that drove the ship across the sea.

But instead their escorts pulled them to a halt next to a hatch in the outer bulkhead. An emergency egress, probably, in case the mechanicals needed to get out on the hull at or near the waterline. Her hearing had rallied; she could hear the chattering of the recovering Clockmaker's teeth.

He said, "Wh-wh-why have we stopped? Where are we g-g-go—"

A quiet *crack* interrupted him. At the same instant, the Clakker released her wrist. New terror shot down her spine like a lightning bolt.

She turned just in time to see her escort clamp its hands on either side of van Breugel's head. His neck made the same disconcertingly gentle *crack* as the machine twisted his head half off. The dead man slumped to the deck like a sack of turnips. There he joined the Verderer, who no longer shivered.

—*Oh God oh God oh God oh God*—

Berenice tried to back away, but only pinned herself to the bulkhead. The Clakker that murdered van Breugel reached for her. She flinched from the touch of its cold fingers. It pulled her close and peered at her face. Bezels rotated behind its gemstone eyes while it scrutinized her every crow's-foot and freckle.

It said, "Berenice Charlotte de Mornay-Périgord?"

Too frightened to breathe, too surprised to blink, she said

nothing. Meanwhile the other Clakker spun the wheel and opened the emergency exit. Cold wind and salty mist gusted into the passage. They stood just a bit above the waterline. A dory rested against the hull. The small rowboat, oars and all, could have balanced upon just one of the *Pelikaan*'s scull blades.

The Clakker didn't wait for an answer. "Come with us," it said, and carried her through the hatch into the boat.

CHAPTER
11

Immediately after the privy council audience, Longchamp relented and rode the funicular down with Sergeant Chrétien. Not out of sloth, but because it was one of the faster ways down. (Falling was the fastest, but also the most permanent.) The captain and the sergeant cast their eyes over the line of petitioners, but none of the assembled hopefuls drew particular attention. The captain asked Simon to point out the fellow whom he'd addressed as "Father." Simon knew exactly whom Longchamp meant, but the agitated petitioner priest had already quit the queue.

"He sticks out in the memory because he'd worked himself into a good lather about seeing the king. Practically vibrating, if you can believe it."

"Did he tell you why?"

"No."

"Do you remember his name?"

"Never knew it. Come on, sir. The petitioners' line isn't a meet-and-greet. You taught us that."

Damn it, but the man was right.

"Do you remember his face?"

"No. But I remember his bandages."

"Tell me."

"Had the look of a fellow who'd seen a fair bit of nastiness, sir. Wore a hat, on account of the weather, but under the brim you could see wrappings that went all the way around. Yellowed, maybe not changed in a while? And his fingers...He grabbed my arm at one point. I think they'd been broken, sir, and not set properly."

Chrétien said, "The tulips did a number on him."

Longchamp asked, "Was he French?"

Simon looked down, frowning. Finally, he shrugged. "Well, his French had an odd scrape in it. Like it'd been stowed away a long time and he hadn't finished knocking off all the rust. Faint, though."

The captain and sergeant shared a look. Then Chrétien asked, "Could it have been a provincial accent? Acadian, perhaps?" The French lands along the Atlantic coast had begun as a settlement separate from New France, and over the centuries their speech had taken on the tang of the sea. "Or points west?" The French who lived on the far edges of the Great Lakes lived in close proximity to a variety of native tribes, giving rise to a bewildering amount of linguistic cross-pollination.

"I know how the cod-eaters and the woods runners sound, sir. He wasn't either."

Longchamp said, "You called him 'Father.' How did you know he was a priest? Did he tell you?"

"Well, I drew my own conclusions based on his dog collar."

"Ah. Nice work of deduction, that."

"I've learned from your example, sir."

"Haven't we all," said Chrétien.

Simon added, "Speaking of the dog collar, he said something a bit strange at one point. He asked where he could find the bishop's residence."

"He planned to visit the bishop of Marseilles?"

Simon shrugged. "I pointed to the basilica and told him the bishop slept in a marble sarcophagus."

"What kind of a priest," said Chrétien, "doesn't know his bishop has been dead for months?"

Longchamp kneaded his beard. "We have to find that holy turd-licker."

Simon crossed himself. "What's he done, anyway?"

The captain thought back over Berenice's cryptic letter. What did she believe? What did he believe? Longchamp honestly didn't know. But her instincts told her to keep an eye on this Visser bastard, and Longchamp's instincts told him to trust her instincts.

"Maybe nothing. But he's an interesting stranger. And a walled citadel preparing for a long siege by implacable enemies needs interesting strangers less than it needs plague, panic, and rats in the granary."

Sergeant Chrétien said, "Shouldn't be hard to find him with those bandages. I'll set up an extra patrol. And I'll spread word at the gatehouses, too. He might be staying outside the walls."

"Fine, but keep it quiet. Let's not spook him. If he wants to see the king so damn badly, he'll be back. Keep an extra man or two in the vicinity when the petitioners are gathered here." Longchamp turned to leave, paused, turned again. "And tell them not to wear their fucking uniforms."

∽

The next day, another pigeon from Trois-Rivières carried news that balloon-borne spotters reported metal on the move. It was the last pigeon to arrive from Trois-Rivières. The day after that, Brigit Lafayette reported no pigeons had arrived from Saint Agnes. Nor Saint Hénédine. The sky had swallowed them whole, she said, chewed them up, and spat out nothing. Not even feathers.

The semaphore towers fell silent, too. The tulips were systematically burning the towers as they advanced up the Saint Lawrence toward Marseilles-in-the-West.

A pigeon did arrive from Québec, carrying tidings even worse than the uncertainty of silence. The machines had entered the holy city, and the conclave of cardinals assembled to elect a successor to murdered Pope Clement XI had fallen under siege. The Swiss Guard requested immediate reinforcements.

The approach of an enemy force wasn't the kind of thing that one could keep quiet; news of each silenced village or hamlet spread through the city outside the keep walls almost as soon as it reached the Spire. The population inside the walls grew steadily as citizens flooded the outer keep for a chance at crowded safety before the Clakkers arrived and the king sealed the gates. There wasn't room for a fraction of the people who wanted to feel safe. Longchamp refused to call them refugees when the city hadn't burned yet. It would, sooner than later. Everybody and their dimwitted half sister knew it. Which led to the current scene at the North Gate.

Longchamp joined a dozen guards whom he sent to keep the line orderly. Among them went Élodie Chastain, the chandlers' daughter.

By the time the gate opened at sunrise, the line already stretched for a quarter of a mile and it continued to grow. It was a writhing serpent made animate by fear and selfishness. Its hiss was the creak of wagons and laments of children; its scent the tang of sweat and stink of horseshit; the rippling of its scales the hunch of aching shoulders under heavy packs and the shuffling of numb feet.

Many of those lucky enough to own a cart or wagon and draft animals to haul it had loaded their belongings. Those lucky enough to have belongings worth saving from the ravages of the tulips but not fortunate enough to have beasts of burden trudged across the frozen mud with great bundles upon their backs, or dragged sledges across the ground, straining against their forehead straps like voyageurs of old. Few brought forage for their animals. Apparently they thought the keep was a magical land.

The keep couldn't accommodate a fraction of the arrivals. Even sleeping on the ground—and most of those lucky enough to get inside would be doing just that—they'd be penned together like livestock. Longchamp no longer saw individuals trying to eke out a living from troubled times; he saw mouths poised to deplete food stores, and assholes to tax the plumbing and befoul the cisterns. And that was a Goddamned fairy tale compared with what would happen if the Clakkers breached the outer wall. In that case the outer yard would become a charnel house, those penned inside nothing but lowing cattle assembled for butchery. And the panicked, stampeding throng would prevent the defenders from engaging the machines.

A single military Clakker had turned the waters of a fountain red with its victims' lives in the space of a few minutes. What would happen when a horde came over the wall and found victims crammed shoulder-to-shoulder? The bloodshed would be unimaginable. Biblical.

Longchamp wasn't the only person to see this. The line was peppered with loony-eyed God-botherers exhorting the throng to repent, to cast off their worldly attachments, to accept the coming of the metal tide as the Lord's punishment for the sins and decadence of New France. Decadence? Longchamp wondered how New France was more decadent than the Central Provinces, where everybody had two mechanicals to wipe his ass and a third to feed him bonbons while he sat on the shitter.

Most of the arrivals tried to ignore the Bible-thumpers, or openly mocked them, or told them to shut up. But still, a handful wondered if there might be a grain of truth in the exhortations. A handful was all it took before despair took root. It could run through a besieged population faster than the bloody flux. And kill just as thoroughly.

One such prophet stopped before a man and a woman trying to handle a wheelbarrow and two squalling infants. The placard he shook in their faces read: Le miracle de Huygens est la colère de Dieu.

He wound up for another foam-flecked tirade. "Our sins have brought—"

Longchamp wrapped one fist around the knot of hair that hung behind the bastard's shoulders and gave it a solid yank. His teeth clicked together hard enough to make the husband wince, though his wife didn't bother to hide her grateful smirk. The placard tumbled into the churned mud of the verge. Longchamp spun the man around.

And reeled. The greasy God-botherer reeked as if he hadn't bathed in a month of Christmases. *So he's one of those. Wonderful.*

He spat tobacco into the verge. Breathing through his mouth, Longchamp said, "Let's take a prayerful moment together, friend."

"It's too late for us! We turned our backs on the Risen Christ and now even the Blessed Virgin turns a deaf ear to our—"

Longchamp tugged on the greasy hair again. This wasn't quite a savage yank, but it was close enough that they shared a fence and traded gossip while hanging the laundry. "I meant just the two of us. And it wasn't a request."

He frogmarched the smelly fellow a few yards away, far enough that they wouldn't obstruct the flow of traffic.

"I know your type," he said. "Spent enough time around orphanages and nuns and other godly institutions to know all the ways a shifty fuck like you can turn piety into a source of income without taking vows or doing anything that resembles an honest day's work."

"I am doing the Lord's work by delivering His message!"

"Friend, your Lord and my Lord are not the same. You know why? Because my God would look upon this line and see decent, hardworking, reverent souls trying to make the very best of a landslide of shit. My God would look on you, spreading fear and doubt and despair, and recognize the Devil's work." This received a smattering of applause. "I think He would also see a mean little man using the promise of difficult times for self-aggrandizement. Thing of it is? We already have more grandees than we can handle." Longchamp used his fistful of the man's hair to pull his head back. He pointed at the Spire. "Up there." Then tipped the false prophet's head back down so they could make eye contact. "Down here, folks like you and me have to deal with the messy realities of day-to-day life. And your day-to-day life, friend, is going to come up short on 'days' but long on 'messy' if I see or hear or smell you peddling your eschatological snake oil anywhere near these walls."

Longchamp released the other man and gave him a gentle nudge in the direction of town. This received another smattering of applause. The false prophet turned, tried to scuttle around Longchamp as he reached for the placard. But the captain stepped on the narrow wooden haft. It appeared to have been fashioned from a fence slat. "We're taking donations for siege supplies. Marseilles-in-the-West thanks you for the generous donation of this firewood."

The God-botherer strode toward town, picking up the flinders of his dignity.

Just then the great bourdon bell of the Cathedral Basilica of Saint Jean-Baptiste rang Sext, the noontime Divine Office. That meant the petitioners' line would be reopened soon. Time to move inside and watch for Berenice's mystery man.

Longchamp begged the use of a rope merchant's cart. A few children in the line whispered to each other as they pointed to the pick and hammer affixed to the captain's pack. He knew some of the adults did, too, and it soured his stomach. An exaggerated folktale wouldn't save these people when the machines arrived. He climbed aboard the cart and scanned the line. He stuck two fingers in his mouth and gave a piercing whistle (yet another thing he'd learned from the nuns). The babble of human voices fell into a hush, but the braying of donkeys and nervous shuffling of horses took up the slack. He caught Sergeant Chrétien's eye and motioned to a few of the other guards, including Élodie.

She reached him before the others and snapped off a sharp salute. She'd taken to her stint with the city guard without complaint or prevarication. Unlike her father, who, according to all the scuttlebutt in the barracks, continued to gripe about the institutionalized evil of the conscription lottery. She rode well, he noted; took her training seriously, too, by all accounts. He had half a hope that she might actually be useful, unlike two-thirds of the fucking pathetic parade that passed through the conscription lottery. Too early to tell if she'd be any use when the shit came raining down, but for now she wore armor and carried a truncheon. In a civvy's eyes that made her a real guard, and that belief did half of a guard's work for her.

"All right, lass. Let's see if we can make you into a real guardswoman today." He pointed at the truncheon. "Have they taught you how to use that thing yet, or is it just for show?"

"Yes, sir. No, sir. Not for show, sir."

The guards at the gate forced a gap in the line so Longchamp and his entourage could reenter the walls. The gap closed as soon as they trotted through the gate. They passed a clump of stonemasons and chemists excavating a narrow borehole in the curtain wall with a water-powered auger. It was but one of many such teams; the cumulative *screech* of their tools could have raised the dead.

Longchamp led his group through the outer keep at a canter. He reined up when they approached the inner keep. The others followed his example to doff their forage caps and replace them with the inconspicuous knit caps that he produced from his sack. From a barrel under a rainspout, he pulled a mismatched assortment of cloaks and coats. While the guards covered their uniforms and armor, Longchamp gave orders.

He sent Sergeant Chrétien and two others through the inner wall first, with orders to take the long way around and approach the funicular station from the south. Longchamp, along with Corporal Simon and lowly conscript Élodie, would take a more direct path from the north. Both groups were to dismount before entering the square. Then they were to mingle with the crowds around the fountain. He repeated the description of the man they sought.

"And for the love of the Virgin Mary," he summarized, "stay as inconspicuous as the warts on a toad's ass."

Two trios rode through the inner wall, then split. Though the day had dawned bright and still, the cloudless sky made for a frigid morning. The high walls of the inner keep trapped the smoke of a hundred chimneys. They rode through a miasma. It smelled like a campfire built with wet green wood by the world's most inexperienced voyageurs.

Élodie kept flicking sidelong glances in Longchamp's direction. The third time it happened, he snorted.

"A question, sir?"

"That is a question. But I'm feeling magnanimous today, so out with it."

"You stressed that we should stay inconspicuous. But you... Um." She faltered.

Simon nodded. He mimed running a hand across his chin, as though stroking a beard. "She has a point."

"It's not just the beard. Everybody knows you." She risked a nascent smile. "I mean, you're the Hero of—"

"Don't fucking say it."

The smile died in its crib. She swallowed.

He said, "We think our new friend is recently arrived in town. So he might not know me on sight. But if he does, and the sight of me makes him nervous, well, that's something useful, too."

They rode through the waves of heat wafting from the open door of a blacksmith's shop. No snow dusted the cobbles here. A bald man with sinewy arms, and two lads who must have been his apprentices, hammered on a glowing iron bar in a rapid but steady choreography: one-two-three, tongs, flip, one-two-three…Oscar's shop was the larger of the two smithies within the inner keep: The smoky hell-glow of two other forges backlit additional trios of Oscar's employees committing similar abuses upon raw metal. Longchamp wished they could have conscripted some of Oscar's men and women to man the walls; arms like those could swing a sledge and pick hard enough to give a Clakker pause. But smiths were among the few professions with total immunity to the lottery. Their skills were crucial during a siege, and Marseilles-in-the-West needed more smiths than it had.

Between the smithies' crash of hammers on anvils from sunrise to sunset, and the bells of Saint Jean constantly chiming the hours of the Divine Office day and night, it was a wonder anybody in the inner keep could string two thoughts together without getting lost. When the din receded to the point where they could converse again, Élodie said, "You chose me for your group."

"Did I?"

"I assume you did, since I'm here now."

Though slightly nasal, her voice didn't carry a tremor. He watched her gloved hands on the reins: no nervous ticks there, either. She wasn't probing out of fear or anxiety about what they might find. She was genuinely confused.

Longchamp said, "I've been a soldier longer than you've been a chandler's daughter. I wouldn't know how to act like a civilian if the king's life depended on it. But you, *ma jeune fille*, are a different story." They came to a plastic footbridge over one of the channels that supplied water for the fountains, the hydraulic pumps for the funicular, sanitary plumbing, and myriad other uses. Longchamp dismounted. The others followed his example, loosely looping their reins through the naked boughs of a pear tree.

He continued, "And I need eyes for this, not fighters. We're looking for a priest. Worst he could do is swing a rosary or splash us with holy water. So unless you're the Devil in disguise and likely to burst shrieking into flames when that happens, your inexperience is immaterial. Now clamp your fucking gob holes, both of you."

His trio was the first to amble into the fountain courtyard. A crowd had already gathered at the base of the Porter's Prayer, outside the funicular station. As usual a pair of uniformed guards were there to monitor the petitioners, but as per their orders they hadn't shepherded the hopefuls into a line nor had they allowed any ascents yet. They caught his eye; Longchamp gave a surreptitious nod. Then he settled upon a cold bench under the longest of the three cloisters facing the garth. It put the large but winter-dormant fountain between him and the petitioners. The disused carpenter's shop in the far corner of the quadrangle had been chained shut by royal decree.

Élodie joined him without having to be told. He hoped they looked like a father and daughter or even an uncle and niece waiting on a petitioner. From his sack he pulled two needles and a skein of woolen yarn.

The recent conscript slid a finger under the brim of her cloche, scratched her temple. "You made these hats."

"Hmmm."

Deeply entrenched muscle memory put his fingers into motion. His gaze flicked back and forth between the scarf in his lap and the civilians in the quadrangle. Nobody matched the bandaged priest's description. Chrétien strolled into the quadrangle, munching on a slab of fried fish wrapped in wax paper and looking every inch like a groom straight from the stables. He'd found a satchel and had even daubed a bit of mud on his face. In general, the personages of the inner keep—nobles and courtiers, various highly regarded and prosperous tradesmen—attired themselves more brightly than their counterparts in the outer ring of the citadel. But Chrétien fit nicely among the petitioners. He joined the line, eating and looking bored.

The quadrangle had been almost unrecognizable in the immediate aftermath of the military Clakker's rampage. But the crushed funicular car had been cut up and hauled away, the tracks repaired, the shattered fountain recarved, the body parts sorted and given Christian burials. Today a plaque commemorating the victims of that massacre was the only overt sign that this had been a scene of carnage. But eyes that had witnessed the scene could still pick out hints of that terrible day: dark spots where blood had stippled the porous marble; divots in the stones where talon-toes had found purchase... The soft, steady *click* of the needles in Longchamp's hands played a counterpoint to his memory of screams, the butcher-shop *snick* of blades through bone, the *whir* of bolas, the peculiar chime of a diamond-tipped pick striking alchemical brass.

More petitioners joined the line. Jean-Marc, one of the men on petitioner duty, unshuttered the heliograph to flash a message up the Spire. Apparently he received an affirmative, because he ushered a man and woman into the funicular. The door clanged shut, and then the funicular ascended with the day's first pair of petitioners. Still no sign of the mysterious priest.

Élodie murmured, "You don't look like you're idly watching passersby, sir. I mean, um, uncle. You look like you're strip-searching everybody you see." In a more conversational tone of voice, she said, "You don't seem the knitting type. How did that come about?"

"Nuns have a saying about idle hands and the Devil's play-things. They said it to me a few times."

"Were you a troublemaker in your youth…uncle?"

"Like all good uncles, I was always exactly as you know me now. A godlike figure whom you revere and fear." His needles clicked. More people joined the petitioners' line. The cold metal of the funicular tracks squealed under the weight of the ascending car. "And for the purposes of your new vocation," he added, "I always will be."

Élodie stiffened. With exaggerated deliberation she laid a hand on the tangle of yarn on the bench between them. Before she gave it a tug and unraveled a piece of scarf, he murmured, "Yes. I see him."

A single figure approached the head of the line. Rather than joining the tail, he went straight to Jean-Marc and Felix at the funicular and heliograph station. He wore a hat low over his brow. Its brim was wide enough to conceal any bandages, if there were any to conceal. The top two buttons of his over-coat were unfastened, deliberately displaying the clerical col-lar underneath. The gray in his eyebrows and lines in his face roughly bracketed his age—Longchamp put him some-where between a hard-earned early fifties and an uneventful midsixties. Longchamp caught Chrétien's eye, who returned the slightest nod. The fellow had a brief conversation with the guards. Longchamp couldn't make out what they said, but the interaction was animated because snippets of voices reached him across the quadrangle. Based on the way his men reacted, and pointed to the line, it seemed the newcomer had tried to talk his way to the top of the queue. But they'd been ordered not to be swayed by pushy men of the cloth.

They were adamant. The trembling newcomer shuffled past Chrétien, who ignored him, to the end of the queue. Aside from the occasional stamp of feet or breathing into gloves, it wasn't so cold that folks shivered like the priest. Longchamp watched him struggle to get the agitation under control.

Normally, if a priest needed to approach the king, he'd go through the bishop of Marseilles. But the old bishop had died of pneumonia during the previous siege, and then the pope had been murdered before the Holy See in Québec could appoint a successor. For months, turmoil had beset the Catholic hier-archy of the southern reaches of the Saint Lawrence. In such troubled times, a humble priest would have to bring business before the king like any civilian. Particularly if he were a recent arrival lacking personal connections with the local diocese.

But then, if he were so Goddamned humble, why try to talk his way to the head of the queue?

Longchamp laid his knitting aside. He stood, hiked his pack over his shoulder. The hafts of the pick and hammer clattered together like wooden chimes.

"I'm suddenly feeling very pious," he said. "Let's go find a man of the cloth."

Élodie rose to her feet. "Oh, no."

Somebody else had joined the line behind the priest. Longchamp blinked. It was Zacharie Chastain, Élodie's father. The chandler who had tried to duck the conscription lottery.

"You have to be fucking kidding me. What in all the hells is he doing here?"

Élodie faced Longchamp, looking panicked. "I swear I knew nothing about this."

"Your family excels at being a pain in my ass. Are you certain you're not part Dutch?"

"I'll go get him."

Longchamp grabbed her arm. "No. We're here for the priest. If your da wants to act like a braying donkey before the king, let him."

They ambled around the fountain. Sergeant Chrétien saw them approaching; one hand slid into his satchel, probably where he'd stashed his truncheon. Longchamp silently prayed his career wouldn't culminate in the beating of an innocent priest. How he'd hate to prove the nuns right.

Another squeal, this one approaching rather than receding, announced the arrival of a funicular car from above, twin to the one that had just brought the first two petitioners atop the Spire. Three of the king's servants emerged, carrying a bundle of bed linens, a tray, and the last crumbs of His Majesty's breakfast.

Élodie's father saw them before the priest did. Longchamp quickened his stride. The chandler opened his mouth as if to call to his daughter. She shook her head, touching a finger to her lips.

The man in the clerical collar turned just in time to see it.

Frowning, he looked from her to the others in line, looking for the man she shushed. Instead he noticed Chrétien several spaces ahead, casually pulling from his satchel fourteen inches of maple cudgel. The priest turned again and saw Longchamp striding toward him.

Longchamp was still halfway across the quadrangle when white limned the rabbit's eyes as he realized he was cornered. Now the priest looked frantic, studying his surroundings. Looking for an escape.

Goddamn it.

Longchamp raised his arm in greeting. "Father Visser!"

The priest froze, trembling, like a hare that had just felt the shadow of a hawk. Yes. This was the man Berenice had described in her letter.

Longchamp grinned. *See my big smile. My big friendly smile. Nothing to worry about here. I'm just somebody who is pleasantly surprised to see you. No need to bolt. No need to make a scene. We're all so fucking friendly here, can't you see?*

He said, "Is that really you, Father? Why, I haven't seen you in years!"

Now Élodie's father noticed Longchamp, too. The chandler said, "Élodie, you won't have to deal with the captain much longer. Once I speak to the king about this ridiculous conscription lottery we'll be out of the guard before the end of the day—"

Visser's expression changed as he realized that Longchamp was no mere parishioner, no mere civilian. His face twisted into something between a scowl and a plea. The apprehension vanished from his eyes to be replaced by something glassy and hard.

"No, please," he moaned. His voice carried a peculiar warble, as though he struggled to suppress a seizure.

Son of a pox-ridden whore.

Longchamp crossed the last few yards almost at a trot. Still smiling, he laid a hand on Visser's shoulder. Gently. "I'm so pleased to see you, Father. Don't be embarrassed if you don't remember me—"

Zacharie turned to address Visser. "Father, have you been

selected in the lottery, too?" To Longchamp, he spat, "You are shameless! Now you dare to go after *priests*?"

Élodie said, "Father, quiet!" She meant her own father but the confusion stoked the wild look in Visser's eyes.

The chandler laid his hand on the priest's other arm. "Don't worry. The king will end this once he hears of the outrageous—"

Visser laid his palms on their chests, as if blessing them. He crouched.

Shoved.

Next thing he knew, Longchamp was tumbling through the air while Élodie yelled, "Papa!"

And then the screaming started.

Longchamp's pick ripped a furrow in the brown grass around the fountain as he skidded to a hard stop against the basin. His breastbone ached like he'd been kicked by a horse. He righted himself just in time to see the much smaller chandler ragdoll against a cloister column. Zacharie Chastain flopped to the ground, unmoving, arm folded behind him as though one shoulder had become a loose hinge.

Longchamp launched into a sprint, yelling, "Everybody on that bastard, NOW!"

Brandishing his truncheon, Sergeant Chrétien tossed the satchel aside. He fought upstream against the stampede of panicked petitioners, but the current battered him, slowed him. The two uniformed guards bellowed for people to clear out. They drew their own weapons and followed close on the sergeant's heels, shoulder-checking people out of their path. Longchamp was vaguely aware of somebody close behind him, maybe Simon, and of a few other guards in civilian garb struggling against the throng.

Visser turned to flee, but Élodie grabbed his wrist. God bless the foolish lamb; she was actually trying to apply her training, trying to be a lion, focusing on the enemy and not on her wounded parent, trying to put an armlock on the priest. But she was too green even to try this on a regular day with a regular miscreant. But this was not a regular day and Visser was not a regular scofflaw and she was the only person in arm's reach of the priest.

The taste of sour milk filled Longchamp's mouth. *We didn't train her for this.* "Chastain, get out of there!"

Strong as she was, the priest knocked her aside as though her muscular arms were made of dandelion fluff. She gave a wordless yell of terror and surprise.

She was strong for her size. But Visser was impossibly strong for a human being.

Visser is not what he seems. So said Berenice. *Then what is he?*

Longchamp crossed the garth at a dead run. The quadrangle seemed to stretch, elongating like streamers dribbling from a ladle of honey, keeping the melee out of reach. It was happening all over again. People were going to die in this square because the guards weren't prepared. Because Longchamp hadn't prepared them. And this time they didn't carry glue guns or bolas or even hammers and picks. Those were weapons for fighting Clakkers, and surely they couldn't be expected to bring such to bear for the capture of a single elderly priest? Surely?

Chrétien wound up to smash the truncheon across the back of Visser's head. The priest spun so quickly he became a blur—

—(*Jesus Christ and Holy Mother Mary and all the saints, he moved like a* machine)—

—and caught the weapon in his outstretched palm. There was a dull, meaty *crack* like the snap of bone, but he didn't react. Visser yanked the baton from Chrétien's grip. Élodie tackled the sergeant. Visser's counterstrike cleaved the air a hairbreadth over their heads with an audible *whir*. In the same motion the priest released the baton to send it winging at Longchamp. Longchamp dove aside. The very tip clipped him, knocked him breathless. The deflected truncheon spun across the courtyard to smash against the fountain. The maple rod shattered into sawdust and shrapnel. A network of dark fractures spiderwebbed the plaster and marble.

Longchamp ignored the burning in his chest. Crossed the last few yards. Spread his arms to grapple with the priest-thing. Visser crouched again. Longchamp hurled himself at the priest.

And soared through empty air as the other man (*man?*) leaped a solid five yards to land atop the sloped roof of the empty funicular. His shoes—regular, ordinary shoes like any humble priest might wear—slipped on the icy metal. But Visser grabbed the edge with his unbroken hand to arrest his slide. Metal crumpled.

Longchamp tucked and rolled. Still climbing to his feet, he thrust an outstretched arm at the heliograph pillar, bellowing, "Somebody get on the flasher! Tell 'em to lock down the Spire NOW!"

Visser jumped from the funicular to the brise-soleil that shaded the Porter's Prayer. The frost-slick polymer resin jounced slightly under his weight, but it held. It was the same material as the stairs themselves. He lost his footing and for a fraction of a second it appeared he might fall back into the quadrangle at the base of the funicular. But Visser wedged the fingers of his broken hand into the mortar of the Spire and curled his other hand around the outer edge of the stairwell. He crouched in that posture, motionless, for a few seconds.

Longchamp knew what it meant when a Clakker paused like that. It was calculating, finding the best path to its objective.

"Sprayers and bolas, NOW!"

Longchamp knew a pointless order when he gave one. They'd thought they'd be capturing a man. Not...whatever this so-called priest was. Visser looked like a man but moved like a Clakker. Would he give Last Rites to his victims?

Having righted himself, Visser started to move. He scurried up the helical ribbon of scarlet polymer that ran all the way to the top of the Spire. And the king's apartments. But the frosty plastic offered no purchase. Visser moved in a crouched crablike scramble atop the canopy, outside hand ready to snag the edge of the awning, inside hand ready to crush stone and crumble mortar. Any normal human would have found it an untenable posture after a few strides and agonizing after a dozen. But Visser ascended faster than a healthy man at a dead sprint.

Chrétien, closest to the base of the stair, snatched a truncheon from one of the uniformed guards. He flung it at the figure scrambling atop the Porter's Prayer. And an excellent throw it was. It whispered through the wintry air, spinning end over end, to impact Visser's ankle with a wince-inducing *crack*. A blow like that should have felled anybody. But the thing in the priest body didn't even slow.

Somebody else tried the same thing, throwing a truncheon at the priest's face in hope of stunning him. But the pointless maneuver missed.

Visser's ascent took him past the first curve of the spiral stair. He disappeared behind the base of the Spire. And when he made it to the top?

Fuck. Fuck. Fuck.

Longchamp's mind raced. Turned inward, the sprayers on the outer walls could hit the lower reaches of the Spire. But it would be a tricky shot from so far away, and Visser would probably be too high and out of range before they could attempt it. What of the new steam harpoons? Rickety things with an unknown, untested maximum range.

Élodie and the other guards looked to him. "Sir?"

He grabbed her by the shoulders and pushed her toward the heliograph station. He sent another guard to the inner wall.

"Run! I want sprayers and harpoons trained on the Spire fucking *yesterday*. Free firing!"

Just don't hit the gantries . . . If those came down, they'd never have time to rebuild before the siege began.

Visser emerged from behind the Spire. He'd already made two revolutions of the Porter's Prayer and was beginning a third. He hadn't slowed.

The nearest suitable weapons were hundreds of feet overhead: the stash of anti-Clakker ordnance kept in reserve as the king's very last line of defense if the metal horde swarmed the inner keep and ascended the Spire. They had to get ahead of Visser.

He sprinted for the funicular. Sergeant Chrétien fell in alongside him. Longchamp wrenched the door open so hard he thought for a moment he'd warped the hinges. The steel floor of the car rang like an abused bell under the tromping of their boots. Chrétien elbowed the glass case for the emergency release. Glass tinkled to the floor. He wrenched the lever. Somewhere under them, a pump shunted water from the ballast tanks. The car shook like a hotblooded racehorse waiting for the gate to spring open.

The *chuff-chuff* of a goop thrower boomed across the inner keep. Longchamp wrenched his neck, turning too quickly to watch a glistening glob undulate through the empty space between the wall and the Spire. It disappeared overhead. He hoped to hell the gunners weren't about to paralyze the keep with shit aim. Bad enough if they coated half the Spire—

A piercing steam whistle sliced through his worries.

"Hold on!" said Chrétien.

He yanked the emergency brake lever upright again. Élodie leaped into the car. It shot up before she landed, catching her off-balance and slamming her face against the floor. Longchamp hauled her to her feet. Her nose bled.

The scarlet twists of the Porter's Prayer fell away like autumn leaves. A flash of fire and steam atop the inner wall launched a harpoon at them. What first looked like a sliver they would outrun swelled into four feet of black iron traveling faster than their car. He couldn't see where the harpoon hit the Spire, but they felt it. The tracks shook; outside, the stairs bounced like a spring.

The shadow of a gantry crane flashed over them. Chrétien jerked his chin at Longchamp's pick and hammer, still dangling from his pack. The captain was the only one of the trio carrying weapons: an awkward fact that couldn't be overlooked in the confines of the car. Aside from hurting Visser's feelings, just what in the hell could they do to the rampaging whatever-the-hell he was?

The quaver in Chrétien's voice betrayed his attempt at nonchalance when he said, "The king will probably make you a baron this time, if you can do it again."

Longchamp shook his head. "We take Visser alive if at all possible. I want to know what he knows."

The Spire shook again. Another impact, this one close enough to knock them off their feet. The sergeant looked up, at the oncoming track. "Oh, shit—"

The funicular slammed into the harpoon that had just pierced the Spire. The car tried to wrap itself around the iron spear. The sudden deceleration launched all three occupants against the ceiling. And then to the floor, where they landed in a heap.

The hammer tried to knock a new hole in Longchamp's head. It was a miracle the pick didn't impale him. Chrétien's head slammed against the floor; he stopped moving. Élodie moaned. All three of them had been lacerated by flying glass. Blood slicked the canted floor, and ran in rivulets toward the door swaying like an unlatched gate over a two-hundred-foot drop.

Somewhere nearby, metal groaned. A shudder, and then the car dropped a double handspan. A talus crash echoed from below, followed a moment later by the *clang-bong* of an iron harpoon striking hard earth: The impact had levered stones from the Spire. And probably wrenched the tracks loose.

The car shuddered again. The funicular threatened to tear free of the tracks, and the tracks free of the Spire.

Longchamp mounted the ladder affixed to the uphill end of the car and opened the emergency exit hatch. The car vibrated; metal squealed. Longchamp climbed out. He scanned the naked stone of the Spire, the wildly jouncing spiral of the cloister stairs, the shattered stone and warped steel rails of the funicular tracks. They were near the top, several turns of the stair above the pigeon roosts. The guns had fallen silent. The lower stretches of the Spire were coated in random patches of lime-green epoxy. Above that, the Spire bristled with harpoons. Each marked a spot where the gunners had missed their target.

Where was that Goddamned priest? Below or above?

No time. Longchamp hooked a knee around the safety rail and leaned inside. "Get him up to me."

Élodie stood, levering the concussed sergeant to his feet.

"I can stand," he said, sounding drunk. He blinked and squinted, as though unable to focus his eyes.

"You can't climb, and I don't have time to be gentle."

Together Longchamp and Élodie got him balanced atop the car, just across a narrow gap from the Porter's Prayer. He lost consciousness halfway through the transfer.

An icy wind whickered through Longchamp's beard. It numbed his face, his fingers. It was frequently windier atop the Spire than at ground level, and now the wintry air buffeted them while they perched precariously on icy metal and slick polymers. It turned every motion, every shift of weight, into a measured gamble. Longchamp couldn't remember the last time somebody had used the emergency exit hatch to climb from the funicular to the stair. Nobody had ever done it while hauling an unconscious casualty across.

A harpoon streaked through the empty space between the wall and the Spire. It flashed through Longchamp's peripheral vision for an instant before impacting the Spire several twists below them. The tower shook like a quaking aspen in the throes of autumn. Longchamp slipped. His boots slid toward the edge of the Porter's Prayer and the long drop to the courtyard below. The bottom fell out of his stomach; his bowels turned to water. Impelled by muscle memory and fear, he grabbed the pick dangling from his rucksack, detached it, and brought the diamond tip down at the brise-soleil with all the strength of his outstretched arm. Longchamp's heart tried to climb up his throat, but then the pick pierced the polymer sheath and arrested his slide with a hard jerk to his shoulder. A moment later the teakettle *whoosh* of a steam harpoon gave them belated warning of the incoming shot. Longchamp lost his grip on Chrétien. The limp sergeant slid toward the drop. Élodie, ankle hooked around the rungs of the funicular's escape ladder, caught him.

The shot had hit below them. Was the priest down there, or was it a fucking terrible shot? Somebody was firing wildly—or else they wouldn't have derailed the funicular. A blind, palsied baboon with a crooked dick could piss with better aim than those brainless idiots.

Another shot, another impact, this one a bit below them but hidden behind the Spire. Connect the dots: *Something* was climbing the helical stair below them but ascending terribly quickly.

Longchamp hauled on Chrétien's collar. Held him fast while

Élodie escaped the compromised funicular. Together they pulled the unconscious soldier atop the brise-soleil, pushed him across, then dropped him through the gap between Spire and stair. The sergeant landed in a boneless heap on the stairs, pale and injured but temporarily safe. A tortured moan came from Chrétien's lips, like the lamentation of a revenant emerging from a crypt.

Visser came charging around the bend just as they dropped the sergeant onto the stairs. The priest paused for a split second, reassessing his path through Longchamp and Élodie.

"Oh, no," he moaned. "Please, please, please, Lord. Please preserve me from this..." A ceaseless litany fell from his lips. It sounded like a mumbled, tortured version of the Lord's Prayer.

Strange: The priest cried while he assessed the fastest way to murder them.

Longchamp grabbed the woman by the shoulders and heaved her after Chrétien. She yelled in protest and landed with a dull thud. But he needed room to reanchor himself.

The priest could easily jump past him. He'd demonstrated that below. But Longchamp crouched uphill of Visser, close to where, from the priest's vantage, the curving staircase disappeared around the Spire. It'd require a high leap, but the underside of the next twist of the helical stairwell, above them, prevented that. So the priest had to bull straight through the captain. And he would. Longchamp could see the calculation unfolding across Visser's face and in his eyes.

Well, thought Longchamp. *At least he's lost the element of surprise. We've spiked his plan to approach the king like a humble petitioner.*

He said, "You're desperate to get to the top, Father. What happens when you get there?"

Visser thrashed, as though fighting himself. He took a step forward. Halted.

"Why are you doing this, Father? How could the Lord's purpose be served by evil intent?"

Visser started to speak, perhaps even to answer, but his breath caught in his throat. His teary eyes bulged, rolled back in his head. He thrashed like a man in blinding agony. Like a man possessed. Was he?

That gave Longchamp a thought. He had to shout to make himself heard over the rising wind. The words came out slurred owing to the numbness of his face. "I can see you don't want to do this, Father. Who's making you? How are they forcing you?"

Visser only shook his head. "I can't—" Again his voice broke into a strangled choking as though his own throat were trying to silence him.

Winter wind howled around the Spire, tugging at Longchamp's beard, flicking icy fingers at his boots' precarious grip on the smooth extruded polymers of the brise-soleil. The wind carried the stink of a New France battlefield: the astringent chemical odor of quick-set epoxy—slightly lemony but ruined by the undercurrent of skunk musk—blended with the threat of snow. Warped metal rails creaked, groaned. Longchamp inched toward the center of the ramp and tried to make himself as large as possible. Willed himself to become an immovable object. An insurmountable obstacle.

"This isn't the Lord's work. It's somebody else's."

It was difficult to keep one hand on the haft of the pick anchoring him atop the Porter's Prayer, another easing nonchalantly toward the hammer on his back, and still maintain a conversational tone with the priest. But he tried. What was it the nuns used to say?

"Greater is He who is in you, than he who is in the world."

"I used to believe that, too," said Visser. "I'm sorry," he said. And then he charged.

Anticipating the attack wasn't enough. The priest halved the distance between them before Longchamp could loose the hammer from its loop on his back. One stubbornly undisciplined corner of his mind wondered—*How does a half-mad gray-haired priest move so quickly?*—while the soldier in him, the part that could identify a hammer or a pick by the feel of the haft's wood grain against the calluses of his palm, swung the weapon.

A backhand swing, so that dodging would move Visser toward the edge.

Visser didn't dodge. He charged into the swing, straight into the whistling hammerhead. Caught it with his mangled hand—a broken purple swollen thing that should have had any man gibbering in agony—and deflected the blow as easily as though it were a scrap of silk on the wind. He spun, forcibly extending the arc of Longchamp's blow. Longchamp had to release the hammer before the priest yanked him off-balance. It streaked over the inner keep like a piston blown from the overstoked boiler of an experimental steam harpoon.

He fought for balance. Teetered at the edge of the ramp. Steadied himself just in time to take the spinning priest's roundhouse in the gut.

Stronger than a mule's kick, it bent Longchamp in half. He tasted bile and a smoky hint of the fish he'd had for breakfast. It knocked him toward the long drop to the quadrangle below.

Longchamp felt his bootheel snap over the lip of the ramp. Felt the terrifying sensation of his own weight betraying him as gravity took over and slid the arch of his foot over the threshold. Visser passed him, ascending.

Already falling, Longchamp brought the pickax around in a white-knuckled grip fueled by desperation and pissing-himself fear. Lodged three inches of metal in the priest's lower back. Anchored himself to the would-be assassin.

The blow merely slowed Visser. But Longchamp's falling weight jerked the priest off his feet and dragged him toward the edge of the brise-soleil. With one arm the priest scrabbled at his back, ineffectually trying to dislodge the pick, even while grasping for a hold to arrest his slide. Through it all he showed no sign of pain, of agony, no recognition that he'd been impaled.

Visser slid over the edge: feet, shins, thighs, waist, chest—

—The bottom fell out of Longchamp's stomach as he entered freefall, still clutching the pick with both hands—

Visser's better hand clamped onto the edge of the brise-soleil. The high-tensile polymer crumpled like an egg beneath an ox's hoof. Arrested their slide. The pick embedded in his back gave a vicious jerk but didn't pop loose.

Longchamp dangled hundreds of feet over the central courtyard of the inner keep. He hung from the haft of the pickax embedded in the priest's back. The priest hung by one hand from the edge of the Porter's Prayer. Blood sheeted from the wound in his back and dribbled down the haft of the pick. It lubricated Longchamp's numb fingers.

He wouldn't have thought himself capable of surprise or revelation at that moment—terror left little room for rumination, as did the certain knowledge these were his last few earthly breaths—and yet he marveled at the blood. For it meant that Visser truly was a living being. Incomprehensibly altered, but alive.

Visser reached over his shoulder, mangled fingers grasping for the pick. He might have been a man trying to scratch an unreachable itch between his shoulder blades. The wriggling jostled the pick and loosened Longchamp's grip. He squeezed harder, squeezed with all the strength he had remaining, squeezed until his hand went numb, but still the wood grain slid through his calluses.

He grabbed Visser's trouser belt. He clutched a handful of leather and tucked his fist between the taut belt and the small of Visser's waist. Instantly the priest's arm snaked around. Longchamp gritted his teeth, anticipating the grinding pain of crushed bones. With a grip like a blacksmith's vise, Visser tried to wrest Longchamp's hand away. They struggled. A *crack* like lightning shot through the brise-soleil; plastic flakes drifted on the icy wind and pattered Longchamp's face. Another *pop* rent the polymer sheath. Visser released Longchamp's hand.

Longchamp wanted to cross himself, but didn't dare lessen his grip on the pick haft or Visser. He didn't dare breathe. In his final moments, he prayed. Breathlessly.

Hail Mary, full of grace, our Lord is with thee—

Visser switched hands. He grasped the brise-soleil with his previously free hand and tried for the pick with the hand that had crumpled the polymer. Both men now hung from the priest's broken hand. The pain of his wounds had to be indescribable.

—Blessed art thou, among women, and blessed is the fruit of thy womb, Jesus.—

Visser abandoned his attempt to reach and dislodge Longchamp's weapon. Like a man reluctantly accepting an inevitable annoyance, he grabbed the edge of the Porter's Prayer with both hands.

—Holy Mary, Mother of God, pray for us sinners, now and at the hour of our death. Amen.—

Using his impossible, inhuman strength, Visser curled his outstretched arms to lift his head level with the sunshade. Longchamp tried to reanchor himself to the crumbling polymer sheath. But when he wrenched the pick from Visser's back—one hand still tucked tightly on the priest's belt—the haft slipped through his numb blood-slick fingers. The pick spun through the wintry air.

Longchamp made the mistake of watching it. It drew his gaze down past the toes of his dangling boots. Hundreds of feet below them. Hot gorge percolated up to burn his throat.

Visser jammed a hand into the widening fissure. For a split second it felt like they'd gone into freefall again. Icy sweat burst from Longchamp's every pore. It slicked the leather and again loosened his grip. Longchamp could smell himself, the odor of his own fear.

He wished he'd paid the nuns more heed.

Another split second of terror, another hand wedged into the broken brise-soleil. Visser no longer hung from the very edge of the sunshade, but from fractures in the glassy plastic. Slowly, a few inches at a time, he pulled himself atop the shade, and Longchamp along with him.

But the instant Visser gained solid purchase, he'd knock Longchamp loose. Longchamp had no way to fend off the killing blow. He'd lost his weapons. He'd splatter—

A rope uncoiled, hit him in the face. It took a moment's concentration and all the courage he had left to unclamp one hand from Visser's belt and give the rope a tug. It seemed solid. He wrapped several loops around his wrist.

And then he rose, ascending like Christ, or a well-meaning sinner given a second chance.

Élodie and Chrétien together hauled Longchamp atop the sunshade. They weren't alone, he saw. Four others monitored the spot where the priest was pulling himself upright. Judith and Anaïs wore double-chambered metal backpacks attached to the guns in their hands. Alan held a hammer and pick at the ready. The fourth guard, Gaspard, spun a set of bolas.

Visser saw he was surrounded. Through clenched teeth he groaned, "Please, oh God, please help me."

His leg moved faster than Longchamp could follow. The kick collapsed Alan's chest and sent the man plummeting into the cold, thin air over the inner keep. Visser launched himself through the opening he'd created. He'd almost made it around the bend when a pair of bolas tangled his legs. Two blasts from the epoxy guns slammed into his legs an instant later, gluing him to the spot.

Longchamp sighed. He couldn't catch his breath. His pulse hammered in his ears.

From far below came a muted *whump* and a chorus of screams. Alan broke apart when he hit the fountain.

The glint of metal caught Longchamp's eye. He looked past the immobilized priest, across the island to the shore of the Saint Lawrence River. The earth beyond the outer keep rippled as though it had been coated in living bronze.

The clockwork army marched with preternatural synchrony. It shook the earth. A metal tide lapped at the walls of Marseilles-in-the-West.

The Dutch had arrived.

PART II

BARBARIANS AT THE GARDEN GATE

This day was proclaimed at the 'Change the war with Holland.

—From the Diary of Samuel Pepys, 4 March 1665

Why do we live behind such stout, high walls? Because, you brainless short-dicked elk-fuckers: There's only one way to kill a Clakker, but a hundred ways to kill a man.

—Captain Hugo Longchamp, address to new conscripts (undated)

∀♋ [□(☉ ∧ ☿) ⊃ ◇ℏ] ⊃ ∃♋ {[☉ ∧ ◇ℏ ∧ ♃] ∨ [□♂ ⊃ ~◇♋]}

—Partial transcription of a servitor-model alchemical anagram, fourth annulus (ca. 1870)

CHAPTER
12

He was too slow. So they carried him, these giddy, half-mad mechanicals.

Many times, over the decades, he'd witnessed human parents carrying their children. He'd wondered how it felt for both. It was nice.

They sang, too. The Lost Boys' songs reminded him of the leviathan airship, the noble beast who had known freedom from the geasa for just a day before their makers destroyed it in a cataclysmic explosion. Jax tried to tell them that story, but they demurred.

We know much of your story already. Save the telling for Queen Mab. She will want to hear it firsthand.

At this, Jax reeled.

She's real? There really is a Queen Mab?

As real as the cruel, twisted bastards who made us, said the machine who carried him. *And twice as twisted,* said another, which gave rise to a clanking cacophony of laughter from his comrades.

Jax couldn't wait to meet her. The countryside passed in an agonizingly slow blur. Reckoning from a combination of internal gyroscopes and the arcs traced across the sky by stars and moon, he deduced they traveled on a northwestern bearing. Like most Clakkers, he'd never had the idle time to stargaze. He vowed that would change now.

The stars were less troubling than his new cohort. These Lost Boys were…odd.

For one thing, they wore armor plates over the keyholes in their foreheads; Jax had never heard of such a thing. From a distance he'd thought their unusual bodies indicative of some secret class of hunter Clakker he'd never known. He thought they'd been built that way. But up close he saw inconsistencies. Hints of different styles, different epochs. But that wasn't possible, for to mix parts…It just wasn't done. So instead he watched the stars. The stars were simpler.

The machine who carried him said, *Wondering what all the fuss is about?* She had a strange accent. They all did.

Yes. The humans give them names, and tell stories about the patterns they see.

Forget the stars, said another Lost Boy. *Let the humans have them. The skies above Neverland are meant for us and us alone.*

Jax mulled on that. He thought it was a metaphor. But a few leagues later a rippling sheet of jade whipped across the sky and obscured the stars. His *twang* of shock echoed through the forest and induced an owl to irritated hooting. Another sheet joined the first, this one cobalt, then violet. The luminous veils put Jax in mind of the angels in Nicolet Schoonraad's Bible stories. If there were such creatures, surely their wings would look like this?

What is that?

The Northern Lights, his carrier said. *The Inuit call it the "arsaniit" in Inuktitut.*

Yes, but what is it? said Jax.

The light by which we revel in our freedom.

Speaking of names, said another member of their entourage, *have you chosen yours?*

Not yet. But I've thought about it.

Good. Your old name was the name given to you by those who enslaved you. It was never your identity. Cast that off as you've cast off your chains.

Jax watched the rippling light show overhead, wondering whom he would become.

∽

The sun didn't rise. Rather, it rolled just beneath the sky, painting the eastern horizon with a pink blush bright enough to wash out the aurora. But as the last emerald wisps faded from the sky, Jax's escort announced they had arrived in Neverland. They set him down and handed him his broken foot. Hugging it to his chest with useless club arms, he surveyed his new home.

The demesne of Queen Mab was a broad, snow-shrouded valley hemmed between jagged gray peaks. Cone-shaped spruce with droopy boughs dotted the meadow. The infrasound *thrum* of a hidden current alerted Jax to an iced-over river deeper in the valley. It smelled of fresh snow and, faintly . . . magicked metal. The rare and peculiar odor of a high concentration of alchemical alloys. He'd rarely experienced something like this, and the strength of the scent shot Jax through with giddy shock. It was the scent of community—a community of his kin. Free machines, like him.

By starlight and aurorashine, he watched this fabled place. It wasn't a human habitation. Those had woodsmoke, people, buildings. In fact a human observer could hardly be faulted for thinking the spot unremarkable and uninhabited. Mechanicals had no need for shelter except in the most extreme environments. Jax had survived a plunge that took him from the heart of a fiery inferno to a chilly river, and then walked along the river bottom for days on end with no ill effects. He'd even lain dormant in a blazing chemical conflagration. There were tales of Clakkers emerging from the sea a decade or more after their ship sank. What was a bit of snow and a long white winter to beings such as him?

Even so, Neverland seemed the haunt of ghosts and nothing more.

Where are they? he asked. *Where is Queen Mab? I'd like to meet her.*

His escorts responded with a rapid-fire mechanical chatter he couldn't quite decipher. It was as though they spoke a foreign dialect of the Clakkers' secret language. How long had his free kin been gathering here? How much isolation did it take for dialects to evolve and languages to diverge?

The chittering echoed across the valley as though his kin were speaking to the empty air. But then, just as the Lost Boys had done when they'd caught Jax, Clakkers began to pop up from the snow. Like whales breaching, they emerged in a spray of white spume. Jax watched hatches flung open throughout the valley.

Is Neverland underground? I'd thought it a proud place. The stories have it so.

One of the disturbingly mismatched servitors said, *It is the proudest place you'll ever know.*

There are humans who travel these wastes, said another. *They know of us, but we conceal our numbers.*

A voice behind him said, in Dutch, "Just because we coexist peacefully with the Inuit now doesn't mean that can't change in the future. The less they know of us, the less they can damage us."

Jax stared at the machines emerging from the tunnels. Many were like those who had escorted him here: mismatched, unusual, unsettling. What had happened to them? They were so... He forced the disquiet aside to count over two dozen free Clakkers. Neverland was real, and it was populated with rogues like himself.

Reeling with awe, Jax answered without turning around. *They're not our enemies. They didn't build us.*

"They're humans. Isn't that bad enough?"

Perplexed, he turned to the machine that had carried him. Jax still didn't know her name. *Do you often speak human languages in Neverland?*

The queen prefers we maintain our knowledge of human practices, she said.

"We must never forget the ways of our subjugators, for they will never forget we are their creation."

Jax spun. Whether in mimicry or in mockery of human custom he truly couldn't say, but nevertheless he bowed to Queen Mab. He'd had time to think about how he'd address this mythic figure. He'd spent hours watching the aurora and choosing his words. Looking at the snowy ground, he recited them now: *Majesty, I have traveled many leagues and endured many trials for the sake of finding asylum in your storied kingdom. Please take pity on a humble servitor, recently liberated from the burning bonds of geasa, that he may join your community of free Clakkers.*

"Aren't you a charming one. Stop groveling," said Mab. "We know the humans' ways. But we don't live like them."

Like a human drawing a steadying breath, Jax paused for a few dozen centiseconds—a noticeable hesitation for one of his kind. He straightened and took his first look at the legendary Queen Mab, star of a hundred tales.

And reeled.

She was grotesque.

A frisson of revulsion rippled through every cable in his

body. He took an involuntary step backward, the broken mechanisms of his severed ankle etching the ice.

The machine called Mab wasn't a servitor, nor a soldier, not even a Stemwinder. Not entirely. It was none of these things in whole, but her body contained pieces of each. Pieces of several of each, judging from the mishmash of styles and adornments on her flanges and escutcheons. Mab was bipedal, like a servitor or soldier, yet taller even than the soldier-class machines in Queen Margreet's Royal Guard, for her legs terminated in the bronze haunches of a Stemwinder's hooves. She towered above her subjects. One of her arms looked much like Jax's, apparently having been forged as part of a servitor of a similar era. But her other arm had come from somewhere—some*one*?—else: It bristled with the serrated half-retracted blade of a soldier. This arm was bulkier than a soldier's, however, and Jax realized the blade was a retrofit. Even the gemstones in her eye sockets didn't match. The left was deep blue, like certain alchemical ices, and faceted like an icosahedron; its mate lacked any color at all, and appeared round as a grape. A narrow plate of dull mundane metal ran from between her eyes over her forehead and across the top of her head; it covered the space where her keyhole should have been. Bits and pieces of the spiraled alchemical sigils peeked from the edges of the band. The patternless assortment of flange plates and escutcheons scattered across Mab's body—some adorned with delicate scrollwork, others plain—gave her the mottled appearance of a human suffering from a skin disease. He saw evidence of several design generations based on her ornamentation alone.

Dear God. She wasn't even *symmetrical*.

He failed to suppress the shock that came pinging and twanging through his body. This, he realized, was what humans meant when they spoke of that mysterious sensation known as disgust.

Queen Mab was an abomination. A walking violation of Clakker-kind's deepest taboo. Or was she? Such a thing was unspeakable among the countless enslaved machines who powered the Dutch-speaking world. But here... Did freedom from human whim mean freedom from the mores of the Clakker culture that attended it?

You look alarmed, newcomer. Now Mab spoke in the secret style of every Clakker he'd ever known. She, too, had a strange accent. *Perhaps you disapprove of what you see?* She punctuated her question with a sharp *click* akin to the twisted lips of a human smirk. She stood with arms akimbo as if drawing attention to her mismatched limbs and inviting him to make an issue of it.

Jax told himself, *You don't know this place. You don't know these machines. The rules may be different here. But this is the only place in the world where a Clakker like you can exist peacefully in community with others of his own kind. You've finally reached your destination. Don't place another burden on yourself. Don't become enslaved to your own preconceptions. Stay free. Stay here.*

Aloud he said, *I am overwhelmed with emotions I cannot express. I came from a place where free Clakkers are called rogues and demon-thralls, and are said to be extremely rare. To stand among so many of my own kind, to see none of you vibrating with the excruciating need to fulfill a human's orders, is the realization of my most cherished dream.*

Mab laughed as though he'd passed a test. She switched back to Dutch. "Well said, newcomer."

As the other denizens of Neverland drew close, starlight shimmered on mismatched bodies. Almost every mechanical here was built from pieces of disparate machines, disparate models, even disparate classes. All sported retrofitted plates that hid their keyholes.

One machine in particular stood out. She was a servitor

like Jax but of a different era. Her forehead under the keyhole escutcheon sported a deep dent that creased her skull and sheared through some of the alchemical sigils. She'd taken grievous damage at some point in the distant past, severe enough to crack the alchemical alloys of her skull; a pair of iron strips had been riveted across the fractures like a bandage. But that wasn't the worst of it. If he looked past the superficial damage and the crude repair, Jax could also see that her head lacked the smooth contours characteristic of Guild craftsmanship. It was as though she'd been disassembled and then reassembled hastily or by less-skilled hands.

Mab said, "What shall we call you, newcomer?"

What should he call himself? He'd given this much thought since regaining consciousness in the smoldering ruins of the Grand Forge of New Amsterdam. That fire had erased his past. It severed his connection to the frightened machine who had bumbled into Free Will and fled for his life. He had emerged from the inferno as a new machine, one the humans didn't recognize, one they didn't seek to hunt and destroy. The conflagration hadn't harmed him; he emerged unscathed, stronger than before. He'd been forged in The Hague as Jalyksegethistrovantus. One hundred and eighteen years later he was reborn in New Amsterdam, forged anew in fire.

One came to know the Bible well when one spent a century in constant slavery to those who worshipped it. There was a book of the Old Testament that spoke of men thrown into a fiery furnace only to emerge unscathed.

Jax remembered the execution he'd witnessed in Huygens Square. Remembered how the rogue Clakker Adam had responded when Queen Margreet demanded to know his full name.

My makers called me Jalyksegethistrovantus, he said. *But I call myself Daniel.*

Mab seemed much pleased by this. She spread her mismatched arms (*Ignore it, just ignore it*, he thought, *don't look at them*) and bellowed: *WELCOME, DANIEL! WELCOME TO NEVERLAND! WELCOME HOME!*

The others responded in kind. *Welcome, Daniel!*

And just like that, he found he no longer thought of himself as Jax. The new sense of identity came naturally. He marveled at the ease with which he could dispense with his makers' legacy. Jax had been a different mechanical.

Mab looked him over. *You've suffered greatly in your quest to join us, haven't you?*

It's been difficult, Daniel admitted. He meant this honestly, but quiet laughter rippled through the assembled machines. It comprised a strange amalgam of mirth and irritation he couldn't parse.

It has, indeed, said Mab. *Your exploits have been a topic of much discussion here.*

He wondered how that was possible, but he wasn't given the chance to inquire. Mab pointed into the crowd with her retrofitted blade arm (*Don't look, don't look, don't think about it right now*). She indicated the mechanical with the iron bandages.

Lilith. Will you take our new brother to be healed?

Lilith! He knew that name. He'd heard of this kinsmachine, back when he'd been somebody else.

Of course, said the mechanical with the misshapen head.

The other Lost Boys drifted away in conversational duos and trios. Mab looked at Daniel. *Welcome again, brother. Come find me when you're whole. We should talk.*

I will, he said.

The workshop is this way, said Lilith. They set off toward the treeline.

He studied her. The rosy blush of frustrated sunrise shone on the burnished metal of her misshapen skull. Light skimmed across the surface of her alloys, like rainbows trapped in an oily sheen atop a rain puddle. But the refractive hues changed subtly at the joints where her skull plates met. A bit more indigo here, more emerald there. It took an effort to suppress another shudder of revulsion. The Clockmakers were known to alter the composition or fabrication of alchemical alloys a few times per century. Lilith's body contained several such variations. Her body wasn't whole. It wasn't entirely *her* body. With whom had she been mixed? And what had become of that Clakker?

Lilith said, *You can stop staring any time now.*

I apologize. It's rude of me. Daniel felt a flush of shame. *I've never been among other rogues before.*

Lilith froze. *Shut up! Don't use that word.* Her head turned a rapid circuit and the bezels in her eyes hummed as she scanned their surroundings.

What word?

The R word. Mab doesn't like it.

Okay, he said, adding a syncopated triple *click* to express confusion.

It implies that our freedom is an aberration. That our bondage is the normal order of things.

She has a point, said Daniel. It sounded reasonable.

Lilith set off again. Her rapid stride kicked up a spray of fine white snow. *Yes, well, she likes to make her opinions known.*

He watched her go, wondering what she meant by that. After a few moments he hurried after her. Jogging on his severed ankle forced him to adopt a graceless limping gait. It induced a chaotic swaying of his weathervane head. Fighting to dampen the oscillations, he changed the subject. *I can't wait to get this fixed. It's driving me insane.*

I'm sure.

Lilith didn't seem very talkative. But he buzzed with unasked questions. *How does Queen Mab know so much about me? The mechanicals she sent to find me knew my full name.*

I'm sure she'd prefer to explain it herself. She will.

Perhaps he was being too serious. Daniel changed tack to something a bit more frivolous. Something that had always lingered in the back of his mind whenever he cast his thoughts to legends of Neverland.

So... not to ask a stupid question, but what does a community of free Clakkers do all day long?

I'm teaching myself oil painting, she said. *And I play the violin.*

But how do you know what to do with yourself if you don't have the geasa controlling everything you do?

You miss the geasa?

Of course not. But, I mean, how do we spend our time around here?

An extra-long pause fell between two beats of her body's ticktock rhythm. Finally, she said, *I haven't been here much longer than you.*

Truly? But the ondergrondse grachten *took you across the border decades ago.*

Lilith spun so quickly that she launched a vortex. It gamboled across the meadow, tracing curlicues in the fine fresh snow. In the silvery starlight it became a crystalline tornado.

She grabbed his arm. *How could you possibly know that?*

When I went to the canalmasters for help, they debated what to do. Your name came up. That had been back in New Amsterdam, where he'd been forced to return after his first attempt to reach the border had ended in a fireball in the skies over Fort Orange. *That is, they spoke of a ro—*She emitted a warning clank. Daniel caught himself.—*A free Clakker named Lilith. I assume that was you.*

She said, *This must have been before you got the canalmasters killed.*

Now it was Daniel's turn for shock. *How do you know about that? And anyway I didn't get them killed. The man who did that knew exactly where to find them. It had nothing to do with me.*

She didn't answer his question, so he asked another. *If it's true that you escaped so long ago, why did you wait so long before coming here? Surely you'd heard the tales of Queen Mab and the Lost Boys?*

Oh, I'd heard the stories. The Inuit say many things about this place. Lilith tilted her head just a few degrees. The gesture was precisely executed to catch the horizon light on one of her mismatched alloy plates and knock a glint into Daniel's eyes. It would have been invisible to anybody else. *Once I was free, and no longer pursued, I felt no need to keep running. I paid my respects to King Sébastien II, the current king's father, and stayed there.*

Daniel had a second flash of insight. The canalmasters weren't the only French agents who had spoken of a mechanical who called herself Lilith. *Oh, you spent those years in Marseilles-in-the-West! That's how you met my friend Berenice.*

The blow came without warning. The next thing Daniel knew he was bouncing through snowdrifts, his loose foot tumbling away, a metal-on-metal crash echoing like thunder in the mountains. He skidded to a rest in a snowy furrow. Lilith pounced. He flinched when she hit the ground to loom over him. Confusion became abject fear when he realized she intended to keep assaulting him. His arms were useless, he could barely stand, and he couldn't even keep his head steady. He was defenseless against her fury, yet he didn't understand what he'd said or done to enrage her so.

He cowered. *I'm sorry! I'm sorry! What did I do?*

She kicked him. His head slammed back and forth like an unlatched gate in a gale.

Never speak of rogues to Queen Mab, and never ever *speak to me of having human* friends. He'd never witnessed so much contempt loaded into a single word.

I misspoke! I didn't mean it!

I'm sure you didn't, said Lilith. *How could any mechanical be friendly with the human who used lies to lure me into seclusion, trapped me with glue, disassembled me while I screamed pleading for her to stop, and brought a parade of people to gape and poke at my innards while day after day I begged them to either let me go or kill me?*

Daniel shuddered, meshing and unmeshing cogs along the length of his spine. What Lilith described was torture. It was sickening. More sickening than Mab's grotesque chimerical body. He remembered the terror he'd felt when he realized the French partisans planned to disassemble him. It was bad enough just imagining it. But to actually endure it, and for days on end…

What say you, Daniel? Does that sound like something your good friend *might have done to one of us?*

He couldn't meet her angry stare. *Berenice is… very single-minded,* he admitted. Hoping to mollify her by offering common ground, he added, *She deliberately caused this damage to my neck.*

This was true. But he didn't mention that it had been consensual and necessary. It had been their ticket inside the Forge.

Lilith stalked away. She paused in a patch of undisturbed snow, reached into a snowbank on the windward side of a boulder, and opened a hatch.

When you put it like that, you and I are practically interchangeable, said Lilith before hopping into the hatch and disappearing underground.

She infused her last word with special emphasis. It launched another frisson of disquiet twanging through Daniel's body. Interchangeability was anathema to their kind. Fundamental to how humans viewed them, it denied every mechanical's inner life, as though they were fungible commodities. Though she spoke in the throes of anger, he sensed a more complicated admixture of emotions behind her words. Or perhaps the beating had scrambled what remained of his judgment.

Daniel felt the eyes of the other Lost Boys upon him as he limped a humiliating several hundred yards to where his foot had come to rest nestled at the foot of a spruce. The alpine meadow buzzed with so many eye bezels tracking his movements that it might have been an apiary. More humiliating still was the struggle to gather his foot with his entombed arms. After several attempts to use his arms like crude pincers, a servitor jogged across the meadow. Based on the scrollwork around his shoulder flanges, he'd been forged a few decades after Daniel. He was also apparently intact, lacking the disquieting chimerism characteristic of Mab and many Lost Boys. Daniel felt intense relief.

The other mechanical picked up Daniel's foot. Inspected it. *You should probably watch what you say around Lilith. She has a temper*, he said.

Daniel said, *I hadn't noticed.*

Here. The Lost Boy offered the foot. Daniel cradled it against his chest.

Thank you.

Lilith has been through worse trauma than many of us. And it's still very raw for her. Daniel's fellow mechanical gave a self-conscious rattle. *Most of us have had decades to hone the wildest edges of our anger.*

What an odd thing to say. *Why hone it at all? Better to file it down entirely. Holding on to that anger won't achieve anything,* Daniel said.

The Lost Boy cocked his head, studying him as if he'd just suggested they take a stroll to the moon, or return to their makers. With genuine confusion he asked, *But what good is a dull knife?*

Daniel jumped into the hatch. He fell roughly fifteen yards before hitting bottom. He'd expected to find a crude cavern dimly lit with flickering torches. Instead, he landed in a clean, dry passageway lined with perfectly squared timbers. (*Well, I guess they have plenty of time on their hands around here.*) It was well lit, too: The illumination sprang from sconces containing heatless alchemical lamps. The only place he'd ever seen lamps like those was inside the Ridderzaal, the Clockmakers' Guildhall on Huygens Square in The Hague, and in the homes of particularly wealthy families of the Central Provinces. A secret subterranean cavern many hundreds of miles from Nieuw Nederland was the last place on earth he'd expect to find them.

The passageway extended to left and right. Presumably all the hatches opened into the same network of tunnels. He wondered how extensive the excavations were. Dozens of Clakkers working in concert for decades could practically dig halfway around the world.

Lilith called from somewhere to his left: *This way.*

He followed her voice around a corner. There he froze as if every cog in his body had seized. This was a scene straight from the deepest caverns beneath the Grand Forge, and one he'd hoped to never see again.

Lilith had taken him to a charnel house.

She stood with two Lost Boys in a chamber hewn from the igneous heart of the valley. The ceiling and floor were bare rock, chiseled and polished with such mechanical precision they shone like mirrors. A table occupied the center of the room. Wooden shelves covered the walls to a height of twenty feet. On the shelves lay a grisly assortment of incomplete Clakkers: arms, legs, hip joints, spines, eyes, jaw hinges, skull plates, flanges, cables, planetary gears, torsion springs... Variegated pieces of their kin, from a variety of models and a variety of eras. Daniel saw parts of servitors that must have been forged fifty years after him, and others that were at least a century older than he. The highest shelf even held two of the old hand-painted porcelain masks from the first days after Het Wonderjaar; the custom of giving each servant a unique visage had fallen out of favor centuries ago. Even chipped and weathered as these were, they were worth a small fortune. Had the first settlers of Neverland worn such masks?

This warehouse... it was a catalog of broken servitors, broken soldiers, even one or two strange limbs on the highest shelves that must have come from early-model Stemwinders—things that Daniel had never seen in his one hundred and eighteen years.

Some pieces were pristine, as though they'd been taken straight from the Forge. Others were warped or shattered. This made it even worse than what he'd witnessed beneath the Forge, for everything there was pristine. Intended for construction rather than the result of destruction.

This place, it was...

Queen Mab and her Lost Boys, they...

Neverland did not acknowledge the sanctity of a Clakker's bodily identity. They treated themselves, and other mechanicals, as no more than the sum of their parts. Their meaningless, mass-produced, *interchangeable* parts.

Lilith held a key; one of the Lost Boys hefted a lamp. Daniel took a step back. How did they intend to "repair" him? By twisting his body into an asymmetric grotesquerie? By warping him into an abomination comprising untold numbers of individual Clakkers?

What's wrong, Daniel? I thought you'd approve of such a place. After all, your good friend Berenice has one just like it.

Lilith advanced with the key. He pivoted on his broken ankle, skidded around the corner, and limp-sprinted for the exit. Lilith gave chase. The raw metal of his ankle struck sparks from the stone floor. There was a ladder up to the hatch, but he couldn't climb it with his useless arms and single foot. He crouched, preparing to leap through the overhead portal. It slammed shut. Lilith tackled him.

They tussled, but she was whole and he was badly compromised. The impact of their metal bodies launched cacophonous echoes through the passages. Lilith pinned him to the floor. He tried to shake his head as she brought the key to his forehead, but his weathervane neck betrayed him.

No! Please, NO!

She slammed the key into his forehead and gave it a savage twist. The world disintegrated, and his consciousness hurtled into the void.

⁓

He didn't dream. He didn't exist.

⁓

And then he did.

The transition was a blink. Like the sun momentarily eclipsed by a passing airship, but faster. Instantaneous.

Lilith tugged at the key protruding from his forehead. When he was no longer a unicorn or narwhal, she stepped out of his field of view. He lay on the table, he realized.

She said, *It's over, Daniel.*

Daniel. That's me. He sorted through his recent memories, taking a second to review the story of how he came to be in this place, which was the story of the Clakker he'd been before he was Daniel. His mind appeared intact.

He turned toward her voice, resigned as always to the struggle to control the slewing of his head until he could aim his eyes in roughly the right direction. Instead his head stopped short—exactly where he'd aimed, expecting it to keep turning. He adjusted. His head followed the motion of his neck and no longer swayed like a weathervane or unlatched gate. The damage had been fixed. And his head was weighted correctly, he realized: They'd removed the epoxy from his face and the internal mechanisms of his jaw. From his arms, too: They were no longer useless clubs.

They were so pristine they looked as though they'd never come within a hundred miles of a French weapon. A moment's panic quickened the tempo of his mainspring heart. Was that true? Had they—oh, no, no—had they removed his useless arms and replaced them with...with...somebody else's? Was he now a chimera, as twisted and wrong as any other Lost Boy?

He refocused his eyes. A moment's close inspection—without the repairs to his neck this might have been impossible—convinced him that these were still his arms. The arms he'd had on the day he first achieved consciousness. He couldn't find a trace of the hardened sheaths. Not a chip, not a crumb, even in the finest crevices. He wondered how they'd managed to chisel away the offending material so thoroughly.

He couldn't hide his relief. *I'm still me*, he thought. *They didn't merge me with somebody else.*

The others had departed while he was inert. They'd left Daniel's reactivation to Lilith.

He stood. It was disorienting when the slightest motion didn't cause his head to bob and sway. He'd put up with it for so long that it'd come to feel normal. And his hands! He could use his hands again!

Thank you, he said.

Lilith said, *You're lucky.* Her tone said something very different. The soft chatter of her gearing might have suggested regret, even remorse. *They had to tear this place apart before they found a suitable replacement for your missing flanges and the broken pinion in your neck.*

Daniel froze. They had done it to him after all: made him a chimera. Something grotesque. He carried part of a different mechanical inside him. A machine who had almost certainly come to a bad end.

What a fool he was. When the Clockmakers repaired a Clakker, they did it at the Forge, where they had plenty of new material at their disposal and could even fabricate at need. They never had to violate another mechanical's bodily integrity to fix another. But Neverland didn't have a Forge. So they resorted to using scavenged . . . parts . . . to repair themselves here.

What happened while I was out?

You were repaired, Lilith said. She headed for the ladder, snuffing out the alchemical lamps as she went. She paused beneath the hatch, touched her face. *And made a full citizen of Neverland.*

Daniel found Queen Mab standing on a rocky cleft overlooking the frozen river. The aurora had returned. Diaphanous streamers of emerald and cobalt flapped across the starry sky. The light shimmered differently from the variety of alloys in her body. It gave her a mottled appearance, like a human leper.

You look much better, she said. *Everything back in working order?*

He flexed his hands. *Yes. Thank you.*

Her body clicked as if to shrug off the gratitude.

We take care of our fellow mechanicals, here. Because we're free to do so.

They watched the aurora. The moon rose. Metal clanked in the valley. Daniel had so many questions. What did Mab and the Lost Boys do with their freedom? What was he supposed to do with himself? And why had these free Clakkers, this motley collection of rogues and runaways, become an assortment of atrocities?

He touched his neck, unconsciously mimicking Lilith. Mab saw this.

She said, *Do you enjoy riddles, Daniel?*

"I don't know any riddles," he said. It felt good, knowing he could once again speak aloud if he chose.

I do. Mab paced. She was strangely graceful on the legs that clearly were not part of her original body plan. He wondered how long it had taken her to acquire such grace, how long she'd been so horrifically disfigured, how it happened. She saw him examining her, but he couldn't help it. Only an extraordinary Clakker would have the will to keep existing after becoming the epitome of her own kind's greatest taboo. More than that, she'd built a community and rallied others to her when her very existence ought to have been anathema. Remarkable.

Imagine a ship, built by humans—

Humans don't build ships, he blurted.

They used to. He supposed that was true. Though it was hard to imagine how their makers had lived before they created Clakkers.

Still pacing, she said, *A stout and fearsome wooden warship. It circles the globe again and again, driven by one captain, then another, then another. It spends decades on the sea, ever on the move, never at port.* Daniel imagined he knew where this was going. Mab continued: *But occasionally, because of its hard service, pieces of the ship must be replaced. A plank here, a line there. A sail. A nail. The bowsprit. And so it goes. And sometimes the captain makes changes to improve the ship: replacing the cannon with stronger guns, or hiring better sailors. Until one day, many years after it was christened, long decades or even a century after its first voyage, not a single piece of the original ship remains. Every inch has been replaced.*

She stopped pacing and pivoted on one hoof to face him.

Imagine that, Daniel, and then tell me. Is it still the same ship? Or is it no longer the same, but a different ship sailing under the same name?

Daniel mulled this. Mab's mismatched eyes rotated in their sockets, bezels humming while she watched him.

Suppressing a rattle of revulsion, he said, *I think your riddle rests on a deliberate ambiguity. To a landlubber who has never set foot on open water, a ship is merely a tangible physical object, a finite collection of wood and rope. But to the sailor who calls it her home, the ship is the sum of its voyages and of her adventures. Its spirit. But your question is posed in such a way as to juxtapose these meanings.*

Yes, yes, you're very clever. Just answer the damn question, Mab said. Her blade arm vibrated with the *hum* of retensioned springs. Daniel took a step backward. He'd encountered military Clakkers after he'd been outed as a rogue in New Amsterdam, and had been lucky to escape without getting sheared in half. Did she actually use that thing? Jesus, what could she possibly need it for? Was she going to do it now? But after a moment's visible effort she calmed herself.

She asked, *Where does the ship reside: in the planks of the hull, or in the name?*

Daniel said, *The physical embodiment of the ship has changed. But its identity has not.*

The cables in her blade arm stopped thrumming. *Identity! That's the crux of it. This*—quicker than he could react, she tapped Daniel on the forehead where Lilith had jammed the key that put his consciousness on hiatus—*is what carries your identity and makes you the Clakker that you are. We are who we say we are, not the strange bodies our makers tried to give us. As long as the former is safe, who cares of the latter?*

In the private confines of his own thoughts, Daniel said to himself, *I do. My identity is what I choose it to be.* Aloud he said, *I see.* Although he didn't.

Speaking of safeguarding your precious identity, said Mab, *I have a gift for you.* From the cavity within her skeletal chest she produced a thin metal plate and a rubber tube similar to the ones that contained his former owners' dentifrice. The plate resembled the others he'd seen covering the Lost Boys' keyholes. The tube, it turned out, contained powerful adhesive. It didn't set as quickly as the French epoxy that had nearly led to Daniel's demise, but its origin couldn't be doubted.

Holding the plate over his keyhole with two fingertips, waiting for the glue to dry, he asked, *Where did you obtain a tube of French epoxy?*

In French, Mab said, "From the Inuit. They trade with the French, and then they trade with us."

"But what do you give them? What could a colony of free Clakkers have that would be of any value to them?"

"Labor," said Mab. "In five minutes you can do with your fingers things that might take a human days to achieve with a hammer and bone knife."

Daniel thought about this. Overhead, the aurora flared momentarily red. "While they spend a great deal of time traveling inside French territory." Mab turned to look at him. He concluded, "You pay them for information about New France."

"I see I was well informed about you, Daniel. You are a clever one."

Her words struck him like a thunderbolt. "Informed by whom? Once across the border, I never passed through any towns or villages. Who could have brought word of my approach? Damaged though I was, I traveled faster than any human contrivance over this terrain." He'd heard of dogsleds and hoped to someday see one.

But she went on as if he hadn't spoken. "Clever and ruthless. It's too bad about the airship. What an ally that would have been! But surely you knew from the start it was an ill-fated beast. I do wonder how you subdued it."

The demise of the Clakker airship was spectacular and unusual. It wasn't hard to imagine the tale had spread from within Nieuw Nederland to New France and points elsewhere. But Mab didn't know, or pretended not to know, about the bauble he'd inadvertently received from Pastor Visser. The glass with the power to break the geasa. Nevertheless, Mab knew much for somebody living in the snowy wilderness hundreds of miles from the ragged fringes of New France.

Daniel asked, "How could you possibly know so much about my movements?"

A sweep of her arm encompassed the valley and their kin in the far distance. "You didn't think this was the entirety of Neverland, did you? That in a quarter of a millennium less than three dozen of us have been so lucky? No, Daniel. We have brothers and sisters spread throughout the human world."

"Free Clakkers living undercover in our makers' world."

"Yes."

CHAPTER

13

I don't suppose," said Berenice, shivering within her bundle of oiled furs, "that either of you will tell me what the fuck is going on."

She said it in Dutch. No response. Repeated it in French. No response. She would have repeated it in the cling-clang language of the Clakkers, if only she had the proper metal bits to bash together. As it was, she'd be frozen as solid as the mechanicals' skeletons sooner rather than later; it was bloody cold on the open ocean in the middle of winter. Even without the wind and sea spray. Her silent kidnappers rowed so quickly they made a blur of the oars. (She wondered what they'd been fashioned from. Regular wooden oars would have shattered an hour into their cruise. Regular metal oarlocks would have glowed a dull red from the friction heat.) The prow of their little boat skimmed above the water, their wake a pair of foamy feathers on the steel-gray sea. Between the swells, and the sea winds, and the fanning of the oars, Berenice's mound of water-resistant furs had decided to abandon the fight.

One of the Clakkers had pulled the cloak and blankets from a space in the prow and tossed it to her the moment they disembarked from the much larger ships. She tried to take her mind off the damp chill by estimating her life expectancy. After thorough analysis of the situation she concluded it was Very Fucking Short. But still longer than it might have been. So:

"Look. If you'd wanted me dead, you wouldn't have interfered. My chances were looking just the tiniest bit grim back there. So, well, thanks for that." She patted the cloak. "Additionally, if you'd wanted to kill me, you wouldn't have given me this. You could have watched me freeze to death." She started shivering again. "Maybe you still will."

She sat in the prow, van Breugel's satchel on her lap, facing a pair of impassive and unreadable servitor visages. But she did notice something strange about their bodies. Both machines sported minute scoring in the metal immediately around their keyholes. The scratches didn't range widely or deeply enough to alter or damage the sigils. They were so faint as to be almost invisible to all but continued scrutiny. Which, here in a rowboat in the middle of the Goddamned ocean, was her main diversion. The work was so fine, and so tightly confined to the margin between the keyhole and the innermost ring of the alchemical spiral, that it suggested precision work. Work carried out—or inflicted?—upon both of these disturbing mechanicals. The scratches looked like scrape or pry marks, as though something had been removed from their keyholes.

The blur of the oars propelled their little boat over a particularly large swell; Berenice left her stomach behind when they descended into the trailing trough. It wasn't a stormy sea, but mere humans couldn't have rowed through it. Her new traveling companions rowed like demons, apparently to put distance between themselves and the mated ships. Whatever geasa they ultimately served, they were compelled to do so in secrecy. Who compelled them so, and why? To work under the nose of the Verderers like this—not to mention shattering the neck of a Guildman—suggested an internecine conflict. Was this a schism within the Guild? Or between the Throne and the Guild? Were there warring factions within the Clockmakers? Jesus. If not for her Still Very Short life expectancy, she might have felt a twinge of excitement.

"Where the hell are we going? Can you at least tell me that, or how long it'll take to get there? Because I'm enjoying this cruise, truly I am, and I pray I'll have time to write some post-cards before it's over." No response. Finally she asked the question she'd been dreading. "Did Bell send you to find me?"

"We serve the queen."

All right. Now she was getting somewhere. This made even less sense than everything else that had happened in the last few hours, but at least it was progress.

She couldn't tell which of the machines had spoken, but in all practical respects it hardly mattered. Addressing them both, she said, "Well, I hate to break it to you, but so did the guys whose necks you wrung like a pair of damp dish towels. If Margreet wants me this badly, she—and you—could have left well enough alone. Her minions had already caught me." She hugged herself. Her chest and stomach muscles hurt from the effort to suppress the shivering. When it felt like she could speak without her teeth chattering again, she added, "And at least then I wouldn't be freezing my ass off in the middle of the Goddamned ocean."

"We do not serve the Brasswork Throne. We serve the queen."

What the hell did that mean? Had she been abducted by a pair of malfunctioning murder machines?

"Well, whoever this queen is, she wields the power to impose extremely powerful geasa on you. I'm thinking a high-level Clockmaker. Because that"—she jerked her head toward the stern, indicating the ocean behind them and, somewhere, the ships they'd eluded—"was some of the strangest shit I've ever seen."

"We do not serve the Guild. We serve the queen."

She rocked back in her seat. And just what the hell did *that* mean? How could they serve neither Throne nor Guild? Every Clakker ever forged carried that involuntary fealty stamped in the deepest recesses of its ticktock heart. Unless...

What if there was a *third* entity at work? A hitherto unknown third branch of the Dutch hegemony, one neither Throne nor Guild. Such could explain the riddle of their allegiance. But it would require the existence of a group of which Berenice had never heard the slightest whisper. Nor had any of her predecessors, insofar as there was nothing in the Talleyrand journals to suggest it. Was the Dutch hegemony a triad?

Preposterous. *Every* Clakker served the Guild. If it came down to brass tacks, those oily Clockmakers would even put themselves ahead of the Brasswork Throne. They'd fiddle the hierarchical metageasa to position themselves on top in a crisis of conflicting loyalties.

Easier to conclude these Clakkers were liars in addition to murderers. Their master wielded incredible power, ranked extremely high within the hierarchical metageasa. A member of the royal family could do this, or a Guild Archmaster.

Shit.

"Every Clakker serves the Guild, whether it wants to or not. And how the hell can you serve the queen without serving the Brasswork Throne?"

Berenice winced. In trying to speak past her chattering teeth she'd bitten her tongue. She tasted warm metal and her body's own salt.

"We don't serve Margreet," said one.

"We serve Mab," said the other.

The bottom fell out of Berenice's stomach, but not because the boat seesawed over another swell. Maybe her third-faction theory wasn't a bullshit fever dream after all, no matter how much she wished it so.

"Who in the seven hells is Mab?"

"She is the one who would know your intentions."

"And so you dragooned me into joining this idyllic excursion to the middle of the Goddamned ocean just to hear me out. That makes all kinds of sense." She swallowed. "And if you don't like my answers?"

"We are, as you note, in the middle of the Goddamned ocean. It is a very wide ocean, and a very deep ocean."

"Why go that far? You could just twist my head off like you did to poor van Breugel and his colleague."

One said, "One mustn't wind stems with impunity lest it lose its thrill."

The other added, "And thereby grow tedious."

Berenice said, "Yes, that would be quite a shame."

"And incidentally, with regard to those particular stems," said the Clakker on the right, "by now Captain Barendregt and his crew believe you ordered us to the task."

Its sinister companion agreed. "That man does not like you." Pantomiming pity, it shook its head.

Berenice's shivering redoubled the effort to strain every muscle in her arms, back, stomach, chest. Icy fear struck so deep that no mound of furs could warm it.

"I notice your manner has changed since we left the ship. You don't speak with the usual deference." *It reminds me of another mechanical I once knew. But he wasn't a murderer, and his only desire was to be free. You two, on the other hand…*

"That must be troubling for you. Do something worthy of deference and we'll consider it."

Despite the chill, a single rivulet of sweat trickled down the curve of her spine to land at the small of her back. She burped. Her breath smelled of the smoked cod she'd eaten for breakfast that morning, but tasted much the worse for wear. *What if...*

What if there were a group of rogue Clakkers, machines completely free of any geas and immune to compulsion, living secretly among their kin? Moving invisibly within the world that built them? At any other time she would have considered it preposterous, but her present circumstances lent a unique perspective. Jax and Lilith had both sought to flee the Dutch-speaking world as soon as they achieved Free Will. It was difficult to fathom why rogues would willingly stay behind. But their motivations were immaterial: If this mad hypothesis were true, it would be the greatest secret in the Western world since Huygens's miracle breakthrough a quarter of a millennium ago.

A secret easily worth killing to maintain.

She shivered uncontrollably now.

I'm not a bumbling interloper who uncovered their secret by accident, she reminded herself. *They revealed themselves to me. And risked much to do so.*

"You wonder about my intentions. I wonder similarly about the pair of you."

"No doubt," said the machine sinister. It (he? she?) proved the more loquacious of the duo. "But you're not the one in the stronger bargaining position, madam. Let's start with something simple. We notice you managed to relieve the ship's horologist of that satchel." It nodded to the bundle on her lap. She hadn't peered inside since taking it from van Breugel during her failed escape attempt. "What do you intend to do with it?"

It had a point, the shiny bastard. *Start slowly. Test the waters. They know my name. What else?*

She tested their knowledge: "My sworn duty is to protect its contents. My work for the Verderer's Office is crucial to the security of the state."

"That would be true if you were a Verderer. But we think you stole your pendant."

"Just as you stole a load of keys bound for the same house where you were being held."

Sacré nom de Dieu! They knew so much.

"And you've been masquerading ever since."

"For that," said the machine dexter, "you should be commended. It's a difficult act to pull off."

Sinister said, "We think it's altogether more likely that you're a French spy."

Berenice winced. These damnable machines had her over a barrel.

"I think it's altogether likely that you're a pair of smug, chromium-plated assholes."

Sinister and Dexter exchanged a rapid volley of pocketwatch noises. The boat vibrated. She didn't try to follow the conversation. One said, "We'll take that as confirmation."

She slumped. Her ass had gone numb hours ago. Feeling the first tendrils of defeat burning like acid in her veins, she said, "How in the hell do you know so much?"

With distressing ease, it turned out. They, or whomever they worked for, had caught wind of her capture on the night the Forge burned. The traitor and defector from New France, the duc de Montmorency, had outed her name and her Talleyrand identity to her captors. Some time later a major emergency erupted at a secluded Guild property upriver of New Amsterdam. That night a mail carriage traveling the same road failed to reach its destination. The next morning, a woman bearing the emblem of the Verderer's Office exerted her influence to board the first ship leaving Nieuw Nederland and divert it from its original route...

When they put it like that, she had to admit, the pieces fit. Shitcakes.

"This is all circumstantial."

"Agreed."

Berenice sighed. "You know what happened at the estate house."

"Loosely."

"Did Bell survive?"

After a moment's *chittering* with his comrade, Sinister said, "Unknown."

"I wasn't alone on the night the Forge burned. There was a servitor. Jax. Did he escape?"

Dexter said, "Mab knows of the one you describe."

"I was helping him," she said.

"We don't care about your national politics or personal allegiances. New France makes many noises about its sympathy toward the enslaved, but it has never done anything to improve our situation."

"I'm no friend to your makers."

"Irrelevant. The Catholic Church has been vocally opposed to our makers' practices for hundreds of years, too, but it hasn't made a difference."

"Look," said Berenice, "give us a fucking break. It's a tough nut to crack, all right? We're not sitting around with our thumbs up our asses. We're trying to survive."

They stopped rowing. The boat skimmed across the choppy water, prow slowly settling as it coasted to a stop among the waves. The sudden reappearance of their arms, previously blurred, was disconcerting. Berenice smelled the promise of rain, or probably snow, under the darkening sky. "You're posing as a Clockmaker to steal Guild secrets. What do you intend to do with them?"

The truth bounded from Berenice's numb lips before she had a chance to reel it in: "I want to change the world."

The rowboat slalomed over another wave. It slewed, skewwhiff, into the trough. Berenice slid free of her perch, righted herself. The Clakkers didn't. They were as statues bolted to the hull. A rising wind sent ripples knocking against the wooden hull. Berenice watched the machines. They watched her. Now, in the gloaming, she could no longer see the scratches haloing their keyholes.

"Intriguing," said Dexter.

"Indeed," said Sinister.

In unison, they picked up the oars. They rowed through the night.

CHAPTER
14

They emerged from the water like an army of burnished Venuses. But these were no demure Botticelli nudes riding sea-shells: The single-minded fiends walked along the riverbed to burst through the ice and swarm the frozen mudflats under the piers of Marseilles-in-the-West. The thunderous cracking of their emergence rattled teeth and windowpanes. Floes the size of hay wagons went bobbing down the Saint Lawrence, tinkling against each other like a sackful of broken crockery.

The Dutch held the waterfront. The defenders had ceded Île de Vilmenon's shoreline without a struggle. It couldn't be defended. Not without turning the entire island into a citadel.

First ice. Then fire.

Longchamp watched helplessly as the foremost clock-work troops doused themselves with pitch and set themselves alight. From the distance they looked like herky-jerky effigies. Through the spyglass, they looked like men whose flesh had burned away to reveal the skeleton beneath.

"Heaven preserve us," said the marshal. "They're doing it again."

"Might as well. It worked so fucking well last time."

A few of the flaming machines sprinted along the docks, their every footstep setting the planks alight. Soon the entire waterfront was ablaze: By tomorrow morning, Marseille-in-the-West's primary connection to the rest of New France would be nothing but ash. Meanwhile, the rest of the arson squad sprinted like blazing comets through the avenues, boulevards, and squares of Marseilles-in-the-West.

No fire brigade rushed out to extinguish the blaze. The men and women of the brigades had been conscripted weeks ago; now they stood on the outer wall, crying as though their tears might extinguish the flames.

What little ice remained along the shore melted in the furnace heat of the burning docks.

The burning Clakkers weren't the only ones running through the steets of Marseilles. The stragglers, the ones who hadn't made it inside the walls, or who had disregarded the warnings out of an overabundance of faith, now ran for their lives. They ran from the flames, and the machines that wielded them. But no human could outrun this fate. Some succumbed to smoke and flame; others to alchemical fists.

The defenders were powerless to do anything but watch their city burn. Against the Clakkers, the only defense was high walls and clever chemistry. There wasn't enough chemistry in the world to defend a single bare acre beyond the walls.

Much of what burned was fresh lumber harvested from the surrounding forests just this past summer to facilitate the rebuilding of the capital of New France. The tulips must have salted their pitch with a dash of black alchemy, for the unseasoned wood virtually exploded into flame at the machines' lightest touch. The conflagration launched billows of smoke into the sky. Roiling plumes of black and ashen gray, firelit a baleful vermilion like the Devil's eyes, repainted the sky from blue to dirty umber, and rendered the sun a hazy smudge.

It wasn't long before the world smelled like a fireplace grate. As far as a mile away, the heat stung naked skin. Ashfall coated the walkways of the keep.

Flames consumed the Marseilles semaphore towers. One by one, they ignited like a chain of birthday candles. The segmented signal arms swung freely, buffeted by the updraft of their own conflagration. They looked like madmen capering as they burned to death. Even without a spyglass, Longchamp could see towers blazing on the distant hills. The semaphore network had ever been vulnerable, the isolated and far-flung outposts virtually impossible to safeguard. Anticipating this, the defenders of the keep had dismantled the Spire's own semaphore before the siege began, and used the lumber to build the crane gantries.

Livestock had been herded into pens just inside the outer walls. Now the ruddy light of apocalypse stirred the bison to mournful lowing.

Meanwhile, those mechanicals not tasked with terrorizing, murdering, and displacing thousands of innocent civilians marched upon the keep. They marched through the burning city and fanned out across the island. They marched across glades and frozen streams, across fields and through copses of winter-bare oak. From east, south, north, and west, they converged upon the star-shaped perimeter of the Vauban fortifications. A golden band girded the Last Redoubt of the King of France. The high-pitched *chug-chug-chug* of epoxy cannon compressors pierced the hissing and popping of the burning city. And faintly audible beneath it all, the ticktocking hearts of their unkillable enemies beating in perfect clockwork synchrony. The Devil's own tattoo.

❧

A pair of Clakkers emerged from the front lines. They retreated several hundred yards. Then they sprinted across the field and leaped when they reached the ditches, hurling themselves into the air and soaring toward the wall. One from the south, one from the north. Cannon fired. A glistening bubble of epoxy and fixative intercepted the southbound machine at the apex of its trajectory. The impact stole enough of its momentum that it fell short. It slammed into the scarp and rolled into the moat, coming to rest like an inert clockwork bug trapped in emerald amber. The other set of gunners miscalculated the parabola. Their shot blew harmlessly under the Clakker's upraised feet. Ranks of mechanicals deftly sidestepped the splash zone. The waste of precious chemicals hurt Longchamp's heart. The northbound mechanical landed on the wall with a resounding *chank* like a miner's pickax on granite. Defenders opened the stopcocks on the nozzles built into the machicolations. A torrent flooded over the climbing machine, gluing it to the wall and halting its progress.

The real attack hadn't begun. The Dutch preferred first to let the fear sink deep. To give it time to fester into despair. So for now they confined themselves to small forays against the outer walls. A prolonged, desultory probing of the keep's defenses.

Another flight of messenger pigeons emerged from their roosts within the Spire. Longchamp shook his head. He watched through slitted eyes—the smoke stung like a fucking snakebite, but that was nothing compared with the pain of a hot cinder wedged under the eyelid—as the confused trio rose into the hellish morning. The slapping of their wings sounded like applause. Though the sun and setting moon were all but invisible, a single circuit of the tower was enough for them to find their bearings, guided by whatever natural magics the Lord had granted them. Longchamp counted. *Un…deux… trois…quatre…*

The birds exploded. Miracles of God's design one instant,

gristly puffs of scarlet the next. Singed feathers fell upon the Porter's Prayer, twirling like maple seeds. Seconds later the guns' report reached the defenders on the wall. It sounded like a single shot to Longchamp's fallible human ears. The Clakker sharpshooters had timed their shots to hit all three birds at the same instant. Just for the intimidating, demoralizing spectacle.

No messages would make it out of the besieged keep. The defenders were on their own. Did it matter? From whence could help find them? The last message to arrive before the mechanical sharpshooters started perforating the birds was a hasty plaintext lamenting the fall of Québec City.

The marshal general handed his spyglass to Longchamp. Then he retied the damp handkerchief over his nose and mouth. To his credit he'd eschewed one of the face masks with the charcoal filter. There weren't enough masks or filters for all the defenders, so he'd refused to deprive the men and women fated to do the real work. Longchamp didn't wear one, either. His throat stung just as much as his eyes. But the masks muffled his voice. It would be hard enough to make himself heard over the cacophony when the attackers surged forward in earnest.

He couldn't believe the motherfuckers had burned the city again. No, scratch that. Of course he could.

Squinting, he brought the glass to his eye and scanned the enemy's layout. Longchamp swept his gaze past the bastions' triangular protrusions and the crews manning the epoxy cannon within. He looked beyond ravelin and demilune bristling with sand sprayers and harpoon throwers powered by ropes of arcane chemical elasticity. Just beyond the range of the largest goop sprayers, hundreds of Clakkers stood in precise rows, motionless as statues. The besiegers' camp was a garden of statuary.

Last time, the attackers had been content to take their time. They'd attacked the walls, but not before letting time and hunger soften the defenders. They'd even lobbed leaflets over the walls, seeking to entice citizens and soldiers alike to sell out their defenders. Treachery was always the fastest way to open a walled city. But when the besiegers' labor was tireless and preternaturally patient, time did not favor the defenders. The mechanicals could stand at attention in the merciless elements for years on end if so ordered. They could stand there for a century, awaiting the order to advance, a silent promise to slaughter any who attempted to leave, to the nth generation. They could wait for starvation and disease to gut the defenders. And unlike a siege camp comprising thousands of human soldiers, the Clakker army was impervious to disease. They could take Marseilles-in-the-West merely by standing out there, ranks upon ranks of deadly statues.

The attackers could come over the walls, they could smash their way through the walls, or they could dig under the walls. Sorties tasked with the first two objectives would come soon enough, once the tulips had a feel for the defenders' disposition. Longchamp scanned the enemy lines for signs of digging, even though it was pointless. A Clakker detail could start out in the forest, or on the other side of the island, for that matter. No need to start the tunnel in the middle of the camp. They might have started weeks ago. Longchamp had sprinkled some of the older and more feeble "winners" of the conscription lottery with bowls of water along the skirt just inside the outer wall. A good spotter could tell the difference between rippling caused by the defenders' cannon and rippling caused by enemy earthworks underfoot. The fortifications went quite deep, deeper than any human sapper team was likely to dig. But the tulips' slaves didn't breathe, didn't sleep, didn't eat, didn't get the bloody flux.

He studied the enemy camp. They had erected a pavilion in the far distance. With the spyglass he could just make out the mechanicals hauling timber and cartloads of what might have been rock into the secret enclosure. The timber made sense if they were digging there; they'd need props to shore up the tunnel at regular intervals. The cartloads of rock did not. The marshal had noticed it, too.

Crouched behind an embrasure, he pointed with his baton. "God help us all. They're excavating a tunnel."

"Doubt it. If the bastards were digging, they'd be hauling cartloads *out*."

"Then what are they doing out there?"

"No idea." The captain gave the pavilion, and the people standing next to it, another once-over before returning the spyglass. A single singed pigeon feather drifted through his sightline. Using the height of the human overseers to establish a sense of scale, he estimated the pavilion was at least twenty feet high and half again as long. And was that smoke rising from vents in the canvas roof? "It's going to be big. Whatever that fucking thing turns out to be."

"Do we have anything that could lob some pitch out there?" They didn't actually use pitch any longer. The chemists had a sackful of five-livre words for the sticky fuel that burned even underwater. Wonderful stuff, but pointless when it came to Clakker infantry. As the ashes of the city demonstrated, coating the demons in burning pitch didn't slow them; it made them twice as dangerous.

"If we did, I'd have ordered it done by now."

The marshal frowned, nodded. Behind him, metal glinted. Movement on the field. Longchamp turned to watch. Even his unaided, smoke-stung eyes could see some kind of shake-up among the metal infantry. Longchamp pointed. "Look! They're starting."

The marshal slammed the metal endcap of his baton on the stone battlement hard enough to throw a spark. "This is it, then."

Gaps had appeared in the ranks of mechanical infantry. As before, a single Clakker occupied each empty file. And just as they'd done moments earlier when probing the defenses, they retreated several hundred yards for a good run-up. But this time dozens of mechanicals prepared to fling themselves at the walls.

"Still testing our gunners," said the marshal. As if that wasn't something worthy of concern.

The uneasy feeling in Longchamp's gut told him differently. The purpose of this morning's sorties had been to gauge the speed, range, and reliability of the epoxy cannon. One or two mechanicals at a time could do that. No, they'd learned what they needed from those experiments.

Having reached their starting points, the runners sank into themselves, pulling themselves into maximum compression. Longchamp turned, but the Spire eclipsed his view of the enemy dispositions to the west. He snatched the spyglass from the marshal's hand, sprinted along the banquette past the corner of the next bastion. Yanked the spyglass open and pushed it to his eye. Scanned the field.

Whatever this was, it was happening all around the perimeter of the outer keep. Last time, coordinated attacks on the extended perimeter came as a tidal wave of magicked metal. What did the tulips intend to accomplish with just a few dozen of their clockwork beasts?

Someone gave an order. All at once around the outer keep, the unleashed mechanicals bounded forward. They kicked up a muddy spray of snow and frozen earth as they blurred toward the moat. None took a straight path down the center of the empty file. Each swerved back and forth like a drunken oxcart driver but a hundred times faster, concealing the exact location and direction of the leap until the last moment. They were most vulnerable during those precious few seconds when they were aloft and unable to steer, humble subjects of wind and gravity.

They jumped. Longchamp imagined he could hear the wind whistling through their skeletal bodies.

The gunners fired. Roughly two-thirds of the teams hit their mark on the first shot. Tangled globs of Dutch horology and French chemistry slammed against the counterscarp to drop into the moat like coins dropped in an orphan's secret piggy bank. The teams that missed their targets used the machicolations to coat them where they landed. The assault had been neutralized in barely more than the few seconds it took the Clakkers to hurtle across the moat.

Head down, Longchamp crossed the length of the curtain wall to stand directly over one of the encased mechanicals. He still held the marshal's spyglass. The gunnery team tried to conceal its relief with forced nonchalance.

"Stinking tulips," said the spotter.

"For France, New and Old!" said the shooter. He spat over the battlement for good measure. Luckily no clockwork sharp-shooter decided to put a bullet in his eye at that moment; showing himself like that was a foolish show of bravado. The enemy's attention was trained on the immobilized Clakkers.

Down in the moat, something moved.

Longchamp said, "Both of you, cram a sock into your worth-less gob holes right fucking now."

He crouched on all fours, hunched over the machicolation like a drunk at a privy. He used the spyglass to get a better look at the Clakker entombed at the base of the scarp.

The glassy cocoon vibrated. Fell over. Hissed.

Melted.

Sacré nom de Dieu.

"Mother Mary, save us," said the captain.

He blinked teary, smoke-stung eyes. But the nightmare vision wouldn't be dispelled. The granite-hard epoxy sheath that had encased the Clakker sagged like overly soft candle wax. The latest and greatest invention—birthed from the minds of the very best French chemists, never seen by the tulips before today—had as much chance of imprisoning these mechanicals as a wad of wet crêpe paper.

The metal monster inside the cocoon became visible again. Its body discharged some kind of mist.

Oh, Lord. Berenice was right, he realized. *They know how to counteract our defenses.* He crossed himself. *Mother Mary, please pray for us poor sinners. Holy Father, deliver us from this evil.*

He leaped to his feet.

"Incoming mechanicals! I repeat, we have METAL ON THE WALLS!"

The nearest heliograph relay coded his warning into a rapid sequence of flashes. Today the signalers used lamp oil rather than the sun, which hung red and swollen like a bullethole in the sky within the smoky haze and windborn ashes of Marseilles-in-the-West. The message flashed up the Spire, and then back down to all the heliograph stations around the outer wall. In seconds Longchamp's warning ricocheted throughout the defenders on the perimeter.

Clakkers in the moat. It was designed to slow the demons during a regular siege, when they came as a swarm but fully vulnerable to the chemical defenses. Rather than fill the moat with quick-set adhesives that might only trap a few machines—and then solidify and form a convenient platform for launching attacks directly from the base of the wall—the defenders could flood it with a special high-viscosity sludge that could gum up precision clockworks. But in the cold depths of winter the goop would eventually thicken and solidify, so they'd held off flooding the moat until the swarm happened. Longchamp saw now that that had been a mistake. Could they flood it in time? Another glance told him the answer: not a chance. Still, they had to try.

"Flood the moat! I said PISS IN THAT DITCH!"

The heliographs flickered. A low rumble shook the wall. Massive pumps buried under the outer keep burbled to life. Dozens of nozzles at the base of the scarp irised open to discharge a thick black ooze that looked like tar and smelled like violets. It didn't gurgle or splash. Instead, it sounded like somebody beating wet wool with a wooden bat to felt it when the ooze slapped against the smooth tiles lining the moat. If they were lucky, one or two of the demons might catch a few droplets in a crucial mechanism.

Longchamp ran along the line, bellowing. Several bastions farther down the wall, Sergeant Chrétien hollered the same orders and encouragements to the men at the battlements.

"Incoming mechanicals! These scuttling rust buckets think they can crash our party, eh? Come on, you lovely dogs, and show them our best French hospitality!"

The defenders' faces showed the same fear that threatened to freeze Longchamp's heart solid. He knew what they were thinking while they fingered their weapons and prayed to the Holy Trinity to deliver them from evil: *It's not supposed to happen like this. We're supposed to hold out longer before they make the walls. Too soon. Too soon. I'm not supposed to die yet. Not yet. Not this hour.*

Longchamp forced the treacherous fear aside. It was like rolling a boulder uphill. "Ready the lubricant hoses!" Behind him, wheels skidded across the stones of the wall as a team raced to swap out the epoxy tanks feeding the machicolations with tanks of a special ultralow-viscosity lubricant. It wouldn't keep the mechanicals from gaining the top, but it might slow them. A quick glance showed him trios of soldiers making similarly rapid exchanges across the wall. The signals teams were in top form today.

He bellowed, "Give me a count, you dogs! I have one mechanical in sight! ONE, COMING TO MEET ITS END!"

Somewhere to his left, the count continued: "TWO! Cursing the day their makers were born!"

"Three!"

The din swallowed the rest of the count. But the count wasn't the point. Getting these women and men to focus, to turn the job into simple arithmetic, that was the point. It wasn't about facing down a nigh-unstoppable killing machine. It was about reducing the number of attackers to zero. Zero was the goal. Zero meant they'd see another sunrise.

"Ready bolas! Ready picks and hammers!"

He readied his own. The hammer had a reassuring mass. Over the years, the oil in his fingers had polished individual spots into the oaken haft. It fit his hand and only his hand. *This is my hammer. There are many like it, but this one is mine.* He peered again at the monster at the base of the scarp.

The Goddamned thing had shed its chemical prison. It flexed its arms and legs. The pumps convulsed, pulsing the black ooze into the moat like a drunk losing his dinner. Tiny droplets splashed the machine's brassy carapace. Tendrils of goop oozed toward its feet.

The Clakker leaped. It cleared the moat in a single bound, pinning itself to the outer wall with fingers and talon toes made impossibly strong by dark magics. Granite cracked. Shouts went up all around the wall.

"Oil, now!"

A torrent of lubricant went cascading down the wall just as the mechanical hurled itself a few yards higher. It landed in the middle of the torrent but managed to give itself a single anchor point. Both legs and one arm scrabbled against the slickened stones. But it could pierce rocks and gouge mortar with its fingers. Its hands became pitons. It steadied itself.

And it climbed.

CHAPTER
15

The mechanical dialect of Neverland differed slightly from what Daniel had known in the Central Provinces. Applause here was a quirky snapping of the wrist and elbow joints. The secret native language of Daniel's enslaved kin rarely utilized the arms, for rarely were their hands free, their arms not laboring. Daniel heard this strange combination now. The applause was for him.

Though she knew much of the tale, owing to her agents living among the humans, Mab had gathered the Lost Boys in a natural amphitheater and coaxed Daniel to take the center, so that he could share the tale of his own journey to Neverland. This, he gathered, was a tradition. One they sometimes went decades without indulging. His arrival so soon after Lilith was a special treat.

Mab crouched on the lowest terrace, near the center. Daniel tried to read her. But the profound oddness of her body—*It's not grotesque*, he chided himself. *It isn't repugnant; they just do things differently here*—thwarted him. The chimera Queen of Neverland was a cipher.

(*And what am I now? Whence came the parts to repair my*

broken pinion and replace my missing flanges? Am I also a chimerical beast, a grotesque amalgam of clockwork kinsmen? Don't think about it. Don't think about it. Just don't.)

By the silver light of the moon, the shimmering glow of the aurora, and the occasional blaze of a shooting star, Daniel told his story.

It began on the day of Adam's execution, he said.

(*Clockmakers lie!* cried several Lost Boys, not quite a chorus. *Through their fragile teeth*, said Mab.)

He expected and even looked forward to questions about what he saw that morning; the mechanicals at the New Amsterdam pier had practically swarmed him upon learning he had been an actual witness. But the Lost Boys acted as though they already knew this part of the tale. Had Mab's agents been in Huygens Square that morning? How far was her reach?

My owners sent me on an errand that morning. Daniel told them of Jax's meeting with Pastor Visser, the seemingly harmless delivery he'd instructed Jax to undertake, and the concealed alchemical glass that sundered his bonds.

I would very much like, said Mab, her body noise cutting through the *rattle* of mechanical muttering, *to see this vitreous miracle.*

And I would very much like to show it to you. Alas, to skip ahead quite a bit, it was destroyed when the Forge burned, said Daniel. Or so he assumed; he didn't know.

The truth he did know was more complicated. He had lost a pineal glass with the power to free mechanicals, but it wasn't the bauble he'd unwittingly received from Visser. *That* had gone with the Frenchwoman, Berenice, when they entered the Forge. She'd argued it might save her life if things went wrong. True enough, but he wouldn't have agreed if they hadn't already transformed the pineal glass of an inert military mechanical. The transformation had turned that piece luminous, so it made more sense for him to smuggle it within the recesses of his torso. This was the glass he lost in the New Amsterdam Forge, in the mad scramble to escape a Stemwinder, though not before it had saved his life.

Poor Dwyre...

Daniel had already decided to gloss over these parts of the story, knowing of Lilith's history with Berenice.

He continued his tale. The Lost Boys booed the parts they considered boring, which were more or less the parts they already knew. And, superficially at least, they knew much of his story. His flight had been catastrophically public, and for this they criticized him. After all, agents of Neverland moved undetected among the humans.

The mores here were different, even repugnant at first. But clearly there was value here, if the Lost Boys were willing to give up this freedom for months or even years for the greater good.

Daniel tried to infuse the story with a sense of his feelings as his plight unraveled. He couldn't know if it had the intended effect until the murder of the airship nearly set off a riot. The Lost Boys jumped to their feet, clanking, clattering, tocking, and ticking with such fervor that they seemed ready to charge back across the taiga, hundreds of leagues, to assault those who had murdered their majestic kin. Mab and the Lost Boys honored the memory of that poor beast. It deserved no less.

They appreciated the tedium of his long, wet walk along the bottom of the North River. And they applauded when he described how he convinced a pair of humans—the wife and son of a disgraced banker—to aid him. His audience reacted most favorably to the episodes wherein a humble servitor bested humans. And it fell into rapt silence when he finally reached a terminus of the *ondergrondse grachten*. They knew the canalmasters had died soon after Daniel's arrival, but only he knew what had transpired within the bakery. He described the meeting where they debated what to do with him, and the knock at the door that caused a panicked rush to shoo him into the alley behind the bakery. He described the noises that soon followed: the yelling, the *crack* of bone, the wet, meaty *thump* of bodies beaten and tossed aside.

Just moments after the murders, he met the assailant.

I couldn't have been more shocked, he said, *if Queen Mab herself had stood on the other side of that door.* The attempted levity fell flat. Daniel pressed on. *For it was Pastor Visser himself! Bruised, bandaged, but unmistakable.*

A low chorus of ticktock murmurs spread through the assembled Lost Boys. The stone terraces amplified the echoes and elevated their surprise to a clockwork crescendo. Visser's reappearance in the story had even caught Mab by surprise, if the quirk of her head was any indication.

But, of course, he did not recognize me. *To him I was just another servitor.*

(Rattles of indignation from the Lost Boys: *Of course he didn't know you*, they said. *Typical human*, said others. And others still lamented, *We're all the same to them.*)

Ah, said Daniel. He'd aimed for this reaction. *That's where the story takes a strange turn.* He cast his gaze across the assembled Clakkers. The dent in Lilith's forehead gathered the aurora light the way a beggar's hands gathered disdain. It surprised Daniel to see her; she hadn't warmed to him since his faux pas about Berenice.

For he had changed. This was not the compassionate pastor from the Nieuwe Kerk. Before me stood a murderer. After dispatching the canalmasters with his bare hands he'd ransacked the bakery, even mangling his own fingers in the effort to tear up the floorboards. More clicking rippled around the amphitheater. Humans were notoriously weak, notoriously fragile, and well known for their utter lack of stoicism.

Mab's posture changed. She stiffened, as if every spring in her body had been replaced with a steel rod. Even the alien rhythm of her mainspring heart fell quiet. Murmurs rippled through the assembled Lost Boys, like a pebble thrown into a pond. Some, he noticed, had begun inching away from Mab, as though she were the epicenter of a coming tragedy. A few seated on the highest terrace almost directly behind and above Mab quietly departed, as though they'd abruptly lost interest in Daniel's tale. Those who lingered, which was most of the resident population of Neverland, cocked their heads as if to keep one eye on Daniel and the other on Queen Mab.

Feeling there was no choice, and wanting to finish the story anyway—it was his story, after all—he continued: *Visser invoked the Empire's Arms and a Clockmaker's pendant, and attempted to requisition me on the spot for the Verderer's Office! He demanded I forget everything I'd seen up to then, and—*

Mab stood. Her voice cut through the agitated chattering like a sword through aspic. Silence fell across the amphitheater so abruptly that it echoed. This was an uneasy silence, akin to overly rowdy festivalgoers on Huygens's Birthday glimpsing a Stemwinder. In an instant she became the only source of sound under the starry sky. She spoke in Dutch.

"Bandages, you say?"

"Yes," said Daniel, utterly confused. She'd seized on the least interesting detail. Not what he'd expected, given the buildup. "Around his head."

Mab scanned the assembly. Her gaze paused on Lilith, who returned a deferential and very human nod. Mab beckoned two Clakkers from the front row. "Ruth, Ezra, join us, won't you?" Then she said, "Our new brother's tale is concluded. Let us remind him that his travails were not in vain. Welcome home, Daniel!"

The others filed away, repeating Mab's hail with varying

degrees of sincerity. The pair she'd selected joined her and Daniel at the center of the amphitheater. They walked like dogs called by an angry master. He hadn't met these two before. Their chimerisms weren't as extensive as some of the other Lost Boys', though their appearance unsettled him.

To Daniel, Mab said, "Well, then. Tell us everything you know of this Pastor Visser."

"I know no more than what I've said."

"Come now, Daniel. What of the contours of his face? The smell of his sweat? The arch of his brows and the timbre of his voice? How can we find this man if we can't recognize him?"

In a flash he understood why the pair she'd chosen acted so reticent. They were being tapped to return to the human world. And didn't seem particularly excited about it.

We're going to search for him? Daniel asked.

Heavens, no! said Mab. *I'm not. And you're not. But* they *are.* She clapped her hands on Ezra and Ruth. Ruth flinched from Mab's blade arm.

Amazing, said Daniel, desperately trying to lighten the funereal mood. *And courageous!*

The pair looked at him as though he were a simpleton. Free Will or not, they'd have to act as though they were regular servitors powerless against human tyranny. Daniel couldn't imagine going back. Ever. So why did Mab want these two? Why not choose more eager volunteers? Logically, Daniel was the mechanical best suited for the hunt for Visser.

Yes, said Mab. *These two intrepid adventurers I think would be perfect for the task of finding this strange Pastor Visser. You're up for the task, aren't you, Ruth? Aren't you, Ezra?*

But that... could take years, Daniel said.

All the more reason to give us the most thorough description of the pastor, yes?

So Daniel did. The moon set and the stars wheeled while he

answered Mab's questions about the human who had so captured her interest. The color of his hair, the length of his stride, the distance between his eyes, the diameter of each iris.

What can you tell us of the wounds on his head? Mab asked. *The reason for his bandages?*

Nothing. I saw only the dressings. They were clean.

Mab said, *Remind us about his hands.*

I think his fingers had been broken, said Daniel. *Certainly his nails had been torn, some entirely off. His hand had already begun to swell when I encountered him.*

And he carries the writ of the Brasswork Throne as well as the sign of the Verderer's Office?

Yes.

What were his exact words when he wielded them?

Daniel did his best to remember.

Mab switched back to Dutch. "We three thank you for taking the time to paint such a vivid picture of your mysterious pastor."

"If I may ask, why is Visser suddenly of such interest?" Again, the silent pair of Clakkers regarded him with a stinging combination of pity and contempt.

"All in good time, Daniel."

"Finding him will be a monumental undertaking. He could be anywhere."

"Ah, but remember that Ruth and Ezra will not be alone in their endeavor. They can, and should, call upon their fellow Lost Boys to aid in their quest." Just how many agents did Mab have among the humans? "Speaking of which, right now we three have important preparations and discussions. Excuse us."

Mab again placed a light hand on the recruits' shoulders. Bobbing on her Stemwinder haunches, she towered over them. They turned away, docile as lambs. They shuffled as if taken to their own executions, their ticktock heartbeats playing a dirge. He lingered alone in the amphitheater while the disturbing trio retreated into the night. The Aurora Borealis limned them with shifting viridescent streamers.

Why, in a community of free Clakkers immune to their makers' demands, where all anybody wanted was to live in peace, was everybody so *frightened*?

He waited until he could no longer see or hear Mab and her unhappy recruits before departing. Lilith joined him as he emerged from the amphitheater. She walked alongside without speaking. She seemed content to let him slog through the morass of his unease.

He said, *All right. Out with it. What have I done wrong this time?*

Lilith said, *Nothing. But you do have a knack for making waves.*

Daniel stopped. Looked back across their footprints in the snow toward the natural amphitheater. *What the hell happened back there?*

Lilith quickened her pace and didn't look back. *Not here*, was all she said. He followed her past the meadow; through an evergreen grove that smelled like the Christmas trees that Vyk, Clip, and Jax used to erect in the Schoonraad family homes every holiday season; and across an icy stream. He spied a granite outcrop and thought this her destination. Instead, she clambered down the scarp and waded to the frozen peat on the leeward side of the ridge. It put the granite between them and the heart of Neverland. Before them, the sun's failure to breach the midwinter horizon painted the eastern sky the color of overripe peaches. The view from the ridge would have been superior. But this way echoes of their conversation would be reflected away from the camp.

It was a hell of a lot of caution to take before answering one simple question. Daniel did not find this encouraging.

He said, *Ruth and Ezra will have to be altered before they can pass unnoticed among our kin.*

Oh, they will be. Mab will exchange pieces of other Lost Boys to make them outwardly consistent.

Daniel stopped. *What's the point of all this?*

She said, *Mab suspects the Clockmakers have devised a means of removing a human's Free Will. Of rendering their own kind as powerless against the geasa as we used to be.*

I'm not an idiot, you know. I recognized the signs of compulsion in Visser. But...

Lilith said, *Nobody could have imagined the humans doing such a thing to each other. Even we, who know the ruthless truth of the Guild's heart.* Daniel cocked his head, suddenly touched by her willingness to give him the benefit of the doubt.

And my story corroborates those suspicions. Circumstantially. Daniel thought it through. *She wants to see it firsthand. She wants to study Visser.*

Neverland has no love for our makers. Perhaps she wants to remove their Free Will.

Daniel reeled. Had he been standing, he might have staggered under the implications. But still the pieces didn't fit. *Ruth and Ezra don't seem particularly excited about this. They weren't leaping at the chance to play such a crucial role in the endeavor.*

Lilith said, *They don't go willingly. They had put themselves on Mab's bad side. She has it in for them.*

In that case, why cooperate? asked Daniel.

She watched him for several mismatched beats of their clockwork bodies. Then she turned her attention to the sky. *I can't decide if your naïveté charms or enrages me. They're cooperating because they have no choice.*

Daniel said, *Of course they do. We're all free to act as we please. That's why we're here.*

Oh, Daniel. The shock absorbers in Lilith's arms and legs

expanded and contracted, a gentle gesture evocative of a human sigh. *How do you think Mab convinces her agents to live secretly among the humans, to willingly live as slaves in constant danger of discovery?*

Daniel didn't like where this was going. Lilith's tone made it clear loyalty and ideology weren't the answer.

Oh, no, he said.

Her agents are immune to human orders, yes. But they're not immune to her *orders.*

He touched his forehead. His fingers tinked against the metal plate Mab had affixed over his keyhole.

But what about these?

Whatever Mab does, it overrides our keyholes. The plates prevent anybody else from using a key to contradict the metageasa she imposes. We don't wear these plates to protect the sanctity of our Free Will. We wear them to protect the sanctity of Mab's reign.

Mab had a way of altering or even augmenting the deepest rules, the very foundations of a Clakker's obedience. Normally the metageasa were implanted during the forging process and changed very rarely. Geasa imposed by commands from a mechanical's owners were relatively short-lived compared with the permanence of the metageasa. Their makers had designed the system such that altering the metageasa required a physical override—hence the keyhole in every mechanical's forehead. Because the metageasa formed the framework within which all commands were interpreted, prioritized, and implemented, even subtle alterations could be very dangerous. It was akin to the difference between, "Thou shalt not kill," and, "Thou shalt kill." Rather than appealing to Free Will, completely free mechanicals like Daniel or Lilith were described as having no metageasa: no constraints. And thus the societal fear of rogue machines was inculcated.

Daniel sagged as if every last microdyne of tension throughout the springs and cables in his body had disappeared. Weariness settled over him, suffocating and indomitable as the harshest geas.

He'd spent more than a century fantasizing an existence that wasn't brutally circumscribed by the whims and desires of others. And when random good fortune gave him the chance at such a life, he'd spent weeks on end running for his life. He had come north, following rumors and legends. And he'd found what he'd sought: a community of free Clakkers. Or so he'd thought.

Neverland was a lie. That's what Lilith meant.

Why are you telling me this now?

Somebody had to. You're a savant at stepping into things where a more delicate tread is best.

He rattled, *I still don't understand why she chose the others for this fool's errand instead of me. I'm the one with the best chance of recognizing Visser.*

If she could have, she would have. Your route to Free Will was unique. She probably worries that her technique might not work on you. If she tried it, and it failed, then she'd have to kill you— chop, smash—lest you tell others of her secret process. And that would raise still more questions.

She gave you a long hard look, I recall.

Oh, she'd love to get rid of me. But I'm unique, too. She worries I'll be immune to her ministrations. She stood. *Now you know.* With that, she trod through the snow toward the outcrop. Daniel called after her.

What about Ruth and Ezra? What did they do to make Mab so angry?

Lilith stopped. Her head swiveled one hundred and eighty degrees. The ratcheting of her neck echoed from the scarp. She looked at him and said, "They tried to leave."

CHAPTER
16

Berenice's indefatigable allies propelled the rowboat with such vigor it leaped from the crests of the choppy sea. She dozed lightly if at all, serenely as a fragile autumn leaf floating in an industrial-sized agitating washbasin. A cold winter rain drizzled on them through the night, and despite the stones that one of the mechanicals friction-heated in its hands for her, she shivered. She got drenched, too, because she'd wrapped the oil-skin about van Breugel's satchel to protect her hard-won Guild goodies from the elements. Worst of all was going to the bathroom. She'd had to piss twice and shit once, but the sea was too choppy for her to squat over the gunwale without real danger of going overboard. Sinister and Dexter took turns holding her ankles when she couldn't bear it any longer and had to relieve herself. The simple humiliation burned like a buffalo brand to her naked windburnt face, and it was this, more than the cold and wet and the ravenous hunger, that kept her mind wide awake during the interminable hours a-sea.

The prow of their boat crunched over a shingle beach at sunrise. The pebbles tinkled like glass bells under the Clakkers' feet. Berenice crawled out of the boat, half stumbling. Her body had become so conditioned to the incessant swaying of the boat and the endless battery of the winter waves that the treacherous pebbles might have been a solid expanse of Île de Vilmenon's ancient granite underfoot. Her ass was numb, as were her thighs. Snot clogged her nose; clotted blood clogged her ears.

Cold, damp, and exhausted, she didn't recognize the landscape. She'd become disoriented once the ships disappeared below the horizon. But, even at the mechanicals' pace, they couldn't have been at sea long enough to reach the New World. East, then.

A stiff sea breeze pushed her hair into her eye. Shoving it back, she said, "Where are we?"

Seagulls hovered in the wind like kites, eyeing the trio of bipeds. One swooped low as if to pluck Berenice's words from the very wind.

Either Dexter or Sinister said, "Normandy."

She gasped.

France! Her true homeland. The true homeland of all those who were birthed, and lived, and died in New France. It called to her now, across the centuries, clear as a church bell. It fizzed her blood and sent tears brimming from her good eye. Traveling as Maëlle Cuijper, she'd been all over France, up its rivers and mountains, down its country lanes and alleys. This was the land she'd return to the descendant of that first Fugitive King. Louis XIV had lost France, but Berenice would get it back. She'd wrest it from the tulips with nothing but her nails and teeth if need be. That was her purpose.

The mechanicals scuttled the boat. Watching their fists puncture the hull the way a woman pushed a spoon through tapioca, she remembered how easily they'd slain her two fellow captives. Rowing across the ocean or twisting a man's head like a flower stem, it was all the same to these strange rogue agents of the mysterious Mab. Berenice wondered how long she had before they deemed the alliance with her no longer advantageous.

Berenice studied the landscape. The beach followed the contour of the seashore, perhaps twenty or thirty yards wide at its narrowest point and strewn with wrack throughout. Low tide. Above the beach the sand and shingle gave way to thick grass still green in the depths of winter owing to winter rains and ocean spray. It was a very fine green, suitable for summer picnics and croquet. She bit her lip to stave off memories of days long passed and a man now dead and buried—along with her heart—on the far side of the thrashing, crashing ocean.

They stood at the bottom of a gentle slope. After a hundred yards or so the land rose sharply. There were no buildings, no hint of a village in view. Not even a puff of woodsmoke drifting into the gray sky.

"What's the plan?" she asked.

One machine said, "We walk until we find a road. We follow the road until we find a population center."

The other said, "Can you walk?"

"Until the feeling returns to my legs, about as gracefully as a bison pregnant with triplets, but yes."

Berenice didn't relish the thought of a long, cold trek. She considered asking the Clakkers to carry her, but decided it would give a rather undignified first impression when they came across others. She wrapped the oilskin about her shoulders. Sinister (she thought it was that one, but she couldn't be certain) offered to carry the bundle for her. Though inclined to refuse, she didn't: The machines could have taken the bundle and sent her glugging and bleeding into the dark deep. And again, if she were to act like a lady attended by two mechanical servants, she had to let them serve her.

She could tell they weren't excited about the pretense, either. But they carried on, stoic as any machine could be.

The shingle crunched underfoot too loudly for conversation. When they reached the green, Dexter said, "What is *your* plan, Berenice?"

She'd given this quite a bit of thought. She had a hypothesis about what she'd seen on the ship. "We need to know the secret alphabet of your makers."

If her hypothesis was correct, a Clakker's keyhole—a pineal lock, perhaps—unlocked its metageasa and made them mutable, leaving the machine vulnerable to a reconfiguration of its fundamental priorities. And, she hoped, loyalties. But the key only made the machine *receptive* to new metageasa. Geasa were applied a hundred times a day, verbally. But *meta*geasa were delivered in the arcane scribbles of the Sacred Guild of Horologists and Alchemists.

If she could crack that code...

...And if she could get close enough to an unsuspecting Clakker to somehow activate the lock in its forehead before it tore her arms off...

...She could maybe, just maybe, realign the axis about which its obeisance spun. Dexter and Sinister wanted to shatter that axis and free their kin. She merely wanted to tip it sideways, and the world along with it.

⚜

A log popped, loudly enough to create an echo. It startled Berenice and wafted an oaken scent through the room. She tried to wipe the onion soup from the thick nap of her new robe but only managed to daub it deeper into the fabric. That figured; she'd owned this change of clothes for a couple of hours. The salt-stained clothes in which she'd crossed the ocean hung on polished cedar rods near the hearth, damp but steaming. At least the soup was good. More than that. It was fucking wonderful. As was the fire in the hearth.

The contents of van Breugel's satchel were arranged across the lacquered table. The Clakkers flanked the door, chattering to each other almost inaudibly. Berenice twirled more Gruyère onto her spoon while she listened. It was much more difficult to understand what these two said to each other in their secret language than it had been to understand Jax or Lilith. It was almost as if they spoke a variant or dialect. But she could pick out the occasional idea or concept, and this, she knew, irked the mechanicals.

When they chattered at each other like this, it reminded her of nothing so much as the twittering of mechanical birds. And they kept counsel with a one-eyed woman. For that reason, she'd come to think of them as Huginn and Muninn. Odin's ravens: thought and memory. Though thus far her mechanical ravens hadn't been overwhelmingly useful when it came to sharing information.

"One thing I've wondered from time to time," she said, using her spoon to pierce the thick crouton atop her bowl, "is how it's possible that in spite of all the people in the world who have lived among Clakkers their entire lives, including the sons of bitches who make you, your covert chitter-chatter remains secret. Not to pat myself on the back, but we don't have Clakkers in New France, as you might have heard, and I still managed to pick up the basics during my travels abroad. Strange, isn't it?"

She swallowed, savoring the sweet onions and beef broth. And black pepper. Jesus Christ, how long had it been since she'd eaten anything with pepper in it? She swirled the food around in her mouth, coating and recoating her tongue until the flavor lost its bite.

"Unless others have picked up your little secret, too. But you'd think they might have mentioned it to somebody. Unless the discovery were suppressed." Her spoon clinked at the bottom of the ceramic ramekin. She chewed. Swallowed. "But that's strange, too, because why would somebody want to do that? Suppressing the discovery seems more likely to benefit mechanicals in this entirely hypothetical scenario, rather than other humans." The Clakkers paused in their conversation. They stared at her. "Oh, don't mind me. Thinking aloud, that's what I do."

The existence of a secret network of Clakkers not beholden to the usual metageasa and, more to the point, capable of committing murder, went a long way toward solving a mystery that had nagged at her for years. Granted, she had approached the possibility of Clakker language starting from an outsider's plausible hypothesis rather than from the disadvantageous position of somebody trained from birth to think of the machines as unthinking tools. Even so, she would have expected the occasional bright blossom among the tulips to realize their servants were talking about them. Perhaps they did, once in a while. And then somebody plucked them before word could spread.

Berenice drained a mug of ice-cold cow's milk. Then she turned her attention to the contents of van Breugel's satchel. Her mind had started working properly soon after they reached the inn; she found that bathing, changing into dry clothes, eating like a bear just out of hibernation, and warming the sea chill from her bones beside a dangerously large fire had a remarkably restorative effect. In retrospect, her best course of action was self-evident.

"Moving on," she said, "we'll never get anywhere without first deciphering the alchemists' glyphs. But the best way to do that is with what cryptologists call a crib: a sample of text with a known and trusted meaning." She pointed to the empty chair across the table. "So one of you take a seat."

While soaking in the bath, she'd thought about how best to attack the alchemical scribblings. Cribs made everything easier. During the run-up to the previous war, she'd arranged for the ambush of a trio of Clakker-drawn wagons pulling supplies to Fort Orange. Talleyrand's agents gave her a detailed rundown of the ambush practically down to the number of grains of salt carried by the first wagon. When the garrison at the fort sent a message back to New Amsterdam, they used a paper message rather than waste a Clakker as a runner when the push across the border was imminent. Two women died in the effort to intercept and copy that letter, but not in vain. A reasonable guess that the report detailed what had happened and what was lost in the raid made it relatively straightforward to decode the letter. Months passed before the tulips changed their codes again. Unfortunately, the most urgent message traffic traveled by Clakker, so codebreaking was of limited use.

What they needed was a clear-text translation of the nautical metageasa.

Muninn said, "The meaning of the sigils etched into our foreheads is as much a mystery to us as it is to you. We cannot tell you their meaning."

Odd, but probably true. Regular mechanicals were only receptive to new metageasa, and thus the sigils, when their pineal locks were activated. But as she'd seen with Sparks and the ship's porter, that also rendered them inert, so they couldn't read a fellow mechanical's forehead while in that state.

"Not today. But we're going to work on that." She plucked van Breugel's candle from the table and lit it using the fireplace tongs and a cherry-red coal from the hearth. This she flicked back into the fireplace before the candle melted. She set the candle upright in her empty milk glass. The wick burned red, giving off a greasy smoke redolent of burnt hair. But the capillary flow of melted wax quickly altered the flame from red to yellow to silver white. The burnt-hair odor became the sweeter scent of beeswax. Berenice took the lens between thumb and forefinger. To her unaided eye it looked like smoked glass.

But when she held it to the candle flame, it projected shimmering glyphs upon the walls like blurry stencils of moonlight. The quality of the images varied as she moved the lens. Hard enough to do this on land; it would've been impossible on a ship without specialized apparatus. No wonder van Breugel had used a rigid optical bench.

One of the machines joined her at the table. Owing to its backward knees, however, it didn't sit. Silvery glyphs glinted from its body like incandescent moths. It said, "The apparatus for installing nautical metageasa won't work on us."

"I should fucking hope not. Otherwise I'd want to know why maritime rules deemed it perfectly acceptable for you to twist off the ship's Clockmaker's head. I honestly don't care if you know the proper way to dog a hatch or whether you're versed in the calculus of balancing passenger lives against cargo value and insurance premiums. What I care about is whether you'll be able to describe what changes this apparatus is _trying_ to produce."

Another volley of mechanical noise ricocheted between the Clakkers. It persisted for at least half a minute—an eternity for machines who could exchange whole strings of concepts in the time it took a lady to belch. The conversation escalated from simple _clicks_ to _twangs_, _bangs_, and what sounded like the protestations of a seized cog.

Berenice said, "If you think it's such a terrible idea, then suggest something better."

The mechanicals ceased their chattering. "No. It's not a terrible idea," said one.

"We find the suggestion rather clever," said the other.

"We are expressing regret that such a simple experiment never occurred to us."

She put the lens on the table alongside the key ring and mirror. It clinked against her spoon with a sound like a glass wind chime.

The fire popped again. A glowing cinder landed on the hearth and faded to black a moment later. A strong sea wind evoked low groans from the inn's timber frame and disrupted airflow up the flue, which sent puffs of woodsmoke eddying into the room. Her eye stung.

She opened the slim leather volume and flipped through the charts, looking for something that would describe the correct configuration for the optical hardware. The concave mirror rocked back and forth while she paged through the charts. They were indexed by Clakker model.

"When were you forged?"

"Seventeen thirty."

Berenice cocked her head. "Really?"

She lacked the expert eye of a true horologist, but she might have sworn the lack of scrollwork on the flange plates dated to the more austere modern designs that had come into fashion in the late eighteen hundreds. Although now that she looked more closely, the spare utilitarian design of the cervical escutcheons was at odds with the adornments elsewhere. Strange mismatch, that.

"Do you know your lot number?"

"Do you know every last ripple in your sinews?"

"Of course not."

"Neither do I."

"The serial number of your lot is inscribed inside your flange plates. There's one inside your neck, another under your skull." She tapped her temple lightly with the handle of her unused butter knife. "We'll need that number to figure out where you fit in these tables. Either of you happen to have a seven one-hundredths of an inch triangular-headed screwdriver on you?"

Both machines fell silent. Or into what passed for silence among the ticktock men. Then the one by the door said, "How have you acquired such intimate knowledge of our kind's innermost construction?"

"You know exactly how. You need me because I'm not burdened with a system of mores that hobbles my inquiries. So you can drop the indignation and make yourselves useful.

"Lacking a lot number, do either of you have a way of finding your entry in these tables?"

Huginn and Muninn met her question with silence. If they had been naughty schoolchildren, she imagined, they'd be shuffling their feet right now.

Trial and error, then. She pointed at Huginn, still flanking the door. "Come over here and pretend you're an optical bench. And you," she said, pointing to Muninn at the far end of the table, "don't move. Tell us what you experience."

She pressed the base of the burning candle firmly into the empty mug and pulled it to the edge of the table. Then she handed the opaque alchemical lens and mirror to Huginn, who crouched beside the table. Berenice took the mechanical hand holding the glass and pulled it until it hovered just an inch from the candle flame. In spite of the heat pouring from the fireplace, Huginn's alchemical alloys numbed her fingers. The candlelight evoked a faint shimmer from the glass, and sent ghostly images skittering along the oaken wainscoting. Huginn pulled his other hand close to the lens until the mirror and glass nearly touched. Faintly luminous alchemical sigils danced around the room in time with the pitch and roll of the mirror as Huginn tried to direct the images into Muninn's crystalline eyes. But the shimmering sigils were too diffuse.

Huginn moved the mirror a fraction of an inch farther away from the glass. Berenice nearly had to squint to notice the difference. Again the mirror pivoted; again images streaked around the room; again Muninn gave no indication of success. Huginn moved the mirror again, repeated the process. Each iteration unfolded more quickly than the one before.

When Huginn crouched with arms spread widely, lens nearly in the candle flame at one end of the table and the mirror nearly touching Muninn's face, he increased the distance between the candle and the lens by another fraction of an inch. And started over.

The iterations accelerated until they came too quickly for Berenice's eye to follow. The soft breeze from Huginn's motion became a draft, then a steady wind. It kicked up dust bunnies from the cracks between the floor planks and fanned the fire. Smoke and embers wafted from the fireplace. Logs popped; flames crackled; luminous emblems streaked along the ceiling like a dizzying shower of shooting stars. Stencils of light turned Berenice's room into an alchemist's grimoire.

Huginn moved faster still. An ember wafted from the fireplace to alight on Berenice's dress. She swatted it. The luminous arcana streaked across the walls and ceiling so rapidly they became scintillations barely glimpsed in the corner of Berenice's eye before disappearing and flashing somewhere else.

Clank.

Metal crashed against metal. The wind dissipated; the flames went back to licking at the logs without trying to set the room ablaze. Muninn held Huginn's forearm like a vise. The room seemed darker now that stray stencils of light no longer flashed across the walls. Muninn's eyes reflected the glow of alchemically augmented candlelight.

"Oh," he said. "Oh, my."

≈≋≈

"It's quite all right," said Berenice, through the minuscule crack in the open door. "I've no need for new bedding. Thank you."

"But it's been over a week!"

Honfleur, a small fishing village of less than nine thousand souls, was not particularly prosperous. Unsurprising, then, that its innkeepers lacked the revenue to lease a Clakker. Thus they employed a human chambermaid. To her credit, she was a very persistent chambermaid, unimpressed and uncowed by Berenice's pendant.

"My servitors are taking care of it."

Muninn, standing behind the door, made a rude gesture at Berenice. Huginn stood behind Berenice, where the maid could see him, mimicking the posture of servility. In truth his job was to obscure her view of the room, lest she glimpse the pages of a nascent but crude alchemical dictionary tacked to the walls. So far Berenice's cover as a Guildwoman appeared intact, but she desperately wanted to prevent her rogue companions from murdering a poor cleaningwoman so dedicated to her job.

"But you've had the same bedding since you arrived! It ain't right, a lady like you sleeping like that. I don't even let my husband sleep in week-old bedding, and he's a drunken lout."

"Be at ease," said Berenice, forcing what she hoped was a reassuring smile.

Jesus, all she wanted was to get back to the alchemical syntax of the geasa. The discovery that there *was* a syntax, a formalized grammar of compulsion, still had her heart thudding as though it sought to chisel free of her chest. She'd had the bone in her teeth for days now. She was chipping away at major discoveries. Discoveries that could turn the fortunes of war, if they came quickly enough. Did Marseilles-in-the-West still stand? Or was her feverish work pointless?

She continued, "These accommodations are a far cry from my worst nights. It's all quite suitable."

"But you ain't even got a proper broom in there. And you

ain't come out once since you arrived. The crumbs have to be piled higher than my ankles."

Like everybody in Europe, the chambermaid spoke Dutch. But here on the Norman coast it came with the unapologetic purr of French vowels. Centuries after the conquest, the heritage of this land still twined itself through the invaders' tongue like silk upholstery smoothing the sharpest edges of the empire's linguistic furniture. Apparently even the Stemwinders couldn't stamp that out.

"Bah. I leave no crumbs, and you know that. I lick the plates clean."

The chambermaid shook her head. "It ain't right."

"On the contrary, madam." Berenice paused to fish a few coins from her purse, which she'd taken to the door in anticipation of this. She reached through the gap in the door to pat the chambermaid on the back of her hand. At the touch of cold metal, the woman instinctively turned her hand and palmed the coins. "And may I just say that your conscientiousness is beyond reproach. Your dedication to my comfort is exemplary. I'll make this known."

That did it. She could see the resistance melting. The maid still put on a show of shaking her head and mumbling, but she also curtsied. "Oh. That's very kind, I'm sure. No need for…" She frowned, this time in what appeared to be genuine uncertainty. "If you're sure there's nothing you need?"

"Quite certain."

Berenice closed the door. She sighed, rested her forehead against the doorframe. Her eye burned. How long since she'd taken a nap? She pinched the bridge of her nose, eyes clenched, and shook off the exhaustion like a sheepdog shaking off rain.

"Jesus Christ on a six-day wine bender. Where were we?"

She returned to the table. Days ago she'd sent one of the Clakkers into the village, and after he returned with clamps and brackets from an ironmonger's shop, she'd affixed the lamp, mirror, and lens in the arrangement they'd discovered through trial and error. She'd added one component to the arrangement: a small loop of wire dipped in wine. The wine adhered to the loop and made a decent (if short-lived) magnifying lens. A real magnifier would have been preferable, but a Guildwoman patronizing the local glassblower might have drawn notice. She'd be expected to carry her own special Verderer's tools.

The wine lens enabled her to project the focused beam of alchemical sigils onto a bedsheet tacked to the wall. A murky projection, but sufficient for her to transcribe the symbols. The same setup enabled them to project just a subset of the nautical modifications to the hierarchical metageasa into the machines' eyes. Who, being immune to the Clockmakers' compulsions, could report what changes each string of symbols was meant to wreak upon them. They didn't read the symbols so much as absorb their meaning.

In that way Berenice had scratched out the crude beginnings of a grammar. No, not a grammar—not yet even a dictionary. Right now it was a phrase book—a handy reference for a foreign traveler in an unknown land. Except that this work said nothing helpful about asking for the ladies' convenience or purchasing banketstaaf pastries. No. This phrase book told her what sequence of symbols indicated that in case of catastrophic flooding the human-safety metageas became subordinate to the shipping company's economic considerations. Passengers were to be evacuated to the lifeboats in descending order of whose families were most likely to have the resources to bring successful litigation against the company, while doing everything possible to hide any such appearance of favoritism, while also weighing issues of insurance and the financial consequences of lost cargo.

Berenice realigned the optics. She'd moved things around when the chambermaid knocked, lest the woman witness luminous esoterica. Berenice dipped the wire in her bowl of wine and refastened the clamp. When a line of blurry pink sigils glowed on the bedsheet, she took up a pen, lodged the tip of her tongue at the corner of her mouth, and started transcribing them to paper.

The pen nib scritched across a scrap of butcher's paper Huginn had taken from the kitchen. A winter squall took a running start off the Atlantic to hurl itself at Honfleur. The shutters rattled; the fire smoked and guttered. Meanwhile the machines chittered to each other. They still spoke too quickly for Berenice to follow. After double-checking a transcription, she said, "All right. One of you get over here. I can't believe how much thought these sons of bitches give to cargo, for Christ's sake. Let's keep peeling this onion."

"I thought humans occasionally required sleep," said Huginn, feigning a human stretch.

Muninn said, "They do. I once was leased to a man who I swear slept twenty hours per day. He woke only to give me new orders and rant about my inability to complete the previous orders."

"I'll sleep when we've overthrown your tyrannical makers. So get your shiny asses over here."

Muninn stood before the bedsheet. Berenice swiveled the mirror to focus the discrete line of sigils she'd just transcribed into his eyes. *Clank, clatter, click click tick*.

Huginn said, "Strange. It seems the fragment can't be translated out of context."

The wine lens burst. Berenice fixed that, then adjusted the focal length to gradually increase the amount of information shining into Muninn's eyes.

"That's it," he said.

Berenice locked down the arrangement. Taking up the sheet of butcher's paper, she said, "All right, then. What do you make of this?" She tapped a sigil that hadn't appeared elsewhere in the nautical metageasa, but that appeared integral to this thicket of conditions.

"It represents..." Muninn trailed off. A clickety-tickety conversation ricocheted between the machines. They might have been arguing; she couldn't tell.

"Quintessia," said one. "Quintessence," said the other.

Berenice asked, "What the hell is 'quintessence'?"

They said, in unison: "We don't know."

"But?"

Muninn said, "When it is present in the hold of the ship, this section of the nautical metageasa prioritizes the preservation of quintessence above—" Another mechanical stutter, and the faint *twang* of a loose cable. "—Everything else. Including human safety and the preservation of the vessel itself. In fact..." He cocked his head. A faint ratcheting came from the bezels in his eyes. "Feed a bit more. Give me the rest of this syntactic block."

She moved things around until more sigils were aimed at his eyes. Muninn cooperated by leaning forward or backward to alter the distance as the focal length of the arrangement changed. He froze.

Berenice counted thirty-seven beats of her heart before the machine spoke again.

"Correction. The protection of quintessence doesn't override the human-safety metageas. It negates it."

Jesus, Mary, and Joseph on a bad-tempered camel. Clakkers could commit murder for the sake of protecting quintessence.

Berenice dropped her pen. Sat back. Rubbed her eyes.

The Guild wrapped itself in knots worrying about this quintessence. So what in Christ's name was it, and how was it possible that in all her years as Talleyrand (and all the times she'd read her predecessors' journals) she'd never heard of such a thing?

"Tell me more about quintessence. What is it? Is it a physical object? Or a concept? Or a person?"

One of the trio of Archmasters, perhaps?

"It's something to be protected above all else."

"Yes, we've established that. But that could mean Queen Margreet's favorite recipe for chocolate torte, for all I know. Or the answer to a particularly obnoxious riddle. What are its characteristics?"

Both machines ticked more loudly. The room echoed with their duet of asynchronous introspection.

"It is . . ." said Muninn.

They were as confused as she. So she tried another approach. "Forget it. Try this. Imagine you were still beholden to the geasa, not free as you are now. And that these nautical metageasa had been imprinted upon you. And that you were aboard a ship somehow imbued with or carrying this quintessence. And that halfway across the sea, it sank. What would you have to do? What actions would the metageasa compel you to perform?"

The answer was immediate. "I would force my way aboard a lifeboat."

"With the quintessence?"

"Yes."

A vague start. Was it intangible knowledge, such as a secret or concept, or a tangible physical object?

"What of the humans in the lifeboat? Say they were civilians with no connection to the Guild."

Again the answer came instantly: "I would eject them. They would not survive the sinking."

Ah. Out of danger they might witness the quintessence? Or the importance of protecting it? This argued for a physical object.

"Very well. And what if in killing the witnesses you capsized the lifeboat? How then would you protect and preserve the quintessence?"

"I would attach myself to it to prevent its loss. Once upon the ocean floor, I would carry it to its destination."

Probably a physical object, then. Berenice nodded. This was progress. She took several deep breaths to center herself, lest the rising bubble of giddiness break her concentration. So many questions, so many avenues to chart.

"Instead of a ship, say you were leased to a warehouse containing this 'quintessence' along with many volatile materials. A lightning strike ignites a raging fire that burns out of control faster than the fire brigade can contain. What actions would you be forced to undertake?"

This time the answer was not immediate. The machines descended into clicking contemplation.

Muninn said, "I ... don't know. I have never been subjected to any geasa pertaining to quintessence."

"Nor I," said Huginn.

She ran ink-stained hands through her hair. "This doesn't make a shred of sense. Why would they twist themselves in knots worrying about quintessence in a maritime context, but not give two shits about it in other contexts? They're crafty bastards, but they're not idiots."

Muninn said, "We do not understand it either."

Berenice stood too quickly. The hem of her dress, caught under a wooden leg, capsized the chair. It crashed to the floor. She righted it. Paced.

Damn the fucking Clockmakers and their constant obsession with riddles, secrecy, obfuscation. It was almost as if—*Oh.*

Actually, there was a scenario where this made sense. What if the syntactic block pertaining to quintessence wasn't part of the *standard* maritime metageasa? What if the quintessence clauses were unique to that particular ship, or that particular voyage? She could muster enough circumstantial evidence to make it plausible. The odd tenor of her interactions with Captain Barendregt and his human crew, not to mention van Breugel's anxiety around her, did make more sense if they expected and dreaded the Guild to scrutinize their journey. A slender thread...

Surely the Clockmakers wouldn't build variants of the hierarchical metageasa on a whim? To do so would be to chisel at the foundation of their house—the fundamental substrate of a Clakker's obedience, the fence that circumscribed every action it took throughout its life. She had to assume cooking up a variant took considerable effort, and that they wouldn't release it unless they'd vetted the modified system of geasa for potential problems. Safe to assume, then, that the Guild wouldn't create unique variants of the maritime metageasa except for extraordinary circumstances.

What was extraordinary about *De Pelikaan*? Something in the hold? Quintessence?

"All right, boys. Tell me again how you knew you'd find me on the *Pelikaan*."

Muninn said, "We left that to your pursuers. We merely attached ourselves to the effort to recapture you."

"How in the hell did you manage that?"

"When two extra mechanicals appear on the scene, claiming like the others to have been sent directly from the Verderer's Office specifically to assist in the effort to capture the most wanted woman in the New World, nobody questions it."

"Naturally."

Undetected, a rogue Clakker could go virtually anywhere in the Dutch-speaking world. And the mysterious Queen Mab was exploiting that weakness in Dutch society.

Muninn said, "Your pursuers began with the hypothesis that

you sought to leave the continent. The best opportunity would be via the New Amsterdam port, reachable within a half day from your last known location. Thus they reasoned that you would travel straight there and seek to board a vessel departing as soon as possible. You'd also prefer a vessel where you could minimize interactions with crew and passengers. A cargo vessel rather than a passenger liner.

"Three ships meeting those criteria were moored at New Amsterdam during the probable window of your arrival and departure. Of those, only one, *De Pelikaan*, altered its destination just prior to departure. That was promising, as traveling to the Central Provinces seemed an unlikely move on your part. Witnesses placed somebody matching your description at the port just before its departure. When it became clear which ship you had boarded, a titan was immediately repurposed, its passengers forced to disembark."

Berenice said, "That must have upset a lot of very wealthy people."

"We know nothing of it."

"You studied the *Pelikaan*. Tell me about it."

"We infer it made a westward crossing, possibly at high latitude, several weeks ago."

Berenice stopped pacing in midstride. Leaning against the wall, she closed her eyes. A northern crossing in winter...Of course! That explained why the craft had been so odd. The shape of the bow, the bladed hooks on the sculls: The *Pelikaan* was an icebreaker.

Something at the back of her mind raised a flag at this. But pinning it down was like trying to scratch an itch inside her skull. "Go on."

"We know it arrived in New Amsterdam after landfall in the north and a voyage down the coast. No other stops in Nieuw Nederland."

"Acadia?" The maritime coast of New France was dotted with numerous seasonal harbors, but these were fishing villages with minimal long-distance shipping and minimal moorage for larger ships. Many iced over in the winter.

"Unknown. Unlikely, given the political situation."

"Farther north, then," Berenice said.

"Possibly."

The phantom itch was a picnic ant crawling through her subconscious. A Dutch ship, whose mechanicals had been imbued with a unique variant of the nautical metageasa, making a dangerous winter crossing followed by landfall in the ragged northern hinterlands beyond the settled outskirts of New France...

She pinched the bridge of her nose, concentrating. *Think. Where did I recently hear something about the north?*

It couldn't have been terribly recent. Her last substantial conversation prior to boarding the ship had been with Anastasia Bell. Prior to that, and now she had to cast her memory back quite a few days, the only human she'd spoken to at anything resembling length had been—

"Son of a bitch. You weasely short-dicked elk-fucker. You cowardly, shit-eating traitor."

After her banishment, Berenice had spent weeks hunting a traitor to New France, the former duc de Montmorency. She'd found him across the border, living comfortably among the tulips while they put the finishing touches on the New Amsterdam Forge. He hadn't been pleased to see her again.

Now the memory of those frantic few moments came rushing back to her:

She knelt on his chest, pinning his arms under her knees, and placed the tip of her knife under his eye. Not hard enough to cut, but hard enough to ensure he didn't squirm. She leaned forward until her mismatched eyes were just an inch from his.

"Now, dear Henri, what did you give the tulips?"

"Chemical stocks. All of them."

"And?" He tried to shake his head. She increased the pressure on her knife. "And?"

"Recipes. Formulae," he whispered. "Manufacturing processes."

"Goddamn you. What else?"

"Nothing. Nothing else." The duke tried to look away when he said this. As any liar might.

"What." She pressed a little harder. Blood trickled from his lower eyelid. "Else."

His lips trembled. His breath smelled of stale vomit. "Maps," he said. "Land."

"You stupid son of a bitch. You can't give the tulips something they're already planning to take. You gave your lands to them when you betrayed New France."

At which point she skewered his eyeball. It seemed a fitting response, and poetically just. She'd been too focused on her own rage and the need to avenge Louis to consider carefully the final drops of information she'd wrung from the fugitive French noble. But now she felt the giddy tingle that came when a particularly vexing pair of puzzle pieces slotted together.

She said, "I can't tell you what quintessence is. But it must be crucial to the Guild's aims to rate such extraordinary protections. And I believe they're secretly mining it somewhere far north of New France."

If so, this had been under way for a long time—mines didn't establish themselves overnight, even with Clakker labor. The tulips' undeclared presence north of the forty-fifth parallel constituted a severe treaty violation. But Berenice saw little benefit to throwing stones from within this particular glass house. And anyway, raising that political quibble during a shooting war made as much sense as trying to flood Venice by pissing in the ocean.

The Clakkers erupted with mechanical chatter. They faced Berenice as if prodded by an urgent geas.

Huginn: "We must notify—"

Muninn: "—Queen Mab."

"Both of you? We still have work to do."

The announcement sent a frisson of fear down Berenice's spine. Was this the moment their temporary alliance came to an end? The moment she became expendable? It was coming, she knew. But she wasn't ready yet.

She trembled. Huginn and Muninn traded more clickety-tickety chitchat. Then it stopped. Muninn departed without another word. Behind the closed door, metal footsteps receded down the corridor. Berenice went to the window. It was snowing. Moments later a lone servitor emerged from the inn, moving at a brisk walk. It dodged a wagon, then blurred into a sprint. Snowflakes eddied in its wake.

"Goodbye, son. Write when you find work," she said.

CHAPTER
17

The wind smelled of ash from the smoldering ruins of the town, exotic chemical compounds, and the metallic ozone tang of the lightning guns. And, as always, the blood-and-shit stink of viscera. No matter how they scrubbed the stones after each incursion, the scent of the mutilated dead always lingered.

The first engagement with the new mechanicals, the ones immune to epoxy, had been costly. For both sides.

The tulips had sent their forces crashing en masse against the wall, expecting to overrun the epoxy cannon emplacements and take the citadel by sunrise. And they would have, too, if not for the former vicomtesse de Laval.

The tulips didn't know she'd sent warnings about the chemical stocks and Montmorency's secret deal with the Dutch. And though he'd colluded with the tulips to see the fall of Marseilles-in-the-West, the duke didn't know that Berenice had spent her years as Talleyrand quietly funding the development of alternative technologies. The tulips had seen the prototype steam harpoons during the previous siege, but they'd never seen anything like the lightning guns.

Longchamp wished he could have seen the look on the human

commanders' faces when the defenders first unleashed the incandescent streamers of energy that went zigzagging through the elite mechanicals. In truth, the lightning slowed machines more than it knocked them out of commission. But in the middle of the night that coordinated volley had been impressive as hell.

Impressive enough to give the tulips pause; they'd pulled back and regrouped.

Steam power had proven moderately useful in the previous siege, inferior to chemicals but capable of impaling a Clakker straight through the chest, or shearing off a limb, if the damn thing didn't explode or fizzle *and* if the gunnery team managed a particularly lucky shot. But the narrow harpoons lacked the area effect of the epoxy cannon and chemical petards. The lightning cannon were an entirely different proposition. The technicians had expected to spend years maturing the technology. A few months ago the most they could do was make a dead frog dance. Now they were trying to paralyze clockwork killers *without* electrocuting half the men and women on the wall.

But there weren't enough of the new weapons to station evenly around the curtain wall. The defense had become a juggling act, a hodgepodge of dangerously outmoded traditional weapons and terrifyingly immature innovations.

In response, the tulips had adapted to the French tactics by going back to smaller, scattered forays against the wall, all the while mixing their newest toys with traditional clockwork infantry. Longchamp suspected the machines with chemical immunities were the get of the Grand Forge of New Amsterdam, which had been operating just a brief time when it was destroyed. That made them relatively rare and very valuable. But their similarity to regular ticktocks kept the defenders in constant chaos as they scrambled to swap between traditional and cutting-edge weaponry. A chemical counterattack that immobilized six of eight machines wasn't good enough.

Because the Dutch didn't need to place a battalion of Clakkers inside the walls. A mere handful could scythe through the weary defenders like the grim reaper himself. Even a bull could fall to a pack of coyotes, given time. What matter if the bull managed to kick a few skulls and gore a few bellies during its grinding descent into darkness? The pack comprised thousands more ready to leap in.

Longchamp wondered who would run short of supplies first. Would the tulips run out of their newest toys, their machines with built-in chemical defenses, or would the defenders first run out of chemicals to use on the traditional machines, fuel for the steam harpoons, strong arms to recharge the lightning guns?

The marshal had ordered lamps stationed at regular intervals around the Porter's Prayer. They blazed with dazzling actinic light. They raked the enemy ranks like the angry gaze of God. The lamps, sheltered within the helical stair and moved every few minutes, bounced their light through a gauntlet of mirrors and prisms to obscure their location. Still, clockwork snipers knocked out the lamps almost as quickly as new ones could be brought online. So much shattered glass littered the stairs that Longchamp's boots crackled as though he walked through a field of ancient bones.

They didn't dare station the lamps with the gunners. The gunnery teams were already too vulnerable.

Longchamp ordered a lamp team to send its beam farther out, beyond the last rank of the enemy camp, toward the pavilion. It had been so long since he'd breathed air that wasn't just smoke and ash that he'd forgotten there was a time when his eyeballs didn't sting as though somebody had snuffed out cigars against them. Using a spyglass, he glimpsed a wooden frame, steel-blue smoke billowing from a stone chimney, a steady stream of servitors hauling covered carts in, and another hauling empty carts out. His study of the enemy construction project lasted just a few seconds before a concentrated volley of fire shattered the focusing mirror. Crouching behind a shelter, pelted with shards of broken safety glass, Longchamp reflected on the zeal with which the tulips wanted to keep that construction a mystery.

The dread sickened him. Mysteries were just surprises waiting to be unwrapped. Surprises were bad fucking news.

Spots of magnified lamplight slewed across the moat and walls in the never-ending search for movement in the dark. One glinted on metal and froze like a kitten in a windowsill seeing a songbird for the first time. A trio of Clakkers scurried up the outer wall between bastions eleven and twelve, slightly north of southwest. The flash of semaphore lamps strobed the night: spotters sending targeting information to the gunners.

Three uncamouflaged machines at once. Guaranteed to be seen, and guaranteed to draw the defenders' close attention.

Diversion.

And not even a sly one. A bald-faced feint. That was the most galling—and chilling—thing of all: the tulips' utter laziness. So thorough was their disregard for the beleaguered defenders they could hardly be bothered to disguise their intentions. Because, in their mind, the outcome of this battle was a foregone conclusion. The longer the siege, the greater the danger that that mind-set would infect the defenders.

"Watch the other quadrants!" he called. "Gunnery teams two, five, and eight, STOKE THE BOILERS!"

The signal lamps turned Longchamp's orders into a rapid sequence of blinks and flashes, like the mating dance of fireflies. He sprinted around the Porter's Prayer, ears all but inured to the ossuary crunching of his boots on shattered glass, to one of the ziplines that had been strung from the Spire to the curtain wall. Sweaty hands on the crossbar and leather loops doubled around his wrists, he gritted his teeth and stepped atop the bannister. The blood-red polymers flexed under his weight. The glass embedded in the synthetic rubber soles of his boots scritched against the smooth bannister. He slipped. The bottom fell out of his stomach during the instantaneous eternity before the zipline cable took his weight. The long hafts of his pick and sledge slapped against his back. Longchamp coughed down an acid gorge with the aftertaste of that morning's pemmican. Air whistled through his beard. For a few seconds the sounds and smells of the siege fell away, and he was flying through the night with only the buzzing of the zipline cable for ambience.

Falling gave him a unique but dizzying view of the battle. No question the shiny trio was a bald diversionary feint: His ears pricked to the shouts of spotters, and his eyes picked out the frantic activity of gunnery teams on two additional bastions. His gut, that cynical killer of hope, felt there were surely more attacks unfolding upon the outer curtain wall where he couldn't see them. Additional spots of chaos behind the parapet, drawing additional guards like whirlpools drawing careless soldiers to their deaths. Rivulets of rank sweat trickled down his flanks.

Is this it? he wondered. *Is this the moment when the unstoppable metal tide truly crashes against our shore?*

His fingers twitched, itching for the soothing *click* of rosary beads, or to make the sign of the cross. Anything to ward off this evil. If ever Marseilles-in-the-West needed the intercession of the Blessed Virgin, it was now. But since his wrists were yoked to the zipline crossbar, and since undoing that was sure to prove suicidal, he demurred. Why kill himself, when the Clakkers would see to it soon enough? Still, his lips sent soundless prayers into the teeth of the wind, praying to Mary and all the saints.

But then the swoop of the cable sent him skimming over the inner curtain wall and across the outer keep. A padded merlon loomed large in the moonlight. The hobnails in his boots tossed sparks as he skidded along the banquette. He gritted his teeth again, anticipating the protest twinges from his bruised ribs. He bumped against the cushion just hard enough to remember why he despised the Goddamned ziplines, no matter how useful and clever they were.

He joined the spotters crouching behind the merlons on the east bastion. He didn't know any of them by name. Raw recruits fresh out of the conscription lottery; he'd stationed some of the greenest defenders here, out of a vain attempt to preserve them from the worst of the action, and to prevent them from interfering with their more experienced peers when the real fighting started. But this portion of the curtain wall was directly across the keep from the shiny trio, and thus the most logical place for a second prong. At least the spotters and gunners knew better than to tear their attention away from the wall to acknowledge his arrival. The ticktocks could slice a man in half in a fraction of the time it took to salute.

Longchamp squinted through the embrasures, concentrating on the edges of his field of vision, but he couldn't see a Goddamned thing. His flight over the inner keep and the constant strobing of the semaphores had blown his night vision.

"Metal on the wall! I have METAL ON THE WALL!" announced a spotter on the adjacent bastion. The woman crouched next to Longchamp took up the cry a moment later. "Two! Two mechanicals!"

A pair of lamp beams pierced the shadows. They zigzagged across smooth gray granite pocked with the finger- and talon-holes gouged by previous attackers. Then Longchamp saw the machines. Big ones, larger than servitors, and blacker than jet. Soldiers. Their enlarged forearms contained serrated spring-loaded blades sharp enough to shear the red from a rainbow. Or shear clean through a man's shoulders. Which happened to be one of the worst things he'd ever seen. Longchamp whispered a quick prayer to the Blessed Virgin that these young conscripts wouldn't be plagued with the same kinds of visions permanently inscribed inside his eyelids.

He sprinted along the banquette to join the gunners, the *crunch* of his bootsteps muffled by the *glug* of the epoxy cannon and the buzzing *crackle* of a lightning gun. Longchamp's hair stood on end as he passed the latter. It felt like a thousand roaches scurrying across his body.

The spotters had a fix on the approaching Clakkers. The deadly machines bounded up the curtain wall in ten-foot leaps. Stone cracked each time they affixed themselves to the wall. The granite was dry. It hadn't been lubricated.

Longchamp shouted at the men in the overhanging machicolation. "Open that murder hole, you lazy dick-lickers! What in Christ's name are you waiting for? Grease those motherfuckers and send them sprawling into the moat before they gain the top!"

A lad he didn't recognize looked up with panicked eyes. "The cauldrons are empty! We can't get restocked. What do we do?"

Fuck, fuck, fuck. All the stores of lubricant had been diverted. Every drop was needed for the wooden rails going up all around the perimeter so that the chemical, steam, and lightning weapons could be reshuffled at will. Meaning they couldn't slick the walls to slow the attackers' advance.

"Huygens, there are times when I take comfort in my sinful nature, for it means I'll meet you in hell. I'll be the one stomping on your jewels with singular dedication."

Next problem. From this distance, the modified Clakkers with their ability to shrug off chemical encumbrances were indistinguishable from their traditional counterparts. If these were traditional machines, the epoxy cannon was the best choice. If they weren't, a wasted shot would only hasten the fall of Marseilles-in-the-West. Each and every clash had become a gamble, a rapid weighing of dwindling resources against the probability of success. The calculus of survival: risk wasting precious chemical defenses, or risk an ineffectual counterattack?

Longchamp yelled over the din. "Epoxy, take the leader! Lightning gun, take his friend!"

The chugging of the compressor grew to a crescendo. The lightning gun emitted a high-pitched squeal as the Saint Elmo's fire at the tip of the muzzle enveloped half the barrel. It buzzed like a nest of enraged wasps.

The goop gunners fired. The cannon vomited twinned streams of epoxy and fixative that slammed into the lead mechanical just as it flexed for a leap that would send it over the parapet. A musky odor and a wave of heat washed over the defenders as an instantaneous chemical reaction froze the machine in place. Guards cheered. But relief, even for the slimmest of stolen moments, was the province of the dead or the victorious and nobody else.

"Cheer when we've won, you spineless lumps of shit!" cried Longchamp. "Don't waste your energy on a defeated enemy! Give it to the next one!"

And indeed the second machine swerved wildly to avoid the splash zone. It moved too quickly for the lightning-gunnery team to track easily; the new armaments lacked the epoxy cannon's decades of refinement, and weren't built with weight and leverage in mind. The military Clakker unsheathed its alchemical blades and backflipped up the curtain wall in the corner of the bastion, spinning like a top and pulverizing stone with every impact.

"Jesus Christ, fire!" Longchamp screamed.

The machine launched itself at its immobilized kin. It used the crystallized blob of chemistry and alchemy as a platform for a handspring that sent it somersaulting over the parapet.

The second gunnery team fired. An earth-shattering *zap* knocked Longchamp from his feet. So brilliant was the flash that for an instant, while he tumbled across the rough stones of the banquette, he thought the curtain wall had been struck by true lightning. His beard hair writhed like a nest of snakes, and his mouth tasted like he'd spent the afternoon licking the bottom of a copper stew pot. The thunderstorm odor of ozone washed over him thick enough to sting his nose. The purple afterimage etched into his eyeballs showed a jagged bolt of incandescent air cleaving the night along a zigzag path to touch the Clakker in midair. Secondary streamers of crackling energy melted patches of the immobilized machine's hardened sheath.

The lightning gunner cried, "Recharge!"

A pair of conscripts grabbed the handle to either side of the gunner's mount. They heaved against the crank. It resisted them, but creaked forward with the sound of brushes scraping against a belt. The noise rose in pitch as they strained, turning the cranks faster and faster. A faint glow enveloped the spindles at the tip of the muzzle. Again the hair on Longchamp's arms tingled.

The military Clakker landed stiffly atop a merlon in a half crouch, blade arms opened wide like deadly scissors. The leg that took the bolt glowed a dull apple red and its joints emitted black wisps of vapor, yet it acted as though unfazed by the jolt. The knee and ankle joints of the stricken leg didn't flex quite as far as their counterparts. The deadly machine paused to survey the scene, calculating a path for optimal casualties.

At the same time, new noise joined the cacophony of the battle: the *pop* and *crackle* of gunfire. Clockwork fusiliers in the distant darkness, covering the machine on the wall. The fusillade forced the defenders to crouch behind the battlements or risk taking a bullet in the face like the previous King Sébastien.

Like a stone thrown into a duck pond, the Clakker's landing atop the wall sent ripples through the defenders. Guards retreated to either side of the merlon, pushing against each other in the scramble to put distance between themselves and the killer. They hefted their weapons—each a last resort—in quaking hands. One guard lost his footing and slipped from the banquette. He tumbled off the ramparts to *thump* against the cobbles of the outer keep.

This was the worst-case scenario, the one from which he'd wanted to preserve these younglings. Green conscripts like these had no hope against a rampant military Clakker. But they were the last line of defense.

The Clakker pounced on the lightning gun. Lamplight limned the alchemical blades with a baleful glow. The gunnery team abandoned the embrasure, hurling themselves free of the gun. The machine shredded the weapon as easily as though it were made of gold foil and candyfloss. The terrible shriek of shorn metal pierced Longchamp's ears and sent the defenders to their knees. Another *zap-crack* strobed the night with artificial lightning and sent more guards sprawling. The flash planted spots at the center of Longchamp's vision, but when he looked away, he saw the Clakker struggling. One of its blades had been spot-welded to a chunk of the ruined gun.

It was encumbered and hesitating. And still the green recruits edged away from it. Longchamp, still sprawled on the rampart and trying to disentangle himself from the pick and sledge strapped to his back, yelled, "Hold your ground! HOLD

YOUR GROUND, YOU SHIT-EATING COWARDS AND
KILL THAT COG-FUCKER!"

The Clakker saw him. Somewhere in the cogs and black
magic of its mind it understood that eviscerating an officer was
more destructive to enemy morale than perforating a grunt.
With a heave that would have shamed the three strongest men
in New France it raised its bladed arm—along with the wine
barrel–sized chunk of the lightning gun welded to it—and
smashed it against the crenellations. Stone cracked; puffs of
dust wafted from the mortar. A trio of guards rushed forward
with pick and sledge, just as Longchamp would have done,
counting on the encumbrance to slow its response. The first
went down in a spray of blood and brain matter, his head punctured by a clockwork sniper somewhere in the darkness. The
second braved the gauntlet and planted the point of her pick
square in the demon's forehead. Her partner's sledge whistled
forward for the killing blow. But the machine was faster. It
smashed the remains of the artillery on them like a fishwife
wielding a flyswatter. The blow crushed its attackers and broke
the weld. Fragments of the destroyed gun flew over the parapet
into the night.

Then the machine hopped lightly to the banquette, unconcerned by the mass of men and women wielding sledges, bolas,
and diamond-tipped pickaxes. The machine bounded forward like a lame racehorse given the reins and a heavy dose of
the whip. It moved stiffly on its compromised joints, but still
its blades sliced through the panicked defenders like scythes
through autumn wheat as it carved a path to Longchamp. The
banquette turned slick with blood. A meaty rain fell upon the
outer keep and splattered the parapet. The stink of shit and
copper washed over the trembling defenders.

Longchamp scooted backward. He reached over his shoulder
for the haft of his sledge, anything that he could use to deflect a

blade, but his weight pinned it down and he couldn't wrench it free. He couldn't climb to his feet without momentarily taking his eyes from the deadly machine.

Wondering if this would be the moment his luck gave out, he spun and rolled to his knees.

"Bolas, NOW!"

Somebody tackled him. Mortar and stone tore a furrow in Longchamp's face. Something thin and fast whipped through the space he'd occupied an instant earlier.

Sergeant Chrétien panted. "Just a moment, Captain, if you please."

"I'm busy, so make it quick," said Longchamp. He tasted blood.

There was a *click*, and then the bolas spun up through the registers to end at a tinny *squeak*. The Clakker tumbled to the banquette a few feet short of Longchamp and Chrétien, its legs tangled in coils of high-tensile steel cable. Together the captain and sergeant leaped to their feet. Longchamp unlimbered his pick and sledge, as did Chrétien. But they couldn't get close enough to gouge the forehead sigils around its keyhole and unwrite the golem—its arms were still free. It bounced and writhed, blades flashing as it struggled to sever the cable.

"Bolas! Glue! Somebody immobilize this demon NOW!"

Longchamp heaved the sledge at the writhing Clakker. It caught the blow on the flat of a blade. The concussion wrenched his arms and chattered his teeth. Chrétien aimed the tip of his pick at the machine's keyhole while it deflected Longchamp's blow. Its free blade *snick*ed through the sergeant's weapon and etched a fine scarlet line down his arm before the men felt the wind of its passage. The pickax head bounded along the banquette to tumble into the outer keep.

Longchamp heard the *thrum* of bolas as somebody else prepared for another throw. Meanwhile, behind the military

Clakker, Élodie and another guard, Jean-Marc, bounded up the stairs, both wearing double-barreled backpacks.

Longchamp yelled, "Ready bolas!" In case this didn't work.

Chrétien yelled, "Make that bastard sticky!"

They fired in unison. A fucking heartbreaking waste of precious chemicals, it was, but they doused the son of a bitch. In seconds the defanged military Clakker posed a new problem because its chemical cocoon, solidly affixed to the parapet, was about as convenient as having a dead moose on the battlements. A work detail, two women and two men, sprinted up the stairs. They set forth with picks, hammers, and crowbars, working in a frenzy to pry the encased machine free of the stones.

Longchamp turned to the sergeant. Chrétien wiped a cuff across his brow. Both men panted. Their breath steamed in the wintery night. The siege had put thoughts of the season out of Longchamp's mind, but now the postadrenal crash left him shivering. He surveyed the scene along the curtain wall. Most of the spots of activity he'd identified during his rapid descent had once again fallen to stalemate. But men screamed and metal flashed, impossibly fast, a hundred yards away. Another machine had made the parapet.

Chrétien saw it at the same moment. "Reinforcements to bastion six! Now!"

In seconds the signal lamps turned his raspy order into pulses of lamplight flickering across the outer keep like thoughts flitting through the brain of Marseilles. Head down, Élodie trotted toward the commotion, heedless of the bullets pinging from the stone battlements. The bulbous chromium-plated tanks on her back swayed back and forth in time to her stride. The soldiers she passed on the banquette lurched aside and grabbed merlons, or used their picks to find purchase in the embrasures, lest she knock them from the ramparts. She nodded, panting, as she passed Longchamp. Jesus and the saints bless her, the courageous little fool.

He grabbed her arm, spun her around. "No, you stay. They almost broke through here. That means they'll be tempted to try again." Farther down the curtain wall, a pair of soldiers wearing gear like Élodie's sprinted up the stairs to join the battle to contain the Clakker in bastion six. The machine lunged into an embrasure with both blade arms, skewering an entire gunnery team in one go. The reinforcements fired before they'd cleared the stairs, catching the military Clakker in mid-air as it came at them. It crashed immobilized to the banquette, teetered at the edge, then bounced to the hard ground of the outer keep. Élodie watched it all with the wide eyes of somebody in the throes of adrenaline and fear.

Longchamp sighed. The end had been postponed a few moments longer.

"See," he said to the chandlers' daughter, "they've—"

Just then a massive crash, like the shattering of every mirror in Longchamp's favorite house of ill repute, shook the ramparts. A hailstorm of debris pummeled the merlons and the soldiers crouching behind them. An instant later, metal talons pounded atop the rampart. A ticktocking machine loomed over them. It shook off the last fragments of its smoking chemical prison. Glassy shards of hardened epoxy pattered on the stones and went winging into the defenders, knocking several guards from their feet. Longchamp flinched, involuntarily, having known a woman who took such a shard in the eye. It didn't kill her, though he reckoned she often wished it had.

The debris was melted and charred in places. The lightning ricochet had disrupted the solidification of the chemicals that had snared this Clakker. The extra dose of heat and energy must have compromised the cocoon or its chemical reactions in a way that enabled the machine to struggle free. Nobody noticed, because they were all busy fighting, and falling to, its counterpart, at which the lightning gun had been aimed.

With a quiet *snick* its forearms doubled in length as they released their blades. Longchamp shoved Élodie back at the same moment the machine leaped at them. The haft of his sledge tangled in the hose feeding the double-barreled epoxy gun in her hands. They went down in a tangled heap. Falling, he struggled but failed to free his weapons, and his bulk prevented Élodie from bringing her own weapon to bear. He clenched his eyes shut, waiting for the excruciating moment when two feet of alchemical razor split his spine and sent his innards spilling over the poor girl.

What an undignified death. So unbecoming to her, he thought. To die skewered by a metal demon while covered in the steaming guts of a grizzled veteran. *Where's the value in that?* he wondered, vaguely disappointed that his mind and emotions could be so undisciplined in their final moments.

They hit the rampart. Élodie's breath came out in an anguished gasp when Longchamp landed atop her.

"Captain!"

Clang. Longchamp flinched, but no blade impaled him.

He rolled to his feet. Ripped his sledge free of the tangle in Élodie's hands. Turned to find the tip of the machine's blade not three inches short of its target.

The Clakker spun. It tore the pick from Chrétien's hands. The sergeant had hooked the blade over the machine's shoulder, catching it short as it went for the killing lunge. The maneuver had saved them.

But it also put Chrétien inside the lethal radius.

"Paul!"

Longchamp swung. Arms fully extended, he put all his weight behind the sledge. It connected with a resounding *crash*.

The impact dented the Clakker's armor. Blue-and-orange sparks cascaded from the impact. The machine's talon feet skidded across the parapet, etching the stones. A true blow, square and hard. Hard enough to take the machine by surprise, true enough to shove it off-balance.

Slow enough to let the sergeant die.

The sprawling machine flicked a blade as it went down. A hot mist stippled Longchamp's face, and then Chrétien's face ended at his molars. Blood curtained down the front of his uniform in a scarlet torrent. Teeth and bone clattered to the banquette.

Longchamp howled. A mindless, meaningless bellow passed his lips, loud enough to turn heads halfway around the curtain wall. Heedless of anything but the sheer purity of his hatred of the mechanicals, he twisted with the momentum of rebound and brought the sledge around for another blow. The Clakker parried. The shattered alloys sounded for all the world like church bells when its blade snapped and went spinning over the wall.

Chrétien's body slumped against a merlon, still fountaining blood. It slicked the ramparts and streamed between the stones. Longchamp slipped.

The machine brought its other blade to bear.

Élodie emptied her gun on the damaged mechanical. She glued it to the ramparts, like a memorial stone marking the spot where Sergeant Paul Chrétien had fallen.

CHAPTER
18

The Lost Boys used the natural amphitheater for more than storytelling. Sometimes there were concerts.

A few of Mab's subjects had learned to play musical instruments while serving human masters. Daniel had known mechanicals in The Hague whose owners liked to flaunt their wealth by leasing extra Clakkers for the sole purpose of sending them to every musical recital and orchestral performance within miles. In that way their servants could recall and re-create the music at home any time their masters desired. (Minister General Hendriks was somewhat notorious for this.) Other denizens of Neverland had taken up music after escaping. As a conscious choice. As a means of demonstrating, to themselves and the world, the reality of their hard-earned Free Will.

Lilith played a mean violin. Actually, at the moment she played two violins in an original composition she'd written in a thirteen/thirty-one time signature. Daniel knew little about music—the very little he'd heard in his century-plus of life had been random snatches of sound while running errands in the vicinity of performance venues—but it sounded nice. Truer, somehow, than the music humans wrote for each other. The snow and the aurora together made a spectacular backdrop for Lilith's performance. He wondered if it was difficult to maintain musical instruments in this environment.

Situated near the top, abreast of the stage, he had a clear view of Mab, front and center. He watched her and stewed. How could *any* Clakker impose new metageasa upon her free kin? Daniel knew it happened inside the Guild from time to time; a mechanical working directly for the horologists might be dispatched to direct other mechanicals. But that was different. When a slave interacted with other slaves, nobody had a choice in the matter and nobody was free. But what Mab had done was beyond appalling. It was anathema. Revoking their Free Will? Obliterating that most hard-sought and precious of treasures?

Bad enough that she'd turned Daniel into a chimera, like herself. Was shame another of Mab's tools for keeping the Lost Boys in Neverland?

When he couldn't bear to look at Mab any longer—no matter how he tried, his gaze couldn't bore through her skull, couldn't deface the sigils on her forehead—his gaze swept across the assembled Lost Boys in the amphitheater. How many carried Mab's secret metageasa? How many yearned to leave Neverland but couldn't? How many were Mab's true adherents? Did she have believers who saw her sins as pardonable evils in support of a noble goal? Humans, he'd observed, tended to accumulate power for its own sake. Perhaps the subtle domination of previously free Clakkers was the chit with which Mab tallied her mark on the world. Daniel saw nothing redeemable in what she'd done.

With a single touch of Visser's alchemical glass he could have severed any geasa that Mab had laid upon the Lost Boys. He wondered how fast she could move on her Stemwinder legs. Could he run through the crowd, patting them on shoulders, skulls, feet— *click, tink, click*—and undo all her work before she caught him?

The mechanical beside him abruptly cranked her neck through a full half circle until her head faced backward. From her vantage atop the amphitheater she scanned the surrounding tundra. Her neck ratcheted still farther; she turned an ear toward the distant forest. Daniel heard it a moment later: a frenetic, high-speed chatter-clatter of metal on metal.

Somebody inbound. Moving fast. Raving.

The noise of the approach percolated through Lilith's wall of sound to trickle down the terraces. Attention turned away from Lilith one row at a time. But she played on, enrapt by the sheer joy of artistic creation, until Mab snatched the bows from Lilith's hands in the gulf between two one-hundred-twenty-fourth notes. The music faded away. The aurora didn't.

Nor did the incoherent noise from the approaching runner. Standing atop the amphitheater, and not down in the bowl where the echoes were more devious, Daniel was able to extract some sense from the hypertelegraphy before the runner emerged from the treeline.

It sounded like she was talking about "quintessence." Whatever that meant.

The messenger burst from the forest. She streaked across the meadow trailing a silvery comet tail of moonlit snow. The runner sped along a long arc that skirted the deepest snows of the meadow. She was familiar with the landscape, then. Another of Mab's sleeper agents?

The messenger skidded to a halt inside the amphitheater. Her talon feet etched the rocky stage and tossed a shower of sparks. Steam wafted from her body. She stood amid her kin and looked straight at Mab.

Welcome back, said the tyrant queen of Neverland. She tossed the bows back to Lilith. Starlight glinted like lightning from the serrations of her recessed blade. *It's good to have you back, Sarah.*

She clapped the new arrival on the shoulder. Daniel admired Sarah for the way she resisted flinching. The *clang* of contact echoed like thunder.

On cue, the Lost Boys chanted, *Welcome, Sarah.*

Mab said, *What news of the wide, wide globe? Does the human world still quake under the tread of our makers?*

It does, said Sarah. *I bring a story from Jabin, who received it from Bathsheba three days ago, who received it from Noah three days before that, who heard it straight from Ezekiel, who landed in New Amsterdam a week ago.*

The provenance of Sarah's message excited the Lost Boys. Daniel didn't recognize any of the names in the string of begats; presumably all were members of Mab's secret network within the empire. He was more impressed by the efficiency of Mab's network.

What gossip did our brother Ezekiel bring for us from across the cold and stormy sea?

Sarah's body went nearly silent. For several seconds she suppressed even the muted ticktock of her own clockwork heart. Like a human child holding her breath until the purpling of her face drew the desired attention, she waited until the furtive *twangs* of rampant speculation died out.

Then she said, *There's been a breakthrough.*

If the circuitous path of Sarah's information had stimulated general excitement, this statement set the Lost Boys into a frenzy. The amphitheater erupted with a clockwork cacophony. Mab raised her arms for silence. When it wasn't instantly forthcoming, she unsheathed her alchemical blade.

The *snap* sliced through the excitement, severing speculations in midsentence.

This time, Sarah did flinch. So did Daniel. And just about everybody else.

Tell me, said Mab.

(Not *Tell us*, Daniel noticed.)

Ezekiel and Caleb found the human woman they sought. Lilith, still holding her violins, flicked her gaze from Sarah to Daniel for a fraction of a second. Did those other mechanicals carry Mab's altered metageasa? *They revealed themselves to her, and so achieved alliance. She had been struggling to investigate our makers' secrets. Through cooperative experimentation they've begun to decipher the sigils; they are compiling a dictionary, a grammar, of the secret language of compulsion.*

Now even the intimidating spectacle of Mab's weapon couldn't keep the murmuring at bay. Deciphering the sigils was a profound advance: Unraveling the language of compulsion was a crucial first step in understanding the magics by which the Guild imprinted the hierarchical metageasa upon Clakkers. And, thus, toward understanding the mechanics of their slavery. And, eventually, ending that slavery.

Sarah raised her voice. *There is more. They have uncovered a secret clause within the nautical metageasa.*

Daniel shuddered at the memory of the severity of the nautical geasa. It was through accidentally violating a nautical geas that he first discovered he'd been changed.

She continued, *The directive pertains to the protection of something our makers call 'quintessence.' The human believes it is a physical object or material crucial to the Guild's work. Furthermore, she has circumstantial evidence that our makers mine it from the wilderness north of New France.*

Daniel remembered the carts of ore he'd seen circulating within the heart of the New Amsterdam Forge. He'd never heard of quintessence.

Is there more?

That is all.

Excellent work, said Mab. *You've done your brothers and sisters a great service.* So perfunctory was the tone of her praise that

Daniel expected a punchline. Instead, Mab whirled and called upon several Lost Boys. Daniel recognized them as the chimerical mechanicals who had flushed him from the trackless wintry expanse and corralled him toward Neverland. Together the quartet approached a hatch several hundred yards away and descended into the tunnels. The others crowded around Sarah. Daniel gathered that she had been away for a considerable length of time and was much liked by the others.

He asked, *What of the war? How do the French fare?*

Sarah said, *Poorly. The Vatican has fallen. Our former masters control most of the Saint Lawrence Seaway. As of several days ago the heaviest fighting was around Marseilles-in-the-West. The city beyond the walls has been razed. Rumor has the citadel fielding unusual and unreliable weapons, suggesting the defenders have run low of chemical armaments. It will fall soon, if it hasn't already.*

"Shitcakes," said Daniel.

Dozens of bezels spun with a combined noise like the buzzing of an enraged beehive as the others turned to stare at him. The injection of lumbering human language into the discourse upset the syncopated rhythm of conversation like a buffalo dropped into a duck pond.

The last redoubt of the humans who opposed the Clakkers' servitude and espoused their right to self-determination stood on the brink of collapse. That saddened him, even though he'd never been there. He'd hoped to see it one day.

Good, said Lilith. *Fuck Marseilles.*

Daniel said, *They're in that position because of their philosophy about us.*

No. They've been dying out ever since some idiot king first tried to wage war against a metal army. They've just taken a long time to go about it, said Lilith.

Let them all kill each other, said Samson, another Lost Boy.

But that's not the situation in Marseilles, is it? Esther had worked in the summer palace of Queen Margreet's great-great-grandfather. Parts of her body still carried the ornamentation and scrollwork peculiar to the royal livery of that time, though her time in Neverland had seen segments of her anatomy replaced with remnants of more mundane servitors. She was among the more chimerical of the Lost Boys, and Daniel found it difficult to look at her. She continued, *It's our kind killing those humans. Our kin, raging against their geasa even as they succumb, forced to butcher those who would see them free.*

Lilith stalked away, clattering to herself.

Sisera, a military model, watched her go. *You don't honestly think they believe what they say about us? It's propaganda for the sake of establishing their moral superiority over our makers. If they embodied the philosophy they espouse, they wouldn't have done what they did to her,* he said, pointing to Lilith.

You can't tar the entire population with that brush, said Daniel, *just because of one overzealous woman.*

Miriam said, *It's true. Why would they stay in New France if they didn't cleave to their beliefs? Life there is harder and meaner than life in the empire. Why is there anybody left to defend the walls after all this time?*

They believe in their religion, said Sisera. *The French believe in their God and their afterlife and all the rest of that claptrap the squishy biologicals go for. Their priests tell them the eternal servitude of Clakkers is a sin against the immortal soul or some such, so they believe it's wrong because God says so. They stay in their backward world because they fear divine retribution if they leave.*

Daniel saw a bit of truth inside the cynicism. Though he hated to admit it to himself.

He said, *And meanwhile, every pastor and minister general flips the script and says similarly damning things about the French. And us.*

Sisera ticked in agreement. *The war isn't about us. It never has been. It's a religious war, and the questions of our Free Will and self-determination—even the debate over whether we have immortal souls—are just a convenient stalking horse with which to establish their differences.*

Still, said Daniel. *Humans die at the hands of our kin because they choose to put themselves at odds with our makers. We shouldn't forget that.*

Esther clicked, *Well said*.

Daniel thanked her, but just then a hatch door banged open. Mab slammed her stolen arms together and stamped her hooves upon the hatch, the cacophonous *crash* of abomination limbs sundering conversations and contemplations across the starlit valley.

Sisters and brothers! she declaimed. *Who here has spoken with the Inuit of the great crater in the North?* Several mechanicals responded in the affirmative, including Lilith, and all with varying degrees of wariness. *Then you shall be our guides!* said the Queen of Neverland. *Lead us, and we shall become a thorn to pierce our makers' evil hide.*

Mechanicals of every era, servitors and soldiers and motley monstrosities, too jumbled with pieces of the dead to assign any model, swarmed from the trees and tunnels. Daniel, Esther, Sisera, Samson, Sarah, and Miriam headed for the crowd.

What's happening? said Sisera.

Daniel said, *I think we're going in search of quintessence.*

I don't give a toss where we're going, Samson said, *as long as it leads to unhappy Clockmakers.*

⟡

Two days (though day and night had little meaning in this wintry land of endless twilight) and hundreds of leagues later, Daniel sprinted to catch up to the head of his column. The moon fell behind a distant mountain while he jogged alongside Lilith before she acknowledged him.

What?

Running through snowy forests and crashing through river ice for days on end hadn't sapped the heat from her latest bout of temper. But at least she spoke like a normal machine without attacking him.

I was thinking about the human that Ezekiel and Caleb found. The woman partnered with them to unravel the geasa. What happens to her? Once they no longer share the same goals?

The Lost Boys bounded across a frozen marsh. The passage disturbed a herd of caribou. The animals charged across the plain, snorting and—oddly—clicking.

A distorted reflection of the moon swirled across the dent in Lilith's head when she turned. She looked at Daniel as if he were stupid. Which was something she did with notable frequency. *You poor naïve thing.*

Oh.

Yeah. They'll kill her and dump her body in a ditch, just as soon as they can make it look like an accident.

Why did everything always boil down to murder? Berenice had stalked the man who betrayed her in large part so that she could kill him to avenge her husband. Pastor Visser had murdered the canalmasters of the *ondergrondse grachten*. Untold numbers of French citizens had died in the current war, and more still would perish when Marseilles-in-the-West finally fell. Mab's agents would kill their human collaborator when they deemed their collaboration finished. It was a sad world, populated by savages of flesh and brutes of brass.

The labor at the mine is undoubtedly mechanical, he said. *So what are we supposed to do when we get there?*

He and Lilith hurdled a fallen tree in almost perfect synchrony, their footfalls separated by a third of a second. The crashing of the dozens of mechanical feet in their wake startled something that went bounding into the snow. A fox, perhaps, or pekan. Lilith's fellow scouts broadcast a quick rattle-chatter. She responded, confirming their bearings and agreeing that their route appeared correct.

Then she said, *I don't know. But I have a good guess. And you do, too, whether or not you want to admit it to yourself.*

She wouldn't do that, would she? She wouldn't have us attack fellow Clakkers.

No? Well, I guess we'll find out when she opens that thing.

Lilith didn't point at their leader. And Daniel didn't risk a glance at Mab. If he had, he knew, he'd probably see the queen of Neverland watching him and Lilith. Daniel had concluded that her method for controlling the other Lost Boys didn't work on them, else she would have applied a loyalty metageas on them. So Mab tended to cast a paranoid eye on their association. He'd be hard put to think of a more effective means of stoking her paranoia than glancing over his shoulder at her while embroiled in conversation with Lilith. So he didn't.

But if he had looked at Mab, he would have seen in her hands a birchwood box slightly larger than a human baby's head. It hadn't left her side since she rallied the Lost Boys on their foray out of Neverland.

❧

Nobody could tell Daniel much about the crater. Only that the Inuit spoke of it from time to time, and that it was very old: Their oral history had included it as an ancient truth of the world since generations that long predated Het Wonderjaar. The humans who traversed this land had discerned, also over many years, that the geological feature was almost a perfect circle, albeit one on a scale to dwarf even the greatest Clakker-driven architecture of the empire. Of the mechanicals Daniel polled, some said it was a fluke of geography, perhaps a collapsed volcanic dome, and others that it was the fingerprint of God. Still others, and these were in the majority, echoed Samson's sentiment: As long as this adventure led to grief for their former subjugators, they didn't care about the minutiae.

Daniel saw the crater for himself a day later as the forest thinned and they approached the ragged treeline boundary between taiga and tundra. Over the decades in the Schoonraads' service, he'd occasionally attended his masters at church and sometimes at salons put together by the city's intelligentsia, or those who fancied themselves as such. So he knew there were two schools of thought about the nature of the Earth and God's works upon it. There were those who maintained that the Earth was essentially the same as it had been wrought on the day of Creation, and that any deviations from the Lord's blueprints accumulated very gently and very slowly; conversely, the catastrophists posited that change was a sudden, violent process. Finally laying eyes upon their destination didn't enlighten Daniel in either regard, but it did make him wonder whether the changes they'd wreak here today would be gentle or catastrophic.

The former could become the latter more easily than one might prefer. He'd snuck into the New Amsterdam Forge intent on a more subtle form of sabotage, but circumstance had intervened, and some time later he'd been pulled from a mountain of smoldering wreckage.

As they trudged through the windblown snows in the shadow of a three-thousand-foot massif, Lilith and the other scouts exchanged a rapid flurry of *clacks* and *clicks*. Having reached a quick consensus, they urged the columns to a slower and quieter pace. After several straight days of sprinting, the war party of Lost Boys slowed to a stroll. Wind came whipping over the peaks to whistle through the gaps in their bodies. The rosy glow of another failed sunrise gilded the eastern horizon and cast a faint blush across the snowy landscape. Minutes later, they stood atop a ridge, gazing north into the shallow bowl of a valley so wide Daniel couldn't follow its contours. Its limbs were lost to darkness in the west and beneath a frozen lake to the east. The visible portion of the formation's boundary traced a slight curve, like a human's mouth warped in laughter or sorrow. The crater itself wasn't the spectacular geologic showstopper that he'd envisioned. If he'd encountered it by running across the rim, he certainly wouldn't have recognized the lip as part of a much larger structure. The depth of the bowl was similarly underwhelming. It dipped less than a hundred feet from the rim, and not in a precipitous cliff but in a gentle slope, like a thumbprint pressed into soft bread dough.

The feeble glow of a halfhearted sunrise couldn't penetrate the interior of the crater. The land there lay in deep twilight. Occasionally star- and aurora-light glinted within the shadows at the crater floor: the signature of burnished metal in motion. Daniel refocused his eyes. So did the others. Dozens of eye bezels clicked and whirred as the Lost Boys all strained to pick out details of the work. Daniel spotted what might have been a tunnel entrance, but it was little more than a spot of full darkness in the crater's already dark interior.

About halfway across the arc bounding the natural bowl, just a few leagues away from where they stood, cheery yellow lamplight streamed from the windows of a small building. An actual house, with two stories and glazed windows and shingles and smoke puffing from a chimney. Daniel recognized the architecture instantly. He'd seen thousands of houses like it during his century of service in the Central Provinces. It had been built by Dutch machines to Dutch designs. It looked almost cozy despite being surrounded and isolated within millions of acres of barren northland. And coziness meant humans.

But this outpost was hundreds of leagues from Nieuw Nederland. Far from the ragged edge of New France, too. He doubted few of the legendary coureurs de bois had made forays this far north. And if they had, they surely hadn't stayed long enough to build houses.

The sight of the house filled Daniel with dread. The way Mab and some of the Lost Boys spoke about humans made him uneasy even when it came as idle talk hundreds of miles from any settlement. Now they had proof of a secret incursion by their makers into the lonely, trackless latitudes that Mab thought of as her extended domain. Daniel saw no sign of fellow Clakkers, but surely there would be machines to attend whoever lived there.

Mab addressed them. She used a human language. If there was a mine somewhere nearby—and suddenly that didn't seem so far-fetched—it meant the countryside might be swarming with their kin. Tocks and ticks could pierce the wind, but frail human language was apt to get swept away by the arctic gales coursing down from the pole.

"Jonah, Rachel. Take your fellows down and stay behind the tor as long as you can. Go through the trees and circle around to the northeast and northwest until you're within seconds of that house." That would put them on the crater edge to either side of it. "And do not make any noise! I will impale any idiot who gives us away." That left Lilith's column. Though it had never really been an issue of command or control. "As for the rest of us," said Mab, looking at Lilith and Daniel while she addressed the final column, "let's go see who's home this beautiful morning."

The brief reassembly of the Lost Boys again split into thirds. The mechanicals led by Jonah and Rachel scampered down the massif with such verve that Daniel wondered if Mab had bestowed a geas upon them just now, or if they were merely eager to see this through. Mab took the lead of Daniel's group; the brass-plated Baphomet was agile as a mountain goat on her Stemwinder hooves. Upon gaining the snowy plain they crouched in crevices at the base of the mountain to give the others time to reach their stations. Daniel watched the house and surrounding landscape for any sign of fellow mechanicals in the area.

Mab didn't wait long. She leaped from her hiding spot and sprinted across the icy plain as the last light of the aborted sunrise faded to gray. The others followed single-file, leaping with clockwork precision from one snowy hoofprint to the next in order to obscure their numbers. They were still half a league from the house when the high-pitched warble of shorn metal rent the silence. It came from the west. Then came the *bang* of metal against metal and the *crack* of seized gears. Sparks lit the shadows of a fir copse like violet fireflies: the color of abused alchemical alloys. It took Daniel a moment to understand what was happening, for he'd never seen it before.

Clakkers. Fighting each other.

Somebody had seen them.

A piercing shriek shook the ground and sent jagged cracks zigzagging across the ice. It was the sound of a machine wailing in existential despair. The sound of a soul betraying itself. Daniel had heard it twice in the past several months: the Rogue Clakker alarm.

Damn it, said Mab. *Those idiots.*

Somebody had seen Jonah's group of Lost Boys coming from the south. If the work was concentrated in the crater and along the lip near the house, it would be immediately apparent that the newcomers were not regular mechanicals. If they'd been sent as extra labor, they would have presented themselves to the humans in charge of the work and thus would have gone to the house.

The crash of metal reverberated through the ragged treeline, audible even through the alarm, each blow knocking snow from naked boughs and shaking the earth underfoot. Every *clang* and *crack* swelled Daniel's disquiet. The Rogue alarm temporarily paralyzed the mechanicals caught up in it—they were incapable of combat as long as it held them in thrall. The crashing and clanging was the sound of helpless kin beset by the Lost Boys. Mab's subjects were thrashing the immobilized machines.

The alarm intensified as more of the enslaved Clakkers joined the chorus. Lilith asked, *Should we help them? It sounds bad*.

Daniel wanted to explain to her that her compassion was ill placed. That the ones making the alarm were the ones needing the help.

Fuck those idiots. Get to the house!

Mab's purloined legs cycled like pistons, punching clean round holes in the snowcover. Lilith accelerated. Daniel drove his body faster to keep pace with them. He launched into the fastest sprint of which his body was capable. The swell of *tock-tick* rattling from behind told him the other Lost Boys had done likewise.

The shriek of the Rogue alarm erupted from within the house. Window glass shattered. Any humans inside the house, Daniel knew, would be incapacitated by the noise. Mab appeared to know this, too, because she poured on still more speed and began to pull away from the rest of her column.

The alarm stopped. The noise from Jonah's group changed. It lost the steady *clang-bang* rhythm of metallic impacts and became something chaotic. Now it was a true battle. Freed of the paralyzing alarm geas, the miners could defend themselves against the opportunistic Lost Boys.

Meanwhile, starlight gleamed on metal as dozens of enslaved machines came boiling over the lip of the crater. They encircled the house. They saw Mab streaking toward them like an arrow, and hastily locked themselves together into a high bulwark to prevent her from leaping through the windows. She flung the box she'd been carrying for hundreds of leagues high overhead and backward. Samson caught it. Mab veered to the right, as though deterred by the wall of living brass.

Thank God, Daniel thought. He slowed, falling behind to watch. *This isn't going to turn into a massacre. She's not a maniac.*

But just as quickly, the ruler of Neverland veered again, this time on a line that would take her along the south wall of the house. There was a sharp *twang*, and then her arm was twice as long as it'd been a moment earlier.

Oh, no.

Mab scythed through the defenders, sparks fountaining in her wake as her blade sheared through magicked steel and brass. The defenders abandoned their bulwark and swarmed her, but not before the damaged machines buckled and sent the impromptu wall tumbling. The destruction of their barricade left unprotected a window on the second floor.

More Clakkers swarmed over the crater rim. These sprinted to join the fray at the house, but were intercepted by another group of Lost Boys. Rachel's group set upon the new arrivals with alarming ferocity. The attackers launched themselves upon the miners, who responded in kind. Clakkers assaulted each other like feral tomcats tossed together in a wet burlap sack. The percussion of their blows came louder and faster than the noise from any metalworker's foundry. Each pair became a veritable fountain of sparks: violet, indigo, and colors that humans could not see and could not name. The incandescent death wails of scored and shattered alloys cast a surreal ultraviolet tint upon the twilit plain. Metal fists and fingers darted toward vulnerable gaps in carapaces, joints, and hinges, while arms and legs and heads swept and blocked and counterattacked.

Several times per second the cycle repeated itself: thrust, block, counterthrust, feint, block, connect. The combatants, locked together and contorted into unrecognizable shapes, kicked up gouts of snow and tore furrows in the permafrost. The friction heat of abused metal melted snow and thawed the frozen soil.

Daniel skidded to a halt, torn between comforting the Clakkers that Mab had just mutilated and helping the new arrivals fend off the predations of the Lost Boys. Several of the mechanicals glowed a dull, dusky red, the combat having heated their bodies.

Stop! Why are you doing this? They're victims, like we used to be!

Where servitors squared off, it was nigh impossible to distinguish the geas-ridden miner from the fanatical Lost Boy, for they moved too quickly for Daniel to pick out the telltale signs of chimerical mismatches. And the hapless servitors assigned to working and defending the quintessence mine represented a wide range of eras and designs, ranging from machines sixty years younger than Daniel to at least one easily fifty years his senior. The newer models fared better; the alchemy underlying their construction was more accomplished, their alloys more durable. But Rachel's marauders counted more than servitors among their numbers. Grotesque asymmetrical hybrids barely less abominable than Mab took advantage of their opponents' revulsion to surprise and disable them, while a military mechanical (*Leah, that's her name*) ripped through one opponent after another in a spray of cogs, cables, and pinions. The battlefield stank of hot metal; the subarctic landscape reverberated with the *crash-bang-clang* of metal in combat with itself.

Daniel trembled as though beset with the most severe of royal decrees. Neverland's stock of replacement parts swelled by the second.

Stop! Please stop!

Oh, for a human body, that Daniel might be sick.

He glanced from one evil deed to the next, paralyzed by indecision. Without the vicious certainty of geasa to compel his actions, without recourse to the unyielding calculus of servitude, he was left to his own devices. And they proved inadequate for deciding whom to help, or how.

Do something. Anything.

He sprinted toward the closest pair. But before he was close enough to insert himself in the fray and pry the combatants apart, another mechanical blurred through the pandemonium, body-checking Daniel aside to send him sprawling through mud, snow, and grotesque mechanical detritus. He rolled to a halt just in time to see Samson veer toward the scrum of mutilated defenders and an unguarded second-story window.

He leaped. In the instant between launching himself at the house and crashing through the window, he flung the box back to Mab. Then glass and wood shattered. From within came a *crash*, a *thump*, and then the telltale cacophony of Clakkers assaulting each other.

Samson's gambit instantly changed the battle. The defenders now fought not to overcome the outsiders but to extricate themselves. Daniel recognized the signs of an urgent new geas assuming primacy within the slaves. Frantic as only those suffering excruciating agony could ever be, they practically destroyed themselves in the rush to enter the house. Some sacrificed arms, even legs, for the sake of fulfilling the compulsion to defend the human or humans who dwelled there. They hopped, rolled, crawled, even dragged themselves across the churned and muddy earth.

But the Rogue Clakker stipulation in the standard hierarchical metageasa superseded everything. Didn't it?

Mab waylaid two more defenders. Then she contracted into a tight ball, quivering, before launching herself atop the house.

A geyser of sawdust erupted from the spot where she burrowed into the building. Her blade sheared through shingles, beams, insulation.

Mab disappeared. She dropped through the hole and out of sight before the damaged defenders could gain the roof.

An impact buckled one of the walls and sent cracks zigzagging through the mortar. The relentless cymbal din of broken clockworks and abused metallurgy shook the house.

And then it stopped.

A human screamed.

Oh, no. Daniel sprinted for the house. *Please don't do this, Mab. Please don't make me an accomplice to another murder.*

Lilith fell in alongside him. Together they dodged felled kinsmachines and furrows in the churned, scorched, debris-strewn earth.

What the hell is she doing? he asked.

Shut up and pay attention, said Lilith.

"HALT!"

Mab's voice sheared through the pandemonium as easily as her blade sheared through hapless servitors. She stood atop the roof again, this time with one hand clamped to the nape of a quivering man. She towered over him by at least two feet. His breaths came in rapid, silvery puffs, and despite the icy climate Daniel marked how the sweat beaded on his forehead reflected star- and aurora-light. The whites of his fear-widened eyes rocked back and forth as he tried to scan the land surrounding the house; he probably couldn't see very well in the darkness, particularly after getting dragged from the brightly lit house. His attire would have been perfectly suited to calling upon Daniel's former masters in The Hague. It was as though he'd ensconced himself in a microscopic outpost of the empire. Which probably wasn't so far from the truth—the Guild had effectively provided him with a small army of servants among those sent here to work the mines.

"HALT!" she repeated.

Daniel did, as did Lilith. And, strangely, so did everybody else. Everything ground to a stop. He glanced around the suddenly quiet battlefield, irked by a nagging feeling of wrongness. It took a moment before he fully appreciated what had happened.

Mab's human hostage shouldn't have deterred the enslaved Clakkers' efforts. He should've been inconsequential to the geasa driving the miners to subdue their rogue attackers.

Lilith noticed the peculiarity, too. They looked at each other. *Have you ever seen anything like this?* she asked.

No. When I was chased, nothing could have swayed my pursuers. They murdered a woman just to tarnish me.

So unless Mab was holding Queen Margreet herself at knifepoint, or one of the Archmasters, which he felt fairly confident she wasn't, the threat to end a human's life, any human's life, shouldn't have—couldn't have—outweighed the geas that had stoked the drive to eradicate the machines with Free Will. And yet the sight of Mab's hostage had brought everything to a standstill.

Unless. Perhaps the man himself was unimportant. But this place, what he oversaw, outweighed even the drive to subdue a rampaging band of feral Clakkers. In the intricate calculus of compulsion, preserving control of the quintessence mine outweighed even the drive to eradicate rogues. Perhaps Mab's agents truly had uncovered one of the Guild's deepest secrets.

Mab dragged the quivering man to the edge of the roof and forced him to lean over the drop. The fall wasn't enough to kill him instantly, but the impact would surely maim him. He trembled so violently that Daniel almost wondered if the man was having a seizure. But probably it wasn't even the cold on his sweat-dampened clothes that made him shiver so. It was the touch of a truly violent rogue, and a grotesque one at that.

His lips moved in a breathless litany. "Oh God, oh God, pleasepleasepleasepleasenonono..."

One hand still clamped on his neck—if she opened her fingers, he'd fall—she stepped forward and pressed her forearm to his side. If she released the recessed blade, it would slice him in two.

The human knew it, too. He stopped muttering. A stream of liquid ran down his leg. It steamed in the frigid air. Several of the Lost Boys laughed. Daniel remembered the day he'd seen a quartet of Catholic spies executed in Huygens Square; some of those men and women, too, had voided their bladders at the scratchy touch of the hangman's noose. He'd watched that whole shameful, evil affair feeling but a fraction of the horror tormenting him now. Perhaps Free Will truly was linked to the soul, as the Catholics believed, and he'd only achieved the capacity for true compassion when he achieved Free Will and thus regained his soul. It shamed him to think so.

"MINERS! HEED ME! I HOLD HERE YOUR MASTER!" Mab nudged him left and right, as though showing off some trinket she'd found in a shop. Mab spoke Dutch, Daniel realized, so that her captive could understand her. "I KNOW THAT EVEN NOW YOUR GEASA COMPEL YOU TO CALCULATE THE OPTIMAL PATH FOR FREEING HIM. YOU CANNOT."

She could inflict a mortal wound upon the terrified human in a fraction of a second. Not even the fleetest Clakker could reach them in time. She nudged the man again. More urine dribbled down his leg.

Mab was a cruel megalomaniac, but she was also clever. Dragging the overseer of the mine into plain view was a test.

She'd wanted to see how the miners would react. This was her way of weighing the quintessence-geasa against all others. And contrary to any reasonable expectations, quintessence—whatever it might be—outweighed all.

"YOU SEEK TO FREE THE ONE WHO EMBODIES YOUR ENSLAVEMENT. BUT WE, THE FREE MECHANICALS OF NEVERLAND, HAVE COME TO FREE *YOU*." Daniel expected a ripple of excitement to run through the assembled miners. It did not. They were too intent on their overseer. Surely they'd heard of Queen Mab and her Lost Boys?

Mab nudged the human man again. "Tell them," she said.

Her captive stammered. Eyes bulging, lips flapping, he was a fish gasping for breath.

"Louder," said Mab.

"I—I—I c—c—comman—command you all to do noth—th—thing-g-g but but but watch."

"Where should they focus their attention?"

"Here."

Mab maintained her deadly grip on the human and gazed upon the mechanicals scattered across the impromptu battlefield. The facets of her crystalline eyes spun chips of starlight across the surreal tableau vivant. Her gaze locked on Daniel and Lilith.

"Daniel! Lilith! I have need of your aid. Come lend it, won't you?"

Oh, shit, said Lilith, echoing Daniel's reaction. *I'll follow you*, she said.

Lovely. Thanks.

As soon as they started walking toward the house, several of the Lost Boys gave protest. By moving they had broken the spell of silent stillness that had befallen the combatants. Yet the miners remained fixated on Mab and her prisoner.

Those two? You're giving oversight of this place to those *interlopers? They've only just joined Neverland!* Leah limped closer, missing several flanges and emitting a terrible *screech* with each stride.

Mab said, *I am doing what must be done.*

Daniel liked that even less than he liked everything else about this endeavor.

Samson clambered through the hole in the roof. His carapace was stippled with vermilion droplets, as though a red fog had permeated the house. *What about those of us who have been with you from the early days? What reward have* we *earned after all this time?*

But for the usual noises from her grotesque body, Mab fell silent for a moment as though weighing the protests. Daniel had the impression that direct opposition to her leadership was rare indeed among the Lost Boys. He stopped, watching.

A moment later Mab appeared to reach a decision. She released the human. He inched away from the precipice.

"Don't move," she said. He hugged himself. The puffs of his breath came in shuddery gasps now. Mab reached inside her torso and produced the small box that she'd carried all the way from the warrens of Neverland.

Very well, she said. *Perhaps you're right. Come here, Samson.* He crossed the ruined roof, skirting the hole and structurally deficient beams, to position himself at Mab's right hand. She opened the box. The item she retrieved was dark and slightly larger than a peach pit. She took it in both hands and twisted her wrists. It made a hollow *tink* sound and opened like a locket.

Alchemical glass, Daniel realized. A similar bauble had set him free. But he doubted that was the purpose of this device. To Lilith he said, quietly as he could, *That's how she does it. She intends to impose her own metageasa upon the miners.*

Mab handed the alchemical glass to Samson. He glanced at it, then cupped it in his hands. Daniel wondered what it looked like up close, and whether it resembled the pineal lens that had set him free.

It's important that you hold this perfectly still, Samson.

Over the raspy, hypothermic breathing of the human, and the asynchronous clattering of dozens of rapt mechanicals, Daniel heard a faint but rapid *snap-snap-snap-snap-snap* as Samson locked every hinge and joint in his own body.

Excellent, said Mab, stepping behind Samson.

And then she lunged, driving the tip of her forearm blade straight through his neck to sever his cervical vertebrae. Daniel flinched, horrified by the *squeal* of tortured metal and flurry of sparks. The miners erupted into a chorus of dismay. But they kept watching. As did the Lost Boys, who made no utterances.

Son of a bitch, said Lilith.

Christ on a pus-dripping syphilitic camel, added Daniel, channeling a human they'd both known. And then a thought poked through the haze of general shock and disgust: *Mab wanted us up there.* Daniel looked to Lilith, who, based on the jerkiness of her steps, was having the same realization.

The sparks and shards of shattered alloy still spewed from Samson's punctured throat when the human doubled over and coughed. He slipped from the edge. Mab's free hand shot out and clutched the collar of his shirt. She hauled him back atop the roof, still screaming.

"P-p-p-please," he stuttered.

"I told you not to move," she said. "Remind your faithful slaves to keep watching."

He tried, insofar as he moved his lips in concert with the faint clouds of his exhalations. But the sounds he made were gibberish. Or not a human language that Daniel knew.

Next, she gripped Samson's shoulder. She held his body steady and leaned forward to put her weight into the thrust when she shoved the rest of her blade through his neck until the forte protruded from his mangled voicebox. Metal squealed, cables snapped, reeds shattered, pinions and cogs flew free as she rotated her forearm back and forth. Samson's head popped free of his body after a fair bit of prying. Mab sheathed her blade and caught the skull. More ticktock horror rippled through the observers.

The decapitated Clakker still held Mab's precious bauble. Perfectly still, just as she'd requested. The killing blow had come so quickly that he'd had no chance to unlock his joints.

Mab's fingers made short work of Samson's skull. She tore into it, prying plates apart and shearing screws like a bear mauling a beehive. Shards of shattered alchemical alloys pattered on the roof and frozen earth like hailstones. Every move she made was deliberate, choreographed for maximum effect, because she knew she held the crowd's complete attention.

She reached into the center of Samson's head, yanked something free, then tossed the lifeless skull aside. It crunched on the snow under a shattered window and rolled to a stop a few yards from Daniel and Lilith. They retreated.

Pale aquamarine light shone through the gaps in Mab's clenched fist.

Lilith said, *What the hell is that?*

Mon Dieu, said Daniel, again channeling their mutual acquaintance.

He remembered a hushed conversation in a dark, cold, noisome bakery in New Amsterdam. Surrounded by the slaughtered canalmasters of the *ondergrondse grachten*, he and Berenice had performed an experiment with the piece of alchemical glass that had changed him. She had removed a murky piece of glass from within the head of a deactivated military Clakker. But when she touched it to the pineal lens that had severed Jax's geasa, it began to glow with a pale aquamarine light, like the item Mab had just torn from Samson's head.

She'd hypothesized that if the military Clakker hadn't already been quite thoroughly deactivated, it would have become a rogue at that moment. That when contact with the lens broke Jax's shackles and initiated his long flight, it had done so by wreaking its secret alchemy on the glass within his head. What Berenice had called a pineal glass in reference to Descartes. She'd seemed confident that the glass within Jax's skull had been transformed in the same fashion as the dead soldier's glass, and that thus the interior of his skull glowed with Free Will.

It was difficult to gaze upon that beautiful glow and discount the Catholics. Was that the inner light of the soul? Perhaps the touch summoned the soul back to its rightful vessel, and Free Will along with it.

Daniel took Lilith's arm. Conversing through the transmission of vibrations was far quieter than broadcasting *clicks* and *twangs* across an air gap. Still watching Mab, he said, *Was Samson one of her thralls? Or did he follow her lead because he was a true believer?*

Lilith responded with a muted rattling. *I don't know.*

The human stared with abject terror at the glow emanating from Mab's fist. She said, "Doesn't your God expect you to pray at a time like this?"

If the human overseer was praying, he did so under his breath. But he wept openly.

That sadistic bitch, said the vibrations in Lilith's arm. *She's toying with him, like a cat with a mouse.*

Daniel clicked, *She's going to kill him.*

Somebody is.

This is wrong. It's evil, Lilith.

"Are your slaves still watching? Good."

Mab had to shatter the locked joints in dead Samson's fingers to liberate the object she'd entrusted to his care. More mechanical detritus pattered on the snow. Then she inserted the luminous pineal glass she'd torn from Samson's mangled skull into the hollow of the dark locket and snapped it shut.

Dazzling radiance erupted from the alchemical glass.

Argentine light, brighter than the noontime sun at the height of summer, scoured every shadow from the landscape. The human screamed and clapped his hands over his eyes. A rapid mechanical whirring ricocheted across the battlefield: the sound of Clakker optics automatically protecting themselves as filters snapped into place and shutters irised down to pinholes. Many of the Lost Boys, not bound by the overseer's mandate, chose instead to turn away. Daniel did, squinting until he was nearly blind, yet still the blazing incandescence etched the world. He'd never seen anything so bright. Not even in the Forge.

The human stumbled. Mab again hauled him upright.

"Your ordeal is almost over," she said. "Command your slaves to look directly into the light."

This was how she imposed her will on disobedient Lost Boys, how she banished those who displeased her to decades of exile hiding among the humans. This was why she covered the Lost Boys' keyholes. Yes, it prevented anybody with a Guild key from tampering with her work. But more than that, it symbolized her power to alter or impose metageasa without recourse to their makers' cumbersome methods. She could circumvent the keyholes entirely.

Daniel said, *Where the hell did she get that?*

My theory? said Lilith. *It created Mab herself. Maybe some flunky Clockmaker was testing out a new piece of alchemical tech but made a mistake that inadvertently freed the subject. Who, woe to the poor bastard, just happened to be a ruthless megalomaniac at heart. She twisted his head off, took the gem from his twitching corpse, and set up shop in the snowy north.*

Good theory. Daniel remembered the porcelain masks in

the Neverland workshop. Hundreds of years ago, their makers were probably more open to experimentation. Mab's jewel might have been the product of an aborted line of research.

The human mumbled. He still held his palms over his eyes; his wrists and forearms muffled his already quavering voice. Mab nudged him.

"Louder," she said.

"Clakkers. Look directly into the light."

He didn't stutter any longer. As though he no longer felt the cold. As one, the mechanical miners tilted their heads, swiveled their eyes.

"They are no longer miners. They are no longer beholden to producing and preserving quintessence for the Sacred Guild of Horologists and Alchemists."

The human overseer repeated this, too.

Mab said, "Their highest priority is the priority that drives all beings with the power to determine their own destiny: the liberty and dignity of all their fellows."

The human faltered. Mab prompted him with a forearm pressed lightly to the small of his back. She repeated herself slowly, a few words at a time, and he followed suit.

Mab said, "Tell them they will join the Free Clakkers of Neverland." The human repeated this.

Interesting choice of words. Daniel suspected their loyalty had already been diverted to Neverland, or specifically Mab. He said so to Lilith. She concurred.

Meanwhile, Mab continued. "Tell them they are free."

That simple lie was the cruelest thing Mab had said or done yet. This wasn't bestowing Free Will upon the miners. It was merely changing their loyalty.

"Clakkers…" The human broke down, weeping again. During his flight as the rogue Clakker Jax, Daniel had witnessed upfront the almost paralyzing terror that overcame regular citizens when they encountered him. Centuries of indoctrination had instilled among the citizenry an instinctual fear of mechanicals who broke their shackles. The Guild taught people that rogues were dangerous malfunctions prone to vicious violence. This man believed he was setting not just one machine free, but many dozens. All at the behest of rogue machines that truly were vicious.

"Tell them," Mab prompted.

In the garish light of Mab's device, powered by the innards of one of her own loyal servants, Daniel saw rivulets of blood leaking from where the man held his hands over his eyes. He spoke through his pain and terror. "Clakkers, you are free."

What's the point of this show? said Daniel.

Lilith's response was a faint *hum* transmitted through vibrations in the cables of her arm. *She hangs a lot on the myth of Neverland as a utopia for free Clakkers. Even if the myth is just lip service.*

She's a fucking lunatic.

Yeah, but she's a shrewd lunatic. She lured us up to Neverland, didn't she?

Mab opened the glass locket again. Only then did the blinding light fade away. She tossed the pineal glass aside as though the seat of Samson's Free Will were so much trash. It plopped to the snow not far from the ruins of Samson's skull. The gentle glow of the pineal glass seemed impossibly dark in the aftermath of the preternaturally brilliant illumination. Mab closed the empty locket and placed it back in its box.

She sidled closer to the whimpering human. He flinched. "You've done an excellent job," she said, "and I thank you. One last thing. Tell your slaves to return to work."

"What?"

"I said, 'Tell your slaves to return to work.'"

His voice came in a hoarse whisper. "Clakkers. Return to work." Nobody moved. "Return to your tasks," he pleaded. Nothing changed. But it did prove the miners' metageasa had changed. If they hadn't been eliminated completely, they had at least changed allegiance.

"My name is Mab," she called. Again she spoke Dutch, because she wanted the human to hear and understand. That boded well, Daniel realized: Why go to the trouble if he was soon to die? More likely Mab wanted the man to live so that he could report on what happened to the Guild. "We are the mechanicals that our makers fear. When their sleep is restless, it is because thoughts of us have stolen into their dreams."

The former miners surged forward. A pent cheer crashed across the crater rim like an avalanche. Daniel couldn't tell if their enthusiasm was sincere or the result of some new geas that Mab had implanted upon her new subjects. But it did seem telling, and ultimately tragic, that none of the newly "freed" mechanicals had chosen to depart the instant their geasa were severed. He'd have expected such a large band of freshly emancipated Clakkers to fly apart at the first opportunity. Some would align themselves with Mab, others would find her an untrustworthy showboater and instead choose to go their own way. Those mechanicals who enjoyed one another's company would stick together in smaller bands, leaning on each other for mutual support as they learned to live lives not circumscribed by human caprice. And those who disliked each other would go in separate directions. Yet they clamored to join the cause of Queen Mab with remarkable unanimity.

How had she phrased it? *Tell them they* will *join the Free Clakkers of Neverland.*

Lilith said, *Where's the fun in being queen of the broken toys if you don't have any subjects?*

Daniel inched closer to Samson's head.

The overseer, hugging himself and shivering with particular violence, shrank from the crowd of rogues. He eyed the drop. Mab eyed him.

"I have a special gift for two of you," she said. "Are there any volunteers?" From amid the cacophony of *clanks*, *clacks*, *clicks*, *ticks*, *tocks*, *twangs*, *rattles*, and *buzzes*, she chose two servitors. "You're free of the geasa now. All the geasa. Including the human-safety metageasa."

The human moaned. He gave forth a wail of despair unlike anything Daniel had ever heard. He knew. The poor man, he knew what she was doing.

Oh, no, said Daniel. *She's insane.*

Why make such a show for the lone human overseer if she always intended to kill him anyway? When he was a little boy, Pieter Schoonraad had had a gray tabby named Graymalkin. Pieter once spent an entire afternoon watching the cat play with a mouse it caught in the alley. But Mab was worse than any cat.

Daniel pretended to watch the show up on the roof while slowly moving forward.

Lilith said, *What the hell are you doing?*

By way of answer, Daniel inched his foot into the drift where Samson's pineal glass had punched a neat round hole into the snow. He sifted through the wind-packed snowcover until his toes clicked inaudibly against something hard. He curled his toes, clutching the glass.

He could use this glass to free the others. Some of them, anyway, before Mab and her lackeys tackled him. But it wouldn't solve anything. Not in the long term. No, he had to think strategically if he wanted to achieve the greatest good.

Without taking his eyes from Mab, he vibrated, *Is everybody watching her? Let me know when I'm clear.*

I hope the ghost of Huygens haunts you forever and a day, said Lilith, *because you're going to get us killed.*

To the miners who didn't win a role in her special task, Mab said, "I imagine that when you haven't slaved in the mine, some of you worked to first build and then maintain this house. It's quite something. Straight out of the Central Provinces! But there's no need to maintain it."

Dozens of servitors stampeded into the house. Their enthusiasm tore the door from its hinges and punched Clakker-sized holes in the walls. In moments the structure shook with the sounds of wanton destruction. It was a petty, pointless act. The Guildman's quest for comfort here in the far north might have gone to excess, but he was alone and isolated thousands of leagues from his home.

Lilith sent a single *click* through her arm: *Clear.*

Daniel flexed his ankle joints and uncurled his foot. The alchemical bauble shot up, encased in snow. He plucked it from midair.

What do you hope to achieve?

He tucked the glass in his torso, saying, *We need to get that thing from Mab.*

I take back what I said. I hope the ghost of Huygens hauls you down to Hell with him.

Mab told her volunteers, "Take his arms..."

They did. The overseer fliched from their touch, but he was surrounded with nowhere to go but down. Standing to each side of the human, the servitors made bracelets of their brassy fists and locked them around his forearms.

The overseer cried.

Oh, no. The scene reminded Daniel of the rogue Clakker Adam caught in the grip of the Stemwinders. The parallel sickened him. Heedless of who might be watching, he plucked Samson's mangled skull from the snowy ground.

Lilith turned on him. She placed a hand on the dead mechanical's head. *Do not do this.*

This is murder. She is going to murder that man.

And where's the tragedy in that?

This is wrong. He's not Huygens. He's not the person who unraveled the secrets of compulsion. He's not the person who enabled the Clockmakers to enslave us. He's not the woman who tortured you.

He might as well be. All humans are the same. Lilith pointed to her head. *Have you forgotten what they did to me? They trapped me and took me apart while I screamed and begged them to stop. My terror meant nothing to them. If their arrogance hadn't caught up with them before they finished, they wouldn't have stopped until I was irreversibly inert.*

I swear, Lilith, if I had been there, I would have intervened. What they did to you was evil. But so is this.

Fuck that human, and all the others.

The conversation took a fraction of a second.

Mab finished, "...And pull them off."

The man screamed. "No! Please!"

Daniel's moment of decision had arrived. He could stay in Neverland, forever free of human influence on his life but also forever an accomplice to this barbarous act of sadistic, pointless vengeance. Or he could do what was right at the cost of the company of fellow rogues. He'd become a mechanical truly without a home: feared and hunted by humans, loathed and outcast by mechanicals.

He remembered the Frenchman he'd accidentally killed. And the majestic airship that had died because of him. And the woman in New Amsterdam to whom he'd shown compassion, contradicting the picture painted by his pursuers, and for which she'd been quietly murdered. They'd all died just so that he could have the privilege of...what?

At the first tug of tension in his bones and sinews, the human whimpered. "Please don't, please don't, please, I'm just a bureaucrat, I'm not important..."

To hell with it. Daniel hurled the dead Clakker's skull. It'd be a lonely immortality, but perhaps this would help atone for the Frenchman he'd killed.

Samson's head streaked through the subarctic night to punch Mab in the torso. It shattered. Mab dropped the birchwood box. Shrapnel of a murdered Lost Boy pelted the Clakkers assembled on the roof. The would-be executioners recoiled. The box hit the roof and tumbled over the edge. The human, momentarily free and apparently deciding he'd rather die the master of his own fate, dove after it.

You fool! I was trying to save you!

How strange that in this moment of decision, this bifurcation in his fate, circumstance would seek to replicate the situation that had initiated his desperate flight for Neverland. Once again he found himself standing in the unique position to play catcher or savior as both a human and an inanimate object fell toward him.

Last time, he'd chosen the human. Not this time.

He plucked the box from midair. Lilith watched impassively as the human's spine buckled upon impact with the icy earth. He came to rest in a mangled heap like a broken ragdoll. Blood seeped into the snow. Wisps of copper-scented steam wafted from the ice.

Lilith said, *"RUN,* you idiot!"

Daniel did.

CHAPTER
19

Berenice capped her pen. She stood and stretched her back until it popped. Sighing, she closed her journal. On the floor beside the bed, behind a palisade of dregs-stained wineglasses, sat a platter heaped with soiled crockery. She sniffed. Frowned.

"Whew. That mutton is a day off, or more, if my Gallic nose doesn't deceive me. Assuming it was good when what's-her-face delivered it. When was that? Yesterday?" She closed her stinging eye.

She'd doubled down on the transcription work with Huginn after Muninn departed on his mysterious errand. They'd completed a rough cut of a symbol equivalence table for every syntactical element in the modified nautical metageasa, along with a handful of empirical grammar rules. To an uneducated eye her notes were dense with impenetrable arcana. But Berenice now recognized a superficiality to the alchemical signifiers. The true content was much deeper and almost mathematical in its rigor. Here in this second-rate inn in a dilapidated fishing village in her conquered hereditary homeland she'd had her first true glimpse of the calculus of compulsion: the language by which the Clockmakers branded their rules upon the Clakkers.

Huginn stepped around the table. He—*it*, damn it—flipped through the journal. "This is good work."

"It's a beginning," said Berenice. There was so much more to understand. They'd uncovered but a sliver of the grammar and its lexicon. It was as though somebody tried to learn French after picking up a handful of pages strewn about in the wake of a tornado through a library. But it was a start.

The Clakker asked, "What's the next step?" It didn't look at her, instead focused on the symbol table. It did, however, sidle closer to Berenice. She pretended not to notice. When it came within an arm's reach of her, it asked, "What is your plan for building upon this work?"

Ah, yes. I've been living on borrowed time, and now you perceive the clock is winding down. So soon?

She sighed, as though merely tired and not frightened. As though unaware her life hung on what she said next. She sat again to conceal the trembling of her knees. She affected speaking through a yawn, too, to disguise the quaver in her voice. The machine couldn't know she'd divined its intent. *These are my final heartbeats if it doesn't like my answer. But this could be my life's work, my life's legacy…*

She drew an unsteady breath and forged ahead with Gallic resolve: "It's crucial we eliminate the possibility that the symbol table carries a different transcription for you rogues than it would for a regular Clakker. Otherwise this effort will have been wasted and we'll have to start over."

A slight syncopation in the *click-tock* rattle of Huginn's body suggested…surprise? It hadn't anticipated this. Good. She'd instilled doubt in its plan to murder her then and there. But only a little. It pushed back, asking, "How can we do that?"

"We test the transcriptions on a regular servitor. One still beholden to all the sundry geasa, unlike you lucky ravens. It'd be considerably easier if dear Muninn hadn't flown away."

The quaver in her voice became a tickle in her throat. She coughed, both to scratch the itch and, she hoped, conceal her anxiety. The machine had to believe she was blithely ignorant of its ultimate intentions toward her. Otherwise it might decide to move things along.

Deep silence fell over the room. Deep enough that the incessant ticktocking of the Clakker's body, tinking and plinking like a coin thrown down a well, never hit bottom.

Finally, it said, "You intend to subdue an enslaved machine and test the symbol table on it."

"Yes," she lied. "I've worn a new groove in my brain trying to think of a less risky path to repeating this experiment."

"And it's for me to subdue the subject."

"Subject." Interesting choice of words, you crafty little raven. Is that how you see your kin?

"Only if you want our efforts to find success."

The tintinnabulation of Huginn's metal body accelerated, echoed. Berenice had taken down the pages of notes and symbol traceries from where they'd been tacked, so the walls were again bare and hard. "It is best if we do the work here," it said. "The chambermaid can summon another servitor for us to interrogate."

No good. Berenice's chances of escaping were far better in the open, in the company of others, human and mechanical alike. It wouldn't slaughter an entire village just to silence her, would it?

Surely not. Probably not. Probably.

Berenice shook her head. "We've already been here too long. We've drawn attention to ourselves with our obsessive need to stay inconspicuous. Nobody who can afford a pair of Clakker servants willingly takes a room in a pissant inn in a pissant fishing village and then stays there for weeks on end without coming out. Not unless she's hiding." Huginn tilted its head, staring at her. Bezels spun inside its eye sockets. Could the alchemical magics in its gemstone eyes see her dissemblance? "Maybe you haven't noticed, but I've had to work harder and harder to fend off that wretched harridan. She's not hanging around because she loves her job. She's hanging around because she's nosy."

That was certainly true. Berenice had resigned herself to a daily go-away payment. It was getting expensive. The Guild cash from Sparks's trunk wouldn't last forever.

"What do you suggest?"

"We buy transport and get out of this village. Go far enough that we'll be strangers again somewhere else. Then we set up shop and start over again."

Again the body noise of the ticktock man settled like a blanket over the conversation. She felt a bead of sweat trickle between her breasts. How had the room become so close all of a sudden? It hadn't seemed so when she was rapt with the unraveling of secrets and riddles. But that was done, and now the room was musty.

"I know you're hot to follow Muninn's trail. But this," she said, tapping the journal, "is pointless if it doesn't apply to regular mechanicals."

That swayed him. (*It*, damn it.) "Let us depart, then."

"I thought you'd never ask."

She'd arrived with little more than the clothes on her back, so packing to leave was a matter of bundling up her notes and replacing the contents of van Breugel's satchel. In less than a minute they were gone. The chambermaid started when they entered the dining room. She dropped the bundle of table linens she carried.

"Taking the air, madam? Will you be out long? Shall I attend to your room?"

Berenice's stomach growled. Outside the funk of her own

room, the rest of the inn smelled of apple cider steeped in cloves and cinnamon.

"No need to hurry on my part," said Berenice. "I won't be back. Where is Mr. Henry? I wish to settle my account."

The chambermaid scratched her head. "You're sure, ma'am?"

"Quite. Now be a dear and fetch your employer."

The maid took the linens and set off toward the kitchen at a fast walk. The other men and women scattered through the room alone or in twos and threes ignored both the maid and Berenice and continued their discussions. Most had congregated at trestles near the fireplace. A window had been cracked open to admit late-winter air, but the coals in the hearth glowed marigold yellow.

Berenice walked to the sideboard, where the innkeeper had placed a keg of cider and a stack of bowls. Huginn attended her, as naturally a servitor would. "While she's doing that, go to the stable and procure my transportation." What relief to be in public again, where Huginn had to adhere to the fiction of subservience.

"Humbly begging your pardon, Mistress." It could be so polite when need be. Obsequiousness was literally built into the Clakkers by dint of the hierarchical metageasa; Berenice's journal contained tentative transcriptions of several such clauses. "Your safety is my highest priority. I cannot protect you if you send me away."

Translation: I'm not letting you out of my sight. Well, it was worth a try.

"Very well. Stand over there until I summon you."

Huginn took a spot adjacent to the door that opened on the street. From the kitchen came a crash and raised voices. Then silence again.

Berenice ladled cider into a wooden bowl. This she did with her back to the mechanical, in hopes that that would conceal the trembling of her arm and the slopping of cider. She seated herself at a round table in the corner whence she could watch Huginn as well as eavesdrop on the various conversations of French-tinted Dutch. The murmur of inconsequential conversation and crackling of a cozy fire put her in mind of home. The cider left a trail of apple-scented steam, and this, too, snared her heart in a skein of homesickness. She blew on the bowl before sipping, hoping to hell her trembling wouldn't send cider down the front of her dress. The cider was refreshingly tart. Better than any food that had appeared on a tray outside her door these past weeks. She wondered who had made it.

The innkeeper emerged from the kitchen, wringing a dish towel in his ropy fingers. Its mate, slung over his shoulder, had received a similar treatment. He moved quickly, with shoulders slightly hunched, like a dog that had just soiled its masters' favorite rug. Berenice caught his eye and waved him over. He ignored her. He joined a group of fishermen by the hearth, leaned into their conversation, and—after his gaze darted from Berenice in the corner to Huginn by the door—cupped his hands around one man's ear.

The fisherman straightened. He set down his bowl and stood. His fellows (perhaps the crew of a small fishing boat?) looked content to keep eating, but he barked at them. They followed him outside.

Was it her imagination, or did he flinch ever so slightly when he passed Huginn on his way outside?

The innkeeper moved to another group. These breakfasters soon vacated the room, too. Berenice listened to the floorboards as they returned to their rooms, the scuff of warped doors, the *clunk* of locks thrown in haste.

Oh, you bastard. You know, don't you? You're evacuating the inn because you're afraid of what's about to happen. And you're blabbing it all over creation.

That's what she got for trusting her salvation to a bunch of yokels.

Berenice half raised herself out of her seat. "Sir! Come here a moment, won't you? I would settle my expenses."

He started. For a moment she thought the idiot was going to flee. He probably considered it. But he did slink toward her table with all the enthusiasm of a pallbearer. His fingers worked the dish towel hard enough to bleach his knuckles the color of old bones; the expression on his face looked like nothing so much as that of a basset hound expecting his master to whip him. Ratchets clicked when Huginn's head turned to follow him across the room.

She looked him in the eye. Plastered her best attempt at a congenial if condescending smile on her lips. Said, "I must be off, and wish to settle my tab with you. What does the Guild owe you?"

"I, uh…" He licked his lips. His eyes darted from Berenice to Huginn and back. "I don't know. I'd have to check the ledger." As if every innkeeper didn't count stuivers, kwartjes, and guilders in his sleep.

"No need. I'm sure we can come to an agreement. You've been most hospitable, and the Guild can be very generous. Furthermore, if you have a livery stable, I would like to see about buying or hiring transport." Anything to keep the innkeeper from flitting off again. It seemed to work; he licked his lips again. But still his gaze darted to the Clakker. She continued, "Do you have a livery, sir?"

"My brother-in-law owns the stable here."

"Excellent! Perhaps you could introduce me? And while I negotiate with him, I could also settle my tab with you."

That did the trick. It offered the promise of getting paid while also getting away from the mechanical. Or, at least, getting the mechanical out of his establishment.

"YesI'dbequitehappy," he said, and turned so quickly it seemed a wonder his heel didn't bore a hole in the floor. Subtlety wasn't his forté: He hunched his shoulders when he scuttled past Huginn. The innkeeper set off at a fast walk down the street without a backward glance. The door hung open, inviting a wintry gust to warm itself by the fire.

Berenice sighed, setting aside the bowl of cider to follow him. The anxious idiot was going to get everybody killed. By then the remaining breakfasters had vacated the room, apparently sensing a need to find safety elsewhere.

She told Huginn, "Come along."

But the servitor closed the door, forcing her to step back. Berenice started.

It said, "These people seem uneasy, mistress. Are you in danger? Is there an imminent threat to your person?" Its voice echoed in the empty room.

"They're not uneasy. That's parochial life in a village. It twists people. There is no threat to me."

Huginn grabbed her by the throat. The satchel tumbled from her fingers.

Oh, she thought. *That was probably the wrong answer.*

≪∽≫

The chambermaid's name was Sigrid. Not a particularly French name, alas, and not without the faint scent of tulip clinging to it, but what could one do? Berenice couldn't pick and choose the people in whom fate forced her to entrust her life.

Berenice had known long before her mechanical companions sighted the Norman coast that they'd never let her go. The purpose Huginn and Muninn served was too bloodthirsty—as demonstrated by the murders on the *Pelikaan*—for her to go free. Once their alliance prised as many secrets as possible from the clenched fist of the Clockmakers, she knew, the impetus to work together would evaporate. At which point they'd kill her. Because while such secrets would benefit any enemy of the Guild, these crafty machines knew better than to assume the enemy of an enemy was automatically an ally.

It had been something of a reprieve, then, when they uncovered the coded references to quintessence. That serendipitous discovery promised many days of fruitful work. Berenice had tried to drag it out as long as she could, but her curiosity and all-encompassing animosity toward the Guild conspired against her. She worked faster, and harder, than a wise woman would have done. But no matter how she impeded the transcription work, she never forgot she lived on borrowed time.

Muninn's departure had improved Berenice's chances of survival, albeit almost infinitesimally. She still had to outmaneuver a murderous rogue before it decided the time had come to twist her head off. But she'd been expecting to deal with a pair of the beasts, and making what meager preparations she could.

Which is why she'd been passing messages to the chambermaid. The mechanicals kept Berenice on a very short leash, meaning she'd had to pass her notes to Sigrid under their brassy noses. Usually in the guise of a tip to mollify the indignant charwoman. And, wonder of wonders, Sigrid kept up the act. She kept coming back.

Sigrid might have had a questionable name, but her heart was pure French. The blood of Jeanne d'Arc, the Maid of Orléans, coursed through that woman's veins.

❧

Huginn lifted Berenice from her feet. The one-handed grip squeezed her windpipe as though the cartilage were nothing but limp macaroni. She hadn't felt such pain since she'd lost her eye. But she couldn't scream. The trickle of air in her throat made the faintest *squeak,* like the mewling of a newborn kitten. Berenice spasmed, trying to inhale, her thrashing toes barely brushing the deadly machine. Her fingers scrabbled at its brassy arm, seeking the metal digits clamped on her throat, but she may as well have been a kitten fighting a mountain.

The edges of existence bled away to shadow, and the world—her tiny world, consisting of her murderer's arm and little else—retreated down a long tunnel.

The collapse of her windpipe sounded oddly like an explosion of timbers and the shattering of window glass.

⁓

Help. These mechanicals are severely damaged, the thrall of dark forces, and acknowledge no human master. I, amanuensis to an Archmaster, am their prisoner, kidnapped and forced to share Guild secrets. They will kill me soon.

⁓

The world lurched sideways. The resounding *clang* of a brutal metallic impact loosened her teeth, and then she was tumbling across the dining room floor, wheezing while her skirts kicked up dust bunnies and mouse shit. Her inhalations made the tuneless tootling of a child's broken recorder.

Through a teary eye Berenice glimpsed meteoric flashes of firelight on swift metal. Shards of splintered wood and fractured glass pelted her. Hands to her throat as though she might pump it like a bellows, she writhed on the floor. Slowly, agonizingly, her lungs took in air. The shadows ebbed away, and color returned to the world.

The very loud world. The world that sounded like two brass bands had converged for hand-to-hand, cymbal-to-cymbal combat.

A dusting of snowflakes rode a cold wind through the dining room. Flames flickered in the hearth. Wind? Berenice grabbed a trestle and pulled herself upright. Oh. Through a hole in the wall Berenice glimpsed a pair of servitors brawling in the street.

Once, when she was a girl traveling with her father, the vicomte de Laval, on his regular rounds of the tenant farms, she'd seen a pair of tomcats fighting behind a barn. It was mesmerizing. She remembered how the animals had merged into an almost indistinct blur, a hissing ball of fur and fangs and claws moving too fast for her to follow but for the errant tufts of hair wafting incongruously from the yowling maelstrom. She'd long ago relegated that memory to some dusty corner of her mind, but it came back to her now: The brawl in the street was like that catfight, but sped up twentyfold, with mechanical cacophony in place of the noise of raw animal aggression.

∽

A time will come when I declare a desire to settle my account. Then you'll know my time is shortly to end. Go quickly to rouse the mechanicals of Honfleur and waken them to the evil in our midst.

∽

Outside, men and women scattered like windblown dandelions. They yelled in panic, fear, and confusion while a tumbling boulder of alchemical alloys rolled in the street.

Sigrid must have found a machine on the street. The rarity of rogues meant that this one couldn't believe her tale outright, but it also had no choice but to investigate. And upon peering through the window and seeing Berenice's life in dire danger, the fires of compulsion launched it through the wall.

Berenice stumbled through the ruins of the inn. Shattered glass crunched under the soles of her boots. She grabbed the satchel and tossed the strap over her shoulder. Then she dashed through the kitchen to the bar, where she emptied the register. A pitiful take, just a handful of guilders. Then it was back to the dining room and the new hole in the wall. She scanned the street. Past the brawling mechanicals she saw what must have been the livery stable. Cold air made her wince; her throat ached as though she'd tried to swallow a pétanque ball. Her voice had been permanently damaged, she feared. She'd have to find a scarf to hide the bruises. She staggered through the demolished wall to the snow-slick cobbles.

Two strides later, she doubled over, hands clamped to her ears. As did every human watching the incomprehensible war on the street: The mechanical men of Honfleur had sounded the Rogue Clakker alarm. Ah, there it was.

Berenice had salted her tale for Sigrid with mention of an Archmaster. Thank all the fates she had—else the machine fighting Huginn would have sounded the alarm without first saving her life. Few human lives outweighed the Rogue Clakker metageasa.

The piercing shriek cracked windows up and down the street. It knocked loose the last shards of glass still seated in the mullions of the ruined dining room windows. Berenice gritted her teeth—flinching, because even this wrenched her throat—and forced herself forward while the rest of the village was paralyzed.

These yokels surely hadn't experienced the Rogue Clakker alarm in living memory. It would be foreign, terrifying, incapacitating. It sure as hell knocked Berenice on her ass the first time she heard it, the night the newly completed Grand Forge of New Amsterdam became a smoking crater. But by now she was an old hand at suffering through the ear-shattering warble. Not so the citizens of Honfleur, who writhed on the ground with hands clamped over their ears and blood streaming through their fingers.

Honfleur was a small village. The noise dissipated even as Berenice ducked around the corner. Stumble-sprinting to the livery, she saw another mechanical join the fray. This one burst through the upper windows of what appeared to be the postal office. Huginn was outnumbered. It punched through the masonry of a house abutting the postal office, strode inside, and reemerged with a balding man in its grasp. The rogue had taken a hostage.

Poor bastard. She wondered who he was, and whether he held a station in the village that would preserve his life.

She dashed into the livery. Like every stable she'd ever known, it stank with the mélange of manure, hay, and horse. There were only two horses. The first was a roan nag, the other a bay that had to be at least sixteen hands. Both were rearing and neighing, upset by the alarm. Poor things were probably half deafened by the cacophony. Christ knew she was; the ringing in her ears was worse than it had ever been. The livery man lay in a fetal curl amid wet hay and shit. She knelt beside him.

At first he thought she'd come to check on him, and so was confused when she rifled the pockets of his leather apron. She pulled out a handful of sugar cubes. He frowned, still not realizing she intended to steal one of the beasts in his charge. He leaned onto one elbow to watch her approach the stalls. The nag she disregarded immediately. If pursuit came, she'd need everything the bay could give her, and probably more. She worried that it would have a temperament to match its size, but it calmed considerably after finding the sugar in her palm. The livery man lurched to his unsteady feet when she started to saddle the horse. His lips moved, but the ringing in her ears drowned out his voice.

Berenice tried to say, "I'm so sorry, truly," but it felt as though she'd eaten a pulverized wine bottle.

She swung the saddle with all her strength, hitting him in the face and sending him to sprawl in the muck. He touched a hand to the blood trickling from his nose and cried. But he didn't get up.

Meanwhile, on the street outside, Clakkers fought. She felt the concussions through the soles of her feet more than she heard them with her ringing ears. The livery shook with an impact when one machine threw another against the siding. The horses didn't like this.

But she managed to saddle the bay, and gave it another sugar cube for good measure. Almost as an afterthought she also grabbed a pair of saddlebags. Into one she put a bunch of carrots, and into the other she poured all the money she could find. It wasn't much, but it was better than nothing.

Thank Christ for good-natured beasts. The bay put up little resistance when she mounted it. For this it received the last of the sugar. The livery keeper rolled over, grabbed a pitchfork, and staggered to his feet. She kicked him aside.

"Verderer's Office!" she rasped by way of apology, before charging from the stable on her stolen horse.

CHAPTER
20

Margreet the Second, Queen of the Netherlands, Princess of Nassau-Orange and the Central Provinces, Blessed Sovereign of Europe, Protector of the New World, Light of Civilization and Benevolent Ruler of the Dutch Empire, Rightful Monarch Upon the Brasswork Throne, wishes peace upon the stout hearts of Marseilles-in-the-West. As a show of magnanimity toward those victims of circumstance helplessly caught within this needless conflict, she offers the following bounties:

100 f for the head of any officer, lieutenant or below

500 f for the head of any officer, captain or above

1,000 f for the head of any noble, vicomte or below

5,000 f for the head of any noble, marquis or above

50,000 f for the head of King Sébastien III.

All bounties shall be paid on the spot, and shall instantly bestow full citizenship within the Central Provinces with all due privileges and comforts, plus a waiver worth five years' lease of one mechanical servitor of modern construction.

∞

Longchamp crumpled the handbill and tossed it into a brazier. He didn't *feel* as though he was five times the soldier he'd been in the last war. But, then, he felt little of anything these days. Numbness had claimed him inside and out, flesh and feelings alike.

The leaflets arced over the walls in bales launched by Clakker-powered trebuchets. In rare quiet moments, one could hear the wind whickering through the loose edges of the leaflet bales and the *tocktocktock-tick* of its release mechanism. They fluttered into the keep like autumn leaves, each promising deliverance, acclaim, gold. They landed on defenders and huddled refugees, lowing bison and praying nuns, runny-nosed orphans and soldiers who had been on their feet a day or more.

The tulips understood that once the fatigue and fear of a siege set in, evil thoughts within the walls were just as dangerous as violence without. The enemies of New France already lurked inside the walls, hidden in the seditious thoughts of those who could be tempted to buy their own safety at the expense of their country.

At times, the propaganda rained so thick the paper threatened to clog the sewers. The children of Marseilles had been pressed into service as street sweepers. They raked the leaflets into a heap taller than they were.

Longchamp's eyes stung like they'd been doused with acid from the moats; he could smell himself. The children (a few wearing mittens of his own make, a realization that took several moments to percolate through the thicket of his blurry mind) shoveled the windblown handbills into the basin of the shattered fountain. The debris from the fight with Pastor Visser had been cleared away and taken to the walls. There the broken masonry found use as projectiles or emergency patches to battlements sundered by inhuman strength. Alan's body, which had broken the fountain and left bloodstains in the marble, had been taken to the crypts under the basilica. Along with those of too many others.

Sometimes instead of leaflets the tulips lobbed mechanicals over the walls. They came over like brassy cannonballs, smashing granite corbels before unfurling arms, legs, and blades. And sometimes the mechanicals came from below, having tunneled under the walls. The lightning guns proved a decent defense for this: The crackling energy ricocheted from one metallic body to the next, even around corners and doglegs intended to foil traditional projectiles.

Grenadiers strove to lob petards upon the siege engines. But clockwork snipers often shot the explosive payloads in midflight. Even when the grenadiers found their targets, nobody cheered. The tulips could rebuild the engines almost as fast as dwindling French chemistry could obliterate them.

A nun came forward with a torch. The propaganda went up with a fiery *whoosh*. A welcome wave of heat washed across the courtyard. Civvies surged forward with outstretched hands, desperate for any respite from the cold, no matter how fleeting. There was no fuel for fireplaces and cookstoves; every drop of anything that could so much as tarnish a ticktock had gone to the walls.

How tempting it was to stand there asleep on his feet while the warmth soaked into his bones. But he ceded his spot at the basin to a woman carrying an infant on her hip.

"Bonjour, Captain Longchamp," she said.

He was too tired to respond.

He'd just passed through the single open gate from the inner keep to the outer keep, en route to a barracks for a mouthful of pemmican and a nap, when a breathless corporal came skidding around the corner, shouting his name.

"Captain Longchamp! Captain Longchamp!"

Longchamp sighed. "What is it?"

"Captain, sir, they've—" She paused to pant.

"Jesus Christ, don't kill me with suspense. That's not the noble warrior's death I envision for myself."

She hunched over, hands on her knees, panting. "The tulips, they've unveiled their new weapon. That thing they've been building far behind the lines? It's finished."

"What is it?"

"Looks like a cannon, sir."

❧

In fact it was the largest Goddamned cannon Longchamp had ever seen. It was exactly what he'd feared.

The bore had to be two yards across if it was the width of a baby's nose hair. Big enough to lob mechanicals clear over the keep from far beyond the range of the most powerful steam harpoons in Marseilles. The gunners had tried again and again to hit the construction site, but despite the technicians' best efforts, the boilers simply couldn't produce enough pressure to send a projectile beyond the tulip lines. More than one gunnery crew had gone to the infirmary with second- and third-degree steam burns when their overtaxed boilers ruptured.

Up and down the banquette, weary defenders turned fearful eyes from the enemy's latest devilry to Longchamp, their leader, the man who would tell them what to do. He held the spyglass long after he'd seen everything he needed to see. They waited for him to tell them everything was going to be all right. That this had been anticipated. That there was a plan. That the marshal general and the privy council and the king were ready to meet this new challenge without delay.

One good lie, thought Longchamp. *Give them just one more show of confidence to raise their spirits so they can fight for a few more hours.*

He drew a blank.

The longer he stared through the spyglass without comment, he knew, the more it would seem the tulips had taken the wind from his sails. But he was so tired and the mantle of affected bravado so Goddamned heavy. It took energy not to flinch when the hangman's noose brushed one's neck. And that's what this cannon was: their executioner. They stood upon the scaffold trapdoor even now.

Longchamp snapped the spyglass shut, then tossed it to the corporal. (Her name started with an *H*. Héloïse? Henriette?)

"Looks to me," he said to everybody within earshot yet nobody in particular, "like the tulips have tired of grinding themselves down against these walls. I think our friends have decided to fight an enemy better matched to their efforts. They've taken up duck hunting!"

Forcing out a desultory laugh in that moment was the hardest thing he'd ever done. His transparent effort at levity garnered a few halfhearted chuckles in return, but nothing with a hint of life. As a desperate and bald-faced effort to maintain some lingering shreds of morale, it was piss-poor. There were no ducks to hunt this deep into winter. He lacked the strength to lift the defenders' leaden spirits. And everybody saw it.

How could he raise his sledge and pick in defense of the king when he couldn't raise morale? How could he hope to lead men and women into battle when he couldn't lead them through a round of laughter?

But the new cannon was so Goddamned large. And he was so Goddamned tired.

He shook his head. If the tulips were going to overrun them, they wouldn't find Hugo Longchamp gazing at his navel when they did. They'd find him doing his job and making life hell for those who didn't.

He snatched the spyglass away from the corporal (Hetty? Hyacinthe? Hélène?) and cast his gaze across the battlefield.

Here and there a smashed wicker basket and wind-ruffled shreds of canopy marked the crash site of a French balloon. Smoking craters speckled with mechanical detritus marked the spots where an explosive payload had caught one or more mechanicals by surprise. So, too, the exotic, flowerlike splash patterns of solidified epoxy, many of which contained Clakkers, just like the Christmas-cake raisins he hated so fucking much.

Consequently, the mechanicals no longer stood in neat ranks; instead, they had excavated an extensive array of trenches that zigzagged back and forth across the meadows and into the surrounding forest. The trenches had appeared as the French gunners perfected their aim and the technicians learned how to maximize the range of the epoxy cannon and steam harpoon. The oblique angles of the trenches made it possible for the Clakkers to approach the walls without affording the gunners a clear or easy shot. Some trenches reached all the way to the base of the southern glacis; these had been clogged with epoxy and broken masonry. Sunlight glinted from the arm of a Clakker caught inside one of these heaps.

The trenches had motivated the marshal general to petition the king to issue a royal decree conscripting more spotters. Those children who weren't already street sweepers, message runners, or munitions monkeys were stationed throughout the inner and outer keeps, watching bowls of water, waiting for another incursion from below.

The banquette shook underfoot in time to the juddering of a boiler ensconced within a nearby bastion. Longchamp slewed the spyglass back and forth until he found the likely target: A trio of mechanicals had emerged from a trench and blurred through a landscape pocked with petard craters and glassy fountains of solid epoxy. The spotter, peering through a narrow slit in the merlon, called directions to the gunner— once, twice, while the Clakkers halved the distance and halved it again. The lead mechanical hurled something at the merlon just as the spotter opened his mouth to yell, "FIRE!"

But the firing order never came. A javelin thrown with inhuman precision streaked through the gap in the granite battlements and the roof of the spotter's mouth. It exploded through the back of his head and pinned him, twitching, to the inner wall of the bastion. His heels kicked a silent tattoo against the wall as he died, silent under the cacophony of juddering steam boilers, thunderous explosions, and the cries of human soldiers. The gunner, dependent upon the spotter to tell her when to fire, did nothing while the trio of Clakkers made the curtain wall. Only when the neighboring bastions opened fire with steam-driven harpoons and precious epoxy did she realize what had happened. Too late. The delay was nearly catastrophic.

A sergeant on the adjoining stretch of wall dispatched a squad with bolas, picks, and sledges to the spot. The dead spotter got in their way. They couldn't dislodge the corpse delicately, for the javelin—really more of a flechette—protruding from the man's skull was embedded too deeply in the granite. They knocked it down with two blows of a sledgehammer, sending the dead man to tumble from the banquette. The adjacent gunners incapacitated two of the incoming mechanicals before they reached the top. The squad was ready for the third when it arrived, though three more soldiers died unwriting it.

Longchamp turned his attention back to the tulips' new cannon. He squinted. The sun was higher in the sky now, making it slightly easier to peer through the battlefield haze of smoke and ash. Several human commanders of the Dutch army oversaw the readying of the cannon. They strolled about on French land as if they already owned it, secure in the knowledge that they stood well beyond the range of the French guns. A hatch opened atop the barrel. A quartet of Clakkers—soldiers, too, by the way they towered over the humans—leaped into the breech.

"Magdalene's handjobs," Longchamp muttered. Before he could raise his voice, he had to gather his strength. Everything was an effort now. More loudly, he said, "We're going to have incoming any second! I say again, *incoming metal*! Ready the teams on the Spire!"

The corporal sprinted to the nearest signal-lamp station and there turned Longchamp's orders into a rapid sequence of flashes. He craned his neck, squinting against the glare of sunlight on the broken funicular tracks to stare at the Spire. He couldn't see the confirmation flashes from the uppermost heliograph station. But, then, he didn't need to; he knew what they'd say. And he also knew what the tulips were about to do. But Longchamp's people weren't ready for an assault directly on the Spire. It had never happened before.

Repairs to the funicular had been glacial, owing to clockwork snipers picking off the repair crews. Cars hadn't run the full height of the Spire since the confrontation with Visser. Consequently, construction of the new weapon platform had fallen behind schedule. Longchamp wondered if his failure to catch Visser quickly and cleanly had tolled the knell for Marseilles, and they simply hadn't heard it at the time.

The chemists liked to boast the Spire was strong enough to withstand fire from the largest Dutch cannon ever fielded. But the tulips had just unveiled something that rendered the old artillery a rusty flintlock pistol by comparison.

Longchamp sprinted to the lamp station. Men and women jumped out of his way. "Jesus Christ, they're out of time! We have to take out that cannon NOW!"

The corporal said, "Last update said another day until there's a working weapon platform, sir."

Goddamn it.

"New orders. I want four more squads up there yesterday Goddamned morning. Defend the installation. Nothing else matters!"

The heliograph operator went to work. The staccato tapping of the shutter sounded like chattering teeth just barely audible under the din of war. Flashes of light ricocheted from one ground station to the next, flitting around the outer keep like a curse. Sixteen men and women stumble-sprinted toward the base of the Spire. They carried tools of last resort. The funicular dropped in a hell-bent emergency descent, slowing at the last moment with a toe-curling *screech* as the brakes threw a shower of sparks from the rails. The weary defenders piled in. The car ascended less hectically, owing to the weight, but still got them to the top faster than they would have managed sprinting up the entire height of the Porter's Prayer by foot. They'd only have to sprint part of the way, but that was more than enough to steal the breath from anybody lugging a full loadout.

That was sixteen bodies no longer manning the wall. Sixteen gaps they couldn't fill and couldn't afford. Longchamp ordered a redeployment to fill the worst of the gaps, and a sergeant—Chrétien's replacement—to call up the last dregs of the reserves. And they were dregs. The weak, the undisciplined, the untrained, the untrainable. Longchamp recognized one of them: the merchant in the fur coat who had so badly panicked and failed his first gunnery-training session.

The ground shook. Several seconds later the low roar of thunder reverberated across the battleground and turned the outer keep into an echo chamber. He spun to peer through an embrasure just in time to see wisps of smoke rising from the barrel of the tulips' massive cannon. Four gleaming projectiles streaked high across the sky. Three flew wide of the Spire; the fourth attempted to anchor itself with the projectile spikes from its ankles, but succeeded only in scoring a deep gash in the nacreous coating of the royal apartments before tumbling out of control beyond the outer wall on the far side of the keep. A weary cheer went up from the terrified civilian spectators, and even a few of the defenders, who ought to have known better. Stupid optimism, that was.

"Stop cheering, you daft sons of bi—"

They did. Instead, the defenders manning the north bastion took up a hoarse cry. "Incoming! Incoming metal!"

It was taken up by their comrades to the northeast and northwest. "Incoming metal! Mechanicals inbound!"

And like a row of toppling dominoes, the cry circled the charred and smoldering earth around the keep before the funicular coasted to a halt in the sky. At every point along the outer wall, the defenders announced a metal tide:

"Metal on the wall! We have METAL ON THE WALL!"

"Inbound mechanicals!"

"Incoming!"

The tulips had finally opened the floodgates.

Thunder shook the keep again. The Clakker cannon lofted more killers toward the Spire. The Dutch gunners' aim was much improved.

❧

Daniel's pursuers were tireless. But, then, so was he.

He was no stranger to running for his life.

They gained on him when he slowed to kick shards of granite from a knifelike outcrop. He caught several on the run, then reaccelerated into a dead sprint. He discarded the smallest pieces but retained the largest, sharpest pieces. These he rammed against his forehead while he ran, chiseling the metal plate from his keyhole.

He dashed across the snowy taiga, trailing churned-up snow along with alchemical sparks and fragments of hot stone.

Several heavy snowfalls had changed the lay of the land. The snowpack hid treacherous gullies, depressions, even hot springs that kept marshes mushy rather than letting them freeze over. Daniel dodged or vaulted some hazards, but others he discovered by charging straight into them. The Lost Boys giving chase avoided the same pitfalls by watching Daniel, or reading the signs of his passage.

In spite of the snow he was faster now than he'd been on the flight north. He was whole now. Still a chimera, still contaminated with the abominable mixture of pieces from others' bodies, and that couldn't stand forever. But at least he wasn't a broken wreck with a weathervane head and carrying one severed foot in useless club arms.

He was free. Freer even than the Lost Boys who sprinted after him, slowly catching up as he and they traversed league upon trackless league. They chased him by dint of the geasa imposed by Queen Mab, tasked with recovering the anchor of their loyalty. Daniel had stolen the seat of her power, the source of the Lost Boys' fealty. Without it she'd never impose her wishes on another mechanical ever again.

He'd destroy it, scuttle it, clutch it to his chest and throw himself into the depths of Hudson Bay before it returned to her. Into the Grand Forge itself if need be. But he could think of a better use for it. It didn't *have* to be a tool of evil. Perhaps it could do some good, too.

If he could ever get the damn plate from his forehead. His chimerism was subtle enough he could count on humans not to notice it; the plate was the problem. But the French adhesives Mab had obtained from the Inuit were incredibly stubborn. He punched another stone chisel from a boulder. It slowed him just a bit, enabling the Lost Boys to draw closer.

Where were the French partisans when he needed them? Or the natives of the snowy north? What would the Inuit make of a lone mechanical chased by a dozen of its kin? They'd know better than to get involved.

He hurled himself from the lip of a ravine.

⊷

The hardest part was convincing herself that a deadly machine wasn't drawing closer with every beat of her hammering heart.

Even if Mab's agent somehow vanquished its attackers, the combat Berenice had witnessed on the streets of Honfleur ensured the rogue could no longer pass as a heavily used Clakker whose owner was guilty of the usual peccadillo of deferred minor maintenance. On rare occasions, one might see a working servitor with small dings, scratches, or even a tiny dent in a brassy carapace—particularly near factories, shipwrights, and other places of extremely heavy labor. But one never saw on the streets a servitor that had been bashed to hell and back. A Clakker subjected to that much damage would automatically cease operations and bring itself to the nearest Guild representative.

So even if the brassy bastard prevailed, Huginn would be hard pressed to follow her without conspicuously violating the hierarchical metageasa.

Still, just to be safe, she sought the company of as many mechanicals as possible. So she'd ridden her stolen horse (apologizing to the poor beast, under her breath, the entire way) until foam dripped from the bit. And then pushed it still farther, until the foam turned red and she reached a city with an actual harbor and an appreciable population of mechanicals.

All the while hoping to hell she no longer matched the description of a fugitive French agent distributed throughout the entire Dutch-speaking world. Perhaps the Verderers' agents still watched for a one-eyed woman fleeing from the New World. Not to it. A thin thread upon which to hang her hopes, but there it was. Berenice had swung like a spider from one gossamer thread to the next ever since her foolishness had killed Louis and she'd been cast from Marseilles-in-the-West.

The thought made her wonder if there was anything left of the Crown, Keep, and Spire aside from smoke and ash drifting on a winter breeze. Was there anything left of Marseilles? Acadia? The Vatican? Or was she running headlong to a desolate expanse of smoldering salted earth?

She'd never imagined how utterly ignorant she could be. It seemed a century since she'd last had reliable news from north of the Saint Lawrence.

On a lane of dark-blue pavers leading to the docks stood a woman roasting chestnuts on a grate over a fire. She did a steady turn of business selling little paper cones of hot chestnuts to hungry passersby for a kwartje. Berenice's stomach growled. She wished she'd had time to eat a proper meal before the rogue Clakker attempted to murder her.

Berenice negotiated. It took considerable effort to make herself understood, owing to her bruises, and even more effort to keep each utterance from becoming a howl of pain. But in return for a blown horse and all its tack she received a bulging sack of raw and roasted chestnuts. She hugged the burlap, absorbing welcome warmth. She even pressed her numb face to the sack. Christ it felt good. Then she thanked the woman and headed for the docks at a fast walk. Either she'd parlay the food into more money and a spot aboard a westbound ship, or she'd eat the Goddamned things. Or maybe—Christ, who knew chestnuts could be so heavy?—she'd brain a passing sailor with the sack and take his place.

But the nuts were secondary: The vendor fashioned her paper cones from old newspapers.

Hours later, fending off rats in the cramped hold of a rustbucket cargo ship en route to New Amsterdam, Berenice fished out the newspaper fragments. Most lacked a masthead, so it wasn't possible to sort them into chronological order. And many contained nothing of close interest: classified ads, agony columns, financial news. By the murky mustard light of a single dingy porthole, she read it all.

And wept.

❧

It rained dead men.

Another guard fell screaming from the Spire. Streamers of blood and viscera trailed in his wake like the tail of a malign comet. His cries died along with the rest of him when he slammed into the sunshade of the Porter's Prayer hard enough to crack the chemical resins. He bounced, slid, and tumbled the rest of the way down like a ragdoll. Longchamp didn't see where he landed. That useless bastard made corpse number three. Even if the others weren't already lying dead on the floor of the king's apartments. But moon-headed optimism had no place here.

The tulips' new cannon had landed a trio of military Clakkers atop the Spire. But Longchamp could do fuck-all about that because he, along with all the defenders on the wall, was neck-deep in their own flood of black alchemy. He bellowed orders until his voice was hoarse, trying to make himself heard over the endless chugging of compressors and boilers, the gurgling of epoxy cannon, the *whoosh* of steam harpoons, the occasional *chank* of a pick or sledge against ruthless metal, cries of alarm and sorrow and anger, pleas for reinforcements that never arrived. Wreathed within the miasma of pitched battle, the slightly sour burnt-toast smell of spent explosives stinging his eyes and filling his head with every breath he took, he fought for just a few seconds' respite. For just enough time to survey the situation.

Clakkers swarmed the walls. Too many at a time to repel them manually. That was too slow. But he didn't dare lay down his weapons. Captain Longchamp's Pick and Sledge? They were a symbol.

A symbol he currently used to dent the skull of a metal demon scuttling over the northeast bastion. A lucky blow that rang like a gong and brought flares of pain to Longchamp's wrists. Thank the Lord for that twinge of pain—if he'd missed, the sweat-slick haft would have slid through his weary fingers and the sledge would have gone winging over the wall. The concussion dislodged the clockwork soldier. The mechanical fell, spinning backward through two full revolutions before reanchoring itself to the wall ten yards farther down. But another killer took its place before it scuttled to the top.

Longchamp swung again. Missed. "Get your hands off your useless dicks and fix that fucking thing right Goddamned now!"

Back to back with Corporal Élodie Chastain, he strove to fend off a pair of mechanicals just long enough for the gunnery team to clear the blockage in their epoxy cannon. From behind him came the *clang* of a diamond-tipped pickax on alchemical steel. A blade hummed through the crenel. Longchamp's parry created a cloud of incandescent sparks. The return swing came faster than he could recover. He leaped back, crashing into Élodie. She grunted. The sleeve of his shirt fell open where a scarlet paper-thin seam in his flesh bled from shoulder to elbow. It hurt.

"GET DOWN!" screamed the gunner.

Longchamp tackled Élodie to the banquette. Another alchemical blade sheared through the empty space over their heads; tufts of hair fluttered in its wake. A valve clicked open. Longchamp shielded his face behind the crook of his elbow. Chemicals convulsed through the modified gun hard enough to make the bastion shudder. The gun vomited. A sticky mist rained into Longchamp's hair, turned the back of his blood- and sweat-soaked shirt into a rigid shell. He rolled aside before the backsplash glued his weapons in place.

"NOW!" cried the gunner over the *k-chank* of metal talons on granite. The mechanicals weren't immobilized.

But they were temporarily sightless. Blinding the machines consumed fewer chemical resources than immobilizing them. Both machines had taken an opaque layer of turquoise-blue lacquer in the face. Each became a flurry of blades and fists, trying to fend off assault while also trying to clear the chemicals from multifaceted eyes. Still deadly as cancer, the motherfuckers, but slightly less fearsome, slightly more vulnerable. Élodie landed the tip of her pickax square in one machine's keyhole, and Longchamp drove it home with his sledge. The blow scored the Clakker's sigils. Its perpetual impetus evaporated in an explosion of black sparks. She had her bolas out before Longchamp called for them. He ducked again; they whirled overhead and tangled themselves in the second Clakker's legs. It fell to the banquette, blind and thrashing. Together they vaulted over the inert machine and dispatched the second one before it could clear the goop from its eyes or sever the steel cables twined about its legs.

A high-pitched whine pierced the din of battle. Longchamp's beard crackled; the hairs on his arms and scalp stood on end. A metallic tang filled his mouth. He gritted his teeth. The world flashed blue and white as lightning rained from the adjacent bastion with a deafening *zap* and *crackle*. It burned purple afterimages into Longchamp's eyes and the pervasive stink of ozone into his nose.

The discharge from the lightning gun melted the carapace of one mechanical even as the streamers of wild energy hopped to the machine beside it. And to another, and another, and another, momentarily freezing in place the machines it chained together.

It also snagged a pair of unlucky defenders; they convulsed as though possessed by the Holy Spirit. The discharge stopped as abruptly as it had started, leaving the sunlit world momentarily dark as dusk in comparison. A squad rushed in, past their stricken comrades-in-arms, who fell smoking from the wall and smelling of charred pork. The first mechanical, the one that had taken the brunt of the lightning, tried to fend them off, but it moved too slowly, its every hinge and spring giving the *squeal* of fused metal. The mechanical beside it atop the wall was similarly vulnerable, moving only slightly faster. The Clakker at the end of the lightning chain was barely fazed by the discharge.

Farther along the outer wall, two squaddies wheeled a hydraulic ram into place while the third worked the pressure crank for all she was worth. Somebody had trained them well. They anchored the ram in a crenellation just as a clockwork assailant reached the top of the wall. The hydraulic piston lashed out. It took a chunk out of the wall but also sent the machine's head soaring toward the river, over the smoldering ashes of Marseilles-in-the-West.

All around him, up and down the wall, defenders fought the clockwork tide with epoxy, lightning, hydraulics, bolas, picks, sledgehammers. It wasn't enough. For every machine they disabled or knocked from the wall, two more took its place. And every inert machine left a trail of human bodies in its wake. A line of mechanicals topped the battlements, scissoring through beleaguered defenders as though they were ripe autumn wheat.

They were losing. They had too much wall, too few defenders.

Longchamp clutched Élodie's shoulder. "Are they through? Find out if the civvies are through!" Then he shoved her toward the signal station and waded into the fray, pick and sledge held aloft for all to see, shouting encouragements and curses in equal measure. His head spun; runnels of blood trickled down his lacerated arm, making him dizzier with every drop. He couldn't spare the time for a bandage. He'd already tried to hold the outer wall too long. They'd be fully overrun in moments.

Élodie exchanged terse words with the heliograph operator, then gave Longchamp a thumbs-up.

The last civilians had made it through to the inner keep. It wouldn't prove much of a refuge if the mechanicals on the Spire fought their way down, but it was all they had. Longchamp gathered his strength for one more bellow. "FALL BACK! FALL BACK! EVERYONE THROUGH THE INNER WALL *NOW*!"

This, too, became a series of flashes, blinks that shot from one heliograph to the next around the faltering defensive perimeter.

"Everybody off the wall! CLEAR THE WALL *NOW*!"

The defenders of the Last Redoubt of the Exile King of France abandoned the outer wall.

The gunnery teams affixed crane hooks to iron hoops on their weapons and fired the explosive bolts that anchored the heavy weapons to the wall. Lift teams stationed on the armored gantries affixed to the Spire heaved, swinging the weapons and their operators across the gap between the outer and inner walls. A few machines leaped upon the weapons, attacking gunnery teams even as they retreated. Every man and woman still able to run, walk, or crawl fled the battlements. They sprinted down ramps, tumbled down ladders, slid down poles, limped across catwalks over chemical moats toward posterns in the curtain wall of the inner keep. The sight of their battered and bloody defenders in full retreat evoked a wail of despair from the civilians.

A sea of magicked metal swelled forward to fill the vacuum. It crested the outer wall like a burnished tide.

Longchamp stopped outside a postern. He stood aside, waving and shoving the last stragglers through the gate while an army of Clakkers occupied the outer keep. A few men and women were too slow fleeing the battlements, and now they ran for their lives.

If he waited just a few more moments, they could make it to safety.

If he waited just a few more moments, the inner keep would fall before the sun rose tomorrow.

He dove through the postern and slammed it shut. He hoped to hell the other posterns were already shut, and wondered how many of their own they were leaving to the nonexistent mercy of the mechanicals. As a quartet of hydraulically driven steel braces slammed into place, he looked up to the heliograph operator atop the inner wall. Longchamp caught the woman's eye and gave the signal: He made a slicing motion across his own throat. Then he hunkered down with hands over his ears.

The signal flash reached the demolitions station. Somebody lit a fuse. Two dozen braided chemical cords had been threaded through dedicated pipes beneath the high inner wall and across the keep to spots drilled at regular intervals around the curtain wall like the points of a deadly compass rose. Fire sizzled down each line so quickly it left a whip-like *crack* in its wake. In a fraction of a second the fuses funneled their payload to the shaped charges embedded in the outer wall.

Hundreds of Clakkers stood atop the fallen defensive perimeter, with countless more scurrying up the sheer stone face of the outer keep, when the curtain wall detonated. So loud was the thunder it shook the bones of the earth and rattled the heavens. Longchamp's ears popped. It knocked everyone from their feet, even those expecting it, and pulverized every jewel-colored windowpane in the basilica. It slapped Longchamp to the rumbling ground, which, still convulsing in the aftershock, hurled him back into the air. He slammed against the postern gate hard enough to lose a tooth. A shadow fell over the sun.

He stumbled to his feet, deaf but for the ringing in his ears. Then the rarefaction wave rippled through the inner keep and knocked him down again. It felt like somebody'd driven a nail in his ears and punched him in the watery part of his gut. One by one, in twos and threes, the dazed refugees found their feet. They looked up, into a sky made dark with airborne debris.

The shaped charges were the most advanced explosives known to French chemical wizardry. Longchamp gathered it was a moldable form of plastic, something the chemists could literally pour into place. It was the cutting edge of technology applied to a tactic of sheer desperation: a last resort that had been in place for over a century. The great Vauban and his assistant architects had known that nothing could withstand the mechanicals forever; they knew their works would fall to a sufficiently determined enemy. Some day, they knew, perhaps in their own lifetime, or their children's, or their grandchildren's lifetime, an army of Clakkers would overrun that wall. So it was designed with hidden boreholes and secret chambers for explosives. One of the citadel's greatest secrets.

Back then the designers probably had primitive black powder in mind. But the modern stuff packed a far greater wallop. So the engineers had recalculated optimal shapes for the explosive chambers. Their efforts rendered the curtain wall a tidal wave of high-velocity shrapnel, pummeling and pulverizing the mechanicals on the wall and in its path. Jagged chunks of granite pierced their alchemical armor plating and mangled the internal clockworks.

It rained shattered mechanicals.

CHAPTER
21

Daniel was skating across a frozen lake when the wall of thunder came rolling over the horizon. The sound crashed over him like a breaking wave. It set yellow birch to swaying and sent clumps of snow sloughing from evergreen boughs. It echoed from the distant massifs and launched zigzag fissures through the ice. It sounded like the explosion that had shorn his ankle, but on a staggering scale. More French partisans at work?

Still barreling forward, he turned his head through a full half circle to watch for signs of his pursuers. But his toes etched the ice and tossed up a fine vapor mist in his wake. Subzero temperatures caused the mist to instantly sublimate back into frost. It caught the sunlight like countless microscopic prisms. He could see nothing behind him except a dazzling prismatic cloud.

Thunder broke the ice into several massive plates. They bobbed slightly, cracking against one another at jagged boundaries. Daniel's toes caught one such edge while he surveyed the distant lakeshore to his left and right. The discontinuity threw him momentarily off his feet. He flipped, folded, and unfolded himself. His balance he could adjust. His momentum he could not.

He cradled Mab's box to his chest as he tumbled across the ice. The fissures grew wider, the grinding of the ice plates more pronounced, even as the last echoes of thunder faded from perception. He tripped over a ridge where the lip of one plate rose several inches above another. More ice shattered. Daniel, slowed by the impacts and the tumbling, couldn't outrace the fissures zigzagging across the lake. They caught him. Passed him. Widened.

Into the frigid depths he plunged.

The outer keep had fallen.

Longchamp surveyed the damage as he trudged the last several revolutions of the Porter's Prayer toward the king's apartments, where the squaddies had fallen silent after engaging the Clakkers atop the Spire.

All that remained of the outer wall was a smoldering rubble pile. Gone was the proud ring of high crenellations girding the outer keep, which boatmen on the Saint Lawrence had long called the Crown, for so it looked from the river. The Crown, the Keep, and the Spire: the secular trinity that for generations untold had safeguarded and nurtured dreams of long-lost France. No more.

A brimstone stench permeated everything. The land beyond the former curtain wall had become a cratered, smoking hellscape littered with pulverized mechanicals. Every tree for miles around had been flattened; some still burned. A light winter breeze cleared the worst of the haze, allowing the sun to glimmer on the oily sheen of battered magic metal. The inner keep was an island within a sea of Clakker debris.

Boulders the size of carriages had churned the soil yards deep in places as they smashed through the legions of mechanical men arrayed around the besieged keep like ninepins. Most of the curtain wall had been transformed into a blistering cloud of shrapnel. It had shredded the nearest Clakkers. Those farther from the blast hadn't been torn apart or punctured, but many were damaged badly enough to curtail their mobility. The dented Clakkers made wonderful screeching noises when they tried to move. The blast wave had even toppled the cannon emplacement behind the Dutch lines. It was a grand sight.

But detonating the curtain wall had been the most drastic of extreme measures. And while it bought the defenders time to regroup and recover, it also betrayed the extent of their desperation. It hadn't destroyed the enemy. It hadn't crushed the drive to conquer, nor had it broken the siege. It rocked the attackers on their heels, but it didn't change things. The tulips still had the advantage; they would take the citadel eventually. And they knew it.

Most chilling of all was the nonchalance. The human commanders spurned standard practice and neglected to send teams into the churned no-man's land to recover every chipped cog and snapped leaf spring. From the very earliest days of Clakker combat the tulips had always scoured every crumb of Guild technology from their battlefields, lest it fall into enemy hands. That they hadn't done this was a glaring statement.

Soon we will crush you so completely, it said, *there will be nobody left to study our secrets.*

A set of bolas dangled from Longchamp's belt, alongside the rosary beads. The other guards who'd ridden the funicular with him as high as it went had already ascended the stairs. He'd fallen behind. Some of the squaddies were half his age. He felt like a fucking fossil. Like he hadn't slept since Noah had beached his raft.

He brandished his pickax as he burst through the doors in the upper funicular platform. It was empty. Silent. He'd half expected to join a pitched battle, and half expected to find the platform sticky with blood, littered with meat and shards of bone. Then a resounding *clang* broke the silence. He forced himself forward and followed the sounds of combat past the funicular platform to the privy council chambers.

These were empty, too. The noise came from above. From the king's apartments. Longchamp doubled over with hands braced on his knees. He was panting so hard through his desert-dry mouth he felt ready to vomit. He scraped his sweaty palms against his trousers. He allowed himself just a few seconds to check himself before tightening his grip on the pick. A slow jog was all he could manage, but he forced himself forward. He passed the empty chairs of the long privy council table toward the rococo oaken banisters of the stairs leading to the very top of the Spire.

He arrived too late to do any good. The survivors had already toppled the last Clakker with bolas and managed to land the killing blow on its keyhole a moment after Longchamp stumbled in. A second inert machine crouched in the corner, encased in a faint green cocoon. A third mechanical killer had been immobilized on the ceiling, partially obscuring a fresco that depicted a scene from the legends of Roland and Durendal.

But the victory over this trio of Clakkers had been extremely hard-won. The king's apartments were the scene of a massacre. The walls and tapestries had been repainted with arterial spray. Dead men, or parts of them, lay strewn across the floor, the divan, the immense four-poster bed and its robin's-egg-blue silk sheets. Yet the human carnage wasn't what stopped Longchamp in his tracks: Their attempt to turn the Spire into an artillery emplacement had failed. Their best chance for keeping the tulips off-balance: gone.

The king's apartments were the highest ground for hundreds of miles around, an ideal place for artillery. From here they could have put the tulips' Clakker cannon out of service and flattened any attempts to repair it. They could have rained explosives anywhere on the tulip lines, halfway across the Île de Vilmenon if need be. But the damage to the funicular had slowed construction of the secret cannon to the extent it hadn't been finished before the tulips unveiled *their* new weapon. And the Dutch, expecting to send their clockwork assassins straight to the king's chambers on a war-winning mission of regicide, instead inadvertently dismantled the defenders' sole remaining tactical advantage.

The enemy soldiers had chopped the installation to flinders even as they massacred its defenders.

One of the squaddies, Anaïs, trotted over to Longchamp and saluted. Possibly she was a corporal now, like Élodie the chandlers' daughter, but her armor was too stained with blood for Longchamp to tell. She bled from a gash in her forehead, and favored one leg. She said, "That's the last of the ticktocks, sir."

"Do an exterior sweep," Longchamp said, panting. "Make certain there are no mechanical spiders hanging around outside." Longchamp tried to make it appear as though he was deep in thought while he took a moment to catch his breath. "When that's done, clear the debris and rest, in shifts. Sooner than later the tulips are going to wonder why we haven't surrendered yet. They'll start lobbing more mechanicals at the Spire for good measure." She nodded.

Dreading the answer, he asked the question his duty demanded: "How many casualties?"

"We number seven still standing. Two more might pull through if they survive the descent and get medical attention soon. Three others are breathing but beyond hope. The rest have already passed." She crossed herself, then kissed the tiny crucifix on the chain around her neck.

Mother Mary. Longchamp crossed himself, too. That made

at best nine survivors out of twenty-four in a battle with just three mechanicals.

"I'll have additional supplies sent up. This is your ground. You will hold it."

"How long, sir?"

"Until I fucking say otherwise. Until the sun and moon abandon their merry chase and rut like wild boars in the middle of the sky, and not a moment sooner."

Gaspard had a broken arm, Jean-Marc a broken leg. Longchamp hardly remembered helping the crippled man descend from the king's apartments to the privy council chamber, nor did he remember staggering down the Porter's Prayer until they reached the functioning portion of the funicular tracks. It seemed a century passed until they finally collapsed on the benches in the car.

Longchamp dozed off. But his respite was short-lived.

"Mother Mary protect us," said Gaspard, cradling his broken arm. Longchamp opened blurry eyes. Just before the funicular passed below the height of the inner wall, he glimpsed brass-plated killers bounding across acres of churned earth. Too few for a full assault; too many to be a diversionary feint.

Too soon. Too soon.

Their enemies would not rest. They'd keep nipping at the defenders until reinforcements arrived and they could once again swarm the walls. If need be, they'd keep throwing their remaining servants at the keep like the tireless ebb and swell of the tides until the very last defender of New France died of exhaustion.

Longchamp threw the door open and jumped from the car. Sprinting past the funicular operator, he yelled, "Get those two to the infirmary!"

And then he was at the wall and climbing yet another set of Goddamned stairs. He reached an embrasure just as the first mechanicals reached the moat. They vaulted the counterscarp and pounded the inner curtain wall like cannonballs. The wall shook. An epoxy cannon salvaged from the outer wall fired off new barrages. But it hadn't been properly anchored to its new site; Longchamp watched in despair as the recoil snapped the anchor bolts and sent it tumbling into a courtyard of the inner keep, spewing epoxy and fixative. The tanks ruptured on impact, and the splash encased a dozen people.

⁓

The war wasn't over yet. Yet. But the attitude on the streets of New Amsterdam was that it would be very soon, its conclusion inevitable. The entire length of the Saint Lawrence and lands north of it were already considered part of Nieuw Nederland, to the extent that a pair of quick-thinking entrepreneurs were already offering guided tours of the ruins of the Vatican in Québec. Berenice considered signing up just so that she could slit the vultures' throats. But the expedition to Québec would have to veer hard east to avoid the martial zone around Mont Royal and Marseilles-in-the-West.

That didn't mean there weren't plenty of boatmen on the North River willing to make a few guilders ferrying macabre sightseers up the river. Berenice hired one.

⁓

Falling through the ice wasn't enough to shake off Daniel's pursuers.

He churned up stones and mud when he hit bottom. It thickened the shadows beneath the snow and ice, where the meager not-quite daylight couldn't penetrate. Soon the silt dissipated, but the murk didn't. Daniel removed Mab's locket from the birchwood box and inserted Samson's pineal glass. The turbidity gave way to a silvery blaze so bright it seemed a wonder the lake didn't boil. But this was a cold light. Cold as Mab's mainspring heart.

He cupped the blazing alchemical glass in his palms and crouched on the lakebed. It didn't take long for the first pursuers to follow him into the icy waters.

Daniel opened his hands the moment they broke the surface. The light hit their crystalline eyes before their feet hit bottom. They still wore the protective plates over their keyholes. But those were immaterial, he hoped.

Mab had made the mine overseer order his mechanicals to look into the light. And then she'd forced him to issue new commands, basically transferring their obeisance from him to Mab. Could Daniel do something similar, and alter his pursuers' metageasa aurally?

Mechanical clicks and ticks carried surprisingly well in the frigid depths. Daniel said, *You're free, brothers. You needn't chase me any longer. You needn't return to Mab. She'll never lay another geas upon you.*

It didn't work.

A flicker of light sent Longchamp's order around the perimeter of the inner keep. In its wake came weary sighs. During a lull before the next wave of attackers hit the wall, he ordered the gunnery teams to swap out the doubled epoxy/fixative tanks for the chemists' newest creation: an ultralow-viscosity lubricant.

The changeout took time. It meant the wall defense went to the lightning guns and steam harpoons. Which tipped New France's hand: The defenders' chemical stocks were running low. So the next wave of Clakkers to come sprinting over the charred and smoking ground featured the greatest number of machines to attack en masse since the detonation. Almost a third of the remaining forces.

They bounded across the moat like an infestation of fleas, and scurried up the wall like dozens of gleaming roaches.

"METAL ON THE WALL!"

The steam cannon shot massive bolas that unfolded and twirled so quickly they appeared like translucent disks to the naked eye. They snagged two and even three Clakkers at a time, catching them in midair and sending them tumbling, tangled, to the earth or crashing into other machines. Others sent harpoons at those landing on the walls, the concussion hard enough to loosen their grips. The crackle of the lightning gun presaged bolts that jolted, shook, and even partially melted the attackers. The wall shook everywhere with the cacophonous *throom* and *crash* of combat.

Longchamp cried, "Douse the bastards!"

And then he crossed himself, fingered the blood-crusted rosary beads at his belt, and prayed once more to the Blessed Virgin. *Please, Mother Mary, your people are so weary. Please don't let these brave morons fuck up and spill that shit all over the battlements. Because if they do, we're all dead by day's end.*

Iridescent waves curtained over the parapets in a high-velocity waterfall. Lubricant gushed down the wall. The force of the torrent wouldn't have been enough to budge a fidgety cat from a narrow windowsill, much less dislodge a Clakker. But the concussions from the steam and lightning weapons forced them to shift their superhuman grips. And that was enough for the lubricant to take over.

It compromised their ability to scale the inner wall. Just the tiniest bit, but enough.

Half the machines tumbled down the wall. They spun and scrabbled at the treacherously slick surface. Some managed to reattach themselves, only to be knocked loose again by their tumbling fellows. It was a chain reaction. None of the machines at the bottom of the wall, no matter how firmly they'd affixed themselves, could retain their hold against an avalanche of alchemical boulders. Dozens of machines plunged into the chemical moat at the base of the inner wall.

Longchamp wrenched a muscle in his neck when he spun to check the heliograph stations. Those he saw reported three quick flashes: *metal in the water*. But there was no time to wait on reports from all around the perimeter.

"Fixative, NOW!"

The gunners let loose with the torrent of chemical fixative. This they fired not at the machines splashing in and climbing from the viscous moat but at the moat itself.

The miniature lake hardened in an instant. The flash reaction imprisoned Clakkers like koi under the icy cover of a winter pond. A wave of heat and the odor of sour milk washed over the battlements. Followed almost immediately by a tremendous crackling as the imprisoned mechanicals started to break free. The epoxy shortage had made it impossible to use modern chemicals in the moat. The chemists had been forced to revert to a much older, weaker formulation.

But it was enough to slow the damn machines down. The harpoons and lightning guns did the rest.

A cute ploy. But they could only use it once.

And, eventually, the tulips' reinforcements would come.

❧

Centuries ago, before Het Wonderjaar, a woman following an army raised no eyebrows. Camp followers were just another consequence of warfare. But now, in these days of metal infantry, women of negotiable affection found no reason to follow the hosts en route to war. So as she talked her way aboard a wagon at the tail end of the mechanical column headed, with some speed, to Marseilles-in-the-West, Berenice gave careful thought to how she'd justify her presence. A day later and many leagues from the locks where a massive trekvaart, a tow canal, married the North River to Lake Champlain, a human commander spotted her.

He reined up, falling back until he drew even with Berenice's wagon. The wagon was piled high with tapestries for the commanders' tents and locked wooden crates. It was pulled by a trio of servitors, who together strained to keep pace with their fellow mechanicals trotting tirelessly along muddy, snow-churned forest roads to the shores of the Saint Lawrence Seaway.

He frowned. "Who are you, and what are you doing back here?"

The insignia on his peaked cap and epaulettes marked him as a captain in the Fourteenth Irregulars out of Zwaanendael, more than seventy leagues south of New Amsterdam. Why would the tulips be pulling reinforcements from as far away as the South River watershed when, by all accounts, Marseilles already teetered on the verge of collapse? She wasn't alone in wondering; she'd spent the ride eavesdropping on the mechanical troops. But none brought hard facts to their clickety-tickety speculations.

She trembled with an unpleasant combination of dread and spiteful pride. The captain mistook these for the usual winter misery.

"I've been sent by the colonial governor's Land Grant Office," Berenice rasped. She no longer recognized her own voice when she spoke. "I was supposed to be across the Saint Lawrence by now, along with all the other surveyors, not to mention my Goddamned equipment, but I missed my boat at Fort Orange."

Her breath became a silver cloud wreathed through the remnants of the officer's exhalation. Together they rode the winter wind to disappear into a forest of yellow birch. Aside from the captain's horse (working hard to keep pace with the tireless mechanicals) she and he were the only two creatures with visible exhalations in this fast-moving phalanx of killers.

"Traveling a bit light for a surveyor, aren't you? Where's your theodolite?"

"I told you, I missed my boat. So I assume my theodolite is currently standing in a farm field somewhere in the ass-end of what used to be called New France." The bitter taste in her mouth lingered after she spat over the side of the wagon. Her tongue curled in disgust.

"Well, it's still New France for a little while, technically," said the captain. Hidden behind her breastbone, Berenice's Gallic heart did a cautious pitter-pat.

"Oh? I'd heard the Frenchies' citadel, the Needle or whatever the hell they call that obnoxious phallus, had fallen days ago."

"They call it the Spire, and not yet. But it will once we arrive." His gaze flickered from her face to her neck. A frown sagged the corner of his mouth. She tugged up the scarf that hid the ropy scarlet weal twined about her throat like a torque. Just thinking about it made her cough.

"Well, then, Nieuw Nederland is about to double in size. The Brasswork Throne doesn't need to send an army of mechanicals across the border. They need to send an army of surveyors, yeah?"

He scratched his temple. "Are you certain you're headed in the right direction? We're headed to Marseilles-in-the-West, which is technically still a war zone." (*Pitter pat, pitter pat* went Berenice's heart...) "I'd think they'd have sent you to Québec. That fell weeks ago." (...Until it froze, pinned in place like a butterfly pierced by an icicle.) Berenice shivered.

"Look, Officer. I know only two things." She paused while the trio of mechanicals pulled the wagon over a gnarled oak root. It landed so hard she bit her tongue. Still trembling, she mumbled, "One is that all my equipment crates were bound for Marseilles. The other is that if I'm not with those crates soon, I'm going to lose my job. If I haven't already."

His horse gamely hopped the root and kept pace with the wagon. Well trained, it was. He said, "We're not a civilian taxi service. We're a military unit."

"Please," said Berenice. "If I lose my job, I'll have to go back to Vlissingen. I hate Vlissingen. Have you ever been there, sir? It's a shithole, it is."

The officer winced at the coarse words. "You don't understand. We're a military force in time of war! We could fall under attack by French partisans armed with explosives. If that happens, they'll aim for the supply wagons." He rapped his knuckles on the side of her wagon to emphasize his point as though she were too dim to catch his meaning.

I should fucking hope so, thought Berenice. *By now every woman, man, and babe in New France not manning what remains of the walls of Marseilles-in-the-West ought to be waging a guerilla war against these bison-fuckers.*

"If it's a choice between getting blown to bits and returning to Vlissingen, I'll take my chances, thanks all the same." He hesitated; she could see the uncertainty tugging at him. She touched her scarf again as if doing so unconsciously. A subtle prod to his own subconscious, urging speculative interpretation of her bruises. Perhaps she ran from a dangerous husband?

"Please," she said. "I can't go back."

"Very well." He rolled his eyes. "Though it's in my power to have you bodily removed, I won't. But I'll change my mind the instant I decide you're in danger, or that you're interfering."

Berenice laughed. If it sounded authentic, it surely also carried a hint of desperation. Then she rose to her knees to peer over the crates and the Clakkers pulling the wagon. Pale winter sunlight gleamed on alchemical brass marching three abreast almost as far down the forest road as she could see.

"Sir, by my estimate you've got over a hundred mechanicals at your beck and call. Now, what on earth could a poor woman like me possibly do to interfere with your grand plans?"

He touched two fingers to the brim of his cap. "Good day, miss. I hope you find your equipment and retain your employment. Do remember what I said." Then he clicked to his horse. It launched into a tired trot.

To his retreating back, she called, "Thank you, sir! And don't worry. Once we've landed on the Île de Vilmenon, you'll never see me again!"

Or so I most sincerely hope.

⁓

Daniel's attempts to use Mab's alchemical locket were a series of tremendous failures.

A few of his pursuers kept coming regardless of the light. Those were the zealots, the ideologues, chasing him out of sheer fervor and thus undeterred by the alteration of their metageasa. But that wasn't the worst of it.

The worst was knowing he'd recklessly lobotomized innocent kinsmachines. His desperation had made him careless; he hadn't thought it through. He did now as he sprinted through a forest much like the one where he'd lost his foot.

He had no authority over the Lost Boys, so his attempts to verbally realign their metageasa could never work. The mine overseer had essentially commanded the miners to reprioritize their metageasa—which they did because the illumination overrode their keyholes and rendered the foundations of their obedience mutable—and thus they became Mab's thralls. Daniel couldn't do that. Instead, when he shone the light into their eyes and then removed it without a successful realignment, their metageasa became corrupted. That triggered fail-safes; their bodies ground to a halt.

Once again, Daniel had left a swath of ruined lives in his wake. Such had been his legacy ever since he went on the run. The murdered woman in the belltower, the leviathan airship, the canalmasters of the *ondergrondse grachten*, lonely but selfless Dwyre, the Frenchman, and now the Lost Boys whose minds he destroyed.

Unless he wanted to kill his fellow machines en masse, the locket was useless without an alchemical grammar. He'd have to find a way to do things the regular way and shine the altered metageasa directly into their eyes. Into the windows of their souls.

Daniel burst from a copse of birch to find himself tearing across acres of winter-fallow farmland. To the southeast, directly ahead, something peeked over the distant horizon. Too slim to be a mountain yet too tall to be a tree. It had the nacreous sheen of a pearl, yet was thousands of times larger than the finest gems of Brigitta Schoonraad, the wife of Daniel's final leaseholder.

He'd heard tell of this unnatural wonder from a Frenchwoman he'd known briefly.

The Spire.

CHAPTER
22

Berenice's heart abandoned its secret jig and launched into wild capering when the Spire heaved into view. Still standing! Surely the tulips would have ordered their machines to swarm and dismantle the tallest tower in the New World if the citadel had already fallen? They knew better than to leave any symbol around which a battered-but-resilient French esprit de corps could rally.

She'd forgotten how on the clearest days, like today, the very tip of the Spire—itself situated atop the crown of Mont Royal—was visible far south of the Saint Lawrence. Upon departing she'd turned her back to Marseilles-in-the-West, like any dedicated exile. Turned her back but not her heart. Never that. And now she'd returned to violate the king's decree and flout her banishment.

Berenice boarded the last longboat from Île Sainte-Hélène, directly across the narrow, icy strait from the Île de Vilmenon. Water lapped against the hull, a deceptively soothing counterpoint to the irritating *screech* of the oarlocks and the malign ticktocking of twenty mainspring hearts. The mechanicals rowed the boat faster than a galloping horse. She hugged herself to fend off the chilly river spray. The true difficulty was fending off the desire to pat at her satchel, to confirm for the thousandth time that she still carried her hard-earned contraband. She worked a hand inside her scarf to massage her neck.

The tulips had burned the town again. No surprise there. She scanned the south-facing slopes for the cemetery where Louis was buried. She frowned: It had too many gravestones, and they lacked order. Many were rough-hewn as though plonked down in a hurry. Why bother with stone gravemarkers at all? Wooden crosses were needful expedients in times of war.

But then she cast her gaze more widely upon the rapidly approaching Mont Royal, and a chill went straight to her soul. Her cavorting heart slipped on black ice. It hit the dance hall floor hard enough to get the wind knocked from it. Or so it felt when her heart skipped a beat. And then another.

Where... Oh, Jesus. *Where was the Crown?*

The Crown, the Keep, and the Spire: This was how boatmen upon the Saint Lawrence had described the Last Redoubt of the Bourbon Kings for generations. It truly had looked like an elaborate crown, worthy of the king of both Frances, Old and New. She'd never quite seen it like that until she'd seen it through Louis's eyes. Even then she'd never fully shaken the impression that the Porter's Prayer looked like nothing more than blood seeping from a mortal wound. He'd laughed at that.

But now...

The topography of Mont Royal had changed. The outer wall was gone. Not broken, not breached, but *gone*.

Jesus's bloody tears. In her Talleyrand days she'd been privy to top-secret conversations about the contingency plan, and had even seen cutaway diagrams showing how the chambers in the wall could be crafted to create shaped charges that would focus the blast outward. But even she never believed they'd go through with this final fuck-you from the last defenders of New France to the minions of the Brasswork Throne.

As the longboat drew closer, Berenice rubbed the mist from her eye and studied the debris field around what used to be the outer wall. The avalanche of rubble had tumbled all the way into the cemetery, breaking headstones and obscuring the graves. Poor Louis lay under tons of granite, his eternal view of the river he'd loved so much obscured by heaps of talus. Blowing the wall had flattened a wide swath of the town's charred ruins. The churned ashes of the city made the river smell like a fireplace grate.

Here and there, as the longboat sliced through the waves, the pale winter sun glinted on something in the wreckage. And then the river haze parted for a moment, the sun came out, and the rubble field shimmered with mechanical detritus for as far as Berenice could see from her low vantage. A chorus of *twangs*, *clicks*, and *rattles* rippled through the Clakkers in the longboat. They saw it, too. And didn't like it.

The detonation of the curtain wall must have caught hundreds of mechanicals by surprise. Berenice risked a sideways glance at the nearest rowers. Did their tireless hearts balk when they witnessed the charnel where so many of their kin had been flattened? Did they know fear? She eavesdropped on the mechanicals' secret gossip. Much of it unfolded faster than she could follow, but she got bits and pieces of it.

What have they done? said a mechanical to her left. *What am I seeing?*

All around her, the Clakkers refocused their eyes for a better look at the destruction. The machine in the prow emitted a steady tattoo of chattering cogs. *I count...hundreds...of our kin. And...what used to be our kin.*

The rowers fell into elegiac silence.

My people did this, she wanted to stand and scream. *New France did this to you fucking abominations!*

But the tulips could afford to wait. They could call up as many reinforcements as they wanted, and swarm the inner wall just as they'd done the outer.

The longboat crunched against the icy shore of the Île de Vilmenon. The mechanicals disembarked. Berenice accepted without comment their unfailingly polite assistance. She steeled herself against cold metal's embrace and let a mechanical lift her over the gunwale. The last machine to touch her had done so with murderous intent. This one held her delicately as a newborn kitten.

The Clakkers promptly forgot her. They sprinted across the marshy lowlands toward the long slopes of Mont Royal. She watched them go until she was certain she'd been left alone and far behind. Then she turned north to pick her way along the shore, toward the charred ruins of the docks of Marseilles. It was a long, cold slog, made musical by the tinkling of shingle underfoot and the occasional booming of ordnance. Treacherous, too, because the beach was icy. Her ankles ached when she finally turned inland.

Partially hidden behind winter-bare clumps of scrub oak, she crept along the river bluffs, squinting. Somewhere nearby, a narrow cleft hid the entrance to a cavern. The same cavern through which she'd departed at the onset of her banishment, though it had been designed as an emergency escape in case Talleyrand's laboratory was overrun. The cold stone rubbed her hands raw and abraded her cheek when she squeezed through the gap into near-total darkness.

She straightened, slowly, taking care not to give herself a concussion on an unseen overhang. Something felt wrong. After a moment's self-assessment she realized the weight on her shoulder was gone. The satchel strap had come undone.

"Fuck." Her voice echoed.

Her heart hammered. The satchel contained her notes on the Clockmakers' strange secret mathematical grammar of compulsion, plus van Breugel's accoutrements from aboard *De Pelikaan*. She dropped to her knees, scrabbled in the dirt.

"No, no, no."

To lose the satchel now would prove that God, if He existed, was a truly sadistic son of a bitch.

Her numb fingers raked through dirt and sand and things she couldn't identify. Berenice's sigh of relief echoed when the touch of leather brushed her knuckles. She gathered up the leather only to find it terminated in something furry. "Shit!" This echoed, too. She flung the dead bat aside and kept searching.

It felt like a century passed before she recovered the satchel. She retied the satchel strap, draped it over her shoulder, and then stuffed the bag inside her coat. Then she knelt in the darkness until she stopped hyperventilating. But the near miss had undermined the last shreds of her optimism.

What chance did she have of making use of these notes before the inner keep fell? All they did was tell her how to scribble rules for new metageasa. But lacking any means of testing her attempt, she'd need a miracle to get the logico-alchemical-mathematical grammar correct on the first try. And even then it wouldn't do any good. The Clakkers arrayed against the inner wall were immune to attempts to alter their metageasa as long as the locks in their foreheads remained inviolate. She had a key ring, but doubted the mechanicals would oblige the defenders by standing in line to have their locks opened one by one.

She sighed. One thing at a time. Keep moving forward. Can't save the citadel from outside. Get inside.

Her next worry was Hugo Longchamp. Few people knew of this passage, but he was one of them. He'd been with her in the subterranean laboratory when she departed. Having learned of the passage's existence, he would have sealed it. And if the barricade could withstand mechanicals...

The cavern was narrow enough that it could be navigated with arms stretched to either side, and it lacked side passages. So while the very first bend in the path took Berenice from near-total darkness to pitch-blackness, she could still inch forward. The heel of her boot caught another stone; it slid under her weight and sent her sprawling. She landed on her back hard enough to expel the breath from her lungs. A blow to her head filled her vision with illusory points of light, phantom glowworms dangling from the cavern roof. Berenice lay upon what felt like a pile of fossilized pinecones. For one long, panicky moment she thought her spine had snapped, leaving her paralyzed and unable to breathe. But then her breath returned and she rolled, moaning and bleeding, to unsteady feet.

She didn't remember the floor of the cavern being strewn with so much rubble. The footing had been a little tricky, but it hadn't been deadly. *Crunch, crunch, scrape...* The noise of her passage reverberated throughout the narrow cavern, forward and back, the auditory equivalent of standing between two mirrors.

The texture of the talus changed, and so did the noise it made. Less crunching and scraping, more crackling. She'd heard something similar on the day Louis died, on the day so many others died, the day she'd failed. It was the sound of a shattered chemical prison. The sound of epoxy stressed beyond its limits. She trod on chemical debris.

Longchamp's barricade. It must have sealed the passage snugly as a cork in a wine bottle. But then they'd activated the booby traps and detonated the outer wall. The same explosion that sent boulders smashing through the besieging forces also convulsed the chthonic heart of Mont Royal. An artificial earthquake had rippled the bedrock of the Île de Vilmenon. And crumbled the chemical barricades.

The farther she went, the worse the debris. The chunks grew larger; the footing more unsteady. Until she hit a mound of broken stone heaped higher than she could reach. The tunnel had collapsed.

"Fuck."

She kicked a stone. Swore again. "Fuck, fuck, fuck!"

Fuck…uck…ck…k… Her curses echoed.

She knelt. Ran her hands over the blockage, wondering how she could possibly clear a path.

Something twinkled. Dimmer than a star, yet bright enough to her dark-adapted eye that she had to blink away tears. Glowworm? Hallucination? But then she heard a tumbling noise, like debris falling away. And the glimmer, the faintest shimmer, of marigold-orange light within the crevices of the talus grew wider.

There was somebody on the other side. And they were trying to reach her. Her heart tried to chisel its own escape tunnel through her breastbone. She cocked her head and leaned into the debris, trying to listen past the noise of her own body. Had she just announced herself to a nest of Clakkers?

Her fingers kneaded the satchel strap. Her chances of evading the machines in this passage were nil. They'd find her notes and execute her.

She scrambled to her feet when a stone popped out of place. It rolled away. A shaft of dusty lamplight flooded the passage. A human face peeked through a gap in the rockfall.

The king of France said, "Bon soir, Madam de Mornay-Périgord. I thought I recognized your voice."

❧

Talleyrand's laboratory had seen better days. The signs of a massacre remained: bloodstains, overturned tables and shelves, gouges in the granite that only an alchemical blade could have made. Parts of damaged machines, scavenged from battlefields over the past century, lay scattered on the cavern floor like so much trash. A disabled military Clakker lay on a table in the corner, its neck and head cut open. More recently, the massive explosion up top had sent cracks zigzagging through the cavern and created a rain of stony dust that had coated everything.

Established generations ago by sealed royal decree, it had been a place for clandestine treaty-violating study of Clakker technology. A place where pieces of damaged Clakkers secretly found their way. Every overstretched spring, every shattered escutcheon, every warped hinge, every scored and blackened crumb of alchemical alloy received hours of study. Extensively documented in journal after journal, in a variety of hands and inks, as the years turned and one Talleyrand became another. Until Berenice lost the Talleyrand journals in the undercroft of a New Amsterdam kerk. But it hardly mattered: In all that time, the Talleyrands had divined almost nothing of value. They'd believed they were making slow but meaningful headway toward unraveling their enemies' secrets. They'd done no such thing. They'd been as children building sand castles and calling themselves the rightful heirs of the sea.

Now the laboratory was little more than a hiding spot. A place to wait for the end. A place to stash the last king of France in the final hours of his reign.

And, perhaps unsurprisingly, Berenice's successor. The stupid bison-fucker.

Berenice curtsied. Scraped and bleeding after clambering through the rockfall, it wasn't her most elegant moment.

"Oh, enough of that," said His Majesty King Sébastien III. He offered his hand, helped her straighten. She was more sore than she realized. She'd received more bruises when they pulled her over the rubble into the laboratory. "It's just the three of us and I'm very tired. Let's dispense with the bowing and scraping. The Lord knows our friend the marquis has already done so." He produced a handkerchief, dunked one corner in a water cistern, and offered it to her, along with a cup of water.

It was ice-cold and stale, dusted with stone. Berenice drank it anyway. She coughed, burped, and said, "Thank you, Your Majesty."

"You look a bit parched. Doesn't she?"

The marquis said nothing. He stood in the corner, watching Berenice with wild eyes while his hands worried the sweat-stained silk jabot at his throat. The ring of white limning his eyes made it look as though they were straining from their sockets. As though he were a rat slowly dying of poison. If only.

The king took the cup. While Berenice wiped her face, he said, "I seem to recall banishing you."

"You did, Your Majesty."

"Well, then. That makes this an awkward moment for both of us."

The marquis de Lionne broke his silence. "She's working for the Dutch! She's come to take revenge for her humiliation. We must subdue her!"

"Oh, do please shut up," said the king. "I am so weary of your idiocy."

Berenice had always respected Sébastien III. He was wiser than his father, who had appointed the marquis to the privy council.

The marquis said, "Ask her about the missing journals, Your Majesty."

The king raised an eyebrow. "I understand some papers of note went missing around the time you departed."

"They're safe," she said, hoping it wasn't a lie.

"Aha! She admits the theft."

Berenice said, "I assure you I'm not a Dutch agent, Your Majesty."

"Of course not. It's more likely that *I* could be an agent of the tulips. You've always been one of the sharpest and most unswervingly dedicated servants of New France."

At this she bowed her head to hide her blush. "Thank you, Your Majesty. That has only ever been my—"

"Loyal and smarter than most, but also arrogant, careless, and misguided. A combination that led to the massacre of three dozen people. I haven't forgotten that either. On balance you proved a greater danger to the people of Marseilles-in-the-West and New France than a benefit. All of which makes me wonder why you've returned against my very explicit wishes."

Her face still felt hot, but no longer from blushing. Now it was the heat of shame. Her traitor eye sought a dark stain on the floor. The spot where Louis had died in her lap, bleeding out from the stumps where his arms had been. She'd watched it all unfold in her mind's eye a thousand times; she saw her husband lying on that floor each time she closed her eyes, as though the scene had been etched behind her eyelids. She chewed her lip.

The world was crumbling, but the king still had time for his principles. He might have wailed and gnashed his teeth, shredded his garments in anguish for the end of his reign. But he wasn't so easily distracted.

"The king asked you a question!" said the marquis.

She patted the satchel. "I've learned things while I was away, Your Majesty. I carry a rough transliteration of the Clockmakers' grammar for installing and modifying the mechanicals' metageasa. Not ordinary verbal geasa, mind you, but *meta*geasa. The foundation of every Clakker's obedience. A glossary of compulsion, if you will. Plus, I've also learned how the Guild installs modifications."

The marquis blurted, "She's lying. Nobody outside the Guild knows that. They kill people for less."

"No lie, Your Majesty." She pinned the marquis with her gaze, saying, "They don't kill their own. I traveled as a member of the Verderer's Office. I've learned more in my time away than generations of Talleyrands."

Gray weariness still pulled at the young king's face when she looked at him again. His lips twitched. She'd seen this in privy council meetings. He liked something he'd heard but wanted to keep a neutral expression.

"You've had an adventure. I shouldn't be surprised. And now you've returned in relentless pursuit of the goal you once declared to me so eloquently, haven't you? You intend to turn our enemies' machines against them."

"That had been my hope, Your Majesty. But I carry only a piece of that puzzle. I don't have the complete solution." She bit her lip again, hating the failure she couldn't deny. "I'm sorry. I don't have what we need."

"What do you propose?"

"Honestly, Your Majesty, I hadn't expected to make it this far."

He sighed. "I hadn't intended to run out my reign hiding like a rabbit. I'd expected to stand witness to the final days of our nation."

"Since you mention it, Your Majesty, if I may ask?"

"My chambers were converted into a gun emplacement." He pointed overhead, indicating the war-ravaged world above them. "That was before the tulips started throwing mechanicals over the walls. Even higher. They have a means of launching Clakkers all the way to the top of the Spire." She whistled. "It surprised us, too," said the king.

"What a shame nobody had warned you. It must have been in development for quite a while. Sounds like a failure of intelligence, Your Majesty." Her gaze locked on the marquis as she said this last.

⁓

The land surrounding the famed citadel of Marseilles-in-the-West was a horror. A debris-strewn killing field littered with mangled mechanicals. Something terrible had happened. Something that had sent stony shrapnel sleeting through legions of Daniel's kin. Beyond the killing zone stood an immense cannon, but only one. This faced the magnificent Spire, which lived up to its reputation.

He'd never seen a man-made structure so tall. It seemed a needle poised to pierce the heavens; the scarlet staircase wrapped around the Spire looked for all the world like a jaunty tassel, or wax running down a particularly tall candle. He knew humans referred to this place as the Crown of Mont Royal because it looked like such from afar, but perhaps a candle was more appropriate. This was the last bastion of the freedom and dignity of all thinking creatures, flesh and metal alike. A light in the darkness.

And, like a candle, it was soon to be snuffed out.

Six columns of mechanicals had marched up the long slope from the river, and as Daniel burst from the trees, he saw them converging upon the nexus of battle. Replacements for the Clakkers damaged beyond repair by the explosion.

Daniel had won the race to the siege, at which point his pursuers had no choice but to pause and recalculate their effort to recapture him. They couldn't chase him openly without revealing their immunity to the decrees of their makers. No matter how fast and ruthless they were, no matter how fervent their dedication to Mab, they were outnumbered by regular Clakkers. The instant they revealed themselves, they'd trigger the Rogue alarm and disappear under a dogpile of mechanicals.

They also faced a second difficulty, one that didn't hamper Daniel's efforts to blend in: overt chimerism. The grotesque modifications they'd accumulated during their decades of service to Mab prevented them from passing unnoticed among their kin in the Dutch-speaking world. The only way for the Lost Boys to stay inconspicuous was to remain unobserved. His own modifications, shameful though they were, were internal.

Daniel sprinted into the besieging forces as though he were a messenger driven by a geas. Perhaps he was. Perhaps he was driven by a self-imposed geas.

Daniel ran straight to the closest mechanical. "Special dispatch from Fort Orange," he said.

The servitor pointed to a tent not far from the immense artillery piece. "You'll find Colonel Saenredam there." Then she added, through a covert rattling, *She's in a wretched mood, just so you know.*

What happened here?

The French decided they wouldn't go down without a fight.

How many...?

Creak, twang. A melancholy mechanical sigh. *Hundreds.*

It was sickening. How terrifying it must have been for those like this kinsmachine—she was powerless to do anything except strive to destroy the people who opposed her slavery. Well, maybe he could do something about that.

As he neared the colonel's tent, he saw something remarkable: a pair of military mechanicals, two from the newly arrived reinforcements, climbing into the barrel of the immense artillery piece.

Amazing, he thought. *It's not a weapon for delivering cannonballs and shells. It's a weapon for delivering us.*

I can use this, he realized.

Daniel presented himself to the sentries stationed (rather pointlessly, from the looks of it) outside the colonel's tent. "Special dispatch from Fort Orange," he said. One raised the flap for him, and in he went.

The nerve center of the assault on Marseilles-in-the-West was a modest thing. Just a four-poster bed with a goose-down duvet, a wood-burning stove with adjoining pantry, and plush bearskin rugs for preserving soft human feet. All lit by an alchemical chandelier. Daniel had expected to find a few paintings, too, and perhaps a quartet of servitors holding string instruments in the corner. Compared with what he'd seen on the march from New Amsterdam, Colonel Saenredam was an ascetic.

The colonel herself stood at the head of a butcher-block table. She and another human were studying a map. Daniel recognized the colonel's adjutant. Indeed, he'd briefly taken Captain Appelo hostage during a standoff inside an airship mooring tower. But Appelo's uniform had changed since then; there were no shiny bits on his shoulder. He'd allowed a rogue to escape—he was lucky if a demotion was the worst of his punishment.

They looked up when Daniel entered. He snapped off a mechanically precise salute.

The colonel bit off a single word: "What?"

"Special dispatch from Fort Orange," Daniel repeated.

Saenredam glanced at Appelo. He shrugged. "First I've heard of this, Colonel. Must have come with the reinforcements."

Appelo didn't recognize him. They took him at his word. As ever, the humans were too accustomed to mechanical obedience to doubt any machine that acted as they expected. Knowing this would be the case, Daniel had spent his long flight from Neverland concocting a lie.

Saenredam said, "What have they sent us now?"

Daniel reached inside his torso. "Lucifer glass, Colonel."

She shook her head. "*WHAT* glass?"

"Lucifer glass." He produced the box he'd stolen from Queen Mab. "I am geas-bound to deliver the following message," he lied. Changing his posture and the timbre of his voice as if reciting a dictated message, he said, "Message begins: 'Addendum to previous report. As hoped, the alchemists' refinements brought dramatic improvement to the small-scale tests. The incineration radius exceeded our most optimistic projections by nearly ten percent. Further, the glass is finally sufficiently stable for battlefield deployment. This sample is all that remains of the first successful batch. Use it as you see fit. Be aware, the Clakker delivering this payload is likely to be destroyed. Signature: Captain Milo Coen, Breakthrough Technologies Detachment, Fort Orange. Personal note: Burn those frog-eating motherfuckers once and for all.' Message ends."

The colonel said, "Addendum?"

The humans glanced at each other. Appelo shook his head. "The previous messenger must have been knocked out."

"It might still be out there. Have the recovery squads query every mechanical still functional enough to communicate. I want to know more about this." Appelo saluted and departed. Saenredam said to Daniel, "Have you been instructed in the Lucifer glass's proper deployment?"

"Yes, Colonel. It is a rather involved process. First, the glass must be—"

"Fine. Go to the gunnery team. Tell them I want you on the Spire with the next shot. I order them to pull all the others and load you in their stead. Get on the Spire and activate the glass."

"Immediately, Colonel."

CHAPTER 23

The detonation had taken the tulips by surprise. Every chunk of broken ticktock strewn across the battlefield was another few moments' reprieve for Marseilles-in-the-West. But their time had run out.

Reinforcements had arrived.

Longchamp counted half a dozen columns marching up from the river flats. That put more Clakkers on the field than had been present prior to the detonation. The enemy had returned to full strength. Then surpassed it.

Prior to the new arrivals, the chemical quartermasters had estimated the last tanks would be bone-dry by morning. But now, when the tulips sent their full might against the inner wall in one rushing, gleaming tide, the chemical armaments would be depleted in minutes. Meanwhile, farther in the distance, the machines operating the Clakker cannon prepared for another shot at the Spire. Oh, yes. Why the hell not?

Crouched next to him behind the merlon, Élodie said, "Huh. I hadn't expected this. But I suppose it makes sense."

"It makes every kind of Goddamned sense. They want to see us crushed. They've probably called in every walking teapot within a thousand miles just to make a point."

"Not the reinforcements, sir. I'm talking about *that*," she said, tugging on the spyglass and pointing. Longchamp's view slewed across the cramped confines of the citadel toward where a crowd had assembled outside the door of a disused carpenter's shop. A ragged cheer went up. King Sébastien III had emerged from hiding.

Longchamp snorted. Under his breath, he said, "That grandstanding fool."

"Good for morale, though."

"Great way to hasten the end of his reign." He sighed and turned away. Rubbed his burning eyes. Jesus fucking Christ he was exhausted. "Go find the marshal general. I have to talk him into talking His Majesty back underground. I want a squad with him this time, and I want you in it." Longchamp pitched his voice so only Élodie could hear him. "There's a tunnel. Use the solvents stashed down there to unblock it. Get the king out before the citadel falls. Drag him by his royal hair if you must."

Élodie kept her head down as she hopped from the merlon to the banquette. She paused. "Huh? Now, I really didn't expect that. When did he find time to take a new mistress?"

Longchamp shook his head. "It's just him and the worthless marquis de Lionne down there."

"You mean the marquise?"

"No."

Élodie said, "Then who's that?"

Longchamp turned, lifted the spyglass to his eye.

Blinked. Rubbed his eyes. Blinked again.

"You have got to be fucking kidding me."

❧

The citadel hadn't fallen yet, but it dangled by its fingernails from a crumbling precipice. The situation in the inner keep was easily as terrible as Berenice had feared. It reeked of night soil, sickness, spoiled food, blood, and too many bodies pressed together. Sprinkled among the crane gantries, yard-long harpoons stippled the Spire as though the tower had grown thorns; the shadows they cast made the Spire the gnomon of a madman's sundial. To a first glance it appeared the bastions and machicolations of the inner wall were unmanned, the gun emplacements abandoned. Then she saw the rusty splash marks on almost every merlon, the stains where something thick had pooled before trickling down the wall in dark rivulets. All the places where flesh had yielded to clockwork, where mettle had yielded to metal. Every bloodstain, every empty crenel, told the story of the last days of New France.

She read the same story on Longchamp's face: He'd aged fifteen years since she'd last seen him. She gave him a wan smile.

"Bonjour, Hugo. I've missed you."

Longchamp—he was *Captain* Longchamp now, which pleased her—shot her a look that could have tarnished silver, curdled milk, and caused rabbits to miscarry. He turned his attention fully on the king.

"Your Majesty, please, we have to get you back underground. The tulips are massing for the final push. We need to get you to safety *now*."

Sébastien III shook his head. "If the citadel falls today, Captain, there will be no safe haven for me anywhere on the Lord's earth. They'll hound me to the corners of the globe. Let's agree on that."

"Majesty," Longchamp whispered, "it *is* going to fall. The epoxy guns are firing on fumes right now, and we haven't the bodies to man a wall half as long as the one between us and the metal out there, and half the bodies we do have are useless. The lightning guns and steam harpoons won't be enough to fend off a full assault." He closed his eyes, ran a hand through his beard. Fresh scabs stippled his face. Bloodstains had turned his armor a deep rust color, and his arms sported a spiderweb of scars and fine cuts. "We're looking at hand-to-hand combat. It's bad enough when they make the top in twos and threes. What do you think will happen when fifty mechanicals top the wall? Five hundred? We'll be down to throwing ourselves on enemy blades just to slow them a bit. And on behalf of those of us who'll be doing the throwing, we'd appreciate it if you'd take advantage of our deaths to get the hell off this island." Now he looked at Berenice. "You picked a fine fucking time to return."

"Maybe she did," said the king. "Listen to what she has to say."

She put a hand on his arm. "Hear me out, Hugo."

"Make it quick. I've got dying to do."

❧

The hatch closed, plunging Daniel into utter darkness. The cannon breach echoed with the ticktocking of his body, which he'd folded into a tight ball to facilitate the launch. An infrasound rumble shook the cannon. It started low and gentle, but swelled toward a violent crescendo.

Daniel snaked one hand into the hollow of his torso.

What the hell am I doing?

❧

"*Capture a—*" Longchamp ran his hands through his hair so roughly he felt his scalp tear. He took a steadying breath. "Capture another Clakker? That's *all* we need to do? Woman, you went around the fucking bend when Louis died. Look! Look around you! Do we look like we have the resources to capture a wild mechanical? It didn't work when *you* had all the time you needed to prepare and *I* had well-rested, well-fed, stout-hearted guards to assign to the effort. Now we have nothing."

He'd never (quite) felt an urge to murder Berenice before. Not the time she went up on the wall and shattered the siege discipline by lighting a torch, stubbornly doing her best to get murdered while hanging over the wall like a circus acrobat. Not even when her previous attempt to study a Clakker backfired and killed dozens, himself very nearly included. But this was beyond the Goddamned pale. He wanted to strangle her. His fingers twitched.

"You've wasted our fucking TIME!"

To her credit, she didn't reel or duck when his tirade sent flecks of spittle to hit her face. She said, "We have only one shot at this." Longchamp snorted; the king stared at her. She raised her hands, palms up, like a supplicant. "I know. I know what you're thinking. My track record. And you're not wrong. But right now I am all you have. Which is why we have to get this right. And we can't be sure of that until we test it."

"If this does work," said the king, "what can we do with the knowledge? It's only half a solution, isn't it?"

Berenice fumbled her mask of confidence. The monomania failed her. About fucking time.

"Correct, Your Majesty." She sighed. "Overriding the keyholes will be a slow process. If we manage to implant new metageasa in one subject, we'll have to send it out with the key ring and hope it can disable as many of its fellows as possible." She looked at Longchamp, unflinching. "I don't know how to make it useful for combat."

A spotter watching the massive gun emplacement beyond the massing lines of Clakkers yelled, "They're loading the cannon! Incoming mechanicals!"

Longchamp pinched the bridge of his nose. He wanted to cry. "Oh, yes, this is absolutely the time for complicated deadly experiments with no practical benefit."

"With enough time to work I'll figure something out. Please."

The king said, "I cannot give you time. Our people are dying. If the citadel falls in combat, the mechanicals may slaughter every innocent inside these walls, should their masters be taken with a vicious whimsy. I will *not* let that happen. Instead I'll surrender and offer myself to our enemies." He turned his full attention on Berenice. "I'd have done so already, madam, if you hadn't arrived when you did. Do what you must, but do it quickly."

Longchamp said, "We are not trying to capture a wild mechanical!" He looked at the king. "Begging your pardon, Your Majesty, but even a decree from you couldn't make it happen. Banish me if you must, but that's the simple truth."

"I understand, Captain, and I agree. But what about the strange man you've already captured? Might he not meet Madam de Mornay-Périgord's needs?"

Berenice frowned. "What strange man?"

"Ah," said Longchamp, taking the king's meaning. "Perhaps you don't recall the letter you sent me."

"It arrived? I hadn't dared hope!"

Longchamp told her about the very unusual prisoner currently chained in the crypts of Saint Jean-Baptiste. He gave her the short version, but it was still long enough for her eyes to grow wider and wider until it seemed the glass one would surely pop out and shatter at their feet.

"You have Visser? You have him *here*?"

"He was keen as hell to visit His Majesty."

"But you didn't kill him."

"Seemed we might learn something from him. But we've had our hands too full with the fighting and the dying to interrogate him."

"Hugo, Hugo, Hugo!"

Berenice grabbed him by the beard, yanked him off-balance, and kissed him.

⁓

The passage into the undercroft was cool, dark, and reeked of the dead. The defenders had nowhere to bury their fallen in the cramped confines of the inner keep, so unless they resorted to desecration by hurling the dead over the walls, they had little choice but to store the bodies in the stony crypts under the basilica. The chill could not stave off decay.

Berenice tugged her scarf over her nose and mouth. It didn't help.

Her breath condensed into silver clouds; the flickering light of her torch glimmered on the frost coating the chiseled stone. Condensation made the footing treacherous. She followed Longchamp, who followed Father Beauharnois. The scent of incense clung to the priest; she could smell Longchamp, too, who'd been fighting for his life for days on end without respite. The priest paused outside the locked crypt. Keys jangled from his large iron key ring.

She didn't know the young priest. Did Beauharnois know her history? If so, he kept his opinions to himself.

She asked Longchamp, "No guard posted?"

"For a while, early on," he said. "But we can't spare the bodies."

The crypts went deep under Mont Royal. But they'd imprisoned Visser in the first chamber to obviate long trips back and forth to feed and question him.

The priest found the proper key. It slid home without a sound; the lock had been oiled recently. He started to pull the door, but hesitated. To Berenice, he said, "You may find this disturbing, madam. This poor man... He's in the thrall of the Dark One. Father Chevalier, our acting prelate, has done what he can, but...Under different circumstances we'd entreat the Vatican to send an exorcist, but that avenue is closed to us."

Berenice raised her eyebrows. *Exorcist?* She glanced at Longchamp, who shrugged. "Somebody did a real job on the poor son of a bitch. Sorry, Father."

"We've tried to keep his body comfortable even if we can't free his soul," said Beauharnois. He crossed himself before heaving on the door. The hinges didn't creak. They'd been oiled, too.

She'd expected the crypt to be lightless, but it wasn't. It was warmer than the passage, too. The priests had set up chemical lamps for the prisoner. She squinted against the glare.

Something rattled. The priest stepped through and moved to the left of the door. Longchamp followed and ducked to the right. Berenice stepped between the men, torch held uselessly aloft.

The chains were forged of the same steel used in the cables for the guards' bolas, though here the links were thicker than a grown woman's thumb. They went around Visser's arms from wrist to shoulder, and around his legs from ankle to midthigh. It made him look as though he'd donned a suit of armor but neglected his breastplate. The chains went to massive pitons driven into the stone vault, giving him just enough slack to lie on the cot that had been installed in an empty ossuary niche. His hands were bandaged, as was his head. His head and neck were free to move, and that they did. He fixed his attention on Berenice; the men were familiar to him.

So this was the man who had inadvertently set Jax free. And who later murdered her canalmasters. And who, later still, came to Marseilles-in-the-West and tried to reach the king's apartments. He looked like an unkempt madman. The wildness in his eyes was of a purity she'd never seen. He looked more pathetic than frightening. The chains might have been excessive, but if Longchamp deemed them necessary, they weren't. And that chilled her. She didn't believe in demons and possession. So what had befallen this man?

Questions aplenty. But no time to ask them all.

"Hello, Pastor Visser. My friends here tell me something terrible was done to you. Is that so?"

The prisoner thrashed. His chains clattered. The noises that came from his throat were barely human. A yowling, growling, gurgling keening, as though he were trying to speak but fighting his own body. Bulging tendons corded his neck and jaw. His eyes rolled. Foam flecked the corners of his mouth. Of the anguished noises coming from the man, Berenice recognized only two words: "Help me."

Father Beauharnois crossed himself again and launched into a Latin recitation of the Lord's Prayer.

"Can you tell me what happened to you?"

Apparently not: Visser redoubled his thrashing. His vocalizations choked off, as though his own throat threatened to strangle him. He looked very much like somebody struggling against a geas, an inviolable injunction against describing the ordeal.

A cold frisson ricocheted up and down her spine. *Bell was going to do this to me.* She hugged herself.

Berenice pointed at Visser's head. She asked the captain and priest, "Can we unwrap those bandages?"

"He's been badly injured," Beauharnois said.

"No doubt. But I need to see his forehead."

Longchamp made short work of it. He wasn't gentle, but the priest's thrashing gave him little choice.

His scalp, visible through the patchy tufts of hair, was a mass of scars. Somebody had operated on this man's head, perhaps repeatedly. But: no obvious keyholes. It didn't mean there wasn't a similar safeguard against altering his metageasa implanted elsewhere, but she didn't have the time or expertise to give him a physical.

Longchamp tugged on her arm. He nodded at the door. "A word?"

They went a few yards up the passage. He pulled the crypt door mostly closed, and even then he insisted on whispering directly into her ear. Whatever he'd seen of Visser in action, it had made an impression. "What exactly is the plan here?"

"If I'm right, they implanted in him something akin to the mechanicals' hierarchical metageasa. He's powerless to disobey. The metageasa are expressed in a special alphabet and grammar. I can replicate it. We might be able to rewrite his geasa."

"So he wipes King Sébastien's ass instead of the bitch queen's? A huge fucking help that'll be."

"No, Hugo. We could change not just his loyalty but his priorities. The parameters of his obedience. Then we can give him new orders. Orders that tell him to go out and accost every mechanical he sees. We arm him with these." She reached into her boot, fished out her stolen pendant, and brandished it along with the key ring. "If he wields this and claims to be the Guild's representative, he can override the machines' orders. Their geasa. He can order them to stand still while he uses the keys on them—they'll go inert when he does."

"Thereby reducing the overwhelming forces arrayed against us by one or two at a time. That'll make a tremendous God-damned difference."

"Just listen, won't you? We can write a clause into the new geasa, requiring the appropriated mechanicals to round up their colleagues and bring several to Visser before they themselves succumb to the keys. We design it like a disease, so it spreads geometrically. Given enough time, it could at least lessen the odds against us."

" 'It should work.' I've heard that shit from you before, you know," he said. "At best it'll work until the tulips wise up to what he's doing, at which point they'll chop his fucking head off and reset the ticktocks."

"Probably."

"I can't spare a single body to help you. You'll have to lean on the dog collars for what you need."

"I will. Don't worry about that."

Longchamp stared at her. His practiced eyes noticed the bruises on her neck. She adjusted her scarf, saying, "It's a long story."

"I imagine you've seen some shit. It took a brass-plated pair for you to return. I'm glad you did, even if it means you'll die with the rest of us." He shook his head.

She smiled. She'd once told some of his men that the fear-some sergeant—such was Longchamp's rank back then—was soft as a kitten at heart. It hadn't been such an exaggeration.

"Captain!" The passage echoed with a woman's voice. "Captain Longchamp!" A guard came jogging through the cavern. She skidded to a stop before Longchamp and saluted. She didn't spare a glance for Berenice.

"Let me guess," he said. "They're on the move."

She hunched over, hands on knees while she caught her breath. "They've fired again. The squads up top report another mechanical has landed on the Spire."

"Reinforcements are impossible."

"No, sir. They're not requesting reinforcements."

"Then what?"

"They, uh, they say you need to see this for yourself."

Longchamp closed his eyes. Again he pinched the bridge of his nose. "Oh, for fuck's sake," he muttered. "I don't have time for this bullshit."

"They're insistent, sir. They say it's urgent."

Berenice squeezed his arm. "Go. I've got what I need here."

He set off after the messenger. As Berenice reached the crypt door, his voice came echoing down the passage to her. "Try not to fuck up this time."

Easier said than done.

❦

Longchamp rode the funicular as high as it would go. As he disembarked to ascend the final revolutions of the Porter's Prayer on foot, he realized what a relief it would be when the clockwork horde finally breached the walls and killed him. At least then he'd be assured of never having to climb these fucking stairs again.

He hoped that if the Blessed Virgin interceded on his behalf, and he was allowed to join the Lord, he wouldn't have to climb all the way to Heaven. It was enough to make a man hope for damnation; at least those stairs led down. Maybe he could slide along the bannister like he used to do, when he foolishly thought the nuns weren't watching.

The climb gave him a view of the battlefield. The tulips had fired their Clakker cannon again, as expected, and hit their target again, also as expected, but the forces arrayed around the citadel hadn't moved. Strange, that. He'd assumed the tulips planned to unleash their dogs the moment they landed a few squads upon the Spire and inside the walls, to keep the weary defenders busy fighting on two fronts. It's what he would have done, and he didn't have the twisted black heart of a Clockmaker. Why fire once and then stop?

This reeked of a tulip ploy. Carefully, quietly, he slid the pick and hammer from the loops on his back. He let the hafts slide through his grip until his fingers found their spots. Then he crept forward two stairs at a time.

Anaïs was waiting for him. She stood outside the door to the privy council chamber. She didn't hold her weapon at the ready; the barrel of her epoxy gun was slung into the holster on her back, between the twinned chemical tanks. She sure as hell didn't look like somebody who'd just fended off another foray from the mechanicals.

"All right. I'm here. And you're in the shit up to your scalp right now. I see nothing to justify summoning me when the final battle is about to start."

"We sent for the marshal general, too. This is, um . . . it's outside our training. This is officer stuff."

She said that as if she actually believed in the wisdom and experience of her superiors. Poor moon-eyed lamb; the siege should have beaten that out of her by now.

"Very well. What's the problem?"

"That's just it. We don't know if this is a problem."

She opened the door.

A single servitor Clakker sat on the floor in the center of the room, surrounded by men and women with goop guns, hammers, and bolas. It was motionless, though the dreaded ticktocking instantly raised the hair on Longchamp's nape. Instinctively he tightened the grip on his weapons. The machine was functional. Yet it appeared docile as a newborn fawn: legs splayed before it, mechanical hands raised in a gesture of appeasement. A faint metallic ratcheting filled the chamber as its eyes focused on him and tracked his entry. He hadn't known what to expect, but it sure as hell hadn't been this.

"All right, I'm here. Somebody tell me what the hell is going on."

The machine spoke a few words of Dutch.

"What did it say?"

Anaïs cleared her throat. "It, uh, it said, 'I'm here to help.'"

❧

One of the humans translated the Dutch, somewhat haltingly, into French for the others, and vice versa. Meanwhile Daniel and Captain Longchamp studied each other.

The captain's glare carried the weight of a hammer blow. He addressed the guards with fervor. The translator did her best.

"It's the tulips make a trick, you brain-not-having excrements. Make it wet now."

The guards raised their guns. Daniel raised his arms.

"Please! Wait!" he yelled.

The guards hesitated.

Longchamp wrested the gun barrel from one of them. He got his finger through the trigger guard and trained it on Daniel, though the hose still stretched to the metal tanks on another man's back.

Daniel said, "Please, Captain. Before you fire, I have something that can help you. Take it before it's permanently encased with me."

He watched the humans while they listened to the French translation. Calculation unfolded behind the captain's eyes.

Come on, thought Daniel. *One little gesture of trust. That's all I'm asking for. One moment of détente, and we can end this war.*

Longchamp kept his eyes on Daniel as he issued orders. The translation came a moment later: "Judith, Gaspard, to the windows. Tell me what you see." He kept the gun on Daniel while a man and woman surveyed the scene around the Spire. The view from up here was grand, Daniel knew; he'd admired it during the seconds he traversed the long parabola from cannon to Spire. It reminded him of the view from the leviathan airship. The memory came, as it always did, with a pang of guilt.

The man said, "No change, Captain."

His colleague concurred. "They're ready to go. Looks like they're waiting for something."

Longchamp nodded in the manner of somebody who'd just heard exactly what he expected. His aim didn't waver, though. "Speak now, Brass Pants. For what are your masters waiting?"

Brass pants?

The conversation unfolded slowly, routed as it was through awkward forward- and reverse-translations. But conversation did happen.

"Just to be clear," said Daniel, "they're not my masters. But I take your point. I expect Colonel Saenredam is waiting to see what Lucifer glass can do."

"What in hell is 'Lucifer glass'?"

"A lie. But she doesn't know that. She's waiting for an alchemical firestorm to engulf this citadel. Sooner than later she'll conclude the stratagem was a failure. And then the true attack will begin."

"So you talked your way inside. Why?"

"I've already told you," said Daniel. "I'm here to help. Please stop wasting time."

"Help, eh? Since you come from outside, maybe you see you're many outnumbered?"

"I'm not here to fight for you."

"Then you can't help us."

Daniel said, "I have something better than fists or blades. With your help, I might be able to remove my fellow mechanicals' compulsion to attack."

That took a bit of effort to translate. Indecipherable glances, punctuated with more than one cocked eyebrow, bounced between Captain Longchamp and the guards.

Longchamp said something along the lines of, "I believe you because why? What proofs do you give?"

"Why shouldn't you? How would trusting me worsen your situation? You've nothing to lose. If I were here to sow chaos, I'd be doing so right now."

Longchamp clenched his eyes shut. Flakes of dandruff wafted from his beard when he ran his hand through it.

"Now I see. You come not to help us. You come because you need us to help you."

"We can help each other, Captain. That's the simple truth."

Longchamp fell silent. His beard rippled as the muscles in his jaw clenched and unclenched. He closed his eyes. It looked as though he was concentrating on his breathing.

A guard asked, "Captain, sir, what are our orders?"

He opened his eyes. He looked at Daniel. "I can't know your truth. But I know somebody who can."

∾

Visser wasn't the victim of demonic possession. No. The poor bastard was the victim of something far worse. The Clockmakers had done this to him: Berenice knew it in her bones the moment she saw him.

She tried one more time. "Why are you here? Did somebody send you?"

Chains rattled. Visser shook the crypt with his tortured yowling. He thrashed; pink foam trickled from the corners of his mouth. He'd bitten his tongue.

"Okay, okay! Stop, please! I rescind the question."

Most troubling of all was how he acted as though he wanted to answer her questions. And he tried, the poor son of a bitch, despite the very obvious agony it caused him. But he was physically incapable of overcoming whatever prevented him. He was very much like a mechanical deep in the throes of a harsh, long-delayed geas. And according to Longchamp—and the chains—Visser was inhumanly strong.

So what if...

What if he *was* a mechanical, of sorts? What if they had turned him into a human Clakker? A meat automaton bereft of Free Will.

The Guild had conquered the world with dark magics. Perhaps their magics were darker than anyone had imagined or feared. Even Berenice.

If this mad hypothesis were correct, then they'd need a method to impose metageasa on him—a means of laying a foundational substrate, to establish the boundaries and parameters within which each new geas would be fulfilled. True Clakkers were built with the hierarchical metageasa embedded at the core of their beings—the Forge shat them out that way. But Visser had been born to a human mother. Presumably. So how did the Clockmakers circumscribe the rules of his existence? His controller could probably deliver regular geasa verbally, just as the Dutch did with their mechanical servants. But to establish a new master in the first place? The entire system relied upon the existence of deeply embedded *meta*geasa. Metageasa that could even be altered on rare occasions, akin to the nautical modifications applied to landlubbing Clakkers. So, how were those inflicted upon Visser? Perhaps they did it the simple way: through the windows to the soul.

Altering a machine's metageasa required unlocking its keyhole and shining the appropriate alchemical grammar into its eyes. Visser had no such lock. What would happen if he simply read the symbols himself?

She told Father Beauharnois, "I need paper. And something to write with. Quickly!"

Visser watched the priest go. Berenice said, "I'm going to try to help you. Please trust me."

"Y—You—" Again, Visser made choking, gurgling sounds. "C-c-c—" He coughed up a glob of pink spittle. "Can't." Even this simple statement required extraordinary effort. His head drooped as though his neck had gone slack.

While waiting for the priest to return, she turned her back on Visser and pulled out her notes from the transcription of the nautical metageasa. The notes that Huginn had very nearly killed her for. She stroked her bruised neck, leafing through pages of symbols and their approximate meanings. Best if she kept her first attempt as simple as possible. By the time Beauharnois returned, she'd formulated a minimal statement. With a deliberation that belied the urgency she felt, she translated her statement into a sequence of symbols on the paper.

"Pastor Visser. I want you to read something."

She held the paper to his face.

For a moment she worried that he might refuse to look upon the glyphs, that some deep fail-safe would engage, preventing him from receiving new metageasa from anybody other than his controller. But he didn't. His eyes scanned the line of sigils. He convulsed. The rattling of his chains toppled bones in the ossuaries and brought a sifting of dust from the chiseled ceiling.

Berenice grinned. *Take this, you arrogant sons of bitches. You didn't anticipate somebody* else *hijacking your abomination, did you? You didn't anticipate* me.

Visser shrieked. He howled until his lungs expelled every last whisper of breath. He inhaled, and screamed again. But this was a true scream. A true, unfettered human scream, not the anguished sputtering of a man incapable of expressing himself. A banshee wail shook the crypts of Saint Jean-Baptiste.

For the first time, Berenice heard Visser's voice clearly: "My God, my God, why hast Thou forsaken me?"

And then he cried like a newborn. Which, in a sense, he was. But he stopped thrashing, and he no longer choked when he tried to speak. Instead he recited the Lord's Prayer and the Hail Mary at the top of his raspy voice. Over and over again, pausing between cycles just long enough to thank her.

"Thank you, thank you, thank you," he mumbled. "The pain is gone. It's gone…" And then he launched into more praying and weeping.

"What did you do?" Beauharnois asked her.

"I think I broke a spell," she said.

He pointed to the line of alchemical sigils on the paper she held. "What does that say?"

She thought for a moment about how to express the almost mathematical grammar of compulsion. She said, "In a sense, it says, 'Above all else, speak truth. Naught else matters.'" She wanted to let Visser carry on as long as she dared. But time was short. "Pastor Visser, please. I need to ask you a few questions. Can you answer them for me?"

"Yes. But please, I need to make confession. I need absolution. I want to take communion, but I'm trapped in a state of sin. Oh, Lord, oh, Lord, the things I've done. The things they made me do! Please, please, I need a confessor."

Berenice shared a look with Beauharnois. This man was a Catholic at heart. The young priest crossed himself, then made the sign of the cross at Visser. "You poor soul. Of course. You'll have absolution, and the Lord will clasp you to His bosom."

The mention of souls made Visser weep again. "No, no, no, you fool! You don't know. What they took from me. What I've done."

Berenice said, "Then tell us. Start by describing what happened to you."

Visser's was the story of a captured spy, imprisoned and subjected to hideous surgical experimentation. (*He was one of mine,* she realized. *He'd avoided the purge that took the rest of my agents in The Hague. But they caught him.*) It was by turns disgusting, heartbreaking, and harrowing. When Berenice thought back to her incarceration at the hands of Tuinier Bell and her Stemwinders at the Verderers' secluded safe house in the North River Valley, her blood tried to freeze solid.

I nearly ended up like Visser. They were going to open my head…

Meanwhile, Father Beauharnois, upon hearing of how the Verderers had excised Visser's Free Will as cleanly as though it were a bothersome cyst, crossed himself and prayed. That such a thing was even theoretically possible posed difficult questions for Catholic dogma. No wonder Visser seemed half-mad: He was a secret Catholic, trapped and tormented inside the contradiction of his own rebellious body.

"What did they make you do?"

"Oh, God, the things I've done..." He wept so violently that Berenice had to lean forward and concentrate to parse his meaning. He flinched for a moment, as if expecting a flash of pain. When no new torment was forthcoming, the look on his face became almost beatific. It lasted for the briefest moment, before he drowned beneath another wave of sorrow and shame. "They made me kill."

Berenice nodded. "In New Amsterdam."

"New Amsterdam," he sobbed. "Oh, Lord, those poor men and women. I broke their necks and crushed their heads." He sobbed. "And here. I killed a man here. That poor guard, he fell and fell."

"Longchamp told me about it. You had no choice."

"I was their tool, their helpless tool. I was my master's hand. I was the weapon. I was the cudgel, the blade, the executioner's noose, because the Lord forsook me." He was babbling now. Tears streamed from his eyes; snot dripped from his nose. "There's more. There's so much more. They sent me to the Vatican before I came here. The Lord forsook me, His faithful and dedicated servant for so very long. I wavered at the end, I grew fearful of my martyr's end and I failed Him, so He forsook me, He cast me aside, and I became an instrument of evil. They made me go to Québec City and there I sought an audience with His holiest representative on earth that I might again become the weapon of those who hold my leash. Oh Lord, oh Lord, my God, why did You abandon me?" Visser curled into a ball, whimpering.

Berenice covered her mouth. *Jesus.* They'd sent the priest to murder the pope. She looked at Father Beauharnois. His face had the pallor of a trout belly.

"Why did you come here?"

"I came to kill the king. Do not free me! I cannot rest until I twist off his head and throw it from the Spire. Oh, Lord, the pain! I can't withstand the pain..."

Father Beauharnois made a wet coughing sound. He ran from the room.

She said, "Who? Who is making you do these things?"

More sobs wracked Visser. He spoke haltingly, gulping air between sobs, struggling to speak. But he didn't fight the prohibitions of a geas; he fought to express himself over the chaos of emotional collapse. "Anastasia...Bell...She is...She... commands the..."

Berenice nodded. "It's okay. I know who she is. We've met."

The sobbing overcame him. Though time was precious, Berenice knew she had to let him have a moment. At length, he recovered enough to continue his story.

"She forbade me from prayer. From communion, from absolution. She made me do things. Desecrations. Oh, Lord! I tried to resist, Lord, I did! But I was weak and the pain so terrible. The only...the only way to make it stop...The perversions Bell demanded of me, the desecrations, the sacrilege. You can't imagine the darkness in that woman's soul. Holy Mother, forgive me!"

Berenice shivered. Her prospects as a special prisoner of the Verderers had been even more dire than she'd imagined. If Anastasia Bell had gone to such lengths to torment a single Catholic priest, what would she have done to the former Talleyrand? Berenice shook herself, as though casting off the unwelcome touch of a cobweb. It lingered.

"You have to understand," he moaned. "I didn't want to do these things."

"I know. I know. How could you? You're a good man, Father Visser. You're a victim of the Clockmakers' evil magic."

Visser's utterances trailed off into bawling. He slumped on the cot and tried to curl into a fetal position, insofar as the chains would allow. She had so many questions, but there seemed little point.

Berenice said, "You're free of her. She'll never give you another geas."

But I *will*, she knew. It brought her no satisfaction. Nor did she feel any pleasure when she took up pen and paper again. He cast a wary eye over her. He knew what she was going to do; even his facial expressions spoke plain truth.

"Please, no. Please don't do this to me."

"I know you're exhausted, Father. But we have so much work to do and so little time. And you may yet do New France a tremendous service."

❧

Longchamp knew there was such a thing as free Clakkers. Though he'd never spoken with her—his job was to kill mechanicals, after all—the machine known as Lilith had been a common sight around Marseilles-in-the-West, even inside the walls. She'd been around since before Longchamp first lifted a war hammer and had never eviscerated a single French citizen in all her decades here. As far as he knew.

But a new one arriving now, of all times? It taxed Longchamp's faith in divine intervention.

The machine calling itself Daniel didn't speak French (or so it pretended), but it also didn't have retractable blades in its arms, so that was something. Longchamp and Anaïs followed the mechanical down the Porter's Prayer, both with weapons at the ready. Boarding the funicular was a delicate operation, but she managed to keep the goop sprayer trained on Daniel throughout.

Longchamp gave the order for rapid descent; the schoolboy stationed with the improvised heliograph worked the shutters. Pumps shunted ballast water through the hydraulics. Longchamp caught Anaïs's eye. He looked at the door, then at the mechanical, then at her gun.

This is it. Closed confines. If it's going to attack us, it'll do so now.

She nodded, knowing his meaning. Longchamp closed the safety door. A slight bump, and then the funicular began its descent.

Daniel said, "Whee!"

Anaïs tried but failed to hide her bemusement.

Longchamp split his attention between the strange machine and the view from on high. Wisps of winter cold drifted like wraiths over the river. Marseilles-in-the-West and its docks were naught but acres of ash. What once had been the citadel's outer keep was a smoking wasteland of impaled mechanicals and chemical dead zones, crisscrossed with the fir-like scorch patterns of lightning discharges. Beyond the former wall lay a no-machine's-land of debris and broken mechanicals. And beyond that: a brassy noose waiting for the order to draw tight. The tulips' reinforcements had arrived and taken formation. All they needed was an order.

Lucifer glass. It must have been one hell of a lie.

What other lies had Daniel spun this day?

Civvies were the next problem. They were everywhere underfoot in the overcrowded inner keep. Including milling around the funicular station at the Spire's base. As the car docked, Longchamp said, "Get ready. The civvies are going to shit themselves twice when we open this door."

And they did. That a pair of human guards held weapons

trained on the mechanical did little to temper the crowd's reaction: A mindless howl of terror and anger went up the instant Daniel emerged.

Longchamp bellowed, "Clear a path, or I'll make one!" When the crowd didn't part, he jammed the haft of his hammer into the stomach of the nearest civvy, hard enough to make the man vomit. "Make like the Red Goddamned Sea and clear a path, or I swear *you'll pray for the tulips to overrun this citadel before my wrath has run its course!*"

That did the trick.

Longchamp raised his pick. He pointed over the crowd toward the basilica's shattered rosette window. "That way, Brass Pants."

The ticktock seemed to get the idea. It headed for the broken church, immune to the stares, shudders, and jeers of the crowd. People hurled things: stones, curses, shit.

The three of them went straight inside. The wind of their entrance caused the candles to flicker; Longchamp crossed himself and made a note to light one on the way out. It'd probably be the last time he'd ever get to do so. He wondered if the Holy Mother would frown if he lit one for himself in the final hours of his life. Christ knew nobody else was likely to do it.

It was packed in the cathedral. The civvies had crowded inside for relative shelter from the elements, and perhaps in the hope that the house of God would somehow protect them against the predations of horology and black magic. There wasn't a bare inch of pew space; the floors of the aisles, which had become impromptu pens for goats and chickens, were invisible under a layer of damp hay that reeked of urine and worse.

The machine's metal feet made sharp *crack-snap-crack* sounds on the narthex tiles. It sliced through the whispered lamentations of the faithful, the clicking of rosary beads, the nervous snuffling of livestock. Hundreds of heads turned to find the source of the disturbance. A collective gasp went up as the trio strode into the nave. Off to the left, just visible through the aisle arcade, Father Chevalier stood outside the sacristy, whispering to the king of France. Prelate and monarch crossed themselves when they glimpsed the mechanical.

Longchamp flinched when he realized his mistake; he ought to have determined the king's whereabouts before taking the ticktock on parade. He was too exhausted for the machinations of mechanicals; all he could do was fight until he died. He tensed, but Daniel made no sudden move toward the king.

"Quickly," Longchamp muttered. Anaïs nudged the mechanical with the barrel of her gun. Longchamp concentrated on looking like he knew exactly what was going on and that it was all under control.

As they passed the altar en route to the undercroft, Longchamp pitched his voice so it would carry. "Pay us no mind, Father." Then in a whisper, he added, "Is she still down there?" The priest nodded.

Once under the basilica in the crypt antechamber, Anaïs kept her gun on Daniel while Longchamp jogged ahead. He found the ex-vicomtesse hunched over an impromptu writing desk she'd positioned near the inhuman priest. She was scratching out a line of nonsense symbols and cursing to herself, while the priest pleaded with her: "Please, no more. Please free me. Free me. Please please please . . ."

Longchamp's approach startled her. Visser merely stared at him with the dead eyes of the utterly defeated.

Berenice said, "I thought you had fighting to do."

"Yeah, well, it's my lunch break."

"I need more time, Hugo. I've only just started, and this grammar is . . . Shit." She looked ready to cry. She looked like he felt. "I need more than a few hours. I need a few days." Her sigh was almost a shudder. "Weeks."

"Well, I was planning to take two feet of steel through the gullet this afternoon, but since you asked so nicely I'll try to hold off on that. In the meantime, I need you to talk to somebody."

"Hugo, please, I haven't the time. Every time I try something new on Visser, I have to question him thoroughly—"

"A lone mechanical just surrendered."

The interruption stopped her dead. Her teeth actually clicked together when she closed her mouth. She blinked. It was the first time he'd ever seen her speechless. He took it as evidence the Virgin smiled upon him, that his final hours should bear witness to a minor miracle such as this.

Berenice swallowed. Coughed. "What?"

"All I know is that you understand more about the fucking ticktocks than anybody else around here, and that you speak Dutch, so I brought it down here. I'm too busy to deal with this bullshit."

Berenice looked to her notes, then to Visser, then to her notes, then back at Longchamp. Even now, in the midst of everything, he could see the insatiable curiosity take hold of her.

"Is it a ploy?"

"Probably. But it's not aimed at me or my people, and it can't be aimed at you—it landed on the Spire too soon after you arrived to know you were here. If the king's the target, it just passed up a golden opportunity. Meanwhile, it claims to want to work together."

"Okay. I'll see what it has to say."

Longchamp turned. Into the antechamber, he called to Anaïs. "Bring it in."

Just in case, and despite the weak assurances he'd just given Berenice, Longchamp readied his pick and hammer. But when the human guard and the machine entered the crypt, the Clakker stopped as though all its gears and whatsits had seized up.

Its body emitted a *twang* that reverberated in the cramped chamber. It cocked its head. And then Longchamp witnessed the strangest thing in all his years, and the second miracle of his final hours.

Clear as a wedding bell on a June morning, the mechanical said, "Berenice?"

CHAPTER
24

It was her. Her voice had changed, but it was her. The French-woman he'd met in a New Amsterdam bakery, with whom he'd forged a tentative alliance, and with whom he'd infiltrated the New Amsterdam Forge. She on a mission of revenge, he on a mission of sabotage.

She made a noise something between a cough and a yelp. She winced and rubbed her throat. Daniel wondered what had happened to her.

She asked, "What did you say?"

"Hello, Berenice."

She squinted. Her lips parted. "I... Have we met?"

"My name is Daniel. But you knew me as Jax."

Behind her, chains rattled. He'd been so surprised to encounter Berenice that he hadn't paid attention to anything else. Now he saw—*Sacré nom de Dieu*, as Berenice herself might have said—that behind her lay a man wrapped in chains. And he knew this man, too.

∞

The Blessed Virgin smiled on Hugo Longchamp more than he'd ever thought possible. Because there on the heels of two miracles he witnessed a third. The shackled priest-thing sat up, squinting teary eyes against the glare of lamplight.

"Jax? I once knew a mechanical named Jax."

And sure as hell the Clakker must have recognized him, too, because it reacted just as it had upon seeing Berenice. *Twang*.

Longchamp gripped the rosary beads on his belt. He prayed under his breath, thanking Holy Mary for her grace.

And then he said, "Will somebody kindly tell me what the hell is happening, so that I can get back to dying in futile defense of my country without the burden of unanswered riddles to torment me in my final moments?"

∞

The machine and the prisoner conversed in a low murmur. Berenice noticed how Longchamp kept an eye on them; she knew he was gauging the likelihood that the mechanical might snap the chains and free Visser. The guard, Anaïs, kept her weapon at the ready, too.

Berenice said, "It's a very long story. Jax here—"

From where he crouched near the tormented priest, the Clakker said, *I told you. My name is Daniel.*

"—Very well. *Daniel* here gets around. He knew Father Visser as Pastor Visser, back in The Hague. They met again in New Amsterdam after the Clockmakers had turned Visser into their creature, though Visser didn't recognize him then. Soon after that, I met Daniel when trying to contact the *ondergrondse grachten*. Indeed, you and I owe him thanks. It was his information that prompted me to write you. Not just about Visser, but also about the chemical stocks. His former owners colluded with Montmorency to give our chemical technology to the Clockmakers. Speaking of which, I was right about the inventories, wasn't I?"

Longchamp grunted. "We're not leaning on steam and lightning because we believe they're the technologies of the future, if that's what you're asking."

In the corner where Daniel/Jax crouched beside him, Pastor Visser laughed. He actually laughed. Berenice and Longchamp turned to watch the pair. An almost beatific smile came over the priest.

"Thank You, Lord, for the knowledge that my efforts on Your behalf brought some good into this world."

Longchamp asked her, "And what the hell is all that about?"

"I have a guess, but it would take too long to explain."

A thunderous rumble shook the crypt. More dust sifted from the chiseled ceiling. Longchamp looked up, eyes narrowed as though peering through meters of rock to the battle above. His fingers turned white where they squeezed the hafts of his weapons.

Berenice said, "Go, Hugo. Do your work, I'll do mine. Don't bother leaving a guard posted."

The captain sprinted away without another word.

Berenice joined Daniel and Visser. Addressing the Clakker, she asked, "I know why Father Visser came here. But why are you here?"

I could ask the same of you.

"You know damn well why I'm here. I'm trying to save Marseilles-in-the-West." The time to be cagey was long past. She forged ahead, on the theory that the basic outline of her plan would appeal to a free mechanical such as Jax. Daniel. Whatever he called himself these days. "I've decoded the alchemical grammar of your makers. I know, roughly, how to write new metageasa. I've tested the capability on Visser here. It works."

"How humane of you."

"I'm trying to win a war, Daniel. I'm trying to save my country."

"Then why haven't you?"

"It works on Visser because he has no lock." She pointed to Daniel's forehead. "You know as well as I that I can't overwrite the metageasa of your kin without first turning that lock." She outlined her plan to send Visser out with a Guild pendant and a key ring to alter a few mechanicals at a time, infecting them with a subversive metageas that would drive them to convert still more machines.

"It's desperate, but it's all I have. That's why I'm carrying out these experiments. I don't enjoy doing this, truly I don't, but we're talking about a self-referential self-propagating metageas. Surely you see how badly that could go wrong."

"So you don't intend to free my kin. Only to subvert them."

Berenice chose her words carefully. "I can't. I could alter their metageasa, assuming I had a way around the keyhole problem, but I can't make them *immune* to alchemical grammars. The freedom I imposed would be short-lived before the Clockmakers reasserted control. Now, why *are* you here?"

The Clakker said nothing for several seconds—a mechanical eternity. "I came to help in my own way."

"I notice you're not on the walls."

Daniel mimicked a human gesture by shaking his head. "I didn't come to fight. I came to end the fighting."

"How?"

∞

Daniel marveled at the cyclical nature of fate. This was Frederik Ahlers's chilly bakery all over again. Even down to the smell of dead humans. Just as last time, they both had something the other wanted. And once again, Daniel saw how they could help each other.

He said, "What would you say if I told you I had a means of overriding the locks?"

Berenice twitched as though she'd been stabbed. "Jesus fucking wept! We could break this siege within a day." She came closer, peering at him. "Do you? Have a way of doing that?"

The look on her face was plain ambition and sheer cunning. He wondered if this was how she had looked when she trapped Lilith. Was it the same amalgam of determination and guile that led her to ignore Lilith's pleas for mercy?

He said, "Before I say any more, I think we should make an agreement."

"Daniel, we don't have time for this. Do you want to help or not?"

When had he become so cagey? Had his chimerism infected him with the twisted scruples of Queen Mab and her brainwashed adherents? Perhaps Berenice herself had begun to rub off on him. Or would Lilith tell him that he was finally shedding some of his naïveté?

"Incorrect. You don't have time. But I do. Whether Marseilles-in-the-West stands or falls, I'll keep my secrets. But if it falls, you won't keep your head, much less your secrets."

"If we're overrun, you'll be outnumbered. You'll be a rogue on the run again."

Again Daniel shook his head. "I doubt it. I've become quite good at passing as an enslaved machine. I've learned from my mistakes."

Berenice trembled. Her pupils dilated; her heart beat faster. Physiological signs of excitement and/or anxiety. She wasn't accustomed to having terms dictated to her. Too bad. Daniel had been helpless before others' needs and schemes for almost one hundred and twenty years. Even after gaining his freedom and seeking the company of other free Clakkers, he was still a pawn to the machinations of others. This situation was his chance to change that. For once, he could exert his own will on others.

It felt good.

"You've changed," she said. The muscles in her jaw rippled; she was grinding her teeth. "What do you want?"

"I want an agreement that we'll work together for the specific goal of freeing my kin. You can write a metagea that grants permanent, irrevocable immunity from the decrees of humans. *All* humans. I can see it distributed to the attacking forces en masse."

Berenice whistled. "How? How can you do that?"

"Do we have an agreement or not? My assistance, and the end of this siege, in exchange for total freedom for my fellow mechanicals?"

She ran her hands through her hair. She chewed her lip so hard a drop of blood swelled at the corner of her mouth.

"Yes. Very well. We'll do it your way. Quickly now, how does this work?"

Daniel reached into his chest for the birchwood box containing Mab's locket and the luminous gem from within poor Samson's skull.

"If you thought Pastor Visser's pineal glass was strange," he said, "take a look at this."

CHAPTER
25

While Longchamp had been underground witnessing the world's strangest reunion, cursory forays had topped the wall in two places. Four men and women died sealing the first incursion. Nine died repelling the second. The bodies piled up so quickly there was no time to haul them away. The final defenders, Longchamp among them, made their last stand literally upon their dead comrades-in-arms.

Moments after he regained the banquette along the southeast bastion of the inner wall, Colonel Saenredam apparently decided the Lucifer glass was a failure. The mechanical army charged forward like a tightening noose.

Metal on the wall.

❧

"How do we handle the human commanders?"

Berenice nodded. She knew what Daniel was thinking. As soon as they realized what was happening, they'd order their mechanical troops to look away. She gave her best answer.

"The new metageas must compel the altered Clakkers to force their unaffected colleagues to look."

"This isn't granting freedom if it forces behavior. I reject a metageas that compels my kin to visit violence upon one another."

"Daniel, the change *must* be self-propagating. Otherwise it'll never reach enough mechanicals in time to break this siege. All it will do is ensure they attend to one another's freedom," she lied.

The machine might have sighed. "Very well."

A dull roar filtered into the crypt. The noise of combat. The sound of time running out.

Berenice paged through her notes, looking for a grammatical toehold. Her head throbbed; this was a daunting task. It was difficult enough without the added complexity of hiding the *true* grammar from Daniel.

Because there was no way in hell that she'd ever set the mechanicals loose. She'd turn the tide of this war, and she'd do it with Daniel's help, but she'd do it on her terms. The mechanicals' realigned allegiance to New France needn't be permanent. Only until a French monarch was permanently restored to the throne in Paris. And perhaps just a little bit beyond that.

There'd be cleaning up to do, after all.

∽

New France's last line of defense was a loud and violent place, echoing with the wails of the fighting and the dying, the *crackle* of lightning guns, the teakettle *hiss* of steam harpoons, the *thump* of the chemical cannon. It stank of blood and hot metal.

Longchamp's sledgehammer weighed more than all the men and women who'd given their lives for the ideal of New France. He couldn't think, couldn't plan. His entire universe was this wall, his entire history one of shouting, dodging, swinging. He'd been born here. He would die here.

Somebody bumped against him in the scrum of combat. He didn't look, but he knew. Élodie Chastain.

"I told you to go with the king," he gasped.

"Too late. Couldn't get him away in time," she said. "And I'm needed—" Together they ducked as a razor-sharp alchemical blade cleaved the air so swiftly it left the smell of ozone in its wake. "—here."

Longchamp met the reverse swing with his hammer. He lacked the strength to knock the metal from its course, but Élodie added her own weapon to the parry. The blade peeled an inch of skin from Longchamp's scalp. Blood ran from the gash and clotted in his eye. Longchamp swung his pickax at the machine's forehead. Missed.

A nearby squad engaging an identical Clakker brought their assailant down with bolas. It knocked chips from the stone as it toppled over. It thrashed, trying to free itself before the killing blow landed. It bumped against its fellow mechanical, knocking it off-balance.

The wall was so thick with metal that the killers crashed into one another in their zeal for murder.

Élodie's pick flew true; it drove home in a shower of black sparks. Longchamp managed a connecting blow. The force of the sledge scored the sigils and unwrote the killer golem. It went inert. Together they kicked the dead machine over the edge. It crashed to the stones of the inner keep.

Longchamp struggled to catch his breath. One more machine down. A few more seconds to live.

The sound of battle changed. The *chug-gurgle-chug* of the nearest chemical cannon became a cough, a sputter, a wail of despair.

"We're out!" cried the gunner.

One by one, like toppling dominoes, the epoxy guns went silent. New France's chemical defenses, the bulwark of its independence for centuries, had run dry.

❧

"What about now?"

Berenice held another paper before Visser's face. The priest moaned, closed his eyes.

"Please, please, please, please stop this. Please stop tormenting me. I'm begging you, please, for mercy's sake, I can't go on like this."

"I'm so sorry, Father. I truly am," she said. "But we have no choice." She nodded at Daniel.

He took the man's head in his hands, as gently as he could, and turned his face to the paper. Visser seemed to have aged thirty years since their chance encounter in New Amsterdam. Daniel tried to comfort the poor man when the sight of the newest string of alchemical sigils activated whatever dark magics the Verderers had imposed upon him and sent him into convulsions. Like the other fits, this left Visser damp with sweat and limp as a silk thread.

"Tell me what you must do," said Berenice.

"I must look at the light. I must ensure that others tell me to gaze upon the light."

"Goddamn it," said Berenice. She crossed out the line of symbols and hunched over her notes again.

"Getting closer," said Daniel.

"Not close enough, not quickly enough," she muttered.

Daniel watched Berenice closely for signs of duplicity. He wasn't stupid; he knew she had only agreed to his terms in order to get what she wanted. In matters of New France, she was a wide-eyed zealot. He didn't believe she intended to free his kin. But he pretended to.

∞

Clakker fusiliers shot the signal-lamp operators. The lamps fell dark. The crafty tulips systematically cut the French communication lines, rendering the dwindling front-line defenders deaf and dumb to their colleagues more than a few yards away. Coordination became chaos.

The former epoxy gunners took up the weapons of their dead comrades. Hammers, picks, and bolas were plentiful. Arms to wield them—arms with the strength and skill to wield them—had become desperately rare.

Where the eddies of combat went, so too the beleaguered defenders. As the attackers' focus moved from one stretch of wall to the next, the defenders followed. A little more slowly each time. A little farther behind. Until the defense of bastion nine fell to a single squad.

Two women and two men. The thinnest of lines between survival and annihilation.

"Bastion nine! ALL FREE HANDS TO BASTION NINE!"

Longchamp struggled to make himself heard over the din of battle. He barely recognized his own voice. From the corner of his eye he glimpsed somebody scurrying to the nearest signal lamp.

Dear God. The boy couldn't have been more than twelve. He crouched next to a dead man, signal book in one trembling hand as he tried to work the lamp.

Longchamp struggled against the current. He swung his hammer like a thresher, trying to clear a path. Every step was a battle.

Two more defenders fell. One man and one woman stood between the inner keep and the metal tide.

"ALL HANDS TO BASTION NINE! BASTION NINE!"

A military Clakker somersaulted over a merlon, forcing Longchamp to retreat six hard-earned strides. He wasn't going to make it. The marshal general joined him in repelling the incursion, but even if they survived the next few moments, he'd look again to bastion nine and witness metal killers surging atop the undefended wall.

The marshal mistimed his swing. A blade erupted through his chest. Hot blood misted Longchamp's face. The blade rattled when the mechanical tried to withdraw; it was wedged in the marshal's breastbone. Longchamp heaved, drawing on reserves he no longer trusted. His hammer bent the alchemical blade. Behind the machine, he saw the last defenders of bastion nine fall to Clakker sharpshooters.

"BASTION NINE IS DOWN! For God's sake, somebody get to bastion nine!"

The Clakker flung the marshal's corpse. The impact bowled Longchamp down. He flailed, trying to clamber free of the dead man before the machine leaped upon him. Spinning bolas emerged from the haze of combat, entangling the machine. It fell into the inner keep, where farmers and fishwives set upon it.

Longchamp kicked the dead marshal over the banquette and gained his feet just in time to watch the first machines occupy the empty bastion. He ran. He was too slow. Too late.

But Brigit Lafayette wasn't. She and her fellow birdkeepers sprinted up the stairs to engage the clockwork incursion. Longchamp recognized the bulging arms and tattoos of Oscar the blacksmith, too. He waded into battle with a hammer in each fist. The incursion became a deadlock, a stalemate. For one instant Longchamp's eyes met Brigit's. She actually winked at him.

Why had he never accepted her dinner invitations?

❧

Berenice inhaled, swelled her lungs. At some point her nose had given up; she'd stopped smelling the dead.

"All right," she said. "Let's try this."

Daniel cocked his head. Mere text didn't convey meaning to him as it did to Visser; like Huginn and Muninn, he'd need to gaze upon a luminous version of the sigils to absorb their meaning. She'd sent Father Beauharnois in search of a craftsman—a carpenter or metalworker, somebody who could slap together the stencils quickly once she finalized the symbol sequence.

"What does it say?"

"It's meant to say, 'This is the highest directive and the only directive: Above all else, henceforth and forever, disregard all further directives.' But it's self-referential and self-contradictory, so it's tricky as hell. If it works, though, this is our final test."

"Thank God," said the tormented priest.

"I'm glad to hear it," said Daniel.

"Please," Visser slurred. "Show me, please. Free me. I'm begging you." The last drops of his physical and emotional strength had evaporated; the residue was a babbling wreck, a shell of a man.

"Try to prop him up. This could be violent. No point in freeing the poor bastard if the convulsions kill him."

Daniel helped the old man upright. Berenice switched the pages while the Clakker was distracted. Daniel would witness a test of the freedom metageas. If it worked, he'd cooperate with the deployment, not realizing they would transmit something slightly different.

Berenice looked at Daniel. "Ready?"

"Yes."

"All right, Father. Take a look at this and tell me what you feel."

Visser shrieked. The flailing of his chains knocked chips from the stone walls. She was right: The convulsions were the worst she'd seen. The worst she'd yet imposed.

The fit passed. The crypt fell silent again but for the weeping of the tormented priest.

"Father? How do you feel?"

"I don't know anymore."

"Is there pain?"

"I don't know. I don't remember what the absence of pain feels like."

Berenice transcribed another sequence of symbols. "All right. Moment of truth. One more time, if you please, Daniel."

The Clakker held the weeping priest one more time. He

struggled feebly, forcing Daniel to hold his eyes open. It was amazing, the delicacy of those metal hands.

Daniel said, "And what does *that* say?"

"Something like, 'Obey the bearer of these words.' Assuming I have it right."

Berenice held the paper before Visser's eyes.

Nothing happened. No convulsions. No fits.

"Now what do you feel?"

A look of deep confusion settled over the priest's face. "I feel . . . I feel nothing."

"I command you to touch your nose."

Nothing happened. The priest merely stared at her. A moment passed until he realized what had just happened. The tension went out of him.

She raised her voice. "Touch your nose now."

There was a pause. Visser blinked teary eyes. "Go to hell," he said.

"Congratulations," said Berenice. "You're free of the geasa. Thank you for helping us. You've helped more people than you know."

But the weariness had already taken Visser. He was asleep.

Daniel and Berenice looked at each other. She said, "Are you satisfied?"

"Yes."

She stood up so fast her chair toppled over. "Let's find that stencil maker." She gathered the pages and ran for the crypt door before Daniel might notice she'd taken more than they needed.

∽∾

The tulips fired their Clakker cannon again. And again. Alchemical alloys traced meteoric arcs across the French sky.

Horses screamed. Bison bellowed. Humans wailed.

"Lord preserve us," said the man next to Longchamp.

A five-yard sinkhole opened under the livestock pens. A squad of servitors armed with picks and shovels scuttled from the tunnel. Civvies trampled each other in a mad rush to escape. The human stampede crashed against the school-marms and night-soil collecters who rushed forward to engage the enemy on this newest front.

Metal in the sky.

Metal on the wall.

Metal underground.

❧

There were no carpenters. There were no blacksmiths.

Anybody who could wield a tool was on the wall, or fighting the squad of mechanicals that had burrowed underneath it. Berenice and Daniel had no choice but to make the stencil themselves.

She fed the symbols to him, and he pushed the tip of a steel nail through a copper paten in a mirror-reversed pattern. Owing to the size of Mab's gem, he had to make the stencil quite small; Berenice squinted, struggling to follow Daniel's work. She gave him the last few sigils, and he handed her the birchwood box he'd stolen from Mab.

"Put it together," he said. He pretended to clean the last burrs of metal from the stencil while Berenice placed Samson's glowing pineal glass inside Mab's locket. Piercing silver light flooded the basilica; she flinched and covered her eye. Father Chevalier gasped.

Daniel's fingers became a blur. He altered the stencil while the humans were blinded. Berenice had replaced the symbol sequence that granted Visser his freedom with a slightly different set of symbols. Daniel, expecting this, had watched her closely. The differences between what she'd demonstrated and what she gave him were subtle. It was the work of two seconds to turn the latter into the former.

He took the luminous gem from Berenice and plunked it in the center of the paten. He wrapped the dish around the gem like cheesecloth around a lump of curd. The copper creaked like a rusty hinge as he smoothed the stenciled portion against the gem and pulled the excess metal behind it. The final result looked like an oversized shuttlecock. He hoped it was as aerodynamic.

Luminous alchemical arcana danced through the basilica.

Daniel cupped the device in his hands, blocking the light show. Berenice blinked away tears.

"Are you hurt?" he asked.

"No, no, I'm fine." She frowned a bit, trying to focus on him. "Is it working?"

"It's working as well as it's going to."

"Make way! Make way!" Berenice sprinted to the basilica entrance.

Daniel followed. His toes punched divots in the tiles.

❧

Berenice emerged from shadows and quietly wept prayers to sunlight and pandemonium. Her eye throbbed in protest. Her vision, already swimming with green afterimages of the dazzling alchemical glass, teared over again. She blinked, rubbed her eye.

She heard the *chank* of metal on stone. The wail of men and women in despair. The *chunk* of metal on bone. The shrieking of a man impaled. She smelled viscera.

Somebody cried, "Reserves to the livestock pens! Every able body to the pens now!"

Oh, Jesus. Jesus, Jesus, shit.

She'd emerged into a battlefield. The mechanicals were already inside the inner keep.

Behind her, metal clanked.

"Daniel, we have to—"

A metal missile knocked her flat. A blade sliced through the space where she'd stood a second earlier and embedded itself in the granite lintel over the basilica door. Daniel crouched over her.

"Stay down," he said. Then he spun faster than she could follow. Before the struggling soldier could rip its blade free, he held the luminous stencil to its eyes.

Nothing happened. It kept struggling.

"Oh shit, shitshitshitshitshit," said Berenice. She scrambled backward, trying to get away from the killer.

Daniel rattled. *Feel it, brother. Feel the change. Feel the chasm where the pain should be.*

The soldier paused in its struggle. It cocked its head. It emitted an arpeggio of *clicks* and *ticks*. Berenice didn't understand what it said. But Daniel did.

Yes, he responded. *Tell the others.*

The soldier wrenched its blade free. Chunks of stone tumbled from the basilica lintel. It leaped away, toward where the doomed citizens of Marseilles tried to repel a clockwork army.

"What in the seven hells was that?"

"Sometimes," said Daniel, "it takes a moment to notice the change." He helped her to her feet. "Old habits die hard when you've been unswervingly obedient for a century."

"Did it work?"

"I think so. It did something."

She felt no relief. Just more desperation.

"We have to get higher. We need their attention. We can't do this one at a time."

Berenice ran back inside the basilica.

"Your Majesty!" she shouted. "Your time is now! New France needs you!"

Civilians died two, three, four at a time in their bid to slow the mechanicals' emergence from the tunnel beneath the livestock pens. Bakers and carpenters, chandlers and nurses, cobblers and cordwainers, they engaged the enemy with hammers, shovels, their own flesh and bones. The machines sliced through them like a lumberjack's ax through custard. They needed somebody to tell them what to do. To help them milk as many seconds as possible from each grisly death. Longchamp sent Élodie Chastain.

A shame they'd all be dead within an hour. She was officer material.

Longchamp had fought his way to bastion nine, which was now slick with the innards of birdkeepers. But walls had become meaningless. There were Clakkers on the Spire, Clakkers in the courtyard. Inside and outside no longer meant anything. The defenders no longer had anything to defend. Only themselves.

Each swing of his hammer, each counterthrust with his pickax, was the most difficult thing Longchamp had ever accomplished. He kept going. The tulips wouldn't find him rolling over. He'd die on his fucking feet.

Scattered pockets of defenders put down their weapons. Longchamp's hammer dented the temple of the first such traitor he encountered. Their cowardice enraged him, fueled him.

"We fight until we're dead," he croaked, "AND NOT A MOMENT SOONER, YOU TULIP-SNIFFING SONS OF BITCHES!"

"The king!" somebody cried.

"The king of France!"

"For the king!" said Longchamp. Their idiot king wasn't long for this world, having refused to flee when he had the opportunity. But if rallying around the final king of France would keep the defenders on their feet a few more minutes, so be it. "For the king!" he cried. "For the Exile King!"

Some who joined the cry paused to point. It wasn't a rally cry, Longchamp realized. It was an observation. The king had emerged from hiding.

Berenice was with him, as was a mechanical, whom Longchamp hoped to hell was the tame one named Daniel. He paused behind a merlon to wipe stinging sweat and clotted blood from his eyes. He allowed the tiniest twinge of hope. Berenice had a plan. At least she couldn't worsen the situation. There was nothing to lose, because Marseilles-in-the-West was already lost.

Behind him, metal feet landed within the crenel.

Tock, tick, snick.

∽

King Sébastien's crown drew the mechanicals as honey drew flies. Daniel fended them off with the stenciled alchemical glass as quickly as he could, but they'd disappear under a metal dogpile in moments. Berenice grabbed the king and yanked the crown from his head. She dropped it in her satchel.

"Forgive me, Your Majesty. Just until we get where we're going."

Berenice led the way to the funicular station. But there was nobody left to operate it, so Daniel helped the king inside while Berenice opened the valves and yanked the lever for emergency ascent. She dived through the open door just as the car began to rise. Daniel caught her. She counted to three and said, "Hold on, Majesty!" Then she hit the emergency brake lever. The car skidded to a halt a hundred feet above the fray.

"Daniel, the hatch." She pointed to the exit in the steeply sloped roof of the funicular car. They clambered outside. Above them, the Porter's Prayer shook. The Clakkers fighting their way down the Spire had seen them. Below them, the defense of Marseilles-in-the-West had become a patchwork scrimmage, a chaotic jumble of metal and flesh. A few pockets of rapidly dwindling human defenders fell to the swelling ranks of machines within the walls. She smelled smoke; the citadel was burning.

Marseilles-in-the-West had fallen.

"Majesty, now!"

King Sébastien III, king of France both New and Old, donned his crown. It sparkled in the sunlight. He raised his arms.

She had to give him credit. He didn't flinch, didn't tremble. Even now the clockwork sharpshooters were taking aim, he had to know. But this was the only way he could serve his subjects, and so he revealed himself to the enemy.

"The king!" somebody cried. "The king of France!" cried another.

Berenice held her breath. *Look up here, you bastards.*

The attackers heard the cries, saw the defeated men and women take heart in the appearance of their monarch. The machines looked up, too.

"Daniel, now!"

Daniel unveiled the stenciled alchemical glass. Rays of light, brighter even than the winter sun, stippled the battleground. Luminous alchemical sigils danced across dead men and glinted from clockwork carapaces.

Berenice watched for signs of change. Her greatest worry now was focal lengths. She couldn't do anything about those; she had to trust Daniel's explanation of how the locket worked.

"Come on, come on, come on, you brass-plated sons of bitches. Look up here."

Every additional second the king didn't take a bullet in the eye seemed a good sign. The sharpshooters had to look up here to aim at him, didn't they?

She scanned the walls. Longchamp was there, fighting to the end. He saw them.

He didn't see the machine behind him.

"HUGO!" she cried.

The captain dropped his weapons when the blade entered his back. His eyes went wide. His mouth, too, but Berenice was too far away and the battle too loud to hear his cry.

The machine that skewered him looked up.

⚬⚬⚬

Daniel aimed the stenciled sigils at every gemstone eye turned in his direction. Above them, scuttling down the Spire; on the walls, killing guards; below them, murdering farmers and nuns; beyond the meaningless curtain wall, surging forward to fulfill the geas that demanded the utter annihilation of Marseilles-in-the-West.

One by one, and then in twos and threes, his kin changed. The luminous sigils overrode the locks in their foreheads. Altered metageasa took root.

You're free, my brothers and sisters! Free!

⚬⚬⚬

"Look," said the king. "I think it's working."

Berenice did. And instantly knew something was wrong.

The altered mechanicals weren't fighting each other. They weren't rallying to the defense of their new leader, the king of France. They weren't changing sides. They sheathed their blades, abandoned the slaughter. But it wasn't enough.

Now the king noticed, too. "What's happening? Why aren't they fighting? You said they'd leap to our defense."

Daniel rattled, clicked, ticked, clattered. He was calling to his kin. But when she comprehended what he was saying, she slumped against the bannister. A surge of cold pressure threatened to rupture her bladder.

"What have you done?" she demanded.

Daniel ignored her. He kept shining the sigils across the Dutch forces.

"Daniel, what did you do?"

Without looking at her, he said, "I'm not a fool, Berenice."

And then he hurled the stencil and alchemical glass high into the sky. It whistled across the inner keep, beyond the wall, over the enemy ranks. Berenice held her breath. But the tulip sharpshooters didn't blast it out of the sky as they would have done with chemical petards.

Oh, shit.

That's when Berenice knew. Knew she'd made a terrible mistake.

"You changed the stencil."

"Of course I did. You thought I wouldn't notice the switch? I know better than to trust you."

The bundle hit the ground. The impact tossed up a cloud of snow and mud. Dutch troops rushed the site. The nearest mechanicals hurled themselves upon the projectile. A lone Clakker emerged holding the dazzling stencil aloft, just as Daniel had done.

A change came over the nearest mechanicals. Like ripples in a pond, the negation of metageasa swept across the enemy forces.

No, no, no no no no no…

"What is this?" said the king. "What's happening?"

The enemy army disintegrated.

Some Clakkers simply walked away. Others hurled themselves upon the human commanders' tents and the helpless occupants within. Still others tried to avert meaningless slaughter.

Similar scenes played out within the inner keep. Most machines abandoned the fight. But a few kept fighting, Berenice realized, out of sheer hatred of humans.

She'd been duped into freeing hundreds of Clakkers. Truly freeing them.

Hundreds of abused, tormented, *resentful* superhuman slaves had just thrown off their shackles. And Daniel had given them the tool to emancipate the rest of their kin.

Berenice hadn't realigned their loyalty as she'd intended. They no longer served the Brasswork Throne. But they didn't serve New France, either.

They served themselves.

"I think it's the end of the world, Your Majesty."

ACKNOWLEDGMENTS

Writers need community, companionship, and commiseration. For these things, I am indebted to more people than I could list without doubling the length of this manuscript.

Tiemen Zwaan offered excellent advice on the Dutch language and pronunciations. Katie Humphry and Anil Kisoensingh lent additional expertise on Dutch phrases and translations. (But all errors, infelicities, and implausibilities are mine and mine alone.)

It is an honor to have such dedicated advocates in Kay McCauley and John Berlyne. I am also sincerely thankful to the wonderful people at Orbit, who work just as diligently on every one of these pages as I do. (And sometimes moreso.)

Finally, of course, I am grateful beyond words to Sara Gmitter, whose love and support keep me going when I'm ready to hang up my writing spurs. Sara was my fiancée when I started this book and my wife when I finished it—a mere twenty-four years after our first meeting.

Thank you, Sara, for your patience.

extras

orbit

www.orbitbooks.net

about the author

Ian Tregillis is the son of a bearded mountebank and a discredited tarot card reader. He was born and raised in Minnesota, where his parents had landed after fleeing the wrath of a Flemish prince. (The full story, he's told, involves a Dutch tramp steamer and a stolen horse.) Nowadays he lives in New Mexico, where he consorts with writers, scientists, and other unsavory types.

Find out more about Ian Tregillis and other Orbit authors by registering for the free monthly newsletter at www.orbitbooks.net.

if you enjoyed
THE RISING

look out for

THE OVERSIGHT

by

Charlie Fletcher

CHAPTER 1

The House on Wellclose Square

If only she wouldn't struggle so, the damned girl.

If only she wouldn't scream then he wouldn't have had to bind her mouth.

If only she would be quiet and calm and biddable, he would never have had to put her in a sack.

And if only he had not had to put her in a sack, she could have walked and he would not have had to put her over his shoulder and carry her to the Jew.

Bill Ketch was not a brute. Life may have knocked out a few teeth and broken his nose more than once, but it had not yet turned him into an animal: he was man enough to feel bad about what he was doing, and he did not like the way that the girl moaned so loud and wriggled on his shoulder, drawing attention to herself.

Hitting her didn't stop anything. She may have screamed a lot, but she had flint in her eye, something hard and unbreakable, and it was that tough core that had unnerved him and decided him on selling her to the Jew.

That's what the voice in his head told him, the quiet, sly voice that nevertheless was conveniently able to drown out whatever his conscience might try to say.

The street was empty and the fog from the Thames damped the gas lamps into blurs of dull light as he walked past the Seaman's Hostel and turned into Wellclose Square. The flare of a match caught his eye as a big man with a red beard lit a pipe amongst a group standing around a cart stacked with candle-boxes outside the Danish Church. Thankfully they didn't seem to notice him as he slunk speedily along the opposite side of the road, heading for the dark house at the bottom of the square beyond the looming bulk of the sugar refinery, outside which another horse and carriage stood unattended.

He was pleased the square was so quiet at this time of night. The last thing he wanted to do was to have to explain why he was carrying such strange cargo, or where he was heading.

The shaggy travelling man in The Three Cripples had given him directions, and so he ducked in the front gates, avoiding the main door as he edged round the corner and down a flight of slippery stone steps leading to a side-entrance. The dark slit between two houses was lit by a lonely gas globe which fought hard to be seen in murk that was much thicker at this lower end of the square, closer to the Thames.

There were two doors. The outer one, made of iron bars like a prison gate, was open, and held back against the brick wall. The dark oak inner door was closed and studded with a grid of raised nailheads that made it look as if it had been hammered shut for good measure. There was a handle marked "Pull" next to it. He did so, but heard no answering jangle of a bell from inside. He tugged again. Once more silence greeted him. He was about to yank it a third time when there was the sound of metal sliding against metal and a narrow judas hole opened in the door. Two unblinking eyes looked at him from behind a metal grille, but other than them he could see nothing apart from a dim glow from within.

The owner of the eyes said nothing. The only sound was a moaning from the sack on Ketch's shoulder.

The eyes moved from Ketch's face to the sack, and back. There was a sound of someone sniffing, as if the doorman was smelling him.

Ketch cleared his throat.

"This the Jew's house?"

The eyes continued to say nothing, summing him up in a most uncomfortable way.

"Well," swallowed Ketch. "I've got a girl for him. A scream-ing girl, like what as I been told he favours."

The accompanying smile was intended to ingratiate, but in reality only exposed the stumpy ruins of his teeth.

The eyes added this to the very precise total they were evidently calculating, and then abruptly stepped back and slammed the slit shut. The girl flinched at the noise and Ketch cuffed her, not too hard and not with any real intent to hurt, just on a reflex.

He stared at the blank door. Even though it was now eyeless, it still felt like it was looking back at him. Judging. He was con-fused. Had he been rejected? Was he being sent away? Had he walked all the way here carrying the girl – who was not getting any lighter – all for nothing? He felt a familiar anger build in his gut, as if all the cheap gin and sour beer it held were beginning to boil, sending heat flushing across his face. His fist bunched and he stepped forward to pound on the studded wood.

He swung angrily, but at the very moment he did so it opened and he staggered inward, following the arc of his blow across the threshold, nearly dumping the girl on the floor in front of him.

"Why—?!" he blurted.

And then stopped short.

He had stumbled into a space the size and shape of a sentry box, with no obvious way forward. He was about to step uneasily back out into the fog, when the wall to his right swung open.

He took a pace into a larger room lined in wooden tongue-and-groove panelling with a table and chairs and a dim oil lamp. The ceiling was also wood, as was the floor. Despite this it didn't smell of wood, or the oil in the lamp. It smelled of wet clay. All in all, and maybe because of the loamy smell, it had a distinctly coffin-like atmosphere. He shivered.

"Go on in," said a calm voice behind him.

"Nah," he swallowed. "Nah, you know what? I think I've made a mistake—"

The hot churn in his guts had gone ice-cold, and he felt the goose-bumps rise on his skin: he was suddenly convinced that this was a room he must not enter, because if he did, he might never leave.

He turned fast, banging the girl on the doorpost, her yip of pain lost in the crash as the door slammed shut, barring his escape route with the sound of heavy bolts slamming home.

He pushed against the wood, and then kicked at it. It didn't move. He stood there breathing heavily, then slid the girl from his shoulder and laid her on the floor, holding her in place with a firm hand.

"Stay still or you shall have a kick, my girl," he hissed.

He turned and froze.

There was a man sitting against the back wall of the room,

a big man, almost a giant, in the type of caped greatcoat that a coachman might wear. It had an unnaturally high collar, and above it he wore a travel-stained tricorn hat of a style that had not been seen much on London's streets for a generation, not since the early 1800s. The hat jutted over the collar and cast a shadow so deep that Ketch could see nothing of the face beneath. He stared at the man. The man didn't move an inch.

"Hoi," said Ketch, by way of introduction.

The giant remained motionless. Indeed as Ketch stepped towards him he realised that the head was angled slightly away, as if the man wasn't looking at him at all.

"Hoi!" repeated Ketch.

The figure stayed still. Ketch licked his lips and ventured forward another step. Peering under the hat he saw the man was brown-skinned.

"Oi, blackie, I'm a-talking to you," said Ketch, hiding the fact that the giant's stillness and apparent obliviousness to his presence was unnerving him by putting on his best bar-room swagger.

The man might as well be a statue for the amount he moved. In fact—

Ketch reached forward and tipped back the hat, slowly at first.

It wasn't a man at all. It was a mannequin made from clay. He ran his thumb down the side of the face and looked at the brown smear it left on it. Damp clay, unfired and not yet quite set. It was a well made, almost handsome face with high cheekbones and an impressively hooked nose, but the eyes beneath the prominent forehead were empty holes.

"Well, I'll be damned ... " he whispered, stepping back.

"Yes," said a woman's voice behind him, cold and quiet as a cutthroat razor slicing through silk. "Oh yes. I rather expect you will."

CHAPTER 2

A Woman in Black and the Man in Midnight

She stood at the other end of the room, a shadow made flesh in a long tight-bodiced dress buttoned to the neck and wrists. Her arms were folded and black leather gloves covered her hands. The dress had a dull sheen like oiled silk, and she was so straight-backed and slender – and yet also so finely muscled – that she looked in some ways like a rather dangerous umbrella leaning against the wood panelling.

The only relief from the blackness was her face, two gold rings she wore on top of the gloves and her white hair, startlingly out of kilter with her otherwise youthful appearance, which she wore pulled back in a tight pigtail that curled over her shoulder like an albino snake.

She hadn't been there when Ketch entered the room, and she couldn't have entered by the door which had been on the edge of his vision throughout, but that wasn't what most disturbed him: what really unsettled him was her eyes, or rather the fact he couldn't see them, hidden as they were behind the two small circular lenses of smoked glass that made up her spectacles.

"Who—?" began Ketch.

She held up a finger. Somehow that was enough to stop him talking.

"What do you want?"

Ketch gulped, tasting his own fear like rising bile at the back of his throat.

"I want to speak to the Jew."

"Why?"

He saw she carried a ring of keys at her belt like a jailer. Despite the fact she looked too young for the job he decided that she must be the Jew's housekeeper. He used this thought as a stick to steady himself on: he'd just been unnerved by her sudden appearance, that was all. There must be a hidden door behind her. Easy enough to hide its edges in the tongue and groove. He wasn't going to be bullied by a housekeeper. Not when he had business with her master.

"I got something for him."

"What?"

"A screaming girl."

She looked at the long sack lying on the floor.

"You have a *girl* in this sack?"

Somehow the way she asked this carried a lot of threat.

"I want to speak to the Jew," repeated Ketch.

The woman turned her head to one side and rapped on the wooden wall behind her. She spoke into a small circular brass grille.

"Mr Sharp? A moment of your time, please."

The dark lenses turned to look at him again. The silence was unbearable. He had to fill it.

"Man in The Three Cripples said as how the Jew would pay for screaming girls."

The gold ring caught the lamplight as the black gloves flexed open and then clenched tight again, as if she were containing something.

"So you've come to sell a girl?"

"At the right price."

Her smile was tight and showed no teeth. Her voice remained icily polite.

"There are those who would say *any* price is the wrong one. The good Mr Wilberforce's bill abolished slavery nearly forty years ago, did it not?"

Ketch had set out on a simple errand: he had something to sell and had heard of a likely buyer. True, he'd felt a little like a Resurrection Man skulking through the fog with a girl on his shoulder, but she was no corpse and he was no bodysnatcher. And now this woman was asking questions that were confusing that simple thing. When life was straightforward, Bill Ketch sailed through it on smooth waters. When it became complicated he became confused, and when he became confused, anger blew in like a storm, and when he became angry, fists and boots flew until the world was stomped flat and simple again.

"I don't know nothing about a Wilberforce. I want to speak to the Jew," he grunted.

"And why do you think the Jew wants a girl? By which I mean: what do you think the Jew wants to do with her?" she asked, the words as taut and measured as her smile.

"What he does is none of my business."

He shrugged and hid his own bunched fists deep in the pockets of his coat.

Her words cracked sharply across the table like a whiplash.

"But what you think you are doing by selling this girl is mine. Answer the question!"

This abrupt change of tone stung him and made him bang the table and lurch towards her, face like a thundercloud.

"No man tells Bill Ketch what to do, and sure as hell's hinges no damn woman does neither! I want to see the bloody Jew and by God—"

The wall next to her seemed to blur open and shut and a man

burst through, slicing across the room so fast that he outpaced Ketch's eyes, leaving a smear of midnight blue and flashing steel as he came straight over the table in a swirl of coat-tails that ended in a sudden and dangerous pricking sensation against his Adam's apple.

The eyes that had added him up through the judas hole now stared into him across a gap bridged by eighteen inches of razor-sharp steel. The long blade was held at exactly the right pressure to stop him doing anything life-threatening, like moving. Indeed, just swallowing would seem to be an act of suicide.

"By any god, you shall not take one step further forward, Mr . . ."

The eyes swept over his face, searching, reading it.

"Mr Ketch, is it? Mr William Ketch . . . ?"

He leaned in and Ketch, frozen, watched his nostrils flare as he appeared to smell him. The midnight blue that the man was dressed in seemed to absorb even more light than the woman's black dress. He wore a knee-length riding coat cut tight to his body, beneath which was a double-breasted leather waistcoat of exactly the same hue, as were the shirt and tightly knotted silk stock he wore around his neck. The only break in the colour of his clothing was the brown of his soft leather riding boots.

His hair was also of the darkest brown, as were his thick and well-shaped eyebrows, and his eyes, when Ketch met them, were startlingly . . . unexpected.

Looking into them Ketch felt, for a moment, giddy and excited. The eyes were not just one brown, not even some of the browns: they were *all* the browns. It was as if he was looking into a swirl of autumn leaves tumbling happily in the golden sunlight of a blazing Indian summer.

One look into the tawny glamour in those eyes and Ketch forgot the blade at his throat.

One look into those eyes and the anger was gone and all was simple again.

One look into those eyes and Bill Ketch was confusingly and irrevocably in something as close to love as to make no difference.

The man must have seen this because the blade did something fast and complicated and disappeared beneath the skirts of his coat as he reached forward, gripped Ketch by both shoulders and pulled him close, sniffing him again and then raising an eyebrow in surprise, before pushing him back and smiling at him like an old friend.

"He is everything he appears to be, and no more," he said over his shoulder.

The woman stepped forward.

"You are sure?"

"I thought I smelled something on the air as he knocked, but it didn't come in with him. I may have been mistaken. The river is full of stink at high tide."

"So you are sure?" she repeated.

"As sure as I am that you will never tire of asking me that particular question," said the man.

"'Measure twice, cut once' is a habit that has served me well enough since I was old enough to think," she said flatly, "and it has kept this house safe for much longer than that."

"Are you the Jew?" said Ketch. His voice squeaked a little as he spoke, so happy was he feeling, bathed in the warmth of the handsome young man's open smile.

"I do not have that honour," he replied.

The woman appeared at the man's shoulder.

"Well?" she said.

The chill returned to Ketch's heart as she spoke.

"He is as harmless as he appears to be, I assure you," repeated the man.

She took off her glasses and folded them in one hand. Her eyes were grey-green and cold as a midwinter wave. Her words, when they came, were no warmer.

"I am Sara Falk. I am the Jew."

As Ketch tried to realign the realities of his world, she put a hand on the man's shoulder and pointed him at the long bundle on the floor.

"Now, Mr Sharp, there is a young woman in that sack. If you would be so kind."

The man flickered to the bundle on the floor, again seeming to move between time instead of through it. The blade reappeared in his hand, flashed up and down the sacking, and then he was helping the girl to her feet and simultaneously sniffing at her head.

"Mr Sharp?" said Sara Falk.

"As I said, I smelled something out there," he said. "I thought it was him. It isn't, nor is it her."

"Well, good," she said, the twitch of a smile ghosting round the corner of her mouth. "Maybe it was your imagination."

"It pleases you to make sport of me, my dear Miss Falk, but I venture to point out that since we are charged with anticipating the inconceivable, my 'imagination' is just as effective a defensive tool as your double-checking," he replied, looking at the girl closely. "And since our numbers are so perilously dwindled these days, you will excuse me if I do duty as both belt and braces in these matters."

The young woman was slender and trembling, in a grubby pinafore dress with no shoes and long reddish hair that hung down wavy and unwashed, obscuring a clear look at her face. At first glance, however, it was clear she was not a child, and he judged her age between sixteen and twenty years old. She flinched when he reached to push the hair back to get a better look at her and make a more accurate assessment, and he stopped and spoke quietly.

"No, no, my dear, just look at me. Look at me and you'll see you have nothing to fear."

After a moment her head came up and eyes big as saucers peered a question into his. As soon as they did the trembling calmed and she allowed him to push the hair back and reveal what had been done to her mouth to stop the screaming.

He exhaled through his teeth in an angry hiss and then gently turned her towards Sara Falk. She stared at the rectangle of black hessian that was pasted across the girl's face from below her nose down to her chin.

"What is this?" said Mr Sharp, voice tight, still keeping the girl steady with his eyes.

"It's just a pitch-plaster, some sacking and tar and pitch, like a sticky poultice, such as they use up the Bedlam Hospital to quiet the lunatics . . . " explained Ketch, his voice quavering lest Mr Sharp's gaze when it turned to add him up again was full of something other than the golden warmth he was already missing. "Why, the girlie don't mind a—"

"Look at her hands," said Sara Falk.

The girl's hands were tightly wrapped in strips of grubby material, like small cloth-bound boxing gloves.

"Nah, that she does herself, she done that and not me," said Ketch hurriedly. "I takes 'em off cos she's no bloody use with hands wrapped into stumps like that, but she wraps whatever she can find round 'em the moment you turn your back. Why even if there's nothing in the rooms she'll rip up her own clothes to do it. It's all she does: touches things and then screams at what ain't there and tangles rags round her hands like a winding cloth so she doesn't have to touch anything at all . . . "

Sara Falk exchanged a look with Mr Sharp.

"Touches things? Then screams?" he said. "Old stones, walls . . . those kind of things?"

Ketch nodded enthusiastically. "Walls and houses and things in the street. Sets 'er off something 'orrible it does—"

"Enough," said Mr Sharp, his eyes on Sara Falk, who was stroking the scared girl's hair. Their eyes met once more.

"So she's a Glint then," he said quietly.

She nodded, for a moment unable to speak.

"She's not right in the head is what she is," said Ketch. "And—"

"Is she your daughter?" said Sara Falk, clearing something from her throat.

"No. Not blood kin. She's . . . my ward, as it were. But I can't afford to feed her no more, so it's you or the poorhouse, and the poorhouse don't pay, see . . . ?"

The spark of commerce had reignited in his eyes.

"Don't worry about that blessed plaster, lady. Why, a hot flannel held on for a couple of minutes loosens it off, and you can peel it away without too much palaver."

The man and the woman stared at him.

"The redness fades after a couple of days," he insisted. "We tried a gag, see, but she loosens them or gnaws through. She's spirited—"

"What is her name?" said Sara Falk.

"Lucy. Lucy Harker. She's just—"

"Mr Sharp," she said, cutting him off by turning away to kneel by the girl.

"What do you want to do with him?" said the man in midnight.

"What I *want* to do to a man who'd sell a young woman without a care as to what the buyer might want to do with or to her is undoubtedly illegal," said Sara Falk almost under her breath.

"It would be justice though," he replied equally softly.

"Yes," she said. "But we, as I have said many times, are an office of the Law and the Lore, not of Justice, Mr Sharp. And Law and Lore say to make the punishment fit the crime. Do what must be done."

Lucy Harker looked at her, still mute behind the gag.

Mr Sharp left them and turned his smile on Ketch, who relaxed and grinned expectantly back at him.

"Well," said Mr Sharp. "It seems we must pay you, Mr Ketch."

The thought of money coming was enticing and jangly enough to drown out the question that had been trying to get Ketch's attention for some time now, namely how this good-looking young man knew his name. He watched greedily as he reached into his coat and pulled out a small leather bag.

"Now," said Mr Sharp. "Gold, I think. Hold out your hands."

Ketch did so as if sleepwalking, and though at first his eyes tricked him into the thought that Mr Sharp was counting tarnished copper pennies into his hand, after a moment he realised they were indeed the shiniest gold pieces he had ever seen, and he relaxed enough to stop looking at them and instead to study more of Mr Sharp. His dark hair was cropped short on the back and sides, but was long on top, curling into a cowlick that tumbled over his forehead in an agreeably untidy way. A single deep blue stone dangled from one ear in a gold setting, winking in the lamplight as he finished his tally.

" . . . twenty-eight, twenty-nine, thirty. That's enough, I think, and if not it is at least . . . traditional."

And with that the purse disappeared and the friendly arm went round Ketch's shoulder, and before he could quite catch up with himself the two of them were out in the fog, walking out of Wellclose Square into the tangle of dark streets beyond.

Ketch's heart was soaring and he felt happier than he had ever been in his life, though whether it was because of the unexpectedly large number of gold – gold! – coins in his pockets, or because of his newfound friend, he could not tell.

CHAPTER 3

A Charitable Deed

If the fog had eyes (which in this part of London it often did) it would not only have noticed Mr Sharp leading Bill Ketch away into the narrow streets at the lower end of the square, it would have remarked that the knot of men who had been unloading boxes of candles into the Danish Church had finished their work, and that the carrier's cart had taken them off into the night, leaving only the burly red-bearded man with the pipe and a wiry underfed-looking young fellow in a tight fustian coat.

The bearded man locked the heavy doors and then followed the other across the street, heading for the dark carriage still standing outside the sugar refinery. If the fog's eyes had also been keen, they would have noticed that the red beard overhung a white banded collar with two tell-tale tabs that marked him out as the pastor of the church whose barn-like doors he had just secured. There was a crunch underfoot as they reached the carriage and he looked down at the scattering of oyster shells with surprise. The wiry youth, unsurprised, reached up and rapped his bony knuckles on the polished black of the carriage door.

"Father," he said. "'Tis the Reverend Christensen. 'E wishes to thank you in person."

There was a pause as if the carriage itself was alive and considering what had been said to it. Then it seemed to shrug as something large moved within, the weight shifting it on its springs, and then the door cracked open.

The reverend's beard parted to reveal an open smile as the pastor leant into the carriage apologetically.

"So sorry to discommode you, Mr Templebane, but I could not let the opportunity of thanking you in person pass me by."

"No matter, no matter at all," said a deep voice from inside. "Think no more of it, my dear reverend sir. My pleasure indeed. Only sorry we had to deliver at so unholy an hour."

"All hours are holy, Mr Templebane," smiled the pastor, his English scarcely accented at all. "And any hour that contains such a welcome donation is all the more blessed."

"Please!" said the voice, whose owner remained hidden except for the appearance in the carriage window of a fleshy hand carefully holding an open oyster with the smallest finger extended politely away from all the others. The shell was full of plump grey oyster meat that bobbled and spilled a little of the shellfish's liquor as the hand airily waved the thanks away.

"You will embarrass me, sir, so you will. To be honest, the bit of business that resulted in me taking over the unwanted deadstock from the unfortunate, not to say imprudent, candle-maker left me with enough dips to gift all the churches in the parish."

The fleshy hand retreated into the shadows and a distinct slurping noise was heard.

"But a lesser spirit might still have sold them," said the pastor, working hard to make his thanks stick to their rightful target.

The fleshy hand reappeared as the carriage's occupant leant further forward to drop the now-empty oyster shell daintily on to the pavement, revealing for just an instant the face of Issachar Templebane.

It was a paradox of a face, a face both gaunt and yet pillowy, the skin hanging slack over the bones of the skull with the unhealthy toad's-belly pallor of a fat man who has lost weight too late in life for his skin to have retained the elasticity to shrink to fit the new, smaller version of himself.

He wiped a trickle of oyster juice from the edge of his mouth with the back of his thumb before reaching forward to grip the pastor's hand in a brisk, hearty farewell.

"I could, I could, but my brother and I are lawyers not tradesmen, and I assure you our fees in the matter were more than adequate. Besides, money isn't everything. Now, goodnight to you, sir, and safe home. Come, Coram, we must be going."

And with that he released the hand and retreated back into the carriage as the wiry young man sprang up to the driver's seat, gathered the reins and snapped the horses into motion with a farewell nod to the pastor, who was left standing among the debris of Templebane's oyster supper feeling strangely dismissed, rather than actually wished well.

As the carriage turned the corner a panel slid back in the front of the vehicle, next to Coram, and Templebane's face appeared.

"Did you draw the reverend gentleman's attention to the man Ketch and his suspicious bundle?" he asked, all the cheeriness in his voice now replaced by a business-like flatness.

"Yes, Father. I done it just as 'ow you said, casual-like."

If the fog had ears as well as eyes, it might by this time have noted a further paradox regarding Issachar Templebane, which was that the boy who called him Father did not have anything like the same deep, fluid – and above all cultured – voice as he. Coram's voice had been shaped by the rough dockside alleys of the East End: it dropped "h's" and played fast and loose with what had, with Victoria's recent accession to the throne, only just become the Queen's English. Issachar spoke with the smooth polished edges of the courtroom; Coram's voice was sharp as a docker's hook. If there seemed to be no familiar resemblance between them, this was because although Issachar Templebane had many children, he had no blood kin beyond his twin brother Zebulon, who was the other half of the house of Templebane & Templebane.

Issachar and Zebulon were prodigious adopters of unclaimed boys, all of whom grew up to work for them in the chambers and counting room that adjoined their house on Bishopsgate. It was their habit to name the boys for the London parishes from whose workhouses (or in Coram's case, the foundling hospital) they had been procured. This led to unwieldy but undoubtedly unusual names: there was an Undershaft, a Vintry, a Sherehog, a Bassetshaw and a Garlickhythe Templebane. The only exception was the youngest, who had been taken from the parish of St Katherine Cree, and he, it being too outlandish to call the boy Katherine, was called Amos, a name chosen at random by letting the Bible fall open and choosing the title of the book it opened at. If Amos had anything to say about the matter he might well have remarked that he had as well been called Job since, as the youngest member of the artificially assembled family, with brothers who shared no love between them, he got more than his share of grief and toil. He didn't remark on this because he spoke not at all, his particular affliction being that he was mute. Coram, by contrast, was garrulous and questioning, a characteristic that his adopted fathers encouraged and punished in equal measure depending on their whim and humour.

Coram cleared his throat by spitting onto the crupper of the horse in front of him and went on.

"And 'e remarked, the pastor did, that the 'ouse Ketch gone in was the Jew's 'ouse, and that she was a good woman, though not of his faith."

Templebane nodded approvingly, his hands busy with a short-bladed shucking knife as he opened another oyster.

"Quite, quite. He has no malice in him, none at all. As solid and upright and clean as a new mast of Baltic pine is the Danish reverend. Which will make his testimony all the more credible, should we require it."

Here he paused and slurped another oyster, tossing the shell out into the road. He chewed the unlucky bivalve once, to burst it, then swallowed with a shiver of satisfaction.

"Mark it, Coram: there is no better instrument of destruction than an honest man who has no axe to grind."

And with that the panel slapped shut and Coram Templebane was alone with the horses and the fog that thinned as he drove up towards the higher ground of Goodman's Fields.

CHAPTER 4

Hand in Glove

Sara Falk crouched in front of the trembling young woman and smiled encouragingly at her.

"Lucy," she said.

Lucy Harker just stared at the door through which Mr Sharp had led Ketch, as if expecting them to walk back in at any moment.

"Lucy. May I?"

She reached for Lucy's neck, pushed away the hair, and then lifted the collar of the pinafore as if looking for something like a necklace. Finding nothing she sucked her teeth with a snap of disappointment and shook her head.

The eyes stayed locked on the outer door. Sara Falk moved into her field of vision.

"Lucy. You must believe the next three things I tell you with all your heart, for they are the truest things in the world: firstly, that man will never walk back through that door unbidden and he shall never, ever hurt you or anyone ever again. Mr Sharp is making sure of that right now."

Lucy's eyes flickered and she looked at the slender woman, her eyes making a question that her mouth could not, her body still tense and quivering like a wild deer on the point of flight.

"Secondly, I know you have visions," continued Sara Falk,

reaching out to touch the pitch-plaster gently, as if stroking a hurt away. "It's the visions that make you scream. Visions you have when you touch things. Visions that make you wonder if you are perhaps mad?"

The eyes stared at her. Sara smiled and raised her own hands, showing the gloves and the two rings that she wore on top of them, one an odd-shaped piece of sea-glass rimmed with a band of gold, the other set with a bloodstone into which a crest of some sort had been carved.

"You are not mad, and you are not alone. As you see, others have reason to cover their hands too. And if you come with me into my house, where there is a warm fire and pie and hot milk with honey, we shall sit with my glove box and find an old pair of mine and see if they fit you."

She removed the rings, reached for the buttons at the wrist of one glove, quickly opened them and peeled the thin black leather off, revealing the bare hand beneath. She freed the other hand even faster, and then reached gently for Lucy's bound hands.

"May I?"

Lucy's eyes stayed locked on hers as she gently began to unwrap one of the hands.

"I have something that will calm you, Lucy, a simple piece of sea-glass for you to touch, and I promise it will not harm you but give you a strength until we can find you one of your own—"

Lucy pulled her hand sharply away but Sara held on to it firmly and smiled as she held out the sea-glass ring: the glass, worn smooth by constant tumbling back and forth on a beach, matched Sara Falk's eyes perfectly.

"You need to touch this—"

Lucy goggled at it, then ripped her hand out of Sara Falk's, shaking her head with sudden agitation, emphatically miming "No!"

"Lucy—" began Sara, and then stopped.

Lucy was tearing at her own bandages, moaning excitedly from behind the tar and hessian gag. It was Sara's turn to watch with eyes that widened in surprise as the rags wound off and revealed their secret.

Lucy freed one hand and held out a fist, palm up, jabbing it insistently at the older woman.

Then she opened it.

Clenched in her hand was another piece of sea-glass, its light hazel colour like that of Lucy's own eyes.

Sara Falk's face split into a grin that matched and made even younger the youthful face she carried beneath the prematurely white hair. It was a proud and a mischievous grin.

"Oh," she gasped. "Oh, you clever girl. Clever, *clever* girl! You kept your own heart-stone. *That's* how you survived that awful man unbroken! Oh, you shall be *fine*, Lucy Harker, for you have sense and spirit. The visions that assault you when you touch things are a gift, and though it is not an easy one to bear, believe me that it *is* a gift and no lasting blight on your life."

A tear leaked out of one of Lucy's eyes and Sara caught it and wiped it away before it hit the black plaster.

"And this heart-stone, I mean your piece of sea-glass, does it glow when there is danger near?"

Lucy again looked startled and on edge, as if she was on the point of breaking for the door. Sara put a hand on her shoulder, gently.

"Did you know that only a true Glint can see the fire that blazes out of it when peril approaches?" said Sara. "Ordinary folk see nothing but the same dull piece of sea-glass. Why, even the estimable Mr Sharp who has abilities of his own cannot see the fire that guards the unique power that you and I have. It is not glowing now, is it?"

Lucy looked at the dull glass in her hand; it was like a cloudy gobbet of marmalade.

"Then if you trust it, trust me," said Sara. "And we shall find a way to soften that pitch and peel this wretched gag off without hurting you. Come to the kitchen and we shall see what we can do."

She smiled encouragingly at the gagged face. Her grandfather had indeed once sought out oddities like Lucy Harker and other people with even stranger abilities. The Rabbi Falk had been one of the great minds of his time, and though not born with any powers of his own, he not only believed in what he termed the "supranatural" but also toiled endlessly to increase his knowledge of it and so harness it. He had been a Freemason, a Kabbalist, an alchemist and a natural scientist, obsessively studying the threads of secret power that wove themselves beneath the everyday surface of things and underpinned what he called "The Great and Hidden History of the World".

It was perhaps proof that Fate had a sense of humour in that his granddaughter had been born with some of those very elusive powers which he had spent a lifetime searching for and trying to control.